WHAT MATTERS MOST

Light *in the* Empire

What Matters Most

Carol Ashby

Cerrillo Press

WHAT MATTERS MOST
Copyright 2021 by Carol Ashby

All rights reserved. No portion of this book may be reproduced, stored in a retrieval system, or transmitted in any form or by any means—electronic, mechanical, photocopy, recording, scanning, or other—except for brief quotations in critical reviews or articles, without the prior written permission of the publisher.

Publisher's Note: This novel is a work of fiction. Names, characters, places, and incidents are either products of the author's imagination or used fictitiously. All characters are fictional, and any similarity to people living or dead is purely coincidental.

Scripture quotations marked ESV are from the Holy Bible, English Standard Version, copyright © 2001, 2007, 2011, 2016 by Crossway Bibles, a division of Good News Publishers. Used by permission. All rights reserved.

Scripture quotations marked CSB have been taken from the Christian Standard Bible®, Copyright © 2017 by Holman Bible Publishers. Used by permission. Christian Standard Bible® and CSB® are federally registered trademarks of Holman Bible Publishers.

Cover and interior design by Roseanna White Designs

Cover images from Shutterstock.com

ISBN: 978-1-946139-30-6 (paperback)
       978-1-946139-31-3 (ebook)
       978-1-946139-32-0 (hardcover)

Cerrillo Press
Edgewood, NM

Be at peace among yourselves. And we urge you, brothers,
admonish the idle, encourage the fainthearted,
help the weak, be patient with them all.
1 Thessalonians 5:13-14 (ESV)

But even if you should suffer for righteousness, you are blessed.
Do not fear what they fear or be intimidated,
but in your hearts regard Christ the Lord as holy,
ready at any time to give a defense to anyone
who asks you for a reason for the hope that is in you.
1 Peter 3:14-15 (CSB)

And we know that for those who love God
all things work together for good,
for those who are called according to his purpose.
Romans 8:28 (ESV)

*To my children, Paul and Lydia,
for their love, support, and encouragement.*

*And especially to my husband, Jim,
who makes every day better just by being here.*

*And most of all, to Jesus.
Soli Deo gloria.*

A Note from the Author

Encouragement. It's something we all need, so why is it so easy to forget what a powerful effect it can have on another person?

Surrounded by a culture that loves to ridicule and find fault, it's easy to get discouraged. It's too easy to focus on the ultimate success or failure, not whether the person tried hard to do their personal best. On the final performance, not the hard work and dedication leading up to it.

But it can take so little to lift up someone who's become disheartened by the challenges of life that are overwhelming them. A thoughtful action, a kind word, a simple "You're part way there already. You can do the rest."—such responses can be a precious gift of encouragement to a weary soul.

Paul knew the importance of encouragement and urged his followers to make a point of doing it. In the fifth chapter of his first letter to the church in Thessalonica, he wrote, "Therefore encourage one another and build one another up, just as you are doing." He stressed the importance of encouragement in his summary of how Christian sisters and brothers should treat each other a few verses later.

"Be at peace among yourselves. And we urge you, brothers, admonish the idle, encourage the fainthearted, help the weak, be patient with them all. See that no one repays anyone evil for evil, but always seek to do good to one another and to everyone. Rejoice always, give thanks in all circumstances; for this is the will of God in Christ Jesus for you." (1 Thessalonians 5:11-18 ESV)

But it's those around us who don't know our Lord who often need encouragement most. When we feel burdened, we only have to pray, and the Holy Spirit will refresh our spirits so we can press on.

Many aren't yet children of God through adoption because they don't believe in Jesus. When life gets tough, they have to bear it on their own. Maybe we can help change that.

Part of showing love to others is the encouragement we can offer them when they need it. What starts as friendliness can grow into friendship, and friendship can open a heart to letting us share our faith.

In *What Matters Most*, Sabina returns home, wounded in spirit by years of bullying. But kindness and acceptance combined with frequent encouragement by her brother's friends help her heal and make her eager to learn about the God they serve. May we always be open to the Spirit's revelation of those in our own lives who need encouragement. Only God knows where our simple act of kindness may lead.

Characters

Roman Names and What They Tell Us

The rules for naming a Roman citizen were well defined, leaving little room for creativity but revealing a lot about the person and their relations.

The Roman familia is the Roman family unit consisting of the paterfamilias, his married and unmarried children regardless of age, his son's children, and his slaves. Wives and freed slaves (freedmen) are sometimes included in the familia.

Romans took names and what they said about family connections very seriously. The three-part name (like Manius Flavius Sabinus) meant you were a Roman citizen of the clan Flavius and family Sabinus. Using a three-part name if you weren't a citizen was actually a crime. Which name of the three you called someone depended on the closeness of your relationship. There were only twenty male first names in common use, and one-in-five Romans was named Gaius. Only close friends and immediate family called you by your first name. Others used your last name, both your second and third names when being formal, and sometimes your first and third names.

When a male slave was freed by a citizen so he became a citizen, too, he took the first and second names of his former owner with his slave name added as his third name. Women were named the feminine form of their father's clan and family names. Married women kept their maiden names because they stayed part of their father's familia, not their husband's.

Flavius Sabinus Familia

Quintus Flavius Sabinus (64): senator and ruthless Roman power broker

Manius Flavius Sabinus (43): Quintus's second son

Septimus Flavius Sabinus (19): Manius's second son

Flavia Sabina (22): Manius's widowed daughter, formerly married to Marcus Aurelius Gallus

Filomena (37): Sabina's lady's maid

Tutelus (26): Manius's Syrian bodyguard, former gladiator bought out of the arena

TITIANUS AND LENAEUS FAMILIAS

Titus Flavius Titianus (30): tribune in XI Urban Cohort, nephew of Quintus Sabinus

Pompeia Lenaea (25): wife of Titianus, teaches in her brother's school

Kaeso Pompeius Lenaeus (19): brother of Pompeia; head of Lenaeus School of Rhetoric

Corax (46): house steward and manservant, made a citizen when Manius bought and freed him

Ciconia (41): housekeeper and cook, married Corax 13 years earlier

Lilia (18): Daughter of Ciconia, housemaid and lady's maid to Pompeia

Theo (12): Son of Corax and Ciconia, now a free citizen.

Melis (16): youth from Titianus's warehouse who helps with investigations

Probus: manager of Titianus's warehouse on the Tiber

THE GLABRIO FAMILIA

Gaius Acilius Glabrio (20): tribune training to replace Titianus as officer over the XI Urban Cohort (father was consul in AD 124)

M'. Acilius Glabrio: consul in AD 91. Exiled by Domitian and executed in AD 95 for treason for becoming a Christian.

M'. Acilius Glabrio, consul in 124, and proconsul of Africa in 139/140, father of Gaius

M'. Acilius Aviola, consul in AD 122, cousin to Acilius Glabrio

THE MARCELLUS FAMILIA

Asinia Marcella (47): mother-in-law of Sabina, daughter of ex-consul Marcellus

M. Asinius Marcellus (43): brother of Asinia, Sabina's ex-mother-in-law

M. Asinius Marcellus (65), consul in 104

THE GALLUS FAMILIA

Marcus Aurelius Gallus (deceased at 29): husband of Sabina for 6 years, killed while hunting in Britannia, son of Asinia

Asinia Marcella (47): second wife of Lucius Gallus, daughter of M. Asinius Marcellus, consul in 104

Lucius Aurelius Gallus (53): former father-in-law

L. Aurelius Gallus (32): first son of Lucius Gallus, consul in AD 146

Other Important Characters
M. Lollius Paullinus Valerius Saturninus (58): Titianus's commander, Urban Prefect AD 124-134, also consul in 125
Q. Marcius Turbo: trusted friend and general for Trajan and Hadrian, Praetorian Prefect AD 125 to 134
Q. Rammius Martialis: tribune of the Praetorian Guard, friend of Titianus
G. Julius Victorinus: less-than-competent tribune of the Urban Cohort
Faustus Cornelius Rufinus (43): politically ambitious senator
Gellius: optio who reports to Titianus at the Subura guard station
Plancus: Titianus's optio at his headquarters office
Lanista Felix: head trainer over the Ludus Bruti
Thrax: gladiator bodyguard from Ludus Bruti

D. = Decimus L. = Lucius, M. = Marcus, M'. = Manius, Q. = Quintus

Many of the characters in this story are based on people in the historical records. For information on the people who are historical rather than fictitious, see the list of literary and historical figures in the historical note at the back of the book.

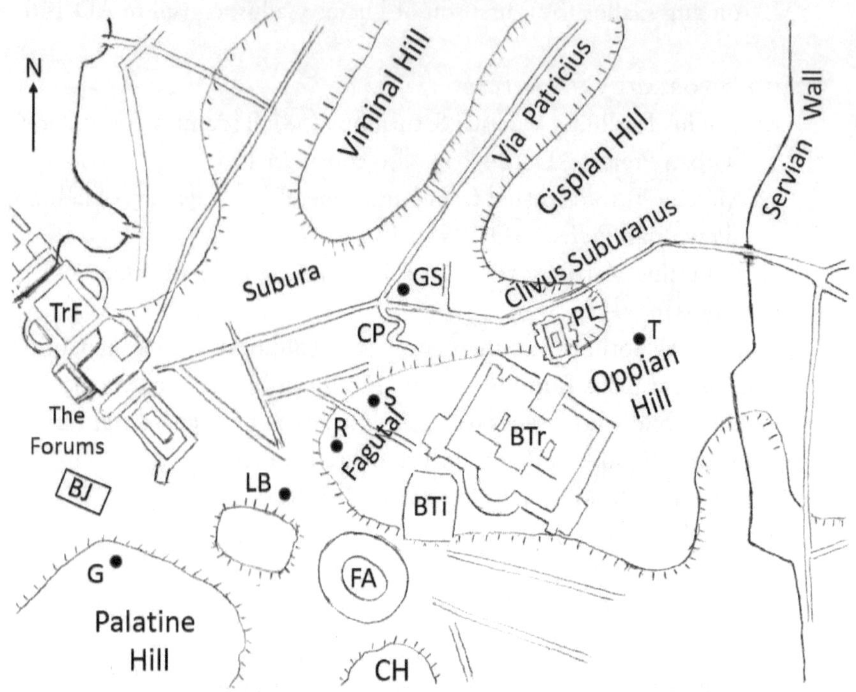

Locations in and near Rome

Glabrio town house on the Palatine Hill (G)

Rufinus town house: in the Fagutal district of the Esquiline Hill (R)

Sabinus town house: in the Fagutal district of the Esquiline Hill (S)

Titianus town house: on the Oppian Hill (T)

Ludus Bruti (LB) near the Flavian Amphitheater (FA)

Guard station (GS): near the intersection of the Clivus Pullius, Clivus Sub-uranus, and the Vicus Patricius

Clivus Pullius (CP): shortest road from guard station to Sabinus town house

Basilica Julia (BJ): large, ornate, public building used for meetings and other official business

Baths of Titus (BTi): imperial bath complex

Baths of Trajan (BTr) imperial bath complex on the Oppian Hill

Forum of Caesar: Forum Iulium or Forum Caesaris

Porticus of Livia (PL): Art galleries and Shrine of Concordia

Trajan's Forum (TF): Rome's "shopping mall"

Caelian Hill (CH)

Beyond the Boundaries of the Map

Praetorian Fortress: outside the Viminal Gate on the Via Patricius

Lacus Sabatinus: location of Gallus estate 20 miles (32 km) north of Rome, now Lake Bracciano

Tibur: town 17 miles (28 km) east of Rome, present-day Tivoli

Via Cassia: major highway leading north from Via Flaminia that enters Rome

Via Clodia: highway leading north from Via Cassia near Veii

Via Flaminia: highway that enters Rome through the Porta Fontinalis

This is Carol's map of important locations in the story derived from Platner's map (1911).

For a detailed map of the entire city: Platner's map of Rome for The Topography and Monuments of Ancient Rome (1911). You can access the full map online at http://bit.ly/DetailedMapofRome

Chapter 1

THE ASSIGNMENT

From his desk drawer, Titus Flavius Titianus lifted the dagger that started it all. The source of soul-piercing grief, but God had used what came after to give him treasures on earth and in heaven that he'd thought were impossible.

He traced the pattern of interwoven vines on the brass handle. There was a certain beauty to it until a man thought about what it had done in Arcanus's hand. But it wasn't the dagger that was evil. It was only a tool. That's all any weapon was. It could be used to defend or destroy. It was the heart of the one who used it that made the difference.

Four more days, and his time of service as tribune of the XI Urban Cohort would be over. He no longer regretted spending his military years catching criminals instead of fighting Rome's wars. He was ready to retire from public life and look after business and family as an ordinary man.

The growl of a throat clearing drew his gaze to the *optio* in the doorway. "What is it, Gellius?"

Only four days, and that would be a question he'd never ask the junior officer again. It was hard not to smile, but he maintained the aloof expression he'd always worn while on duty.

"Prefect Saturninus is here to see you."

Titianus drew a deep breath and stopped short of releasing it as a sigh that Gellius would hear. He could count on one hand the times Saturninus had come to one of his guard stations in the last three years. He'd always left Titianus with a thorny problem needing an immediate solution. What could the urban prefect want from him with only four days left?

He returned the dagger to the drawer and shut it. The last thing he needed was questions about it from Saturninus. The murder of a teacher of rhetoric had interested his commander only because Titianus suspected the freedman of the prefect's friend who wanted to be consul. When Arcanus was robbed and murdered before Titianus could question him, Saturninus had ordered the investigation dropped.

The prefect's glare as he told Titianus to spend no more time on an unimportant matter made that an order he wouldn't risk disobeying. Justice had been mostly served, and his main suspect was conveniently dead anyway.

"Bring him to me." Not what he wanted to say, but today he had no choice.

Wearing a frown that was more than halfway to a scowl, Saturninus entered alone.

Why hadn't he brought the young tribune who was to be Titianus's replacement?

Titianus stood. "Prefect." He struck his chest with his fist. "How can I help you?"

Saturninus closed the door behind him, slid the bolt across, and pointed at Titianus's chair. "Sit."

An odd command, but Titianus lowered himself into his desk chair. With so many years of practice, he could keep his mouth straight and his eyes calm, but his heart rate ramped up with each step the prefect took toward him.

Saturninus stopped at the edge of the desk. He was already looking down at Titianus, but he tipped his head slightly to press the point of his superior rank home. "My acceptance of your resignation…I'm withdrawing it."

Titianus fought the urge to cross his arms. Instead, he clasped his hands and rested them on the desk. Saturninus didn't like questions from subordinates. Silence was the best way to wait for this commander's explanations.

The slight flare of Saturninus's nostrils revealed the prefect was not eager to keep him around. So had the beaming smile when he toasted the end of Titianus's years of faithful service at the last monthly dinner for the tribunes of the Urban Cohort and the Praetorian Guard.

Saturninus cleared his throat. "Hadrian has learned there may be … irregularities in how some imperial business is being conducted. When Turbo and I were reporting on situations worth his notice in Rome, you came up." His snort was soft, but the disapproval was clear. "Your reputation for incorruptibility seems to have impressed the praetorian prefect, and he told Hadrian you were the man for this task."

The corner of Saturninus's mouth twitched. "So, it appears you have one more case before you can resign."

Titianus steepled his fingers and rubbed the side of his nose. Irregularities in imperial business. A tactful way of saying someone of great importance in the governmental hierarchy had done something he shouldn't. Someone with power to strike at anyone who got in his way, and that could come directly or through his supporters.

A year ago, he would have welcomed this assignment. Any chance to clean up corruption would have fired his enthusiasm and sharpened his focus. If he made enemies doing what was right, so be it. But a year ago he was a single man with no one who would be hurt if his investigation exposed someone too important to punish.

But if he refused, would that start the questions about why he'd changed? About Who had changed him? Would his faith be revealed and his whole *familia* be put at risk?

Turbo's recommendation had pinned a target on Titianus's back. Only one answer to an emperor's request was possible.

"My return to private life can wait until I serve Rome and Emperor Hadrian by resolving this problem. I withdraw my resignation for now."

"Good. Officially, you'll still report to me, but Turbo will provide you the details to begin. He'll expect you in his office at the fortress tomorrow morning."

"I'll be there, Prefect."

"That conversation shouldn't take very long, so your replacement will be waiting in your office after you finish with Turbo. You can teach him what's required to do the job like the other tribunes." The corner of his mouth lifted. "Do not try to make him into another one like you."

Saturninus stepped back from the desk and walked away. Titianus rose, but he didn't salute. "As you wish, Prefect."

When Saturninus closed the door behind him, Titianus sank into his chair. Elbows on the desk, he clasped his hands and rested his forehead against them.

God, help me do whatever I must, but please protect those I love from the anger of powerful men if I succeed.

Chapter 2

Freed, but for What?

The Gallus villa north of Rome, morning of Day 1

At the desk by the bedchamber window overlooking the flower garden, Sabina set aside the silver-tipped pen. Her brother Septimus had given it to her as a wedding present. At the Lenaeus School of Rhetoric, he'd used it daily with the inkwell made of lustrous red clay encircled by cream-colored vines. He'd told her to remember him every time she used them. Who would have thought such trifles would become treasures, bringing back memories of a happier time?

She capped the inkwell and blew gently on the papyrus until the shine on the last letters vanished, proclaiming them dry. With the sheet held at arms' length, she scanned her latest poem. Another ode to add to the collection no one would read but her.

Almost no one. Filomena, her lady's maid, would read it to her later so she could hear with her ears the cadence of the words that had sung inside her head.

A movement drew her gaze to a break in the curtain of leaves in the closest tree. A newly fledged bird wiggled its wings, its chirps rising in pitch until its mother pushed a moth into its mouth. Then mother flew away to find another insect, and baby stilled to await its mother's next gift.

Oh, to be as free as the creatures of forest and field. Sabina drew a deep breath and released it as a sigh. Six years ago, at the age of sixteen, she'd moved with eager anticipation from her father's town house to her new father-in-law's villa.

It wasn't a love match, but she'd never expected one. She was a Flavius

Sabinus. It was a political alliance between two leading senatorial families. Grandfather had arranged it, as he did almost everything. She'd met her betrothed only once before the marriage ceremony. Marcus Gallus was twenty-two, handsome, and muscled, and he laughed at all the right places as he and his father conversed with Father and Grandfather.

Each time he looked at her, his eyes lit with approval. That triggered a blush, and a teasing smile joined a raised eyebrow or wink before his attention returned to the older men.

She'd said almost nothing. Nervous as she was, her voice would have betrayed her. With close family, her stutter was barely noticeable. With strangers, it slowed her speech until some looked away and started talking with someone else. With her newly betrothed, magnificent in his shiny brass cuirass and aura of confidence, she'd feared it might make him think her too slow-witted to wed.

Mother always said the stutter wouldn't matter. Just listen attentively, nod in agreement, and make herself silently pleasant. She was pretty and graceful, and that plus the Sabinus name was enough to make any young nobleman eager to marry her. Father said more than a dozen fathers had asked Grandfather about uniting the two families. She was a matrimonial prize.

But being desired for the wrong reason was far worse than no one wanting you. The last six years had proven that.

Beside the desk sat a small wooden chest carved with vines and flowers. After lifting the chain holding its key over her head, she unlocked it and added the sheet to the stack. Tomorrow she'd write an ode to the nestling and the faithfulness of its mother. Her mind would fill with wonderful words, whirling and dancing inside her. With pen in hand, she'd wait for just the right ones to capture the tiny creature's attempts to leave its tree-bound existence and fly.

If only it were that easy for her to be free.

The door swung open, and Filomena stepped through and closed it. "A horse courier just came. Terrible news from Britannia. Master Marcus… he's dead."

Sabina's hands flew up to cover her mouth. "How?"

"Vitula said it was a hunting accident. His horse threw him when a boar charged, and his neck broke."

Sabina sank into the desk chair and closed her eyes. She'd been counting down the days until he would return from Britannia, but it wasn't because she wanted him back.

The handsome young man who made her feel wanted with winks and smiles before the marriage ceremony had come to the bridal bed two hours late and stumbling drunk.

With slurred words, he declared what he wanted, and when she tried to speak, the words wouldn't come. As she struggled to get past the sticking letters, he mimicked each repeated sound and every pause. That only made it worse.

When he told her it wasn't worth the wait to hear what she might say, she stopped trying.

What should have been the happy beginning of a shared life together became something to be endured until he would join the Legio VI Victrix in Britiannia six months after they wed.

She would never say it aloud to anyone, not even Filomena, but his death inspired no grief in her. Knowing she would never again be in his company, ridiculed and rejected—that only brought an unspeakable feeling of relief.

"Where is his mother?"

Asinia Marcella thought Marcus the embodiment of all perfections. She joined her son in mocking Sabina's speech, and they thought it good sport to see who could be meaner. When he left for Londinium and no grandchild was on the way, she proclaimed Sabina at fault and sought consolation in continuing to berate Sabina for her many defects, real and imagined.

If she'd been an ordinary Roman woman, she wouldn't have had to bear it. But she knew better than to ask Grandfather to let her divorce him. He would never sanction a disruption of his alliance with Lucius Aurelius Gallus merely because Gallus's wife was meaner than a weasel.

Asking Father to ask Grandfather wouldn't have changed that. Family reputation was more important to both of them than her happiness.

But no matter how cruel Asinia had been, no mother deserved to lose her son.

"I heard wailing coming from the atrium."

Sabina rose and took Filomena's hand. "Ss-stay here out of sight. I don't want Asinia doing something to you to strike at me." She squared her shoulders. She'd never gone to the games to watch gladiators fight, but was this how they felt before walking out onto the sand?

Onto the balcony and down the stairs, her feet carried her where she didn't want to go. The philosophers claimed true courage wasn't the absence of fear. It was doing what should be done in spite of it. Grandfather and Father would expect her to rise above personal feelings and speak condolences to her husband's grieving mother, even if some part of her wasn't sorry she'd never see Marcus again.

The wails Filomena heard had quieted into sobs, but Sabina was still able to follow them into the peristyle garden. Asinia sat in her favorite wicker chair, face in her hands, shoulders shaking.

What to say? If Marcus had been a man she could love or even one she could like, Sabina would have knelt at her mother-in-law's feet, taken her hands, and joined her in heartfelt tears. But any display of grief on her own part would have to be faked, and Asinia would know it.

With slow, deliberate steps, she approached the grieving mother. Five feet from her, Sabina stopped and cleared her throat. "I'm s-sorry."

That was both true and short enough that she sounded almost normal.

Asinia's hands dropped to the arms of the chair and gripped them tight enough to whiten her knuckles. "Sorry? No, you aren't." Pain vanished from the woman's eyes. It was replaced by fury. "You never cared for Marcus. You were worthless as a wife. You utterly failed in your duty to give him an heir. It's your fault I have no grandson to love as I loved him."

She pushed off the chair arms and rose. "I should never have let my husband bring you into this house just to seal an alliance with your grandfather."

Sabina clenched her jaw. It wasn't her fault Marcus had failed to father a son. Even when he condescended to lie with her, he left as soon as he finished to take his pleasure with someone else. How she longed to argue with the vixen who'd made sure he had access to anyone he wanted, but the words hung in her throat. Past experience had taught her it was better to say nothing, anyway.

Asinia took a step toward her, and Sabina stepped back.

As Sabina moved farther out of striking range, Asinia shook her finger at her. "But maybe you would have ruined any child by passing on your defects. A noble Roman must be an orator, and no one wants to ll-listen to ss-speech like yours."

Sabina's eyes narrowed. For six years, she'd put up with this woman's abuse because Grandfather had decreed it. But Marcus's death ended the formal alliance. She was free to return to her father's house…until Grandfather decided otherwise.

"Ll-lend me your carriage and bodyguards." She tipped back her head to look down her nose as Asinia had done to her every day since she came. "I'll leave today."

The woman who'd tormented her for six years swept the tears from her cheeks and scowled. Her nose wrinkled as if smelling something five-days dead. "Nothing could please me more. Take only what you brought when you came. Nothing my son gave you will leave here."

What her son gave her? Only cruel words and physical neglect. He'd preferred the slave girls to their marriage bed, and she didn't even have a child to make up for six years with this gorgon and her son.

But perhaps that was better. Grandchildren belong to the *paterfamilias*, and Lucius Gallus never refused his shrew of a wife when it was easier to give in to her demands. Asinia would have kept every grandchild to ruin as she'd ruined her son. Sabina would have been forced to leave them behind with the jewels that were only given to her to show off the family wealth at banquets.

"My gg-grandfather's money bought the Horatius ss-scrolls." She took a deep breath. "And Ss-statius's *Silvae*." Another deep breath. "I'm taking them all."

Shoulders squared and head high, she strode from the garden.

One small trunk for the scrolls, the chest holding her own poetry, two chests for the personal items she'd brought with her, and another trunk for everything else. She and Filomena could be packed in an hour and on their way back to Rome.

Like the baby bird in the tree, she was on the verge of freedom. She stepped into her room, closed the door, and tipped her head back against its sculpted panels. Filomena stared at her, but she couldn't keep her lips from curving into the happiest smile in years.

Freedom. That would be the glorious theme for tomorrow's first poem.

Chapter 3

WHAT THE FUTURE HOLDS

On the way to Rome, midday of Day 1

With arms crossed, Sabina watched the house slaves slide her trunk into the carriage. They shoved it against the front wall to leave room for her and Filomena to slip past and reach the padded seat in the rear. Beneath that seat were the only things worth taking with her—her scrolls of Horatius and Statius and the poems she'd written herself.

She motioned for Filomena to climb in first, then squeezed past the trunk to sit beside her. Two mounted bodyguards rode past, one on each side, and took their place ahead of the mule team.

It would have been customary and proper for Asinia to bid her farewell, but no one except the stable slaves were there to see her leave.

She was glad of it.

With a jerk, the *raeda* carrying Sabina from this place of torment started the journey home.

Home. Maybe that wasn't the right word. Her grandfather's town house in the elite Fagutal neighborhood was where her father and Septimus now lived. But it had been almost six years since she'd even visited there.

Within a week after the marriage, her father-in-law sent her and his son to join Asinia at their estate north of Rome. She'd stayed there ever since.

Lucius Gallus had arranged the marriage to cement his political alliance with Grandfather. Father hadn't questioned Grandfather's choice; he never did. It was enough that Gallus was a rising young senator who'd already commanded the III Gallica legion in Syria.

Securing Grandfather's support had paid off for Gallus. The Senate made him governor of Gallia Narbonensis for a year and then prefect over the distribution of grain in Rome. He was now prefect over the public treasury. Given Grandfather's influence with Hadrian, Gallus expected to become consul within two years.

Neither Father nor Grandfather had cared enough to travel the twenty miles to visit. If they had, would Grandfather have been content to leave her with the vixen that Gallus himself avoided by living in Rome when not serving in some distant province?

A deep sigh escaped. Without a doubt. He would never have risked a valued alliance for the sake of her happiness. A Sabinus was expected to serve Rome, and the only way the Sabinus women could serve was by supporting the political careers of their men.

Had Grandfather ever asked why she never came to Rome in the last six years? Or was he glad because he was ashamed that any granddaughter of his stuttered horribly when she got nervous? She'd given him frequent opportunity for embarrassment because she got nervous around anyone except immediate family.

The views from the carriage window as they headed south along Lacus Sabatinus were lovely—worthy inspiration for future poems. But the images blurred when the grief she'd held in check finally broke through.

Grief for her father-in-law at the loss of his son. Lucius Gallus had always been pleasant to her, but he let his wife have her own way at the estate and never reprimanded his son when he was being beastly.

With an older son who'd already given him two grandsons, the Gallus family line would continue, even with Marcus dead. Maybe that was what Lucius cared about most. If so, it should help him bear the loss.

Tears welled in her eyes, but she fought their attempt to escape. A Sabinus knew how to hide emotions. She'd mastered the skill since showing distress only made Asinia pick at her more.

Why hadn't her husband been more like his older brother? Her brother-in-law had seemed a decent man when he came from the bigger Gallus estate just east of Rome for a visit. He never laughed when Marcus and Asinia mocked her. He'd even ordered his wife to stop when she joined the laughter to curry Asinia's favor. But Asinia was only his stepmother. What she thought didn't matter to the man who knew he'd be the next paterfamilias.

And it didn't matter to Sabina anymore.

She flicked away the tear that escaped, but it wasn't for Marcus, his mother, or his father.

Six years—six wretched years—more than a quarter of her life. What should have been the best years of her life had been wasted at the Gallus estate because she'd only sealed a political alliance between Grandfather and Lucius Gallus.

Tears over her uncertain future trickled to the edge of her jaw, where she wiped them off. Filomena took her hand and squeezed. Concerned eyes above an encouraging smile made words between them unnecessary.

Sabina's closest friend belonged to Grandfather. He could take her away and sell her, and Sabina would be powerless to stop it. How ironic that he had just as much power over Sabina's fate.

She returned a shaky smile and turned her face back to the window.

Would she be used again as a bargaining chip when Grandfather arranged another political marriage?

She bit her lip. Might it be possible to remain a widow in her father's house where she wouldn't have to endure the scorn and pity of people who thought her stumbling speech meant a slow mind that limited all she could ever be?

In the silence of her mind, she was as eloquent as the greatest orators. When she wrote, words flowed like spring water sparkling in the sun as it cascaded over a rock ledge. Father had even told Grandfather at a family dinner that her writing was better than Septimus's, and they both thought him exceptional in every way.

And he was. Smart, funny, generous, loyal, a gifted orator, an excellent swordsman—he was everything a young nobleman should be. Best of all, he loved her because…just because.

They'd been more than brother and sister. Only three years her junior, he'd been a true friend for as long as she could remember. He never teased her about her stutter, so she seldom stuttered when it was only the two of them. He was the one person who cared enough to wait until the words finally came out and then thought what she said was worth remembering.

He'd been a precocious youth of thirteen when she left. He'd be a grown man now. But if Septimus was at Father's town house when she got there, maybe it would feel like coming home.

The Titianus town house, evening of Day 1

Kaeso Lenaeus unrolled the scroll on the library desk and traced a line of letters with his fingertips. The theme of Book VI of Quintilianus's *Institutio Oratoria*, was the use of humor as a tool of persuasion. Of all the tools for rhetorical brilliance, this had been Father's favorite.

It seemed like yesterday when Kaeso had stood at the back of the room, chuckling with the students as Father demonstrated before asking each youth to try making everyone laugh. But it had been almost a year since Father's murder. Whether he felt like it or not, tomorrow Kaeso would be the one teaching the sons of noble Romans how to make men laugh.

He closed his eyes and rubbed the back of his neck. But even the violent acts of evil men can bring some good to those who love God. His sister Pompeia had found the perfect husband in the equestrian tribune who hunted Father's murderer, and Titus Titianus had become his brother in Christ.

The school had moved from the small rented town house to Titus's spacious atrium, and soon his brother-in-law would retire from the Urban Cohort to teach history, geometry, and arithmetic while Kaeso taught philosophy and rhetoric, allowing the Lenaeus School of Rhetoric to serve twice as many students.

Father had always said Titianus was one of the finest young men he taught. For him to join both their familia and their faith—nothing would have pleased Father more.

Kaeso looked up when Titus, still in full armor, entered the library and closed the door. He crossed the room and sank into the chair opposite Kaeso before moving the helmet from his head to the desk and swishing his fingers through his hair.

"Only three more days." Kaeso tapped the bronze crown of the helmet with his knuckles. "Then you won't have to wear all the metal, but we do teach in togas." He grinned at his brother-in-law. "Perhaps that's not an improvement."

"I can't quit in three days." Titus rubbed his mouth, and a frown remained when he stopped.

"Why not?" Kaeso's grin vanished as he read the worry in Titus's eyes.

"Saturninus came to the Subura station to tell me he wouldn't accept my resignation yet. Apparently, he and Turbo were briefing Hadrian, and

Turbo wanted to borrow me to investigate some 'irregularities' in some imperial business. Hadrian agreed. So, I have one last case to solve."

"That doesn't sound too bad. What will it take, maybe a week or two?"

"Time isn't the problem." Titus blew his breath out slowly. "To attract Hadrian's attention, they must suspect someone important is involved. Someone politically powerful. Simply making the inquiries will draw too much attention to me. If I find something, I'll make some powerful enemies among the friends and allies of whoever is responsible."

He rested his elbow on the desk and his jaw on his hand. "Saturninus doesn't like Turbo, and I could tell he was angry that my departure's been delayed because Hadrian gave Turbo my services for one last case. When the praetorian prefect requests a subordinate of the urban prefect to conduct an investigation, it's got to be something unusual."

With eyes closed, he shook his head. "If someone starts looking for my weak spot to apply pressure, they might discover my faith." His gaze locked on Kaeso. "That would put us all at risk…Pompeia, you, the whole familia. Maybe even Torquatus and Glyptus."

"Pompeia was afraid of that when you started looking for Father's murderer." Kaeso wrinkled his nose before squeezing his neck. "God protected us from you discovering our faith before you were ready to make it your own." He drew air between his teeth. "If the emperor wants you to do this, you can't say no. We'll just have to ask God to keep special protection over us all."

"True, but I think we need to warn at least some in our house church about what's happening. Torquatus, Glyptus, maybe Corax. Everyone in this house is careful so the students won't find out. Maybe the usual caution is enough for them."

"God always knows the details we don't know, so when we ask for His protection daily, those prayers will cover this as well." Kaeso shrugged. "You couldn't refuse, and you can't blame Hadrian for wanting his best investigator involved." He leaned across the desk to nudge Titus's arm. "Truth and justice above all else. That's what they expect of you."

Titus's mouth twitched. "It was easier to be cold-blooded in the pursuit of justice when I didn't care so much about other people and my own death wouldn't matter to anyone. Hadrian ordered me to remain on duty to investigate this because I'm supposed to be immune to the human emotions that lead to loyalty to family and friends and concern about rank."

He snorted. "Since becoming a Christian, my circle of brothers and sisters has gone from two half-sisters I had no special feelings toward to more than a dozen people I care about deeply." He squeezed the back of his neck as his mouth curved down. "If leading senators are involved, I could make some dangerous enemies at the highest levels."

"What if Quintus Sabinus is part of it?"

"I doubt that, but I've been surprised before." His teeth clenched. "I hate to think what it would do to Manius and Septimus if I were the one to bring harm to Quintus."

A knock on the door was followed by a pause. Then the door opened just enough for Pompeia to stick her head into the room. Kaeso waved her in.

She strolled over to Titus. "I love visiting my old students. Sanura's boy is walking well now."

With her hands on the shoulders of his cuirass, she leaned over to kiss his cheek. "You two look serious."

"I'm going to be serving as tribune a little longer."

Her laugh was followed by another kiss. "Just when Kaeso was looking forward to having your help teaching history, you've changed your mind?"

"Hadrian won't let me retire until I finish one last investigation."

Straight lips replaced her smile. "Will it be dangerous?"

"Maybe. It depends on who's guilty. I don't want anyone investigating me and maybe discovering our faith." He tipped his head to look up at her. "I've been trapped into a politically sensitive investigation that's bound to make me more enemies, and that could increase the danger of following Jesus for all of us."

She moved one hand to stroke his jaw. "When you do your job well, that's always a risk. We'll all ask God for extra protection until you finish this and Hadrian sets you free."

He placed his hand over the hand still on his shoulder and entwined their fingers. "Tomorrow I meet with Prefect Turbo to find out what I'll be doing. Perhaps it won't be a serious problem after all."

Titus stood, and Pompeia began unlatching the clasps on the side of his body armor. Kaeso leaned back in his chair and crossed his arms. Surely God hadn't blessed these two with each other, only to end their life together so quickly.

It wasn't time to worry, but it was always time to pray.

Chapter 4

Coming Home

The Sabinus town house, late evening of Day 1

With his father's Syrian bodyguard Tutelus by his side, Septimus Sabinus entered the town house stableyard. Dinner with Kaeso was always a time for good food and relaxation as he talked with trustworthy friends. Grandfather might prefer to spend his time with the great men of Rome, but Septimus preferred dining with good men like Kaeso and his cousin Titianus.

He was almost to the portico when the jingle of harness announced an approaching carriage. When it tried to enter the stableyard, one of the men guarding the gate grabbed one mule's bridle while the second approached the raeda window.

Septimus didn't catch the words, but a woman's voice made the guard step back and signal the other to release the mule. The carriage came through the gate and stopped.

"See who that is." Septimus tipped his head toward the raeda.

Tutelus strode over to stick his head and massive shoulders through the carriage door. When he stepped back, he held out his hand to steady a young woman as she stepped down. She was dressed in a red linen tunic with a blue *palla* wrapped closely around her and pulled up to cover her hair. Her lady's maid followed her.

It had been six years since she'd left with her new husband, but Septimus would know his sister anywhere. "Sabina!"

Arms spread, he walked toward her. "Welcome! It's good to see you, Skylark."

Sabina closed the space between them and slipped her arms around him as his completed the embrace. Then she stepped back.

"I've come home. The raeda needs to return to the Gallus estate tonight."

Septimus looked past her to Tutelus. "Get her trunks up to the room Pompeia used."

After a silent nod, Tutelus entered the peristyle and returned with four men. The lady's maid who served Sabina took charge of them.

They pulled out a large trunk and a small one and carried them into the house. Her maid disappeared into the carriage. One by one, she handed two small chests to Tutelus, and he placed them on a bench in the portico. When she climbed out of the carriage, she carried a third herself.

With her arms crossed, Sabina watched in silence.

Her maid placed the chest with the others and joined them. With hands clasped in front of her, she bowed to Septimus before lowering her eyes. "That's all, mistress."

Sabina squared her shoulders and raised her chin before waving her hand toward the gate. "You three can r-return to the estate now."

The driver snapped the reins, and the mule team turned the carriage around. As quickly as they'd arrived, the raeda and guards disappeared into the dark street.

When Sabina slipped her arms around Septimus again, the last thing he expected was for her body to shake as if she were sobbing. She made no sound as she clung to him.

Why had she come with only her maid, and why wasn't she wearing the stola of a married woman?

With both hands on her upper arms, he eased her away from him until he could see her face. His fingertips swept some tears from her cheek. "Let's get you settled in your old room. When you're ready, you can tell me all about it."

"I'm r-ready now." Sabina's lips quivered, then steadied into a smile like she used to give him.

With one arm wrapped around his sister's shoulders, Septimus guided her through the peristyle to the library that had always been her favorite room. He motioned her to take one of the chairs by the game table.

After bolting the door, he sank into the chair across from her. "What's happened?"

"My husband is dead."

Septimus leaned across the table and took her hands. "I'm so sorry."

Her face hardened. "I'm not."

His head drew back.

"I sh-shocked you. I know I should grieve, but I can't. The p-past six years have been horrible. M-marcus and his mother…" Her jaw clenched. "When I tried to speak and the words stuck… From the first day they mocked me. Said I wasn't worth listening to. Asinia told me to keep my mouth shut at dinners with more than the family there. She didn't want people laughing behind her back and wondering if her son's heirs would stutter like me."

"Did you tell Father this?"

"No." Her lips tightened. "Grandfather wanted the alliance that my marriage sealed. Father approved of it, too. It was my duty to do my part, even if no one wanted me there." Her chin quivered. "I tried, but I failed to bear a son."

Tears welled up in her eyes "But Grandfather would never have allowed a divorce. So, Marcus's death was the only way out."

"You should have told Father. He would have done something."

"And risk upsetting Grandfather?" She snorted. "A Sabinus daughter cements political alliances. That's just how it is. Father won't oppose any-thing Grandfather wants to do with me."

She covered her mouth and nose with her hands. A tear escaped, and she swept it aside. "What if Grandfather marries me off to another beast like Marcus?" She bit her lip. "Or worse. At least he never hit me."

Another tear followed the first. "But words can wound, too." Then a stream of tears washed over her cheeks. "Oh, Septimus! I don't know if I can bear it again."

Septimus stood and drew her out of her chair. He nestled her cheek against his chest and placed one hand on the back of her head. She'd never minded if something messed up her hair, so his fingertips started a light massage.

"Don't cry, Skylark. Father won't be home until late. Let me talk with him before you do. He's different from how you remember him. I think his response to this will surprise you."

Sabina sniffed and swept away the last trace of tears. "Do you think that will make any difference?" Skepticism coated her words.

"I do. Now, have you eaten dinner?"

As she shook her head, the corners of her mouth drooped. Was she still questioning what he said about Father or saying she was hungry?

He took her hand. "Even this late, I can at least get you some bread and cheese and fruit."

He unbolted the door to find Sabina's lady's maid sitting on the bench outside. Sabina curled her fingers to summon her, and they headed toward the kitchen off the peristyle.

Sabina rested her head against his shoulder as they walked. Her steps dragged, like a weariness far beyond her twenty-two years was weighing her down.

But he'd do what he could to restore what she'd lost since they parted six years ago.

Father had changed a lot in the last three years. Some of it was from his friendship with cousin Titus. Father teased him about being the incorruptible man of honor, but he truly cared about Titus's opinion of him.

But Kaeso's father and Marcus Brutus were really responsible. They'd taught Septimus to always ask what honor required. When he started telling Father that honor, not political advantage, would guide his own life, Father began to change.

The Sabinus town house, nearly midnight of Day 1

When Manius returned home just before midnight, Septimus was lounging in the peristyle garden. His son was reading with a rack of oil lamps on a branching stand behind his chair, but he rolled the scroll and stood when Manius entered.

"Good evening, Father. Was it a good dinner?"

"Informative, as your Grandfather's banquets always are, but I suspect you enjoyed more congenial company."

Manius closed his eyes and rubbed his neck. "I'm getting too old to do this too many nights in a row."

"You'll never be old, Father. Neither will Grandfather. He'll seem young until the day he dies."

To the young, life could seem limitless, but Manius knew better. "Don't tell him we've been discussing his death. He might suspect we're looking forward to it."

Septimus chuckled. "I doubt that. He couldn't have a better son than you, and he knows it." Septimus's gaze dropped to the scroll in his hand before returning to Manius. "But even the best son doesn't always do exactly what his father wants when that could hurt someone else in the family."

So, his son hadn't waited up for him without a reason. "Someone else in the family?"

"Lucius Gallus's son died. Sabina came home tonight. She's asleep in her old room." He tipped his head toward the atrium doorway. "Let's talk in the library."

Manius followed his son into his favorite room in the house. When Septimus closed the door and bolted it, Manius sat halfway on the desk and crossed his arms. "There's more to this than young Gallus's death."

"There is." Approval of his perception lit Septimus's eyes. "She never said anything because she didn't want to disappoint you and Grandfather. From the first day of the marriage, her husband and his mother mocked her stutter. They made it a game between them. Asinia did everything she could to make her feel unworthy to be part of their family. She made her stay silent if anyone but their family was around. Mocked her when she stuttered, which made her stutter more."

Septimus's teeth clenched. "But my sister's all Sabinus. No one can totally crush the spirit of any of us, no matter what they do." He took a deep breath and flexed his jaw. "But she's carrying deep scars from what they did. She's stuttering worse than I ever remember, even with me."

"She should have told me." Anger surged at the thought of them torturing his daughter. "I would have talked with Lucius Gallus, and he would have put a stop to it…or else."

"That's what I thought you'd do, but it's too late to fix what's already happened. It's not too late to keep it from happening again."

"Most Roman widows remarry promptly. As soon as the news of Gallus's death spreads, men will approach your grandfather to ask for a marriage."

"But Seneca wrote that our ancestors allowed women to mourn their husbands for ten months. After Augustus died, women were allowed a full year. Surely Sabina can have at least ten months before Grandfather uses her to seal an alliance again."

"But if she had no love for him, she isn't mourning."

"No, but here in Rome, no one knows that except us. She's afraid what happened with Asinia could happen again."

Manius rubbed his lip. His daughter's fear was not unreasonable. Even though Emperor Claudius was a scholar who wrote well-respected histories of Carthage, the Etruscans, and the Republic, he was ridiculed for his stutter. No one had expected him to become emperor. Many were surprised when he proved a good one. Except for wounds received in battle, Romans made little allowance for physical defects.

"I'll talk with her in the morning to see what she wants."

Septimus sucked air between his teeth. "She might be afraid to tell you."

"I understand more about young women than you give me credit for. I'll give her the choice of staying here with me or at the estate with her mother for at least a few months."

"Don't give her a choice. She'll ask to hide away at the estate, and that's not what she needs now. Keep her here where I can help her become like she used to be. Pompeia could be a huge help in that."

"Titus's wife is good medicine for any problem of the heart. She certainly helped him discover he had one." Manius stood. "I'll invite the two of them and Kaeso for dinner tomorrow. I have no prior engagement then."

"Maybe wait a few days before thrusting her into company with people she doesn't know. That will give me a chance to tell her what good friends they are. I'll get her comfortable with meeting them."

One corner of Manius's mouth curved. For one so young, Septimus was surprisingly good at recognizing what could get someone to do what he wanted. Even better than he'd been at that age. "It also gives me a chance to convince Father that she needs some time with us before her presence in Rome becomes gossip fodder. I can make no long-term promises about what he'll do, but I can sway what he does right now."

Manius unbolted the door and opened it. "Both of you join me for breakfast. We'll set her mind at ease before I hold salutation. Setting her heart at ease…I'll leave that to you and your friends."

Chapter 5

The Final Case

The Praetorian Fortress, morning of Day 2

As Titianus approached the columns fronting the Praetorium where Prefect Turbo would be waiting, he fastened his helmet strap. He seldom did that except at formal reviews of the troops, but a battle-ready helmet might be expected by the brilliant general who'd directed the main Roman fleet during Trajan's Parthian war, put down revolts in Egypt, Cyrene, and Mauritania, commanded the legions on the Danube, and governed first the two Mauritanias and then Dacia.

For the last two years, Hadrian's most trusted general had commanded the Praetorians, who served as imperial bodyguards and kept watch on any political unrest in Rome. Turbo was a man of honor dedicated to serving Rome and the emperor, and Titianus would show all the respect he deserved.

To be personally recommended by such a man was an honor, but Titianus would rather not have been chosen for this delicate mission. It put too many people he cared about at risk, and that was true whether he succeeded or failed.

A guard in full armor stood on each side of the open double doors. Their fists struck their chests as he approached them.

Up the marble steps and through the doorway, he kept his face emotionless. He strode across a courtyard flanked on each side by several rooms that grew smaller as he neared the *tablinum* of the Guard's commander. Two soldiers stood on either side of the closed door, legs spread, shields in their left hands and right hands on their swords' hilts.

He stopped six feet in front of them. "Tribune Flavius Titianus of the XI Urban Cohort to see Prefect Turbo."

Two right fists struck their brass cuirasses, and the larger soldier opened one of the two doors that were carved with the thunderbolts and eagle wings of the Praetorian emblem.

He stepped inside, and the door was pulled shut behind him.

Quintus Marcius Turbo sat behind a massive desk with three wax tablets open before him. Silver frosted the curly black hair that proclaimed his Greek origin from Epidaurum in Dalmatia. Broad shoulders and muscled arms declared him fit for battle.

The prefect closed and stacked the tablets, then handed them to the optio who stood at attention at the end of the desk. "Leave us. We're not to be disturbed."

The optio saluted, spun on his heel, and strode past Titianus. The door opened, then shut behind him.

Turbo pointed at the chair across the desk from him. "Sit."

Titianus lowered himself onto the front half of the seat but kept his spine at attention. Before his marriage, he'd lived in tribune quarters at the fortress. The evening usually ended with a few games of *tabula* or *latrunculi* with one of the Praetorian tribunes. But his game with Martialis was often interrupted because his friend was summoned long after sunset by the still-working Turbo.

Saturninus hosted a monthly dinner for his Urban Cohort tribunes and the Praetorian tribunes. Whether he invited Turbo as well was a mystery to Titianus, but Turbo had never joined them.

Titianus wouldn't have attended himself were it not a useful time to glean information about the private activities of noble Romans. Saturninus served good wine and plenty of it. As the drinkers' inhibitions washed away, he'd often learned what they would never have shared fully sober.

Like him, Saturninus watched and listened. Perhaps his commander hadn't wanted Turbo to do the same.

Turbo leaned back in his chair. "You're probably wondering why I asked you here. My tribune Martialis tells me you have an uncanny ability to find the truth even when it's well hidden, that you don't stop digging until you uncover it."

Titianus's mouth twitched before he could stop it. He didn't like flattery, even from a superior, but the honest praise of a friend…a man had to appreciate that. "Truth and justice matter to me, Prefect."

"So I've heard from your commander." Turbo tightened his lips to stop a smile. "Sometimes that's…inconvenient for him, but that's precisely what this matter requires."

Turbo leaned forward to rest his elbows on the desk and steepled his fingers against his lips. With his gaze locked on Titianus, he fell silent.

Titianus's jaw clenched. Was he supposed to ask what his assignment was, or would Turbo think that insubordinate?

Most people couldn't stand silence, but Titianus wasn't one of them. So many times, he'd learned what someone hadn't planned to tell him because they couldn't bear him simply watching them.

Turbo's suppressed smile broke free, accompanied by a chuckle. "Martialis told me silence is among your favorite tools for getting someone to talk. It's a weapon you wield with skill." He leaned back in his chair. "I sometimes use it myself."

The prefect picked up the brass stylus and rolled it between his fingers. "But it's time to focus on the problem for which I summoned you. What did Saturninus tell you?"

"That irregularities in how some imperial business is being conducted had been discovered. That you recommended that I be the one to investigate because I have a reputation for learning the truth, regardless of the importance of the ones who want to hide it."

Incorruptible was what Saturninus had said, but repeating the word to Turbo felt too arrogant.

"Hadrian and I thought it wise to make the problem sound financial. It makes it easier for you to report the details of your progress to me instead of the urban prefect. In truth, it's political and of the utmost urgency."

Titianus stopped himself before he swallowed too hard, but he'd give almost anything to leave Turbo's office, once more request approval of his resignation, and walk away from what could easily get his whole familia killed. But that was not an option open to him.

Perhaps "utmost urgency" was an exaggeration.

With three fingers and his thumb, Turbo rotated the stylus end over end. "I understand you've served in the Urban Cohort since just before Trajan died. He adopted Hadrian and declared him the next emperor before he crossed the River Styx, but there were some who questioned that because it thwarted their own political ambitions."

"The four ex-consuls." Titianus's heart rate rose despite his attempts to slow it down.

A political problem of utmost urgency…was he really saying a plot against the emperor's life?

Many of the elite had questioned whether Praetorian Prefect Attianus had fabricated the evidence he used to force the Senate to order the four men's executions. Hadrian denied telling Attianus to remove them, but many thought he was lying. Celsus and Palma were his long-time enemies.

Hadrian had stripped Quietus of the governorship of Judaea and the command of his ruthlessly effective Moorish cavalry. Quietus was on his way back to his home province of Mauritania when he died en route. Rumors that Hadrian had him assassinated had rippled through Rome.

One corner of Turbo's mouth lifted. "I expect you know I replaced one of them as governor."

Turbo's pause commanded a response.

"Nigrinus in Dacia after ending the revolt in Mauritania after Quietus's death." Titianus cleared his throat. "And you were putting down the Jewish revolt in Egypt while Quietus was ending it in Judaea. Trajan valued you both highly."

Perhaps he shouldn't have said that. But perhaps it would release him from this assignment before he was told more than he wanted to know.

Turbo's half-smile didn't warm his eyes. "You're a man who knows Rome's history."

"Evenings in tribune quarters lend themselves to reading."

"And tabula when I didn't call your opponent back to work with me. Martialis thinks there's no one more worthy of trust than you." The prefect's smile broadened, and his eyes warmed. "He has a bright political future; I knew his father well in Egypt."

Turbo set the stylus down. "A letter in the imperial post was intercepted. It appears that at least one ex-consul or his son and an unknown number of accomplices are plotting to remove Hadrian as emperor. We know the name of one conspirator. We do not know how many others are involved or who they are."

He unlocked the desk drawer and withdrew a metal box.

"You know about the four ex-consuls, so I assume you know the Senate still harbors animosity toward Emperor Hadrian for the man who'd been Trajan's praetorian prefect getting the Senate to vote for their execution."

He reached inside the neck of his tunic and pulled out a chain with a key on it.

"Your emperor would prefer that the men involved be identified without anyone realizing they are under suspicion until the evidence to convict them is in hand."

He unlocked the box. "My own men would normally do this, but since I don't know who else is involved, I can't risk one of them warning a conspirator."

From the metal box, he lifted a wax tablet.

"But if you are the one investigating, anyone will assume it's merely a criminal matter under Saturninus's jurisdiction. It's common for you to be digging into some problem and looking for connections between people to find those of interest."

He held out the tablet. "Your integrity is beyond question, and your dedication to Rome has been proven repeatedly these last ten years. I have no concern that you'll be revealing anything to someone who shouldn't know it."

As Titianus took it, Turbo leaned back in his chair again. "If you read that, you will have agreed to find out exactly what is planned and identify those involved, no matter who they might be. Hadrian doesn't know who among his regular informers can be trusted, so we think it best to draft the incorruptible tribune of the Urban Cohort to find out."

Titianus held the tablet in both hands. If he opened it, what dangers would he be exposing his family and close friends to? But even if he didn't open it, he'd already been told too much.

He opened the tablet.

At the top where the greeting would normally be, the wax had melted and solidified again. He glanced at Turbo. Intercepted in the imperial mail? It looked like someone had tried to destroy it before anyone else could read it, but a quarter of the way down, some faint writing remained.

> I have in mind a play, like the Greeks staged of old, and we all know the perfect one to play the role of the tragic hero, for so he views himself. Hero, that is, not tragic, and a lover of all things Greek.
>
> Perhaps a tale from ancient Athens. Hipparchus would suit.
>
> Or maybe a Macedonian tale. Philip would do.
>
> There are many eager to play the leads, as we did in the days of our youthful studies.

For a third of the length, another section of wax had melted. Titianus tipped the tablet at an angle to see if anything could be seen. For most of it, any letters that had been there were gone, but there was one strip where a shadowy impression remained. He tipped his head back and held the tablet above him. First slowly, then quickly, then slowly again, he changed the angle. There, visible only when he peered at the right angle along the almost flat surface, could he see it.

> Marcellus agrees about the proper response to an insult to a sister. I'll ensure there's no bodyguard who'll prevent instead of help.

For a short distance there was nothing. But near the bottom of the frame, he could make out more words.

> As M's ancestor would attest, when it's a matter of will, there's nothing that can't be changed. As we all know well how to serve the greatest good and long to do so, may the gods guard our safety.

When he finished, Turbo reached out, and Titianus handed it to him. The prefect returned it to the box and then to the drawer, locking each in turn.

With arms crossed, he leaned back in the chair. Silence filled the room as the prefect watched him.

Titianus controlled his breathing, but it was a struggle to slow his heartbeat. He knew Greek history too well to miss what the allusions meant. Hipparchus was the tyrant of Athens who was assassinated at the Panathenaic Games after disgracing the sister of one of two men he'd made his enemies. Philip of Macedon was murdered by his own bodyguard at the celebration of a royal wedding.

The four consuls had failed, but someone was planning to try again.

"Your thoughts?" Turbo's quiet words startled him.

"An assassination, possibly at a public celebration, and at least two men who are bent on revenge are involved. The comment about changing the will…is this Marcellus related to the consul found guilty of forgery whom Nero spared because of whose great-grandson he was?"

A smile curved Turbo's lips, but his eyes stayed cool as a boulder after midnight. "Martialis was right to recommend you. That's how Hadrian and I read it. Your job will be to find all who are involved so I can stop them."

Turbo leaned on the desk and steepled his fingers again. "Any questions?"

One deep breath, blown out slowly, summed up Titianus's feelings better than any words could. "Not right now, but I may have some as I proceed."

"I expect that. One more thing." Turbo's jaw twitched. "You are not to share any details of your investigation with Saturninus."

Not tell his commander what he was doing? It took all Titianus's self-control not to suck air between his teeth. He'd kept details to himself before until he was ready to make an arrest. It had irritated Saturninus when he'd done it. It would infuriate him this time. If his commander knew he was obeying Turbo's order to shut him out...

"Do you suspect Saturninus is involved?"

The prefect's eyes veiled. The silence wrapped around Titianus like a serpent. Without moving a muscle, Titianus waited.

"Until I know better, I suspect everyone except you." Turbo settled back in his chair. "I'll expect a report on your progress in a week, sooner if you uncover something important. You're dismissed."

Titianus stood and struck his chest. "Yes, Prefect."

He executed a parade-style turn and strode to the door. He opened it and stepped through, and the guards saluted his passing.

As he walked across the courtyard, past the columns, and down the stairs, he willed his heart rate to slow. Saturninus would be waiting to hear what Turbo just told him. What would satisfy his commander without revealing too much?

God, you know I'm ready to be through with all this. With your guidance, I can solve this final problem. But how am I going to walk the line between what Turbo wants and what Saturninus will demand?

If I uncover the plot Turbo suspects, what will protect those I love from men who think nothing of killing an emperor?

Chapter 6

THE NEW TRIBUNE

Titianus's office, headquarters of the Praetorian Fortress

Titianus reached the entrance to the Principia with that question still gnawing at him.

As he walked past his own office toward that of the prefect, Plancus, the optio who served him at headquarters, fell in beside him, matching his stride.

"The prefect isn't in his office, Tribune." Plancus lowered his voice to a near-whisper. "He put the new tribune in your office and then left headquarters."

Titianus fought the smile. He wouldn't have to answer any of Saturninus's uncomfortable questions today.

"Did he say when he was returning?"

"No, Tribune."

"Then follow me, and we'll both meet my replacement."

A young man in full body armor whose shine declared its newness sat in the guest chair by the desk. A pair of wide purple stripes on his short tunic declared his senatorial lineage.

Titianus kept nothing important at the Principia where someone could get at what he didn't want them to see. His would seem like an unoccupied office to the young tribune. The young man stood when Titianus entered.

"Prefect Saturninus didn't tell me who my replacement would be, but welcome." He flashed a fleeting smile. "I'm Titus Flavius Titianus, currently tribune of the XI Cohort."

"Gaius Acilius Glabrio."

Titianus acknowledged the name with a nod. Glabrio's father had been consul only three years earlier. Saturninus was probably delighted to have the son of such an important man reporting to him.

Palm up, Titianus gestured toward Plancus. "This is my optio at headquarters, Memmius Plancus."

Plancus stood at attention and saluted Glabrio. "It's my duty and pleasure to serve you, Tribune."

Titianus placed his hand on Plancus's shoulder. "Plancus can answer any question you have about headquarters protocol and many about the officers and men who work here. When you are commander over the XI Cohort, he'll do what he can to help you care well for your part of Rome. You could have no one better to help you do that."

Even though the words were spoken without a smile, Plancus's face flushed with pride. "I'll do my best, Tribune."

"I know. Leave us."

Plancus struck his chest twice, once for each tribune, executed a parade-turn, and left the room, closing the door behind him.

Titianus released his chinstrap and lifted the helmet off his head. He looked over his shoulder at Glabrio as he set his helmet on the side table. "The only purposes this serves are projecting authority without having to do anything and impressing whoever watches us on parade. Feel free to remove yours in here."

Glabrio left his helmet on.

Titianus settled into his desk chair. "This office is yours now. I have an office at each of my guard stations and those will be sufficient until I retire."

Glabrio's brow furrowed. "Do all the tribunes have offices in their stations?"

"No. We all get written reports from our centurions. Some read all of them; some don't. I prefer to read them where I can get more information right away if I need it."

Glabrio tipped his head back to look down his nose as a skeptical smile curved his mouth. "Prefect Saturninus said most of his tribunes rely on their centurions for day-to-day matters. They are, after all, professionals who've done this for years, and this is a temporary posting for most of us before we move to more challenging assignments."

"Our prefect is more interested in the political part of this job, and he's a man who excels in that arena. But my responsibility for almost ten years has been the safety of the people of Rome. I never had political ambitions."

"My family has served Rome at the highest levels since the Republic. My father has recently been consul. That's my goal as well. I expect to move on soon."

The line between smug and confident was thin, and deciding which better described Glabrio's smile wasn't worth Titianus's effort. He'd be moving on soon as well.

"No matter how long you plan to serve in the Urban Cohort, knowing your centurions and *optiones*, who's particularly good at something, who might need some help…you only achieve that if you spend time with your men. They will tell you what they're reluctant to put in writing if they know you as a man, not just as the tribune who's over them.

"Hmph." Glabrio's eyes narrowed. "But you have the reputation of having no heart inside that cuirass."

Titianus allowed a fleeting wry smile before straightening his lips.

"You don't have to be a friend. They need to know you expect they will do their best, that you appreciate it when they do. They need to know you're a man who can be trusted to do what's right. Rank, wealth, whose friend or relative a man is…that shouldn't be what decides who is punished and who isn't when they've broken the law of Rome."

Glabrio chuckled. "Prefect Saturninus mentioned your unique perspective on that."

"I'm not surprised." Titinus kept his face unreadable. "By law and custom, the punishment for a crime depends on citizen or not, noble order or not. That can't be changed. But the victim of any crime deserves at least enough justice that the one who did wrong is identified and punished as the law dictates."

Titianus stood. "I'll take you to the stations now to meet my…your centurions."

He led Glabrio from the Principia toward the Via Principalis, past the sound of fists hitting chests when the guards saluted as they passed.

As they headed toward the fortress gate, Titianus's hand swept the row of tribune houses lining the street. "The larger ones are for the Praetorian tribunes. That one…" He pointed at one of the smaller ones. "That one is now yours."

"Prefect Saturninus said he allows his tribunes to stay where they want in Rome as long as they're at the Principia when they're on duty."

"He does. I moved back to my town house when I married." He glanced at Glabrio. "I'm equestrian. I preferred the rent I earned to any political advantage from entertaining senators at my own home."

"I make valuable acquaintances at the dinners in my father's town house." A wry smile tugged at one corner of Glabrio's mouth. "Saturninus is among them. My father was consul the year before the prefect was. I hope to serve Rome in the consulship someday as well."

Family pride lit Glabrio's eyes, but he didn't mention his grandfather. That was no surprise. Kaeso had told Titianus about several prominent Romans who'd paid dearly for following Jesus. Glabrio's grandfather had also been consul during Domitian's reign. Then he was exiled. Four years later, a Praetorian centurion had taken a troop to execute him for the treason of becoming a Christian and brought his head back to the emperor in Rome.

What did his son and grandson know of the faith? Were either of them Christians and hiding it like Torquatus had been forced to do for the last thirteen years?

The Sabinus town house, morning of Day 2

Sunbeams played on the wall painting of Diana on a hunt. Her arrow was nocked, the bowstring drawn back, and the doe she was about to kill kept grazing, blissfully unaware of her impending death.

Sabina rolled onto her back and stared at the ceiling. Septimus would be knocking soon, ready to take her down to breakfast with Father. Unlike the deer, standing so calmly when she should be fleeing, Sabina felt like fleeing, even when she was as safe as she'd ever been.

She swung her legs off the bed and stood. Filomena, a sky-blue tunic draped across her arm, came forward to help her dress. Should she wear a stola over her tunic? It declared her a married woman, but did a widow wear one? Did that depend on whether the marriage had been pleasure or pain?

But this was Father's house. No one who would care what she wore would be at breakfast. She could send a letter to the estate later today to ask her mother all her questions about the proper behavior of a senatorial widow.

Filomena had wrapped her torso with a braided silver cord to give shape to the tube of fabric that was held in place at her shoulders by a row of silver clips, each shaped like a small forest animal. The squirrel, the bunny…she'd loved them as a girl.

She was a widowed woman of twenty-two. Her childhood was long past, but when Filomena found the clips in the small drawer in the cabinet where she'd left them on her wedding day, she couldn't resist using them one more time. Maybe they'd transport her back to a time when life seemed full of possibilities and she didn't feel so old.

Old and a failure.

Mother had always told her anyone would be lucky to form a tie with the Sabinus family by marrying her, and her stutter wouldn't make that any less true. She was a smart, capable girl, and a noblewoman could run her household well without making difficult speeches.

To cure her stutter, Father had hired teachers who tried the methods of Demosthenes and the remedies listed in Celsus's medical treatise. But when those didn't help, her mother advised her to listen attentively, nod in agreement, and make herself silently pleasant. She was pretty, and that plus the Sabinus name was enough to make most young noblemen want her.

Sabina had married when Mother still enjoyed playing political games alongside Father, and she mostly shielded Sabina from public life where her stuttering speech might make her an object of jest. Most were afraid to say anything when Mother or Father were present, and that had helped her control the stutter.

In private, her parents had waited for her to speak a little, and then finished her sentence as a question so she could just nod. But that didn't feel like they thought any less of her. They were only being helpful, and her father had told her many times she was a matrimonial prize for all the elite men who wanted a connection with the Sabinus family.

What would Father say now?

Two knocks, a pause, then a third knock. It had been the secret code she and Septimus used with each other as children. He'd remembered, and that drew her smile. Shoulders squared and head high, she opened the door.

He'd grown into a handsome man, but the grin he gave her was still boyish. "I waited up for Father, so he knows why you've come home." He offered his arm, and she placed her hand on it. "I often join him for breakfast before he starts the salutation. You're welcome to do that any time you want." He patted her hand and led her to the stairs. "Our cook rivals the one at Grandfather's house. Everything he makes is tasty, but what he makes for Father is better than what he makes for me alone. It's worth dining early."

They had reached the ground level, and the peristyle *triclinium* was just ahead. She hadn't intended to, but her hand gripped his arm tighter with each step forward. She willed her fingers to relax. It was only Father inside that room, not Asinia or the beast she'd married.

As they entered, Father rose from his couch and walked toward her. "Welcome home. It's been too long."

He spread his arms, and Septimus's hand on her back guided her into them. When they wrapped around her in a gentle embrace, she relaxed against his chest. The tears she never intended to shed burst forth, and even though he might have a wet spot there for all to see when he went to the salutation, he placed one hand on the back of her head and held her close as if it didn't matter.

Almost as quickly as they came, the tears ended.

Father placed his hands on her upper arms and moved her back enough to see her face. A smile slowly lifted the corners of his mouth. "It's good to see you, too."

His fingertips wiped away a tear. "Let's eat." His hand swept toward the center couch, the one where a guest of honor would recline, and he returned to the one on the left.

When they had all settled on the couches. Father took two plates from the serving table between the three couches and handed her one. "Septimus told me some of what's happened. You can tell me more when you want to, but I don't need to know everything yet. It's customary for a widow to withdraw from general society for a few months, and I want you to do that here with me."

Sabina stared at him as if he'd grown a second head. Septimus said he'd changed, but for Father to offer a place of refuge where she wouldn't have to deal with the snickers of the women and the pitying looks from the men—that was so far from what she expected she almost pinched herself to see if she was dreaming.

"Th-thank you, Father."

His reply was a smile and a nod. "Try the rosemary honey rolls. I have them every morning. I think you'll find them exceptional."

As Septimus and Father began talking about this and that and nothing in particular, Sabina nibbled a roll. Father was right. It was exceptional.

As she reached for a second one, the last bit of tension drained away. She'd truly come home.

Chapter 7

An Unexpected Opportunity

The Baths of Trajan, late afternoon of Day 2

After several hours at Titianus's side, Glabrio couldn't remember a day when he'd walked so far. He'd asked why they hadn't ridden when Titianus dragged him on foot through the warehouse district on the Tiber. His mentor's reply—his men wouldn't be riding, and he needed to know what it was like to patrol each of their precincts of Rome.

He'd rather not have known.

Titianus had introduced him to every centurion and optio under his command and to some centurions who commanded the fire-fighters of the *Vigiles*. He only remembered the names of half of them.

Although the Praetorians were on guard at the Flavian Amphitheater during games, the Urban Cohort policed the area around it. They could have skipped that part of Rome since Glabrio had trained at the Ludus Bruti for five years. But the infamous tribune without a heart had insisted on a thorough tour after introducing him to the optio Gellius at the Subura guard station that served the amphitheater, the elite Fagutal region near the Baths of Trajan and Titus, and the area north of the amphitheater where the scum of the city lived with the people too poor to live elsewhere.

Titianus droned on about the kinds of crimes that were common in that area as they walked around the Baths of Trajan, and Glabrio caught maybe three words in ten as he pretended to listen.

They were passing through the changing room on the way to the exit when—

"Titianus." The voice behind them caused his escort to turn.

Freshly draped in a purple-edged toga, Manius Sabinus strode toward them with a manservant trailing behind him.

The closest thing to a smile that Glabrio had seen flitted across Titianus's face. "Manius."

Glabrio masked his surprise. This equestrian tribune who'd lived in officer quarters so he could rent out his town house was on a first-name basis with the favorite son of one of the most influential men in the Senate?

Sabinus stopped when he reached them. "I hadn't expected to find you here, cousin. With only three days left, most would have given up their old duties." He chuckled. "I should have known you wouldn't." He gestured toward Glabrio. "Your successor, I presume?" He directed a friendly political smile at Glabrio.

"Yes. Manius Flavius Sabinus, this is Gaius Acilius Glabrio, latest tribune to join the Urban Cohort."

"Glabrio…I know your father. It's good to see you beginning your own service to Rome."

Glabrio squared his shoulders. "I look forward with pleasure to serving here."

"Titus will be a difficult man to follow, but you'd do well to try."

"Prefect Saturninus already told me about the high standard that's been set for the XI Cohort by your cousin."

Sabinus's chuckle raised Glabrio's eyebrow. "I can easily imagine what Saturninus told you. Don't believe all of it."

Sabinus's gaze returned to Titianus. "I have no prior engagement tonight, so why don't you join me for dinner and bring your protégé?" He cast a fleeting but friendly glance toward Glabrio. "Septimus might join us as well. He wasn't sure of his plans this morning."

Titianus stiffened. The cool gray eyes that seemed to take everyone's measure locked onto Glabrio.

"I've been showing Glabrio his new domain today. It's important to know those who live under his jurisdiction." One corner of Titianus's normally straight mouth lifted. "He might as well start with one of Rome's leading senators."

Titianus turned toward Glabrio. "I have some matters to attend to at the Subura guard station, but you don't need to be there. Perhaps Manius can show you where he lives, and I'll see you both there later."

"Of course." Sabinus swept his hand toward the exit. "I also have some matters that need my attention before evening, but I'll show you where the house is and expect you both back for dinner."

Sabinus and Titianus parted without further words.

As Glabrio walked beside Manius Sabinus, he could scarcely believe how Fortuna had smiled upon him. Who would have thought the equestrian tribune who irritated Saturninus so much would be the tool she would use?

It was only a few blocks to the Sabinus town house, where two bodyguards who looked like gladiators stood by the entrance to the stableyard.

He and Sabinus were still in the street when his host stopped.

"When you return, tell my guards you're joining me and Titus for dinner. Someone will escort you to us."

"Thank you. I look forward to it."

Sabinus's only acknowledgement was a tip of his head. As he started through his gate, he glanced back. "Titus will come in a short tunic and possibly still in armor. Come dressed however you wish. My father prefers to dine in a toga. I do not."

As Glabrio headed toward his own father's town house on the Palatine Hill, he couldn't stop the grin. The prospect of establishing a friendship with the favorite son of Quintus Sabinus was deeply satisfying. Quintus was one of the lions of Rome who knew everything about everyone. His support could be a deciding factor in anything political. His son Manius was the old man's favorite son and expected to be the heir of that influence.

Why had Saturninus concealed his tribune's family relationship? Titianus was notorious for his single-minded dedication to enforcing the law, no matter who might be affected. For such a man to be the nephew of one of the most politically savvy and sometimes ruthless men...that was the last thing Glabrio expected.

This opportunity to start his own friendly acquaintance with Manius Sabinus was one which would delight his father when he went home to trade his armor for a riding cloak. Titianus might enjoy walking through Rome like a legionary, but he much preferred having a horse carry him wherever he wanted to go.

Subura guard station, late afternoon of Day 2

When Titianus reached the station, he entered his office and closed the door. He'd left Glabrio with Manius outside the Baths, and Manius had taken him away not a moment too soon. Titianus needed to sort what remained in his desk and cabinets at the Subura station before Glabrio had a chance to sift through it.

Before their dinner, the new tribune would return to his family town house on the Palatine Hill, nestled in a neighborhood filled with the houses of the great aristocratic families of Rome. If Titianus were a betting man, he'd wager Glabrio would return in a long tunic and toga for a formal dinner. Eating with Manius was usually a pleasure. Adding Glabrio to their party was likely to ruin that. But once Manius issued the invitation, he had no choice.

He wasn't impressed with his replacement. Saturninus was getting his politically sensitive tribune over the XI Cohort. But perhaps it was too much to expect another man to take the risks he had for the sake of justice.

As an equestrian, Titianus had no political ambitions that could be thwarted by making powerful enemies. He never had the pressure of living up to the expectations set by generations of ancestors who'd shared in ruling first the Republic and then the Empire.

The turn of a key unlocked his desk drawer, and he took out the dagger that had killed Lenaeus. It was high quality, too good to throw away, but he couldn't take it home where Pompeia might see it.

He drew his thumb lightly across the razer-sharp edge of the blade. If it had a sheath, Melis could use it. His warehouse manager had bought the boy to train as his replacement, but Titianus had discovered his exceptional skill as an investigator when he used him on the Lenaeus murder case. The youth would appreciate the weapon, including its history.

He'd give it to Melis as soon as the station's optio got it a sheath. Then he'd teach his eager assistant how to use it for defense. He'd use the youth one final time as his second set of ears and eyes to learn the truth as seen by the slaves of a suspect's household.

He rubbed the back of his neck before giving it a final squeeze. Saturninus would try to use Glabrio as a spy to learn what he knew. The young tribune would be too eager to please their commander to be trusted with any sensitive information.

But how could he keep Glabrio from following him around as he dug into the Hadrian assignment?

Titianus drew a deep breath and blew it out slowly. Glabrio was going to be an obstacle that required caution to navigate, not a helper for getting to the truth in this last case he'd solve to serve justice in Rome.

God, please give me wisdom as I attack this problem.

He'd be a fool to think he could do it safely on his own.

The Sabinus town house, late afternoon of Day 2

Curled up in a large wicker chair in the peristyle garden, Sabina rolled the scroll to expose the next panel. She'd missed the extensive library of her father's house. Asinia was no reader, and the dust that settled on the few scrolls that were at the Gallus estate was only disturbed when Sabina touched them.

Father came through the archway leading to the stableyard. He chuckled as if telling himself some private joke. Then his gaze landed on her, and he strode over.

"I trust you had a restful day."

"Yes, Father."

He tapped the wooden knob on the scroll rod. "What are you reading?"

"Ph-Pharsalia." She held the scroll out to him.

"What fired your interest in the civil war between Julius Caesar and Pompey? I know only one other woman who might choose that one by Lucanus from among my scrolls."

"Not b-battles." She swallowed. That sometimes helped the words come faster. "The money you sent for my b-birthdays—I bought scrolls. Horatius. Statius." She cleared her throat. "Statius wrote an ode to honor Lucanus. I wondered why."

"I'm glad my gifts were well spent." Father took the scroll and scanned where she was in it. "Too bad Nero had Lucanus executed at twenty-five. He might have surpassed Horatius in time."

He handed back the scroll. "If there are any of Lucanus's works that aren't in the library already, ask my steward to get them for you."

"You love poetry, Father?"

"Some epic poems, but my taste runs more to history than poetry for poetry's sake."

That wasn't surprising. She'd never been brave enough to show him the poems she wrote before she married. Looking back at them, she was embarrassed by how clumsy they were. Septimus had liked them, but he'd liked everything she ever wrote.

"I ran into our cousin Titianus at the Baths. He'll be joining me for dinner. I also invited Acilius Glabrio. He's the new tribune Titus is training to replace him. Glabrio's father was consul three years ago. I expect Septimus will join us. You're welcome to join us as well."

Son of a consul. The last thing she wanted was to meet a man who might look on her as a ticket to political advantage. "Are they m-married?"

"Titus is. He convinced Pompeia to marry him in this house. She and her brother Kaeso slept here under my protection while Titus hunted their father's murderer. Her father was the tutor Septimus studied with until he was fifteen."

Sabina looked at the scroll to avoid Father seeing her surprise at him inviting such unimportant people to live there."

"It was Septimus's idea. Kaeso is your brother's best friend."

That explained it.

"An inauspicious way for a man and woman to meet, but how fortunate for her." For the daughter of a mere tutor to snare an equestrian husband…that took feminine skills she didn't have.

"Don't think her a predatory female. She wasn't trying to trap a husband." A wry smile accompanied a shake of his head. "It was most amusing watching her try to discourage him until someone tried to kill him. He stayed here while he recovered. She has a kind heart and read to him while he convalesced. By the time he got his strength and vision back, he got a wife as well."

"And the young tribune?" He was almost her age and from a consular family. Her stomach knotted. Exactly what would appeal to Grandfather.

Father's chuckle raised her eyebrows. "Glabrio. He didn't say, and I didn't ask. I enjoy dining with Titus when I have no other engagement. He's wise in ways you might not suspect and one of the smartest men I know. Honest to a fault, too. That's a refreshing change from dining with senators. What I saw tells me Titus isn't impressed with his replacement. But I expect it will be both entertaining and worthwhile to observe the young man and draw my own conclusion." His smile drifted toward a grin. "Perhaps not as amusing as watching Pompeia intrigue Titus while trying to discourage him, but I can't expect such rich entertainment often."

Father enjoyed watching romantic entanglements grow? Had she missed seeing that because she was too young to recognize it, or had he changed in the last six years?

He tapped the scroll. "You'll probably find Lucanus more interesting than watching a politically ambitious young man curry my favor. If you wish, you can have your dinner served in your room instead of joining us. Your mother tired of all the political maneuvering at dinner that's unavoidable if you live in Rome. It's why she mostly stays at the estate now."

"I'll d-dine alone." Father probably didn't want anyone watching a daughter of his struggle to speak, but no matter why he'd given her the choice, being allowed to say no was pure relief.

"I'll have someone tell the kitchen. I'll see you in the morning."

As Father climbed the stairs to the master bedchamber to shed his toga, Sabina rolled up the scroll and stood. By the window in her room, there was a chair almost as comfortable as this one. If her cousin or Glabrio came early, she might have to talk with them if they caught her down here.

She suppressed the shudder before she headed upstairs to the sanctuary of her room.

Chapter 8

First Dinner with Manius

The Sabinus town house, evening of Day 2

When Glabrio rode up to the Sabinus stableyard gate on his gray stallion, one of his father's bodyguards rode a mule behind him. Even in the best parts of Rome, any man who was out alone after dark was a fool. If dinner ran as late as he hoped, he'd be going home by moonlight.

Only one of the gates was open, and a muscular German at least half a head taller than his own guard stood blocking it. "Who seeks entry?"

A second German almost as tall as the first stepped into view.

"Gaius Acilius Glabrio."

He expected that name to move them out of his way, but the bigger one only rested a hand on his dagger and raised one eyebrow.

"I'm expected for dinner."

The guard's head tipped back so he could look down his nose at a mounted man. His mouth curved into a sneer. "Who's expecting you?"

"He's expected, and his bodyguard can enter as well." Glabrio startled at the voice of authority just behind him. He turned in the saddle to find Titianus. He'd come alone on foot and in full armor, as Sabinus had predicted.

Had Titianus been working since they parted, or did he merely like to wear the armor for effect?

Titianus looked up at Glabrio as he walked by. "Brummbar and Barin are always cautious about letting someone in the first time."

The Germans stepped aside to let them enter, giving a nod of respect to Titianus and pressing lips together to control a sneer as Glabrio rode past.

Father would never allow such disrespectful behavior by a slave toward any guest. But the German's Latin carried a heavy accent, so maybe he was a recent purchase not yet schooled in proper manners toward senatorial men, no matter their age.

Titianus stood, mouth straight and arms crossed, as Glabrio dismounted and the stable slave took his horse.

A chuckle behind him made Glabrio turn. A younger version of Manius Sabinus was walking toward him with a tall, smiling Syrian beside him. Beside, not behind. The Syrian was saying something, but Glabrio couldn't make out the words. Septimus Sabinus chuckled again, and the guard's own smile broadened.

But when the Syrian's gaze settled on Glabrio and his still-mounted bodyguard, the smile vanished, and suspicion narrowed his eyes.

"*Salve*, Titus." Septimus looked past Titianus, and recognition lit his eyes. "Glabrio. A pleasant surprise. I didn't see you this week at the ludus."

Glabrio straightened and hoped his smile toward the younger man carried the right level of friendly superiority. "It's my first day as tribune of the XI Urban Cohort. Your father invited me to join you for dinner."

"You're in for a treat. Our cook is excellent, and Titianus is an entertaining dinner companion."

Septimus's mouth twitched; it was obviously a joke. Saturninus had said Titianus might know the meaning of the word "humor," but he never engaged in it himself.

"Has your guard eaten yet?" Septimus leaned sideways to examine Glabrio's protector.

"I don't know."

"Then Tutelus will take him to dine with our men. There's always room for one more at a Sabinus table."

Glabrio nodded permission at his man, and he slipped off the mule to follow the Syrian toward a cluster of tables and benches where a number of slaves were eating.

As they walked into the peristyle with Septimus in the middle, he turned a smile on Glabrio. "I don't envy you trying to take over the renowned Titianus's responsibility for the heart of Rome with all the public buildings and the commercial activity on the river. Add Subura, and you've got a heavy load."

Glabrio's eyes narrowed. "Aren't the centurions fully responsible for policing their districts?"

The warm chuckle that greeted his words raised one eyebrow. "Who told you that?" Septimus nudged Titianus's arm. "I'd be willing to bet it wasn't Titus."

Glabrio was saved from answering when Sabinus strode through the atrium archway. Palm up, his hand indicated where they would dine. They entered a small triclinium with three couches and two small tables holding gameboards of inlaid wood, one each for tabula and *latrunculi.*

Titianus set his helmet on the floor and ruffled his hair before taking off his brass cuirass and standing it beside the helmet. Then he shed the skirt of leather strips, leaving only his tunic and his belt bearing a sheathed dagger.

Sabinus pointed at the center couch. "Titus there." Septimus joined his father on the host's couch to the right, leaving the left couch for Glabrio.

He settled with a smile onto the couch for the least honored guests, but that wasn't where he should be. The senatorial son of a former consul outranked an equestrian who was only a tribune like himself. He should have been offered the center couch, but perhaps it was because Titianus was a relative, or perhaps it was because he was closer to Sabinus's age.

Four gold-lined goblets sat on the low table that was centered between the three couches. As the wine slave mixed water and wine in a two-to-one ratio at a small wall table with three carved fauns for legs, Sabinus turned to Titianus. "I've been to the estate to inspect a new Spanish stallion and four mares that had been bred with the stallion's sire. I expect the foals to be exceptional. You can have first choice when they're born."

He picked up his freshly filled goblet. "Julia said you need to come visit next week after you've retired from the tribunate. You can bring your new wife and spend a few days. Septimus has claimed for years that his friend's sister is exceptional, and she wants to meet the paragon of womanhood who captured the heart of the tribune reputed not to have one."

Titianus took a sip from his own. "That's one pleasure that will have to wait. I'm not retiring when I expected."

The goblet froze halfway to Sabinus's lips. "Why not?"

"I have one final assignment to complete first."

Without words, Sabinus's raise eyebrow asked what that might be.

Titianus's shrug was the only answer.

Glabrio swirled his wine and breathed in the aroma. Was there no answer because he was present, or was Titianus always that discrete about cases?

Saturninus had told him to report what Titianus was doing on his final assignment, which seemed more than a little odd. He'd had to wait that morning for Titianus to finish an interview with Praetorian Prefect Turbo, but Titianus was the urban prefect's tribune, not Turbo's. Perhaps he should ask his father what to make of that. Father had been consul the year before Saturninus. He knew both Hadrian and Turbo well.

The salad course was served, and silence descended on the group as they ate carrots in a white wine sauce.

As the servers carried the dirty dishes and uneaten food away, Septimus licked his lips. "That new sauce is excellent. I should tell Pompeia about it. She's always looking for something new to teach her students."

Glabrio looked down so no one would see his surprise. Her students? What possible reason could there be for the wife of an equestrian in Sabinus's inner circle to be teaching? Who and what would she teach?

Sabinus dabbed at his mouth with a napkin. "I'm dining with Father tomorrow, but Septimus should invite the three of you. He can have the same dish prepared, and Pompeia can judge for herself."

"Do you have plans for tomorrow?" Septimus offered Titianus a hopeful smile.

"I don't know yet for myself. I'm not sure what time I'll get off duty, but I can come late."

"We'll leave some for you. Maybe. That sauce is so good." He grinned. "But there's always some bread left. If Kaeso and Pompeia come early enough, we can get in a game of tabula before eating. Sabina used to beat me more than half the time, so I think she'll enjoy Pompeia as an opponent."

Glabrio lifted his goblet for a sip, his gaze shifting between Septimus and Titianus.

"Your sister's visiting?" Titianus's raised eyebrows left the rest of his face unchanged.

"No. She's come home. Her—"

"She'll be staying with me for a while." Sabinus's eyes gave Septimus a command to be silent. His smile dimmed, and he said no more.

Glabrio avoided looking at any of the three as he took a drink. Who was the daughter of Manius Sabinus married to? Did she divorce him? Did he die? Father would know. Either way, an old alliance sealed by the marriage might be broken, and a new one might be possible. He was neither married nor betrothed.

Titianus broke the silence. "I'll be coming from the station, but you'll have four for tabula even if I'm late."

The second course came, and conversation faded away as each sampled the roast pork in a red wine sauce. It was even better than the salad course, but Septimus made no comment on what Titianus's wife would think. Perhaps she'd had it before. Did she dine there often because Titianus did?

Glabrio's father had often told him the wise young man listens much more than he speaks. As he rises in importance, that ratio of listening to speaking would change, but only a fool failed to be silent when it was important to learn what others weren't that eager to tell.

If Fortuna smiled upon him, this would be the first of many dinners at the Sabinus town house. He glanced at the man he'd soon be replacing in the Urban Cohort. Being included in Titianus's social circle might become the most valuable result of his first post as a tribune of Rome.

The second course was cleared, and Sabinus tapped his goblet for the wine slave to refill.

"This is from my estate north of town. The general vintage from there is good, but I have a small part of the vineyard where I grow some special varieties for my family's personal use." He took a sip. "This is one of those."

Glabrio swirled the wine in the gold-lined silver cup and inhaled its aroma. "I thought it was Falernian." He took a sip. "Or possibly Marcus Brutus's special vintage."

Sabinus's mouth twitched before a political smile appeared. "No one, once they've tasted Brutus's 'vintage for the honorable,' could mistake another for it."

Glabrio felt his neck heat. He'd been caught in his clumsy attempt to flatter Sabinus, but he didn't expect to be called on that so openly. "Father hasn't given me a taste of it yet. I just assumed—"

"That I'd be among those rich enough to buy it second hand?" Sabinus's smile broadened. "The men who qualify to receive it are too honorable to sell it to those who don't." He held up his goblet, and the wine slave refilled it.

The political smile turned into a chuckle. "Your father might not have had a taste of it himself. Very few who reach the pinnacle of Roman power can do so without compromising their honor more than Brutus considers acceptable."

Sabinus lifted the goblet to his lips, and Glabrio caught the quick flick of his gaze toward Titianus and back. "It's too late for me, but a young man like yourself can still aspire to it."

After a sip, he set the goblet down. "So, why did you choose the Urban Cohort for your posting? Most want the adventure and opportunity for military glory of a frontier legion."

"Father isn't away from Rome governing a province at the moment, and he thought it a good time to introduce me to many of the men who have served Rome so well."

"A wise choice, although not many young men would willingly trade the excitement of battle for policing the city."

Was that a criticism of his lack of ambition or a word of praise for taking to heart his father's sage advice? Sabinus's smile was relaxed and friendly, but his eyes were like a merchant sizing up a customer before setting a price.

"I plan to be urban prefect someday. I'll gain invaluable knowledge on how to run the city over the next year or so. There's plenty of time to serve at the frontier after that."

"Ha!" Sabinus picked up his goblet and raise it toward Glabrio. "To your noble quest to serve with distinction! May Fortuna smile on you as you pursue it." He drank the toast and set the goblet back on the table. "You could have no better teacher than Titus for however long you serve under him."

Glabrio offered the smile he knew Sabinus expected before he stole a quick glance at Titianus as he drank the toast in response.

He wasn't serving under anyone but Saturninus, but Sabinus had no way of knowing that. Perhaps Titianus would figure that out soon, but the face of the tribune Saturninus couldn't wait to get rid of was as impassive as a Greek statue right now. Perhaps the so-called best investigator in Rome wasn't as perceptive as he tried to make people think.

The dessert course appeared, and platters were placed on the table where all could reach.

Silence descended again as each sampled the variety of fruit-filled pastries. Glabrio still held the last in his fingers when Sabinus swung his legs off the couch.

"A most enjoyable dinner." Eyes lit with amusement swung toward Titianus. "Bring your young friend again, Titus, if you have him working late with you."

Titianus's reply was a slow nod.

"I need to attend to something before I retire." Sabinus waved his hand toward the door. "Shall we?"

As Glabrio followed Septimus into the peristyle with Titianus and Sabinus behind him, he didn't even try to stop his smile. Father would be delighted to hear about his first dinner with Manius Sabinus and of the invitation to return in the future. Perhaps Father's decision to keep him in Rome for a stint as an Urban Cohort tribune was much wiser than he ever expected.

◆

To let the evening breeze pass through the room to cool it before bedtime, Filomena had opened the door to the balcony. She'd pulled out the silver picks that held Sabina's long, twisted hair in an elegant arrangement, letting it cascade down her back. She'd just tied the ribbon to secure Sabina's tresses in a thick braid for sleeping when male voices came from the peristyle below.

Sabina recognized Septimus's and Father's voices. Then came the quiet, deep voice of a stranger calling her father Manius. Only close friends and family called a Roman man by his first name, so that must be her cousin Titianus.

She'd be meeting him soon over a family dinner in the small triclinium off the peristyle where Father entertained his closest friends. Would it be easier to speak if she already knew what he looked like?

Putting her finger to her lips, she slipped past Filomena onto the balcony. On tiptoes, she crept closer to the balcony railing. The shadows were dark enough she should be able to see without being seen.

Father and Septimus had their backs to her. A dark-haired man about Septimus's age stood to the side, his profile lit by the lamps hanging under the opposite side of the balcony.

Sabina's nose wrinkled. Glabrio carried himself like her husband had. Spine straight, chin high, slight smile as if he found those around him amusing. Not a kind smile, but one that made you feel he's analyzed you and found you lacking.

Cousin Titianus was just past Glabrio and straight across from her. With his short-cropped military haircut and the muscled arms of a soldier, he was ruggedly handsome. But as he listened in silence to Glabrio telling Father how much he'd enjoyed the dinner and that he hoped to have a chance to reciprocate soon, her cousin's face showed no emotion at all. It seemed less human than the death masks of the Sabinus ancestors lining Father's tablinum walls.

She would have sworn she made no sound, but the steel gray eyes that had been focused on Glabrio turned upward, even though his head barely moved. As his gaze met hers, those cool orbs warmed and for the briefest moment, the corners of his mouth turned up. Then, before Father or Glabrio would notice, his gaze returned to Glabrio, and his mouth relaxed back to a straight line.

Sabina eased back from the edge so the men below couldn't see. She slipped along the wall and into her room, closing the door softly behind her. With her back against the carved panels, she shut her eyes. It was a silly, girlish thing to sneak a peek at the dinner guests of her father. She'd turn six shades of pink if Father said anything about it to her.

But in that brief moment when she looked into her cousin's eyes, he seemed like a man who would never reveal she'd been watching them. When she first met him in the company of Father, she needn't fear what he might say.

Chapter 9

TRAINING HIS SUCCESSOR

The Praetorian Fortress, morning of Day 3

After Titianus dropped his stallion off at the stable, he headed toward his old office in the headquarters building. Before he got close enough for the Praetorians guarding the door to hear, he released a deep sigh.

Dinner with Manius was usually a relaxing time of honest conversation with his cousin and often laughter when Septimus joined them. The younger Sabinus had mastered the teaching Pompeia's father had given him on humor as a tool of persuasion. He was always on target and never went too far.

When Manius invited Glabrio to an impromptu dinner when they met at the Baths, Titianus had already had enough of the overconfident young man for one day. Maybe enough for a week.

Last night had been even less enjoyable than Saturninus's monthly tribune dinner. For the most part, he'd seen what he expected. But it had been informative when Manius asked why a consular son who could have had any posting he wanted chose the low-prestige Urban Cohort. He'd probably suffered some teasing over that from his equally ambitious peers.

But his father's decision to introduce him to his network of friends and associates as soon as he could was politically astute. That his son appreciated that fact boded well for his rapid rise in the ranks of the politically powerful.

His eager acceptance of Manius's invitation showed he would look for advantages beyond what his father provided. That was the last thing Titianus needed when embarking on the most dangerous case of his career.

Saturninus was no fool. As soon as he realized he wasn't being told everything, he'd tell Glabrio to stick to his trainer's side like a burr in the fleece of a sheep with a lazy shepherd.

A few more strides up the steps and past the saluting Praetorians took him into headquarters. He'd told Gellius to send some reports up to this office for Glabrio to start familiarizing himself with the Subura district. He'd have some time alone while the young man did that. Six districts with two stations each—that should give him twelve days for digging into Turbo's problem without Glabrio's observation.

He didn't expect Plancus, his headquarters optio, to be waiting near the entrance. "Tribune." His right fist hit his chest. "Optio Gellius sent up some reports, and I volunteered to get the district map for Tribune Glabrio." His voice dropped to a near-whisper. "Prefect Saturninus is with him."

Titianus's nod was the only response visible to others in the courtyard, but Plancus read the thank-you in his eyes and almost smiled in response.

When Titianus entered his office, Saturninus was seated in his desk chair with Glabrio in the visitor chair across from him.

He fisted a salute. "Prefect. What may I do for you?"

A smug smile curved the prefect's lips. "What you've apparently already begun doing." He picked up Titianus's stylus and inspected it before placing the plain brass tool atop the stack of tablets Gellius had sent. "I had several consuls and senators to dine last night, and young Glabrio's father told me you'd taken him on his first tour of his district and arranged for him to dine with Manius Sabinus."

The smile warmed to almost friendly, but his eyes didn't. "I'd like you to continue in that vein. He should accompany you each day to learn more. Let him watch your investigative procedures up close so he'll be properly prepared to take over when you're through with your assignment with Turbo."

Titianus's stomach clenched. He'd expected Saturninus to use Glabrio as a spy, but he hadn't expected him to be so blatant about it. "Very well, Prefect. I'll teach him what he needs to police Rome well, and within the limits set by Prefect Turbo and Emperor Hadrian, he can help me with that matter."

Saturninus's jaw twitched as his eyes narrowed. "You report to me, Titianus."

"And we all report to the emperor." That might be a dangerous thing to say, but there was no avoiding it or Saturninus would expect information that he would never give. "I'll do my best to serve Rome well."

Glabrio's eyes widened as his gaze shifted from Titianus to Saturninus and back, and the proud smile he'd worn until then vanished.

But perhaps it was good the young tribune had heard that exchange. If he dined with his father like Septimus did with Manius and his grandfather, he would know something about many of the men Turbo would consider "of interest."

The big question: could he use Glabrio to help him learn what he needed without any of them discovering he was asking?

Saturninus stood. "Carry on, then. I'll expect to hear from you as information becomes available."

He shifted his gaze to Glabrio. "From both of you."

Glabrio stood. "Yes, Prefect" His fist hit his chest, and Titianus copied him without speaking.

With a final narrow-eyed glance at Titianus, Saturninus left.

Titianus walked past the stacks of tablets and lowered himself into his desk chair. "So, it appears you'll be trailing me around the city at least part of the time. But you also need to familiarize yourself with the daily activities around each guard station."

With the stylus, he tapped the topmost tablet of the rightmost stack. "These will get you started on that."

"There are a lot of them." Glabrio settled back into his chair.

"There are. As your men get to know you, they'll help sort what's important from the unimportant to keep the stack that needs your attention shorter." He let one corner of his mouth lift into a quick, wry smile. "Learn their names." He let the smile appear again. "All of them. They'll serve you better when you do."

Glabrio glanced away, then back. It was obvious he hadn't expected to be called on his inattention yesterday.

"And you'll want to learn about your fellow tribunes, their strengths and weaknesses."

"With only four of us, that won't take long." The confident tilt to Glabrio's chin was back.

"There are fourteen, counting yourself. The prefect has a monthly dinner for his four and the ten of the Praetorian Guard. Get to know the

Praetorian tribunes since you want to transfer to a fighting legion. Some of them have useful insights and contacts in the regular legions."

Titianus rolled the stylus between middle finger and thumb. "It's worth attending sober. You'll learn more."

Glabrio stiffened. He'd drunk enough at Manius's to be incautious with some of his words, but he clearly resented Titianus's warning.

Then the confident smile reappeared. "Father says it's the wise man who leaves a banquet sober, no matter how good the wine."

"The wise man also knows whom to ask questions and whose advice is worth taking." It was hard not to smile as he spoke his next words, but he managed. "Some men provide good examples to follow. Others are good examples of what not to do. Their advice can be valuable as long as you do the opposite."

"You speak of an Urban Cohort tribune?"

That was a good question to pretend he didn't hear.

"The favorite of your superior isn't always chosen for intelligence and skill."

Titianus suppressed the chuckle that the furrow between Glabrio's eyebrows triggered. His replacement would figure out soon enough that Victorinus's incompetence was only exceeded by his political ambition. He'd regard Glabrio as a threat.

Glabrio's forehead smoothed. "I take it you're not the prefect's favorite."

"I've never tried to be."

Glabrio's chuckle was unexpected. What he'd said was no joke.

"Have you ever wondered why the men commanding legions have personal bodyguards?"

The furrow was back.

"They're not for protecting them from attacks by the ones with whom Rome is at war. A legate's most dangerous enemies might be wearing Roman armor. It's not wise to be too quick to trust any man."

"Including you?"

Another question Titianus would ignore. Glabrio's cynical smile and the tilt of his chin proclaimed his condescension. Perhaps he should advise the arrogant senator's son to school his face to hide the feelings and thoughts best kept to himself. But that could wait until his last day of service. Glabrio's lack of discretion was too useful for his own protection from this spy.

"Your fellow tribunes might not want to work together to achieve a safer Rome. You are their competition, and not all are honorable in the way they compete. The less skilled a man is himself, the more likely he will resort to trickery and even treachery to get what he wants."

"Can you tell me who warrants watching?" Curiosity had replaced condescension in Glabrio's eyes.

"Not today. But you'd be wise to earn the trust of your centurions because they have their fingers on the pulse of Rome. You want them to feel they can tell you in confidence if they sense something amiss. That's why I took you around my…your district. Any of the men I introduced you to might make the difference between success and failure for you in this posting."

The final trace of a smirk that had lingered on Glabrio's lips for much of their conversation disappeared.

Titianus leaned back in his chair and crossed his arms. "I know you remember fewer than half of them. Make the effort to know them all. Show them all the respect they earn. It might save you. Not all men who lead deserve the privilege, and some would gladly sacrifice you for their own advantage."

"Including Prefect Saturninus?"

That was a question too dangerous to answer for the son of a former consul who was also on intimate terms with his commander. Manius's father once told him Saturninus was not to be trusted, and no one was better positioned to make that judgement.

"He's your father's friend. That will influence how he treats you. He has his favorites. You'll be safer if you're one of them."

"Safer?" Glabrio snorted. "Are you trying to make him sound dangerous? He's dined with our family many times, and I can't count how many times I've dined with his. He's a great Roman and an honorable man."

"Then your years of service under him should go smoothly."

Titianus stood. "I'll return shortly. The tablets should entertain you until then."

As he passed through the door, he glanced back. Glabrio held a tablet in his hand, but his eyes were fixed on Titianus, and his lips had settled into a frown.

Glabrio had scanned three tablets, and Titianus hadn't returned. Had he left the fortress to begin his investigation? Saturninus had told him to stay close so he could report who Titianus was talking with and what he was asking.

The urban prefect was his commander, and normally it would be right to obey him without question. But if Hadrian wanted Titianus to report to Turbo instead, what should he do himself?

If it were anyone but Saturninus, Father could advise him. But close friendship meant an obligation to watch out for each other. What if there was a good reason that Hadrian didn't want Saturninus to know what Titianus found?

Chapter 10

Surprising Beginnings

The Sabinus town house, morning of Day 3

Sabina had lain in bed, waiting for the sky to change from black to light gray. When the words came, it was important to capture them as soon as possible. Filomena was still asleep in the slave quarters when she swung her feet off the bed and strolled to the writing desk by the window. With a pen freshly dipped in ink, her hand hovered over the blank papyrus sheet.

Sometimes at the estate, an owl would hoot in the brightening dawn. Had that been Minerva's owl? Had the goddess of poetry sent him to encourage her all those times when she'd cried herself to sleep over the futile dreams she'd had of children to love and a husband who appreciated her?

A small brass statue of an owl stood on the corner of the desk. With the hand not holding the pen, she picked it up. Barely five inches tall, it had been a gift from Septimus when he was twelve. He'd told her anyone who wrote poetry like she did needed an owl like Minerva had. Then he said he'd rather have a falcon than an owl himself, but he hadn't convinced Father yet.

It was so good to be back with him. He'd hugged her so often when he was a child. She'd loved it then, but the best of those hugs were nothing compared to standing in the stableyard with his arms around her, comforting her like the man he now was.

Why had she let Asinia keep her from visiting her family? Why had she been so certain Father would never help her escape the prison she'd been trapped in?

At least for a few months, Father had promised her a safe haven with him. Maybe he had enough influence to keep Grandfather from betrothing her to another man like Gallus.

But any man was bound to be disappointed the first time she tried to speak. How could she entertain his Senate colleagues like Mother had for years with her insightful comments and satirical wit?

She shook off those thoughts and closed her eyes to summon one of the views from her trip home. That would inspire today's poem.

Black and white shorebirds had stalked along the water's edge when the driver stopped to check the mules' harness. So graceful as they took each step, they'd suddenly pause before plunging their thin, sharp beaks into the water. Sometimes they caught a meal, but she couldn't see what. But when something startled the group and they took off, the flash of midnight-black wings rising and falling as they lifted the snow-white bodies caught her breath. With long pink legs trailing behind them, they'd circled out over the water, only to return to shore and hunt again.

While those images still danced in her mind, she wrote the first words that would capture their beauty and freedom in an ode.

Her pen was poised to start the second line when a pattern of knocks told her Septimus sought admittance.

Filomena had not yet come to help her dress and turn her braided hair into an elegant hairstyle. But it was only Septimus and Father she'd be dining with. Nothing special was needed for them.

She capped her inkwell and stood. "Come in, little brother."

As she moved toward the dressing table, she wrapped her braid around itself. From the box inlaid with woods of different colors, she extracted several silver hair picks. She'd seen Filomena drive the picks in to hold the braid in place so many times. It was a simple matter to do it herself.

Septimus came and stood behind her. "Can I help?"

She looked over her shoulder at him. "What do you know of fixing a woman's hair?"

"I know it's easier to take it down than to put it up, but I can do what you tell me."

She pushed the last pin into place. "It's done."

"Then let's join Father." He offered his arm, and she rested her hand upon it. Together, they descended the stairs and strolled to the family triclinium.

Father sat at the game table, fingering a polished stone game piece. His smile grew when they entered. "I trust you enjoyed your solitary dinner and more time with Lucanus."

"I did, Father." She took the left-side couch. "Were your d-dinner companions engaging?"

"I found Titus's protégé amusing, but I doubt you would have found the conversation as diverting as I did."

He settled onto the host's couch opposite her. "But for tonight I've arranged some guests I'm sure you'll enjoy."

Guests she'd enjoy? Beyond her own family, there were no others she wanted to see. Certainly not now, and maybe never.

"Regrettably, I have to dine with Father and several of his friends. But Septimus and some from Titus's household will be here. Pompeia is Titus's wife, and Kaeso is his brother-in-law."

"And my best friend." Septimus settled onto the center couch. "You'll like Pompeia. She's a teacher. Ask her a single question and she can carry on a conversation about anything."

"Mm-meeting new people…" She bit her lip. "Must I?"

Father took the plate of hard-boiled eggs and offered it to her. "Yes. You'll thank me for this tomorrow morning."

She took an egg and nibbled the end of it. After being shut away so long at the Gallus estate, the thought of meeting strangers made her stomach churn.

"He's right." Septimus reached for some raisins. "By the end of dinner, you'll see why there's no one in Rome I'd rather spend an evening with."

A nod was all the response she made. They both meant well. Maybe it wouldn't be as bad as she feared.

But she doubted that.

The Praetorian Fortress, late morning of Day 3

Glabrio had just opened the next-to-last tablet, and there was still no sign of Titianus.

But the tablets hadn't been entirely boring. He hadn't expected the number and range of petty crimes and citizen complaints that one station had to cover. He scanned the tablet that lay open before him. More of the same with an occasional twist.

What should he do next? He could ask the optio—what was his

name?—to bring him some tablets from the station that served the Forums and Trajan's Market. Those should expand the variety of criminal activity, but he was already sick of sitting there, shuffling through official records filled with abbreviations he could only guess at.

Where was Titianus? He could ask the optio and if the man knew, have him take him to the tribune who chose which prefect he would obey. But if centurions and optios were loyal to the man who treated them like men worthy of trust, would Titianus's optio tell him where his old commander was, even if ordered to? It would be easy to feign ignorance. He'd seen enough of Titianus to know he'd never reveal himself whether his subordinate's ignorance was real.

He was about to call the man in when he heard a fist hit a chest.

"Tribune."

The word was followed by Titianus walking through the doorway. His gaze swept the desktop and lingered on the large stack of tablets on the opposite side of the desk than they were when he left. The steel-gray eyes that reminded Glabrio of Plutarch's description of the dictator Sulla focused on the last tablet.

"You've made excellent progress." Words of praise, but they were not accompanied by a smile. "Any observations?"

"Yes." Glabrio moved the last unopened tablet to the stack he'd read. "'The gleam of his gray eyes, which was terribly sharp and powerful, was rendered even more fearful by the complexion of his face.' Plutarch could have written that about you as well as Sulla."

He'd meant to irritate his trainer, but Titianus's mouth twitched, as if a smile almost escaped. "You're not the first to make that observation. It's amusing among friends." One corner of his mouth curved. "Such eyes are useful when interrogating someone who's not eager to tell you what they know. Since your parents failed to equip you with eyes cold as ice, you'll have to figure out how to make ordinary brown eyes have the same effect."

Titianus rested his hand on his sword, fixed his gaze on Glabrio, and froze like a statue.

Like a boy who'd been caught misbehaving, Glabrio fought off the urge to squirm under that intense gaze. Then what Titianus was waiting for hit him.

It was still Titianus's chair in which Glabrio sat, and he probably should offer it to its owner. But if he did, he'd be telling Titianus he saw him as his superior instead of the man he was replacing. He leaned back in the chair and crossed his arms, mirroring what Titianus had done.

"How often do people not want to talk with you?"

"If they have something to hide, almost always." The cool smile was the most emotion Glabrio had seen on Titianus that day. "You'll spend more time talking to victims than to the ones who broke Roman law. Some want to tell you everything when they think you'll help them. Some talk merely because they like to talk. Some talk because they can't stand the silence as you stare at them. Your job is to sift what they say to find what's true. The eyes, the mouth, the hands…they'll betray the ones who are lying."

"Hands?" The urge to move his hands into his lap where Titianus couldn't see them was almost irresistible.

"Not all Saturninus's tribunes get involved like I do. For the slaves and noncitizens, they use their precinct torturers and don't go beyond that. But someone will lie just to end the pain. I prefer to give them the chance to tell me the truth because they want to."

"An interesting approach. Does Saturninus agree with it?"

"You can ask him yourself. I do what I think is honorable and right."

From a cabinet in the corner, Titianus removed a satchel and a pair of unused wax tablets. "I told the stableman to get our horses ready. There's a problem in the warehouse district." A subdued smile flitted across his face. "I won't make you walk there this time."

Glabrio pushed back from the desk and stood. Choosing what was honorable and right—that was what any prefect should want from his officers. So, why was Saturninus so eager to get rid of one who did? And why had Hadrian himself picked the man Saturninus despised for the problem that could not be discussed?

Chapter 11

Making New Friends

The Sabinus town house, evening of Day 3

As Filomena pinned the last of several braids in place atop Sabina's head and adjusted the many tight curls she'd made with the curling iron around Sabina's forehead, a shuddering sigh escaped.

"I w-wish Father hadn't decided I needed to meet these people. When Septimus finished his training today at the ludus, he was going to cousin Titianus's house to fetch them. They must be almost here." Sabina chewed her lip. "It's too hard to talk with people who aren't family."

Filomena dabbed some lavender-scented oil behind Sabina's ear and in the hollow of her throat. "But Master Septimus said they'll be unlike anyone you've met before. Maybe they'll be easy to talk to, like he thinks."

"Nothing's hard for Septimus or Father." Sabina massaged her neck. "I should have gone to Mother at the estate. Then I wouldn't be trapped into this dinner."

But Mother had no influence with Grandfather, so maybe she'd have been forced back into Roman society immediately. This dinner couldn't be as bad as that.

A soft knock on the door made Sabina turn. One of the housemaids stood in the doorway. "Master Septimus is here, mistress."

Sabina dismissed her with a flick of her wrist. Then she reached for Filomena's hand. A reassuring squeeze from her closest friend, and she was as ready as she'd ever be.

Like a legionary marching toward an enemy arrayed for battle, she headed downstairs.

As she approached the triclinium doorway, a man's chuckle that didn't sound like Septimus's reached her ears. Perhaps that boded well. A man with a good sense of humor was easier to listen to than a man without one, and she planned to listen as much as possible without talking. But her brother could make anyone laugh once he'd known them long enough to tease out their interests and dislikes. Maybe that chuckle didn't mean a thing.

When she stepped into the room, Septimus and his friend were seated at one of the game tables while a stola-clad woman about her age stood with arms crossed, watching them.

Septimus rose upon her entry and walked over to place his arm around her shoulders. He drew her with him to the table.

"Sabina, this is Kaeso Lenaeus."

Kaeso stood and bowed his head before raising his eyes to meet hers. That was what she'd expect from a man not in the noble orders.

"Septimus promised us the pleasure of meeting his sister tonight. I offer our condolences on your husband's death."

She tipped her head to acknowledge his words and tried to make her face look suitably regretful.

"But returning to family like Septimus and your father can only help."

She should say something, but—

"And this is Pompeia Lenaea. She's Cousin Titus's wife now, thanks to me."

She could have hugged Septimus for sparing her from speaking a response.

"I brought him home when an assassin tried to kill him. She read to him while he recovered, and he decided he couldn't live without her. So that makes her a cousin by marriage as well as my best friend's sister."

The warmth in Pompeia's eyes matched her smile, creating an impression of calm friendliness. "We're delighted to meet you. I can imagine what a challenge it was growing up with a tease like Septimus as a little brother. Kaeso had his moments, too." She directed an affectionate smile at her brother. "But laughter is good for us all, and they provide plenty of it."

"I asked for dinner to be served later than usual to give Titus a chance to join us while it's hot. So…" Septimus spread his arms toward the two game tables. "I told them how you used to beat me regularly at tabula. My favorite way to wait for the last dinner guest is matching wits with Kaeso. Perhaps you and Pompeia would care to join us. When Titus is coming straight to dinner when he gets off duty, it's hard to predict when he'll get here."

Sabina's gaze shifted from Septimus to Pompeia and back to her brother. What he proposed was so much better than trying to talk with strangers. She gave him a hug with her eyes before seating herself at the second table. Palm up, she invited Pompeia to sit across from her with only her hand.

Pompeia seated herself and offered the box of game pieces to Sabina. "Please choose your color. Septimus and my brother like to talk while they play, but I much prefer a silent partner. I find it less distracting. Titus made a good opponent when we first met because he didn't force me to carry on a conversation. I hope that's acceptable to you as well."

"It is." Easy words to speak, even with her stutter. She glanced at Septimus and caught his wink. Had he told them already that she found talking hard?

Nothing in Pompeia's words or eyes suggested anything but her own desire for a quiet game. If she'd made the offer out of pity, even the most astute observer would not have known.

"Septimus always lets the guest go first." Pompeia's smile was playful. "I think I'll claim that privilege. It will give me a better chance for victory." The smile drifted toward a grin. "I should warn you. I always play to win."

As Pompeia moved her first white stone on the tabula board, Sabina felt the tension flow out of her. She moved her own black piece and leaned back in the chair to await Pompeia's next move. Perhaps Father and Septimus were right. She might find some enjoyment in the company of strangers like these.

It had been years since Sabina played tabula, but as she warmed to the game, it was as if it was yesterday. Each time she glanced at her opponent's face, Pompeia sensed it and withdrew her gaze from the game board to focus on Sabina and offer a swift smile. Then her gaze locked on the board again.

It was as comfortable as playing Septimus and just as challenging.

The tapping of hobnails on a marble floor announced the tribune's arrival before he stepped into the triclinium. Titianus arrived in full armor, but as soon as he was in the room, he took off the helmet and placed it on the floor by the wall.

Pompeia made her final move, winning the game. "Thank you, Sabina. Septimus was right that we'd be well suited as opponents. I hope we'll get to play again soon."

"Indeed." Another word that was short and easy to speak perfectly.

Kaeso's sister rose from the table and went to her husband. On tiptoes, she kissed his cheek, and the smile he directed at her said more than mere words could.

Starting at the top, she undid the clasps on one side of the brass that encased his chest. When she released the last one, he placed the cuirass beside the helmet. She stepped back as he took off the padded linen vest that had been beneath it. After he removed the skirt of leather strips and set it with the rest of his armor, she wrapped her arm around his and guided him to the game table where Sabina still sat.

"We decided to play tabula while we waited. Your cousin plays like you—focused on the game without trying to distract me with too much conversation." She directed a smile at Sabina. "My favorite way to play."

"I've never had the pleasure of playing with her." The broad smile his wife's hug had triggered relaxed to a slight curve at the corners of his mouth. "I've not even had the pleasure of meeting my cousin before."

Septimus came from his table to rest his hand on the tribune's back. "I can change that. Titus Flavius Titianus, renowned tribune of the Urban Cohort, this is my sister Sabina."

"It's a pleasure." His eyes were steel gray, but the smile he gave her made eyes that were the color of winter storm clouds feel warm. "But don't believe Septimus. He's well known to exaggerate for a joke. My commander would call me notorious rather than renowned and looks forward to my retirement as soon as possible."

"Now that Titus is here, we can eat." Septimus sat and patted the host couch beside him to invite Sabina to do the same. Titianus and Pompeia took the center couch while Kaeso reclined on the couch opposite.

As their goblets were filled by the wine slave, the servers placed the salad course on the table and handed each a plate of carrots in a white wine sauce.

Septimus inhaled the aroma with eyes closed. "Father had this served last night, and it's so good you might want to add it to what you teach your Egyptians, Pompeia."

"And serve it at our table." Titianus placed a spoonful in his mouth and licked the sauce off his lips.

Pompeia took a bite and raised her eyebrows. "It's delectable. I'll ask Ciconia to come by and talk with your chef."

Sabina took a sip and looked at Pompeia over the goblet's rim. Teaching Egyptians? Why would the wife of her cousin be teaching anyone, let alone Egyptians?

"I see Septimus didn't tell you that Kaeso and I teach. We run the Lenaeus School of Rhetoric. Septimus and Titus were both students of our father. Since we married, the school meets at Titus's town house."

She thought her glance had been inconspicuous. Apparently not, and now she would have to carry on a conversation about it.

She drew a deep breath. "What do you teach?" With relief, she released the remaining breath that she hadn't needed to speak those words.

"I instruct Roman girls in literature, music, philosophy, and history. I also teach peregrine women who want to learn Latin and how to behave in Roman society. Kaeso teaches everything you'd expect in a school of rhetoric." She looked over her shoulder at her husband. "After Titus retires, he'll join Kaeso and start teaching history, geometry, and arithmetic to the boys."

Sabina stopped her eyebrows rising, but did she do it before anyone saw? It would be impolite to ask why an equestrian like Titianus would start teaching Roman youths like a common citizen or a slave.

But Pompeia's lips twitched as if stopping a grin. "I see your surprise, but Titus is not the kind of man who can sit around doing nothing." She leaned back against him and stroked his jaw before turning eyes back on Sabina. "Our school is Quintilian, and there's no better man than Titus to teach young noblemen to value truth and honor."

"You should read some of Sabina's poetry. She writes as well as Statius." Septimus swept his finger across his plate, then licked the sauce off it.

Pompeia's face brightened. "You do? I try to teach my Romans how to write poetry. I would love a true poet to help me improve so I can teach it better. Right now, my poetry is mediocre at best. Do you think you could read some of my poems and tell me how to make them good examples of what personal poetry should be?"

Sabina's gaze bounced between Septimus's eager nods and Pompeia's hopeful eyes. "I ss-suppose I could."

Why had she used an S-word? They always gave her problems.

"When can you come to our house and start helping me? Tomorrow after lunch?"

Pompeia showed no sign of noticing the stutter. Her brother must have forewarned his friends of her defect.

"I hadn't p-planned to leave the town house. Father has no litter here."

Reading the poems in the sanctuary of Father's house was one thing. Moving around Rome where she couldn't avoid being seen and might be forced into a conversation…she suppressed a shudder at that thought.

"It's not too far to walk, and you can avoid the busy area around the Baths." Septimus took a grape from the fruit bowl on the table, tossed it in the air, and caught it in his mouth. "Tutelus would love to escort you there and back and stay however long you want. Their steward's son was teaching him to read Latin and Greek when he was escorting Kaeso and Pompeia back and forth for a while." He picked up another grape. "I'll take Pardus as my guard instead."

"Well…" Sabina bit her lip before she thought what she was doing.

"Please say yes." Pompeia clasped her hands as if she truly cared about the answer. "At least come to our home and critique my work and the best my students have written. If you think I'm a hopeless case who can't be taught, you can tell me. The truth about the quality of my work—I'm not afraid to hear it. You'd be doing me a great favor if you'll come."

"Do it, Sabina. As a favor to me. I think you'll be a great help." Septimus tossed and caught the second grape. "Not that I think you're a horrible poet, Pompeia, but Sabina's poems really are amazing."

With Pompeia's hopeful eyes directed at her and Septimus poking her in the ribs before reaching for the fruit bowl again, did she have a choice?

"I'll try."

The grateful smile Pompeia gave her confirmed the wisdom of her reply. Besides, Septimus was so persistent once he set his mind on something, many days could pass before he'd give up. An afternoon looking at poetry now was better than days of Septimus nagging her to do it before she finally gave in and did it anyway.

◆

Kaeso lifted his goblet, but it wasn't just for a sip of wine. It would let him contemplate Sabina without her realizing where his gaze was focused.

Septimus's sister had a regal gracefulness in her bearing and a face that was classically beautiful, but in her eyes, he could see the fear of meeting them left by six years living in a hostile house that was not a home. She'd joined them for dinner only because Manius decreed it, and a father must be obeyed.

When he offered his condolences, those eyes had veiled. She wasn't sorry her husband was dead, and knowing what Septimus told them as they walked over from Titus's town house, he couldn't blame her.

A husband should protect his wife from others, not join in tormenting her about something she couldn't control. But there was an underlying streak of cruelty in many Roman men that let them enjoy the suffering of others. Fifty thousand would gather in the Flavian Amphitheater for imperial games, but there were dozens, maybe hundreds of amphitheaters one tenth that size across the empire that fed the bloodlust of too many more, Roman and otherwise.

Septimus had tried to explain to him that it wasn't the death but the courage and skill of a gladiator that made him and his friends cheer, but that wasn't the whole of it. They enjoyed watching the executions during lunch as well. They enjoyed the animal fights in the morning, where men would prod and wound and torment an animal before finally making the kill.

But some women enjoyed that, too, and the Vestal Virgins, who tended the supposedly sacred fire of Rome and were symbols of purity and chastity, screamed their demands for the murdering of men on the sand right in front of them.

Septimus had fumed as he described what Sabina had told him of her six years as Marcus Gallus's wife. Perhaps her husband and his mother considered it sport as they tried to crush her spirit.

Kaeso set down the goblet and picked up a fig.

God had commanded a man to love his wife as he loved himself. When he did, she would love him the same in return. And even though Mother never decided to follow Christ herself, Father had loved her as Jesus commanded. She'd loved him dearly in response.

He bit one end off and ate it before slipping the rest into his mouth.

Help Sabina become what she'd been before Gallus stole her confidence. That had been Septimus's plea as he passed on Manius's dinner invitation even though Manius himself couldn't be there.

They were counting on him and Pompeia to draw her out of the protective shell she'd grown to survive.

But what did he know about women, other than his sister? And she'd be the first to tell him with a laugh that she wasn't normal.

He glanced at his brother-in-law and felt the start of a smile. No one understood better than Titus the way men thought, both good ones and evil, but he'd been at least as clueless as Kaeso was about women when he dined with them the first time.

"Sabina."

Pompeia had just extracted a promise of a visit from her. Maybe they could turn one visit into daily visits. Maybe the love and acceptance they would show her could drive away fear and leave her comfortable if not confident once more.

"Yes?" The natural smile Pompeia had inspired became more like the rigid lips of a smiling statue.

"Thank you for being willing to help us. Pompeia will share with me what she learns, and maybe it will change some of what I teach as well."

She opened her mouth, and no sound came. It was as if something had frozen her throat. But everything thawed if you waited long enough.

So, he kept the smile on his lips and his gaze on her eyes.

He counted to ten as her eyes widened and her brow furrowed. However long it took, he'd wait for her answer. He counted five more before she cleared her throat.

"Ss-septimus p-praises me more than I deserve."

"No, I don't." Her brother patted her shoulder. "If anything, I don't praise you enough. They'll soon know which of us is telling the truth." He picked up a grape and bounced it off Kaeso's chest. "You can always expect truth in the Titianus household, and that's how it should be."

Kaeso chuckled as he looked down to find the grape. But he smiled at Sabina again before he ate it.

All eyes turned on the doorway as the servers entered to clear away the dishes. They were followed by others with the main course of fish in a golden sauce. As portions were placed on clean plates and set before them, Kaeso felt Sabina's eyes on him. When he raised his head and acknowledged her with a tip of his head and a warm smile, she lowered her eyes. But the trace of her smile that had mirrored his remained.

Chapter 12

A Good Start

Sabina watched Titus put his body armor back on by himself while his wife held his helmet.

As Septimus leaned against the wall, he crossed his arms. "I'd offer Tutelus to escort you home safely, but if you think no one wants to assassinate you today, you won't need him."

"If a tribune in full armor can't walk safely through Rome at night…" The quick grin Titianus cast her brother proclaimed it a running joke between them.

Pompeia's husband was so different from the stern man she'd seen when she spied from the balcony. Last night she'd seen his chosen facade. She'd seen the real man tonight, and even though he didn't speak much, it was obvious why Septimus called him a good friend. Fortuna had smiled so brightly on Pompeia when she got him as her husband.

But theirs was a marriage founded on their own choices, not forced on them by a paterfamilias. Being born a woman in a senatorial family had stripped her of the choices an ordinary woman might have.

She sighed. There was no reason to think the future held anything different.

Pompeia left her husband's side and came to Sabina with happy eyes and a broad smile. "We'll be looking forward to your visit tomorrow. I teach until lunchtime, so coming in the early afternoon would be perfect."

"I'll be there." Sabina returned the smile, still wondering at how a stranger could seem like a long-time acquaintance after a single dinner.

Titianus claimed his wife's hand to place it on his arm. "Perhaps I'll see you tomorrow, too. I can't be certain how late I'll be working. But you're always welcome at our home, whether you bring Septimus or not."

Kaeso moved to Pompeia's other side. "It might take many days to make Pompeia a better poet, so we hope you'll come often."

A playful slap on the arm was his sister's answer. "You're used to Septimus, so you know just how seriously to take my brother. *Vale*, Sabina."

The party, led by Septimus, headed toward the stableyard where Titianus had left his horse, leaving Sabina to climb the stairs to her room.

Filomena would be waiting for a report on how it had gone. It was good to know she had pleasant things to tell her.

As Sabina entered her room, Filomena's raised eyebrows asked the question.

"I'm glad that's over." Sabina settled into the dressing-table chair, and Filomena began pulling out the silver pins holding her braids in place.

"How did it go?" The last braid tumbled down, and Filomena's fingers kneaded the tight muscles by Sabina's neck.

"Surprising in many ways."

"Good surprises?" Hope in her dear servant's voice made Sabina pat Filomena's hand as the massage continued.

"Yes. I played tabula with my cousin's wife while we waited for him to come off duty."

Filomena's fingers began undoing the many small braids.

"Pompeia said she preferred to play without talking. It was fun to match wits without having to make conversation. But it got more interesting after Cousin Titus joined us."

With the last braid unwound, Filomena ran her fingers through the newly freed hair and picked up a brush.

"His wife is a teacher of women in a school of rhetoric, of all things. When Septimus mentioned I wrote poetry, she asked me to look at her poems and make suggestions. So, I'm going tomorrow afternoon."

She picked up one of the silver picks and fingered the butterfly on the end of it. "I never expected to have an appointment to visit someone I just met before I climbed back up here. They live a short distance past the Baths, so we'll walk there with one of Father's bodyguards tomorrow."

"Will I be carrying any of your poems to show her?"

"I haven't decided yet. I'll look through them tomorrow and maybe pick out a few of the simpler ones to share as examples. Something short will do nicely. I won't have to tell her I wrote them."

"You write as well as Statius and Horace. She won't guess if you don't reveal it."

Sabina smiled at Filomena's compliment and saw Filomena return her smile in the mirror. From many slaves, that comment would be lying flattery, but she'd told Filomena to always speak her true thoughts about her poems so she could improve. The comparison probably wasn't true, but her faithful handmaid thought it was.

As Filomena swept the brush through her hair over and over, Sabina closed her eyes and let every muscle relax.

Septimus had been right. His friends were like no one she'd met before.

Cousin Titus didn't talk much, but what he said revealed an intelligence equal to Father's. No wonder her father liked to dine with the tribune who laughed at Septimus's compliment, claiming he was more notorious than renowned. But what really stood out was how every look and every word he addressed to his wife revealed genuine love and respect.

She'd expected respect from Marcus when they married, even though she failed to get it. But she'd assumed love, if it ever came, would grow slowly during their years together. That's what had happened with her mother and father.

The brushing was finished, and Filomena began making one large braid for sleeping.

Pompeia was so different from the women she'd known. Why did she become a teacher instead of marrying young, as Sabina had? There were other schools for Roman girls whose fathers wanted them to study, but why had she decided to teach non-Roman women how to host banquets for their husbands to impress Roman guests?

She contemplated herself in the mirror, and her approving nod drew Filomena's smile.

Kaeso Lenaeus…perhaps he'd surprised her most. The longer she watched him, the more she could understand why Septimus had picked the son of his old tutor as his best friend. He shared Septimus's playful sense of humor, but he could be serious, too. Cousin Titus seemed to enjoy his company as much as Septimus did.

Filomena removed the clips that held the tunic at her shoulders, and the tube of fabric fell down when she stood. She stepped out of it, and her maid lowered a sleeping tunic over her head.

But what was strangest was how Lenaeus waited however long it took for her to say something, as if what she would say was too important to miss. No man had ever done that except Septimus. And Lenaeus's smile had made her feel like she had as a maiden, not like a scorned woman who'd succumbed to the winks and smiles of a handsome young man, only to be betrayed.

How ironic. She'd worried about the dinner all day, but she was actually looking forward to visiting them tomorrow rather than dreading being in the company of strangers again.

Father would be asking how the dinner went at breakfast. She squeezed her lips tight to keep from laughing at the face she imagined he'd make when she told him.

On the walk home to Titianus's town house

Titianus's stallion had been left in the stable, and the trio had walked a block from the Sabinus town house before anyone spoke.

"Septimus was right." Kaeso crossed the street first, stepping from one concrete block to the next one that had been spaced across the street to let people cross without stepping into whatever muck might be on the road-bed. "Sabina was afraid of us when we first came."

"I like her." Pompeia gripped the sides of her tunic and lifted them high enough to keep the fabric clear of the ground as she followed him. "I'm going to enjoy playing tabula with her again. I don't think she'd played for a while because her first moves weren't well planned, but that changed quickly. I'm not sure I'll beat her next time."

Titianus crossed last and resumed his place beside his wife as they continued walking. "Manius will be pleased when he hears how it went."

The sidewalk was only wide enough for two, and Kaeso looked over his shoulder at the pair. "Asking her to come see your poetry and advise you was brilliant for getting her out of that house."

"It seemed the perfect opening to start a friendship. Besides, I can use the help, and if she's as good as Septimus claims, I'm sure I'll learn something I can use."

Kaeso turned to face them and kept walking backwards. "If you can get her to keep coming, maybe to help with other things, it can only be good for her. She might be too shy to work with the Romans, but she could do something with your Egyptians. Something where she doesn't need to speak too much at the start but can do it more as she gets comfortable."

His heel caught on an uneven spot, and he started to fall. Pompeia reached for his hand, but he caught himself and chuckled as he resumed his backward walk.

"She's so graceful. Maybe she can teach me not to be so clumsy."

"Maybe she can teach you to pay attention to where you're going. That's all it will take." Pompeia's smile was as broad as his own before he turned to walk forward again.

Pay attention. That was good advice, and not just for walking. Listening to her struggle to get a word out was painful, and she'd looked surprised when he waited the first time for her to finish what she was trying to say.

But it had been worth the wait to see the happiness in her eyes each time he did it. By the end of the evening, she was conversing with him as if it were the most comfortable thing in the world, even with the long pauses and the stuttered words.

Septimus had said she'd stuttered only a little before her marriage. She came back to them struggling with it and trying to speak as little as possible.

She'd been like a flower bud starting to open as Pompeia chatted with her and he listened patiently to encourage her to share what she was thinking.

If he could keep her coming to spend time with them, that bud might blossom into what God meant her to be.

The Sabinus town house, morning of Day 4

Father was halfway through his breakfast when Sabina joined him.

"Your brother left already." He picked up a hard-boiled egg and dipped it into his favorite sauce. "Did you enjoy my young friends?"

"Yes, Father. The evening was very pleasant." She sat on the couch and swung her legs up. "I'll be going to their house this afternoon."

A self-satisfied smile curved her father's lips. Not quite what she expected. Had Septimus already told him what happened, or had Father played a part in planning it?

"If it turns into an invitation to stay for dinner, be sure to accept it. I've eaten with them many times, and their cook is more than adequate.

If I don't end up with another commitment, I might drop in for dinner myself."

"Drop in?"

"I have a standing invitation to join them any time. I often avail myself of it when I want a truly relaxing evening with no one expecting anything from me except my company." He took a bite and dipped the egg into the sauce again. "I used to wonder why Septimus ate there so often until I started myself."

"I doubt I'll be invited. I'm a virtual stranger to them."

"Perhaps not, but you should dine with them if you are. It's no wonder Titus married Pompeia. As an equestrian, he could follow his heart in his choice of wife. She's as good for him as your mother is for me."

As Sabina nibbled on a rosemary honey roll, she eyed her father.

Follow his heart. That wasn't a freedom Grandfather was likely to give her. Wealth and power were all well and good for men, but the cost to daughters like her could be painfully high.

Chapter 13

A Willing Protégé

The Praetorian Fortress, morning of Day 4

As Glabrio walked past the offices of the three other tribunes of the Urban Cohort, it was slightly past the time Saturninus said he expected his tribunes on duty. Glabrio's counterparts from Cohorts XII to XIV were seated at their desks.

Titianus had yet to introduce him to them. Perhaps he assumed Saturninus had. But they'd made no effort to introduce themselves to him, either.

The first two were focused on tablets lying open on their desks, but the third was leaning back in his chair, hands on his head as he stared at the ceiling.

Was he lost in thought or merely lost in a post-orgy haze? His eyes were half-glazed, like Glabrio sometimes saw when wine flowed too freely at a celebratory dinner with friends.

Then the man saw him. He leaned forward, and his eyes chilled. His eyebrows lowered as the corners of his mouth plunged. As quickly as the hostility appeared, his face blanked, and he opened a tablet like the other two, keeping his eyes from meeting Glabrio's gaze.

As Glabrio walked the remaining twenty feet to his own office, a wry smile grew. Titianus wouldn't have to tell him which was the tribune he should keep an eye on.

Plancus sat at the optio desk in the antechamber of the tribune office. He stood and struck his chest. "Good morning, Tribune."

Glabrio tipped his head toward the office he'd just passed. "Who's the tribune next to me?"

"Julius Victorinus."

Glabrio eyed the optio. Titianus said his centurions had their fingers on the pulse of Rome and would try to keep him safe because they trusted him. Surely this optio would know the men who worked in the Principia better than that.

Was he also loyal to Titianus?

He closed the door to the courtyard. "Plancus."

At least he remembered this man's name. He'd start learning all the others.

"Yes, Tribune?"

"What can you tell me about him?"

Plancus's eyes locked onto him, but the optio's face revealed no more of what he was thinking than Titianus's did.

Glabrio leaned his back against the door and waited. Titianus claimed that most couldn't stand silence for too long. Was Plancus one of them?

"Tribune Victorinus does his best to serve Prefect Saturninus."

Safe words, spoken without revealing any emotion. He'd learned well from Titianus.

His statement could be interpreted at least three different ways, ranging from a snide comment on the man's limitations to praise for the tribune's dedication to duty to a warning that Victorinus would do anything to curry the prefect's favor.

He opened the door and continued on to his private office. On the desk was another stack of tablets.

"Plancus."

The optio rose and came to stand at attention before him.

"Yes, Tribune?"

"What are these tablets?"

"The reports from the Trajan's Market Station."

Glabrio's lips tightened. Titianus said he'd need to look over these, but this stack was even taller than that from Subura.

He picked up one of the tablets, opened it for a moment, then snapped it shut.

Plancus's head jerked and his gaze fixed on Glabrio.

"Why isn't Titianus here?"

"He was, Tribune. He came early, and when you weren't here, he left."

"Where did he go?"

"He didn't say, Tribune, and it's not my place to ask."

"But it is your duty to keep track of that if I tell you to do it. Next time, if I'm not already here when he comes early, tell him I want to speak with him before he vanishes for the day."

Plancus's jaw twitched. "Yes, Tribune."

"You can go." He flicked his hand toward the door. Plancus struck his chest, made a parade turn, and strode from the office, closing the door as he left.

Plancus would tell Titianus what he'd been ordered to do, but would that make any difference at all in what his assigned mentor did?

Saturninus wanted him to track Titianus's activities on the Turbo case. That was impossible if the man slipped in and out before he even saw him in the morning.

Father always wanted to talk at breakfast, and a good son didn't end the conversation until his father was ready. He massaged his neck. He'd barely been on time, even by keeping his horse at a trot most of the way. He'd almost run over a small boy who'd dashed out in front of him, and a string of his mother's curses had followed Glabrio up the street.

Titianus was coming from his own house that was an easy walking distance from the Sabinus house in the Fagutal. Even on horseback, it should take him almost as long to reach the fortress as it did Glabrio coming from the Palatine.

He picked up a stylus and drummed on the desktop.

One way to make certain he was waiting for Titianus when he arrived was to live even closer…and he already had the perfect place. Within the fortress and a short distance down the Via Principalis were the tribune quarters, and the one where Titianus used to live was now his.

It shouldn't be long until Titianus finished whatever it was Turbo wanted; then he'd retire. Until then, moving into quarters was the ideal way to thwart Titianus's plans to leave him behind with an unending stack of reports to scan.

When Father asked about his morning absence, he'd tell him Saturninus needed him there early for a while. As long as that work-obsessed equestrian didn't keep him too late, he could still make the dinners Father wanted him to attend and ride back here to sleep.

He took his helmet off and placed it on the side table before settling into what was now his chair. Titianus could use the guest chair when he showed up. The optio would start doing things his way, not the way his predecessor wanted it.

He leaned back in the chair and rubbed both sides of his nose. If Titianus saw that as the challenge it truly was, he'd never be allowed to "help" investigate, as Saturninus had called it.

What felt good at the moment wasn't worth failing in his first special assignment from his commander. Perhaps it was time to act the dutiful junior officer until the XI Cohort was entirely his.

Titianus had at least one close connection he'd like to have himself. Simply being with him had inspired an invitation to dine with an important senator who was also the favorite son of one of the most powerful men in Rome. His supposed trainer might provide entrance to the private circles of other men as influential as Manius Sabinus.

Glabrio opened the first tablet and placed it on the desk in front of him. The sooner Titianus thought him a willing protégé, the sooner he'd get access to everything Saturninus wanted and to introductions to Titianus's other politically valuable friends.

Winning a battle could lead to a celebration, but there was no triumph for a general until he'd won the war.

Chapter 14

The Newest Teacher

Early afternoon of Day 4

As Sabina left her father's stableyard, her stomach began to knot. She'd been too nervous to eat much for lunch. Perhaps she shouldn't have eaten any.

Ahead lay the massive building complex that housed the Baths of Trajan and Titus. It had been six years since she'd last been there, but what if an old acquaintance recognized her as she walked by and wanted to talk?

But before they reached the edge of the gardens between Trajan's and Titus's Baths, her Syrian bodyguard veered away and guided them down a narrow street that ran parallel to the busy walkway along the massive wall of Trajan's Bath. He kept them on the uncrowded street until they were well past the Porticus of Livia, where its galleries of artwork drew gatherings of people eager to see and be seen.

She could have hugged Septimus. He usually took Tutelus as his bodyguard, and her brother must have told him of her concern about having to carry on a conversation, even with old friends. He kept them on side streets until they reached a door carved with flowering vines. A small wooden sign hung inconspicuously on the lintel. In capital letters too small to read from the street, it proclaimed her cousin's town house to be the home of the Lenaeus School of Rhetoric.

Her bodyguard knocked with a special pattern, and the door opened. Inside stood a grinning boy in a toga who was just starting his growth spurt.

"Rhetor Lenaeus said you'd be coming so I told Graptus I'd watch the door while he ate." He swung the door wide open, and Tutelus motioned

Sabina to pass through ahead of him as he scanned the street one more time.

"I have to join the class now. Will you be here when we finish?" The boy's eager words behind her confirmed his happiness at seeing her escort.

But why would one of Kaeso's students be that fond of an ex-gladiator Father owned?

Sabina stepped out of the vestibulum into the atrium as the door closed with a thud and two metal bars slid with clicks into the catch plates on the door frame.

"Maybe." Tutelus's deep voice had been lowered to scarcely above a whisper. "We'll leave when Mistress Sabina says."

"I'll tell Pompeia you're all here." The youth scurried past and vanished into the passageway to the peristyle.

So, was he part of the familia since he entered the private portion of the house like he belonged there? And why would a boy in a toga be answering the door like a slave?

"Welcome."

She startled when a man's voice sounded right behind her.

"I'm glad you could come." Kaeso Lenaeus, wearing a toga as befitted a teacher, greeted her with the same warmth in his eyes that she'd seen at last night's dinner. "I wasn't thinking last night, or I would have invited you to join us for lunch before you and Pompeia analyze her poetry."

"In my opinion…" He lowered his voice. "She writes much better than she thinks, but Septimus says you're an expert. It's been my observation that no matter how good I am at something, I can always improve if I listen to those who are better than me."

"S-septimus is my brother. He cares for me, so he's not unbiased."

His chuckle was not what she expected. "He's been my best friend since we were fifteen. That's never kept him from telling me the truth about my own strengths and weaknesses. I'll take his word about yours."

She opened her mouth to respond, but the words stuck. As he had the night before, Kaeso waited.

"Yes, well, he b-believes what he said."

"And so do I." He swept his hand toward the passage where the boy had disappeared. "Pompeia should be here shortly. She spread out some of her work in Titus's tablinum last night. He doesn't hold a salutation, so it's waiting for you now."

"Sabina." Pompeia emerged from the passageway with the boy behind her. "Thank you for coming."

When the pair reached them, Kaeso rested his hands on the boy's shoulders. "I'll see you after class is over and the boys leave."

Together, they entered a classroom. "As I was saying, we study history in part to learn about past mistakes so we can avoid future ones."

Pompeia waved her hand, palm up, toward the tablinum. "I've selected a few of mine for you to critique." She pointed at the packet in Filomena's hands. "I hope you brought a few of your own to show me. Septimus swears they're amazing."

With a knowing smile, Filomena held out the packet, and Sabina took it and held it against her chest. "Yours first."

Pompeia's light laugh was unexpected. "Very well, but you can't leave here until you share some of yours with me."

"I will."

"And perhaps you'll stay for some tabula and dinner. Septimus said he'd likely join us this evening."

"P-perhaps."

Pompeia's smile triggered Sabina's own. Father had said she should accept a dinner invitation. If Septimus was going to be there as well, how could she refuse?

◆

Filomena sat on the bench in the atrium, silently observing the people of Titianus's household. Mistress Sabina was reading Pompeia's poetry and suggesting different words to improve the meter and flow of each poem. It had been too long since she'd seen her mistress so relaxed and happy.

Not since the morning of her wedding six years ago, before the arrogant brute she married came to her drunk and told her to shut up before having his way with her. She'd held her mistress in her arms as the poor child cried herself to sleep that night, and if she'd had a dagger and could have slipped into his room where he lay in a drunken stupor after having one of the housemaids, she would have made Sabina a widow the same day she became a bride.

Her jaw clenched. Breaking his neck when the horse threw him had been too kind a death. He deserved to have the boar rip him open with its tusks so he'd die slowly in agony.

It would only have been just. He and his mother had tortured Mistress for years.

Mistress Sabina had been only twelve when Domina Julia moved Filomena from serving as one of her handmaids to being her daughter's lady's maid. At twenty-seven herself, she was old enough to be the mistress's mother. That was a decade ago, and she'd loved watching Mistress grow from a child into a young woman. Then came that marriage. At the Gallus estate, she'd seen Mistress withdraw behind a protective barrier against all except her. She'd become Mistress's closest friend during their exile. Since it was so far that no one came to visit, perhaps her only friend.

These friends of Master Septimus seemed to enjoy her company, but what if it was an act, like that of Marcus Gallus when he was courting? What if they only wanted to use her for some selfish reason not yet revealed?

This Pompeia was too friendly. She'd only met Mistress last night. She was acting like they'd been friends since they were girls. Filomena had served in the Sabinus houses all her life, and no one she'd ever watched did that. She'd had plenty of chances to see; elite Roman women visited Mistress Sabina's mother all the time.

Mistress was like a flower bud opening today, but that would end if she was betrayed again. A second betrayal could crush her spirit so she'd never recover.

Tutelus would be no help in spotting the danger. He was Mistress's bodyguard, but you'd never know it from how he'd behaved since they came into this house. He lounged in a wicker chair just outside the classroom, listening to whatever Kaeso Lenaeus was teaching. Each time laughter came from inside the room, his mouth curved into a smile.

His loyalty to Master Septimus seemed genuine enough. They even seemed to like each other. Did that extend to Septimus's closest friends? The boy's puppy-like enthusiasm over seeing Tutelus at the door suggested that.

Sabina was merely the daughter of the man who owned him, not someone special to him. He'd do what any bodyguard would if someone threatened her physically, but was that all?

But for Filomena, Mistress was the one person she'd defend from anything and anyone, whatever the cost. She was much more than a kind mistress. She was the one person Filomena loved.

Chapter 15

RETURNING THE FAVOR

The Praetorian Fortress, early afternoon of Day 4

When Glabrio finished the last tablet from the last stack of reports Titianus had left for him, he snapped it shut before moving it to the opposite side of the desk.

With lips squeezed tight, he stood. Titianus still hadn't returned. So, what was he going to tell Saturninus when he made his first report about Titianus's secret investigation?

Titianus was deliberately giving him busywork that would seem to some to be a reasonable introduction to his new responsibilities. But even though nothing about the man's eyes or lips said he was laughing at his replacement being tied to the desk reading mundane reports, Glabrio knew he was.

An equestrian whose ancestors had never done anything notable had no right to think himself better than Glabrio, with three consuls in the last four generations, and he'd make that four when he got old enough to qualify.

He settled the helmet atop his head and fastened the strap. It wasn't comfortable, but it was supposed to be worn, at least for inspections. Titianus left his hanging loose, but did he do that partly to irritate Saturninus by the subtle disrespect it conveyed?

Plancus was trailing his finger down one of the report tablets from yesterday, occasionally stopping to make a mark on another tablet. He stood and struck his chest when Glabrio stopped by his desk.

"I'm going to the prefect's office. If Titianus shows up, don't let him leave until I return."

Plancus stared at him, but what the optio was thinking was anyone's guess. "I'll give him your message, Tribune."

Glabrio strode out the door. Plancus would give him the message, but whether that would get Titianus to wait…he wouldn't bet on that.

The door to the prefect's office stood open, so he marched past the saluting guards.

Saturninus looked up and pointed to the guest chair with his stylus. "Close the door and sit."

Glabrio settled into the chair and waited. Although Saturninus had always been friendly at Father's house, here he was the commander. The right level of familiarity to assume…he had no idea what that was.

Saturninus leaned back in his chair and crossed his arms. "Report."

Eyes that had been friendly at Father's last banquet held no warmth now. Formal, not familiar, was in order.

"Titianus has been having me familiarize myself with the station reports, and yesterday I accompanied him to the warehouse district to talk with a merchant."

"What about?"

"He'd been delinquent in paying customs on his full cargo. He claimed he was importing a cheap wine, but he was packaging and selling it as an expensive one. Selling in flasks that usually held more and labeling some to look like they belonged to another merchant who sold the higher quality wine. So Titianus gave him a choice. He could pay the higher tax that was due for the quality and quantity he'd claimed he was selling, or he could personally inform his largest customers that he'd defrauded them and return what he stole. He would also post in several public places that he'd defrauded his customers so others who might have bought from him could come for a partial refund."

Saturninus chuckled. "Titianus makes his own money importing wine in bulk and packaging it for resale. Only a merchant would understand what would inflict the most pain on another." Disdain coated his voice as he said merchant. "So, what was the cheater's response?"

"He chose to pay the higher customs on what he had sold in the last three months. He promised to sell the wine for its real value in the future and faithfully pay the tax on its true value. Titianus wrote that down in a tablet and had the merchant sign it. He had me witness it. Then he told the merchant that I would be replacing him soon and that his retirement did not mean he could return to his cheating ways."

"Amusing and effective." Saturninus's wry smile faded. "But this didn't have anything to do with Turbo's problem. A tax cheat wouldn't draw Hadrian's personal interest." His eyes narrowed. "What else did Titianus do yesterday?"

"That's all I saw. He left early and didn't return for several hours, and then we rode down to the Tiber."

The remaining trace of a smile turned into a frown. "What has Titianus done this morning?"

"I came at the time set for your tribunes to be here." Glabrio squared his shoulders, but maybe that wasn't a wise move since Saturninus's frown deepened. "Titianus came very early and left before the rest of us arrived. He didn't tell his optio where he went or when he'd return."

"Why weren't you there early so you could accompany him?" The edge on Saturninus's voice was one Glabrio had never heard at his father's dinners.

"He lives somewhere near the Baths of Trajan. That's almost as far as where our house is on the Palatine. I didn't think he would get here that early and then leave, but I have a plan to keep it from happening again."

"How?"

"I'm moving into the tribune quarters tonight. Titianus said he lived there for years, and one of the Praetorians is there, too."

"Martialis. He's the reason Turbo wanted Titianus. I certainly wouldn't have recommended him if Turbo had asked me."

"So, if they're friends and Martialis already reports to Turbo, will Titianus get him involved in the case?"

Saturninus frowned. "Friendship, family obligations, the privilege of rank…none of that means anything to him. He doesn't trust anyone with details until he knows who's guilty."

"Then how do you recommend I get him to trust me enough that I can learn what you want?"

"Your father says you're a bright young man. I leave that for you to figure out." Saturninus rose. "I'm meeting some senators at the Baths before we go to dinner."

Glabrio rubbed under his chin. That was all he could reach with the cheek guards in the way. "Does Titianus go to the Baths in the afternoon?"

"I've seen him there in armor, not relaxing with anyone. He used the fortress baths when he lived here." The prefect's nose scrunched. "He ate the garrison food as well. There's a kitchen in the tribune housing, but he was too miserly to have his own chef. He even said he rented out his town house because using it himself would cost him too much money."

"Perhaps I can get past his aloofness if I invite him. I can suggest that he might learn something by watching who talks with whom and about what. I'll invite him to dinner as well, maybe get him comfortable talking with me about…whatever so he'll consider involving me in the case."

"He's a wary one." One corner of the prefect's mouth lifted, but it was more sneer than wry smile. "At the tribune dinners, he listens instead of talks and always stays sober. Suspicion comes naturally to him. You can see it in his eyes when he's watching you." He stood. "I doubt you'll succeed, but it's worth trying. Keep me posted on what you learn."

"Yes, Prefect." Glabrio struck his chest as Saturninus strode past him. Then he followed the prefect out the door.

One thing was now clear. Titianus had good reason for thinking the prefect might not be safe to work for. Saturninus disliked, maybe even despised the man. He'd be wise to figure out why and try not to make the same mistake. Saturninus being friends with Father wasn't the same as being friends with him, and becoming too friendly with Titianus would be unwise.

He snorted. Titianus becoming friendly with him was as unlikely as a snowfall in July.

But he still needed to get Titianus to trust him enough that he could learn what Saturninus wanted about the investigation for Turbo.

He released the chinstrap as he walked back to his office.

Father was planning a banquet with a large guest list. Tonight, he'd ask if he could invite Titianus to return the favor of being included in the dinner with Manius Sabinus. If any of the men there were of special interest in the Turbo case, he'd see a reaction from Titianus. Or would he? And if there was no reaction, would that tell him anything at all?

Midafternoon of Day 4

When Titianus rode through the fortress gate, he erased the frown that had grown as he rode up the Via Patricius on his way back from the warehouse district. In his saddlebags, he had a selection of reports from the station there. Those should be enough to keep Glabrio busy for the rest of the afternoon. He'd arranged for the later delivery of a stack large enough to keep Saturninus's spy busy tomorrow morning as well.

He needed time alone to focus on Hadrian's problem, but how should he start? He was used to dealing with petty crimes mostly committed by ordinary people, not the rulers of the empire. He was no closer to a good plan of attack than when he left Turbo's office two days earlier.

He had the name of one conspirator from the damaged letter. But for success in removing an emperor, Hadrian's enemy would need a group of like-minded men he thought he could rely on. Who did Marcellus know so well that he would trust them enough to involve them?

The first men to consider might be Marcellus's freedmen clients who owed him everything. Gellius, his optio at the Subura station, was good at combing through records without drawing attention to what he was looking for. He'd figured out the complete network of one senator's freedmen when Titianus was hunting the killer of Pompeia's father. He'd already done that again for this case.

It helped that his suspect was not a generous man who freed many of his highly skilled slaves after they turned thirty. In the twenty-three years since the elder Asinius Marcellus had been consul, he'd freed only three, and his father had only freed four more in his will.

He would look into those seven, but how likely was it that any of them would be loyal enough that either Marcellus could risk them knowing he wanted the emperor dead? Not just wanted, but was willing to act on that desire.

He reined in at the stable, and a legionary trotted over to take his stallion.

"Will you need him soon, Tribune?"

"Feed and water him, but leave him saddled for now."

"Yes, Tribune." A fist to the chest, and the pair headed for an empty stall. Titianus headed for the Principia.

The freedmen were probably innocent, but Titianus didn't have any place else to start. If only he had some way to find out who at the highest levels was both close enough to Marcellus and unhappy enough with Hadrian to join a conspiracy to murder the emperor.

He needed some way to see where and with whom Marcellus spent his time without his target knowing he was watching. But how does a man who was never comfortably part of a social circle himself get where he can watch and analyze the circles of others?

He paused to let a *turma* of calvary pass before he crossed the street. It was headed for the drill field just west of the fortress. When the last of the 30 horses with their riders in dress armor cleared the way, he continued toward headquarters.

Most likely, the conspirators would be senatorial men of the highest rank. The only man he knew well in that group was Manius, and his cousin would never be asked to take part in an assassination.

Would Manius's father? If it were another emperor, he couldn't rule it out before he investigated, but the elder Sabinus and Hadrian had been good friends for years and Quintus had been loyal to Trajan before that.

He shifted the saddlebags on his shoulder. It was hard not to smile as he anticipated the look on Glabrio's face when he handed them to him.

Glabrio…son of one consul, frequently in company with several others. He moved in the social circles Titianus needed to understand to stop a would-be assassin. He'd been thrilled with the chance to add Manius to the important men with whom he dined. Could he be induced to return the favor with invitations to meet and dine with men of interest to Turbo?

But how could he get Saturninus's spy involved without him knowing who was the person at the center of the network of men he needed to identify?

God, if Glabrio can be a help instead of a hindrance, please give me some sign. Show me how to enlist his aid without revealing what he shouldn't know.

He reached the headquarters building and received the usual salutes as he passed the guards.

As he approached his old office, Plancus emerged. "Tribune Glabrio has just returned from the prefect, and he wants to speak with you before you leave again."

Titianus patted the saddlebags. "I brought something for him. I'll talk with him now. You can take a walk for…half an hour."

Plancus's salute was accompanied by a chuckle before he walked away.

When Titianus entered the office, Glabrio was straightening the stack of tablets Titianus had dropped off that morning.

"I see you've made good progress." He set the saddlebags beside the desk. "I've been in the warehouse district, and I brought you some that include a range of problems you haven't seen yet."

Glabrio opened his mouth, then closed it without speaking. He opened the bag and took out a tablet. "I'm sure I'll find these instructive."

He summoned a smile that was not quite genuine, but it almost looked it. "I've been thinking about your recommendation that I get to know my junior officers well. I agree that it's important if I'm to do a good job."

After glancing inside, he closed the tablet and set it down to start a new stack. "It's probably not possible to know too much about each district, including those who live there. People like your cousin Manius Sabinus. I would like very much to be introduced to other prominent men as your replacement so they'll know whom to alert if something isn't quite right and feel comfortable doing that."

Titianus crossed his arms and waited to see if that would stop Glabrio speaking what seemed a carefully rehearsed request or merely make him proceed with greater pretended deference.

"While I'm fortunate to know a number of Father's friends, my own acquaintance outside their number is limited to the few men I've met training with Brutus's gladiators. I know Septimus Sabinus from the ludus, but I'd never met his father."

"What do you propose?" Titianus set his helmet on the side table beside Glabrio's before half-sitting on the table edge.

"Perhaps a visit to the Baths this afternoon would be a good place to begin."

Titianus tightened his lips to stop the smile. He'd asked God for help, and he'd just been answered.

"I trained with Brutus as well. Many of the men I met there are serving Rome with distinction now. I can introduce you to some, and perhaps you can return the favor. My brother-in-law runs the Lenaeus School of Rhetoric where Septimus and I also studied. After I retire, I'll be teaching there as well. It might prove helpful for getting new students from top senatorial families if I'm acquainted with their grandfathers and fathers, especially those from consular families."

He tapped his cuirass. "But being in armor is not the best way to start an acquaintance, so we'll leave ours at Manius's house, along with our horses. It's a short walk from there to Trajan's Baths. Have you eaten yet?"

"No."

"We can get something there. A few exclusive *tabernae* serve senatorial diners."

Titianus scooped up his helmet and returned it to his head. "I left my horse saddled. As soon as yours is ready, we can ride to the Sabinus town house and begin expanding our circles of acquaintances."

As Glabrio smoothed his hair before positioning his helmet and securing the chinstrap, the young tribune smiled as if he'd won a sparring match. But Titianus knew who'd won the real victory in going to the Baths for introductions, and he gave thanks to God for opening the first door on the way to completing his task.

Chapter 16

NEW SOCIAL CIRCLES

The Baths of Trajan, afternoon of Day 4

Although Titianus selected a taberna that catered to the wealthy, none of the diners was known to either of them. Rather than linger in an unfruitful hunting ground, he ate quickly, answering Glabrio's attempts at casual conversation with as few words as possible.

When he summoned the girl for the bill, she sized them up and offered it to Glabrio. His protégé's eyes widened at being selected as the more likely to be paying. But the whiteness of the wool of his tunic and the intricate inlay on his dagger sheath proclaimed to anyone who served senators that he was far richer than Titianus, or at least more likely to spend his money freely.

Her tone as she invited him to come again conveyed more than the offer of another good meal. Glabrio flashed her a smile and paid more than she asked for.

Titianus would speak to him later about not doing that when he was in uniform.

They entered the street, and he took from his purse the amount he'd owed for the meal. With the coins wrapped in his fist, he held them out to Glabrio.

"I got it." Glabrio's smile had slipped toward superior again.

Titianus shook the coins in his hand. "Be careful about judging what a man has by how much he spent on what he's wearing. It might only tell you that he wants to make people think he has more than he does."

Glabrio's eyebrows dipped. "Or less in your case?"

"People will talk to one of their own class more freely than to one who looks too rich or too poor. When you're in uniform, the armor is all most will see, but if you take the armor off, you'll learn more if what you wear fits in."

A slight smile accompanied Glabrio's slow nod. "I'll remember."

He took the coins.

They entered the bath complex and wove through the crowds to the changing room. Titianus hired two slaves he knew to be honest to carry their towels, oils and strigils and the bags into which they'd placed their tunics and daggers.

They were strolling through the *tepidarium* when—

"Titianus?" A voice Titianus seldom heard but couldn't fail to recognize spoke behind them.

They turned to find Quintus Sabinus, Manius's father and one of the most feared powerbrokers in the Senate.

"I wondered if that was you. Seeing you in here this time of day and without your armor...I almost didn't recognize you."

Titianus nodded his greeting. "I'll soon know if that's a problem for others. I have a few minor problems to solve before I retire, but I'll be leaving public service soon."

Sabinus scanned Glabrio from short brown hair to sandaled feet and back before his gaze returned to Titianus. "Who's your young friend?"

Palms up, Titianus held out one hand toward each of them. "Quintus Flavius Sabinus, this is Gaius Acilius Glabrio, newest tribune of the Urban Cohort. He'll replace me commanding the XI Cohort."

Glabrio squared his shoulders. "It's an honor to meet you." A confident smile accompanied well-pleased eyes.

"I suppose it is." Sabinus rested his hand on Titianus's shoulder. "Titianus will be a hard man to equal. Are you going to try?"

Glabrio's smile stiffened, but he kept it from vanishing. After two rapid blinks, he cleared his throat. "I'll do my best to serve Rome well."

Sabinus's mouth twitched, and Titianus felt sorry for the eager young man. Quintus was silently laughing at him, but did Glabrio realize it?

"That's all Rome can ask, but whatever is the best from each man can be vastly different. Your father's best has been good enough. Perhaps yours will be as well." The laughter reached Sabinus's eyes. "I'll be watching."

He removed his hand from Titianus's shoulder. "For whatever reason you're here, try to relax some as well." He tipped his head toward a gathering of senior senators by the exit. "I'm expected."

Titianus answered with a silent nod, and his uncle, who knew the hidden secrets of half the leaders of Rome, walked toward the men who were almost as dangerous as he was if anyone crossed them.

"That went well." Titianus dropped his usual tribune's mask and let his mouth relax into a natural smile, like he did at home.

The less he displayed his old tribune ways, the more likely he was to overhear secrets among men who forgot he was more than an equestrian of limited means. But it would take some practice to act like a normal man again.

"It did?" When Glabrio's gaze shifted from Sabinus to him, his protégé's eyes widened. Whether that was because of his words or the smile he'd not let Glabrio see before, he couldn't tell.

"He said he'd be watching. He respects your father, and he'll soon decide whether you might earn his respect, too."

Meeting Quintus Sabinus was enough to make it a successful afternoon for Glabrio. Now it was his turn. The intercepted letter identified Marcus Asinius Marcellus as lead conspirator. He knew that name. Even though he'd never talked with either of them, he recognized on sight both men who bore it.

But he didn't know if it was the elder Marcellus, who was consul twenty-three years earlier between Trajan's Dacian wars, or his son, who was now in his forties. Because of the elder Marcellus's age, if he were a betting man, he'd bet on the son. But old men had plotted against emperors before, so he'd keep both as suspects.

He scanned the small groups of powerful men, and he spotted the younger Marcellus talking with Faustus Cornelius Rufinus. Two men the right age to be consul, but Hadrian hadn't picked either yet.

He stroked his jaw. How could he start a conversation without it seeming suspicious?

"Glabrio."

His protégé responded with raised eyebrows.

"Who are the men here from consular families that you can introduce me to?"

Glabrio scratched above his eyebrow. "Any of the men I've dined with at our house, I suppose." He scanned the tepidarium. "In here, I see Verus, young Marcellus, Antoninus, Macedo, Capella, Nepos, Aviola—he's our cousin—and Saturninus, but you know him already. Rufinus talking over there with Marcellus...it's very likely he'll be consul soon." With tips of his head and waves of his hand, he pointed out each one without making it obvious.

Titianus's smile grew as Glabrio rattled off the list. "That's more than enough for today."

But there was one problem. Marcellus was talking with Faustus Rufinus. It was not a good time for an introduction with Rufinus there.

Rufinus glanced his way, and their gazes locked. The warm expression he had conversing with Marcellus chilled.

Rufinus had never taken friendly notice of Titianus, and it used to feel like being ignored wasn't personal. But since Rufinus's freedman Arcanus had been killed, the emotion he stirred in Rufinus had gone from indifference to poorly concealed resentment. Arcanus's murder during a robbery led Saturninus to order him to stop investigating Gnaeus Lenaeus's murder, but the death of the man who drove the dagger into Pompeia's father may have let other guilty men go free.

"So, to whom do you want me to introduce you first?"

"How about one of those? His hand swept toward the three groups away from Marcellus and Rufinus. It was better if Saturninus didn't see him talking to his target.

His unwitting assistant rubbed his neck. "My cousin was consul five years ago. Manius Acilius Aviola. He's over there talking with Saturninus. Let's start with him."

Glabrio led them past small groups of chatting men until they approached the pair. He raised his hand in greeting and received a welcoming smile in return.

"A pleasant surprise, cousin. Is your father here?"

Saturninus's back was to them, but he turned at Aviola's greeting. The friendly political smile he wore hardened into a formal one as his gaze fell upon Titianus.

"No. Tribune Titianus was introducing me to some of the leading citizens with town houses in this district. I'll be replacing him shortly as Tribune of the XI Urban Cohort."

Aviola's smile broadened. "The infamous Tribune Titianus, whose very name makes the criminals of Rome tremble. I didn't expect to meet you."

"Those who live lives of honor seldom do." Titianus smiled as if he were speaking to Manius.

Aviola's chuckle was the response he hoped for.

"My young cousin will be an able replacement, but how will a man like yourself, accustomed to hunting the law-breakers of Rome, stand the boredom of retirement?"

"A man of many interests is never bored. I'll enjoy having time to pursue some of them."

"Titianus is better than most at understanding how the common Roman thinks. He is, after all, a merchant who'll be returning to his family's trade after this interlude in the service of Rome." Saturninus's nose twitched at the word "merchant."

Titianus chuckled before switching his gaze from Aviola to Saturninus, and the prefect tensed. "Understanding both noblemen like ourselves and the common man has proven very useful these past ten years. I've enjoyed serving, but I'm ready for something different."

He fixed his gaze on Aviola alone.

"I have an estate with a vineyard that produces some of the wines I sell. I also import wines and some foods from other estates and package them for sale."

He tilted his head and raised on one finger, as if a thought had just struck him. "I've received a shipment of amphorae just this week from one of Hadrian's estates in Campania. It's worth trying if you haven't had it before. If you send your wine steward to my warehouse on the Tiber, have him ask for Probus. Tell him you're interested in the vintage Quintus Sabinus likes best." He shrugged. "My uncle finds it convenient to have me import it."

He fingered his lip. "I can send a message to my manager to hold an amphora for you at the friend's price, if there are any left."

Special treatment, but limited—that and the mention of kinship ties were the way to start any political relationship. Men valued more what was harder to obtain.

"I regret I must limit it to one. Most of this shipment is already committed to my regular customers. These tend to sell fast, but there will more in the future."

"I'll certainly send him. I've eaten with Sabinus often enough, and I think I know which wine that might be. It would be worth paying full price."

Aviola nudged Saturninus. "I might serve it to you, my friend, next time you join me for dinner."

Saturninus forced a chuckle, but any appreciation of the congenial words shared between his friend and his despised tribune was lacking.

A quick glance at Glabrio almost made Titianus laugh. Glabrio was staring at him as if trying to decide whether an imposter had taken Tribune Titianus's place.

To shift so suddenly from masking all emotion to smiling like a normal man…it was almost too great a shock for Glabrio to bear.

Or perhaps it was Saturninus's obvious displeasure with what he meant as an insult turning into Titianus getting to do Aviola a favor that he wouldn't forget.

But it might be him choosing not to mention the school. For the moment, it was unwise to draw the attention of anyone who might be connected to Turbo's problem to his connection with it. The case could turn deadly.

Until his first child was born, he'd made Kaeso and Pompeia his joint heirs with Manius as executor of his will. His cousin could be trusted to watch over his property and protect Pompeia and the rest of the familia any way he could.

There was plenty of time to recruit new students after he was through with this case and the dangerous men he might implicate had been punished as befitted their crimes.

◆

As Glabrio walked beside Titianus on their way back to the Sabinus town house, he couldn't have been better satisfied with their visit to the Baths.

Quintus Flavius Sabinus, of all people, had been pleased to meet him and had expressed an interest in his career.

At least, that's what Titianus said, and surely a man that skilled at interpreting what others really meant would understand his own uncle well enough to know.

But seeing Titianus smiling and joking with Aviola—that was the last thing he expected. Until this afternoon, he'd seen nothing but serious eyes and straight lips, even during their dinner with Manius Sabinus.

Which was the real person…the stone-faced tribune or the friendly man who could make a stranger chuckle?

He glanced at Titianus and found the sober face of the tribune as they walked in silence. Was that a deliberate choice or just habit? Was the man only an actor who could seem human when he chose?

For as short a time as they'd be working together, did it really matter?

Whatever the case, Titianus had already provided two useful introductions. Building on those was Glabrio's immediate goal.

As they approached the Sabinus town house, the first opportunity for that waited inside the stableyard gates.

The two guards looked like the ones who'd been there when Manius showed him the house. They stepped back, and Titianus raised a hand in greeting as they passed through.

"Will you be joining your cousin for dinner?"

"Not here." A twitch of his lips—what did that mean?

As they headed toward the portico, a stableman slipped into the stall where Titianus's horse stood munching on hay. He led it out and tossed the saddle on its back.

Their armor awaited them in the small triclinium where they'd dined with Manius. When Titianus picked up his skirt of leather strips, Glabrio began donning his armor as well. There would be no chance to work on a friendship with Manius Sabinus tonight.

When they returned to the stableyard, both horses stood saddled and ready.

Titianus gripped the reins and a handful of mane, then tossed his leg over the stallion's back. "We made a good start at the Baths. We'll visit again tomorrow afternoon." His calves tensed, and the horse started toward the gate.

Glabrio stepped in front of him. "And in the morning?"

"Read the reports I brought you until I get there." His mouth curved into a fleeting smile. "Enjoy your evening."

"As I hope you enjoy yours."

Another brief smile accompanied a nod, and Titianus trotted out the gate.

Glabrio mounted and followed him, heading toward the street that would take him down off the Oppian Hill. It was a short ride from there to his father's town house on the Palatine.

He'd gather a few things he'd need for the morning. His manservant, an underchef, and some house slaves could bring the rest tomorrow when they moved to the tribune quarters to take care of his needs. Titianus might have been content to live at the fortress with nothing more than a soldier on campaign. He was not.

But tomorrow morning, he would be sitting in that office when Titianus first came. He would not be left behind again.

Chapter 17

THE WRONG KIND OF PEOPLE

The Titianus town house, evening of Day 4

Sabina followed Pompeia into the peristyle to a dining room more spacious than the one Father used for breakfast. There were three couches, but there were also three tables large enough for four pushed against wall. On two of them were gameboards.

One had intricate inlays of different woods around the gridwork of lines that was the playing area for latrunculi. Each game piece was a polished stone, white jade or onyx, with the kings shaped like four-sided pyramids.

Pompeia picked up one of the kings. "This one belonged to Titus's father. He had it at the tribune quarters to play with his friend Martialis. Titus found living in the fortress convenient, and Martialis's family estate was too far away for him to ride back and forth."

Pompeia returned the king to its place by the elegant board and moved to the other table. "I prefer this one. It's the one Father taught Kaeso and me to play on."

It was plain wood, and a vine with faded flowers encircled the playing area. Etched into it were the opposing rows of triangles for tabula. Beside it were many thin slices of an antler, half dyed blue, for the game pieces.

"There's a latrunculi grid on the back side if you'd rather play that."

"Tabula." Sabina's tabula skills came back quickly enough, but the more complex military strategy game…she needed to play it with Septimus before she tried it with anyone else.

Pompeia settled into a chair and invited her to sit with a wave of her hand. "You don't want to play latrunculi with Kaeso. He and Titus play it so often that either of them is guaranteed to beat me now, even though I used to beat my brother half the time."

Kaeso joined them at the table, and Sabina bent her head back to look into his eyes. The hint of laughter there…it was kind and friendly, nothing like she'd seen too many times in the eyes of so-called friends who only saw her as Quintus Sabinus's granddaughter or Manius Sabinus's stuttering child.

"She plays much better than she's telling you. As I tell my students, only with practice can you achieve your best. And practicing with the best can make both of you better."

He placed his hands on his sister's shoulders and squeezed. "But it's teaching something that gives you a greater understanding of it, even if you thought you knew it well before."

"I n-noticed that when making suggestions to Pompeia."

Pompeia patted his hand. "I learned so much today, but I would love to learn more. Septimus was right that your poetry is as good as Statius's."

"You should hear her sing her lyric poetry." Sabina startled at Septimus's voice right behind her. "Never a problem with any words sticking. She has a beautiful voice. It's why I started calling her Skylark when we were younger."

"Really?" Pompeia picked up a blue rondel and rolled it between her fingers. "I can play the lyre well enough to teach it, but I'm not a good singer. Would you be willing to help me with one of my special students? Khepri wants to learn how to write poetry and perform it for her husband."

"I c-could never do that. If s-someone started gossiping about me thinking I was a poet…" Sabina's ears heated. "I don't want to embarrass Father or Mother."

She suppressed the shudder. If Grandfather heard of it, he might think it ridiculous, and who knew what he'd say.

Pompeia's head drew back. "But you are a poet. A wonderful one. As for people who know you hearing about it…that wouldn't be a problem. We can easily keep it secret from the Roman students. Khepri is Egyptian, and she can come in the afternoon after all the girls leave. We'll meet in the peristyle garden where none of the boys are allowed."

"Well…" Sabina bit her lip. It was true that she never stuttered when she sang. Showing Pompeia how to improve her poems had been easy. But could she actually teach what she knew to a stranger?

Septimus placed his hands on her shoulders and leaned over her head to look at her face. "Try it, Sabina. Father always told me I wouldn't know if I could do something until I tried. Only then could I decide if I wanted to do what it took to do it well."

"I g-guess I can."

Pompeia reached across the game board to touch the back of Sabina's hand. "Thank you. I'll let Khepri know tomorrow and see when she'd like to begin. But I still have many poems for you to help me with, so please come whether she'll be here or not."

Sabina's nod drew Pompeia's biggest smile.

Another quick squeeze, and Septimus removed his hands. "I saw Titianus at the Baths. He said he might be late so go ahead and eat if it's more than an hour." He pointed at the other table. "We'll have time for tabula while we wait."

As Septimus flipped the board, Kaeso took the seat where Sabina could see his face.

"The guest goes first." Pompeia's nudge drew Sabina's gaze back to the board. But after they'd exchanged three moves, she glanced at the players at the other table.

Kaeso's head was down, lips straight, brow furrowed as he moved an onyx stone. Then his gaze rose to meet hers, and the smile that lingered on his lips most of the time broadened. Septimus completed his move, and Kaeso's eyes lowered to the board once more.

But not before Sabina felt the pleasure of merely being in Kaeso's company, and it seemed like he enjoyed hers.

"I heard good news at the ludus today." Septimus tossed a stone in the air and caught it. "Before he moved to Germania, it was always my goal to spar with Africanus. Felix said he and Brutus might be coming back for a short visit later this month. He said I might be good enough now. Africanus never fought anyone he didn't think was skilled enough to keep from being injured."

Kaeso forced one of Septimus's pieces off the board. "Keep thinking about that, and I'll beat you for certain."

He looked at her again, and a single bounce of his eyebrows made her blush.

"I'm glad you could join us." Titianus's voice came from the peristyle. "We'll join them as soon as I shed this armor."

She froze with her next game piece six inches above the board. Why did there have to be another guest to disrupt the comfort of a meal with friends?

"Father said he saw you at the Baths today."

The worry drained away as she finished her move. That was her father's voice.

"He did."

"He said you had your replacement with you."

"Glabrio was very pleased to be noticed by one of the lions of Rome."

Father chuckled. "I imagine he was. He did tell us it was his ambition to follow in his father's footsteps."

"He was just as pleased to meet you. We left our horses and armor at your house. When we went back to get them, he was fishing for an invitation to dine with you again."

"I found him amusing company. I'd welcome him at my table again, assuming you join us."

"We'll be going to the Baths again tomorrow. If you see us and it's convenient, invite us. He'll consider it the perfect end to his day."

When they entered the tablinum, Pompeia rose and went to her husband. With one arm wrapped around his, she beamed at Sabina's father. "It's so good to have you join us." She waved a hand toward Sabina. "I learned so much today, and Sabina's coming back tomorrow to teach me more."

Father walked to the middle couch and summoned Sabina with a curl of his fingers. "I'm glad to hear it, and I'm not surprised. Septimus says her skill is exceptional." His smile wrapped around Sabina like a warm embrace. "I'll have to read some tomorrow."

With Pompeia settled beside her husband and Kaeso on the third couch with Septimus, Sabina joined her father on the couch of honor between them. Soon the ebb and flow of conversation among friends enveloped her as the servers carried in the first course.

Each time she joined in, she barely stuttered, and even when she did, everyone waited until she got the words out.

As the salad course was cleared and the second course brought in, she couldn't remember a time when she'd felt more at home and content.

The Sabinus town house, late evening of Day 4

Since Master Sabinus and his son had both come for dinner, they had been a large party walking back from the Titianus town house. Bodyguards walked before and behind them, but Filomena still felt uneasy. Master Septimus's friends treated Mistress Sabina well, but that might be worse than if they hadn't.

Mistress had spent too much time helping Pompeia. The longer they looked at the poems and the more they talked and laughed together, the more it bothered her.

She'd eaten with the servants and house slaves while Sabina was in the triclinium. There was something very odd in how this household was run. The boy who'd worn the toga was there with what must be his mother and father, but so were the housemaids and the stableman, who were obviously slaves. The cook was the boy's mother, and who knew what relationship she was to the girl who was the kitchen helper. Tutelus and the other three bodyguards talked to the others like they ate there often.

Now, in the quiet of Mistress's bedchamber as she prepared for bed, Filomena could learn whether anything said during dinner had shown to Mistress Sabina and her father that these were the wrong kind of people, unworthy of Sabina's notice.

As Filomena pulled the silver pins to release the coiled braids, Mistress sighed. But it wasn't a sad one like Filomena had heard too often in the last six years.

"It was a lovely day." Mistress smiled at her in the mirror. "Pompeia's poems were quite good, but I was able to help her make them better. Trying to see the right way to do that…it was as satisfying as writing one of my own. I liked the challenge."

Filomena nodded. "She should be grateful that you helped her today. She'll do better alone in the future."

"She won't be doing it alone for a while. I'll be going back until we work through everything she's written."

Filomena began unwinding each braid. "That shouldn't take long."

"I don't know how many there are, but I'll still have something to do there. One of her students wants to learn to write poetry and perform it for her husband. I'm going to help with that."

For a husband? Then it couldn't be one of the Roman girls she'd overheard Pompeia describing.

"Who?"

"Kepa or Kepri or something like that. She's Egyptian. Her husband is a merchant here in Rome."

The Egyptian wife of some merchant? Such a person wasn't what any lady of the Sabinus family should be spending her time with. Not at all. And teaching one? That would be scandalous. Teachers might be educated, but they were commoners at best and often slaves. And what if the woman wanted to become one of Mistress Sabina's friends? Her husband might be rich, but he probably wasn't a Roman equestrian, and she wasn't even Roman.

"What would your father think of that? Teaching…it's not suitable."

"It was Father's idea for me to spend time with Septimus's friends, and they're both teachers. He thought it was an excellent idea for me to help Pompeia with her poetry. Helping her student isn't much different."

She reached over her shoulder to take Filomena's hand, which still held a half-loosened braid. "It's not like I'm taking money for it. Maybe there will be something that inspires a poem. I've never met an Egyptian before." She gave two pats before lowering her hand. "It will be fine."

Filomena started on the next braid. It was clear Mistress wouldn't listen to reason. Pompeia had blinded her to what was proper for a senatorial woman. Even being acquaintances would have been beneath Mistress Sabina if the teacher hadn't married Titianus.

But since returning to Rome, she seemed too open to almost anyone who was kind to her. And with the woman being a cousin by marriage and the brother being…nothing really except her brother's friend. He wasn't rich or handsome or the kind that could charm a woman with flirtatious ways like Gallus had.

Filomena stifled a sigh.

She couldn't do anything right now to discourage the friendship with Titianus's wife, but at least her mistress falling for the teacher wasn't something she had to worry about.

Chapter 18

Not According to Plan

The Glabrio town house, evening of Day 4

The aroma of a good dinner wafted through the peristyle garden when Glabrio entered from the stableyard. When his father wasn't already in the triclinium, he continued on to the most likely place to find him, the library.

His father looked up from the scroll on his desk when Glabrio entered. "You look pleased with yourself."

"I'm pleased in general. Titianus might prove more valuable to know than we expected."

Father rolled the scroll and leaned back in his chair. "What did the terrible tribune do today to inspire that?"

"I suggested going to the Baths for him to introduce me to some of the important men who live in the districts he patrols. He agreed immediately, and we spent most of the afternoon there."

He lowered himself into the guest chair. "He introduced me to a few senators he knew from when he studied at Brutus's ludus, mostly men about his own age. But…" He paused to build suspense, and Father raised an eyebrow.

"When we first got there, Quintus Sabinus came over to greet Titianus, and he introduced me as his replacement."

"Sabinus knows too much about many in the Senate. That makes it desirable to be on his good side."

"He did remark on how well you've served Rome."

"I'm pleased to hear that. More than half the Senate is afraid not to heed his opinions. He had Trajan's ear and now has Hadrian's."

"He also said he expected the same from me. He said he'd be watching."

Father slapped his arm. "Excellent. It looks like my hope that you'd start developing valuable relationships during your time with the Urban Cohort will be fulfilled."

One corner of Father's mouth lifted. "It's ironic that Titianus is making those connections for you. Saturninus doesn't like him, but he's never said why." His brow furrowed. "Keep your eyes open in case there's good reason for that hostility."

"I already know what it is." Glabrio picked up a stylus and rolled it between his fingers. "Titianus views upholding the law as a matter of black and white instead of shades of gray."

Father's chuckle raised one of Glabrio's eyebrows. "His family has never served in the Senate. Negotiation. Giving up something to get something more valuable…he's had the luxury of not having to do that when it's necessary for the good of Rome. To help rule the empire, a man has to accept there are many shades of gray, and what looks like black in one light can be white in another."

"Scratch my back, and I'll scratch yours. I think he's more open to that than Saturninus thinks. He's already introduced me to Quintus and Manius Sabinus, and we're going back to the Baths tomorrow. I'd like to return the favor. May I invite him to join me at the next banquet?"

"I can't see why not." The twinkle in Father's eye appeared before his grin. "It might be amusing to watch Saturninus when your newest friend shows up."

"I did get to introduce him to Cousin Aviola, and the two of them got on well. I thought I'd introduce him to more of the men who dine with us regularly. He might find the introductions useful someday."

"I don't know why an equestrian like him would want to meet men so far above him, but I daresay many of them will be curious to meet him in person, given his reputation. The banquet should serve well for that."

The why was no mystery to Glabrio, but Titianus had chosen not to mention the school when speaking with their cousin. That he wanted to be introduced to consular men so he could get students in the future—Titianus didn't say that was shared in confidence, but it was Titianus's right to share that or not with any of the men he met.

There was enough difference in rank it might be a problem for some of them, especially since he was planning to become one of the teachers. That was not a career goal his father's friends would respect.

"There's another thing I decided today."

His father asked the question with a raised eyebrow.

"I'm going to move into the tribune quarters at the fortress for a while. I'll go there alone after dinner, but I'll need my manservant, one of the underchefs, and some house slaves who can serve in the kitchen and do whatever else is needed to care for the place. They can come tomorrow."

"Why?" The stylus Father had been playing with froze.

"Saturninus asked me to do something that requires being there very early, so it's easier to sleep there. But I should be able to dine with you here or meet you to dine somewhere else on most nights."

"A special assignment so soon?" Father returned the stylus to its tray and relaxed in the chair again. "Such things provide valuable opportunities. I'm glad my old friend is already giving you one."

A girl appeared at the door. "Dinner is ready, master."

He waved her away with a nod. "Talk to my steward before you leave, and he'll take care of selecting the right people and getting them there."

He stood. "If there's anything else I can do to help, I'll be glad to speak with Saturninus."

"I appreciate that, Father, but I'm confident I can do everything that's needed on my own, and I'd prefer to do it that way."

"I felt that way myself. Succeeding on your own initiative—I know how important that is. But if you ever need help, I'm here."

Glabrio thanked his father with the broadest smile as he rose. "I'll keep that in mind."

Side by side, they strolled to the triclinium for the pleasure of a family meal, where no one was trying to get anything from them and all pretension could be cast aside.

The Praetorian Fortress, morning of Day 5

Titianus rode through the fortress gate onto the Via Principalis and reined in. Just ahead, Glabrio in full uniform emerged from Titianus's old quarters and strode down the main street toward headquarters. Titianus turned left to put one of the larger Praetorian tribune houses between him and his eager successor.

He should have been well ahead of Glabrio's arrival so he could drop off the latest set of reports before heading to the Forums at the center of Rome. He would have been if Glabrio had ridden up from his father's home on the Palatine.

Moving into his old quarters—he never would have expected Glabrio to give up the luxury of his father's town house for the Spartan accommodations of the fortress.

He fought a smile. If he had been told to follow a man who got there too early and slipped away before he could come from home, he'd have done exactly what Glabrio had.

But years of experience had given him stratagems and tools a new tribune wouldn't expect. He had work to do that morning that Glabrio shouldn't see, and he'd make certain the eager spy didn't see it.

He guided his horse to the back side of Martialis's house, staying out of sight from anyone surveying the camp from the Principia. When he tried the slave entrance, the door was unlocked.

He slipped inside. "Martialis?"

"In here." Martialis lounged in a wicker chair in the library, and he set aside a scroll as Titianus entered. "This is a pleasant surprise." His hand swept toward a small table with its tabula board. "That's been sorely neglected since you moved out."

"You're as good an opponent as my wife, but playing with her includes other pleasures."

"I would bet on it." Martialis grinned. "Why are you sneaking in here so early?"

"I have a favor to ask." He patted the satchel slung from his shoulder. "Can you get this to Plancus?"

"Trying to avoid Saturninus or your replacement?" Martialis held out his hand, and Titianus slipped the strap off his shoulder and gave it to his friend.

"Mostly Glabrio, but actually both."

"I'll have my optio deliver it to Plancus so Glabrio won't know how it got there."

Titianus offered a smile. "Thank you. I need some time to check into something before I take Glabrio with me this afternoon."

Any trace of amusement faded from Martialis's eyes. "I won't ask what you're doing. I don't want to know, but if there's something I can do to help, just ask."

"You're doing it." Titianus tapped Martialis's arm. "I'll see you later."

He returned to his horse and left the fortress. He nudged the stallion into a trot as he started down the Vicus Patricius. On the other side of Subura, that road ended at the Forums at the center of Rome.

He'd spend the next few hours wandering among the senators and others gathered there, seeing who was talking with whom and whether they seemed to be nervous, both before he let them see him and after he walked away.

As Glabrio walked past the other tribune offices, no one had arrived yet. He couldn't help smiling when he turned into his own and found Plancus missing as well. No new stack of tablets awaited him on the desktop.

He'd outsmarted the wily tribune. Wherever Titianus went today, he'd have the watchful companion Saturninus had told him to take everywhere.

He put the helmet on the side table and settled into his chair. It shouldn't be a long wait.

The click of hobnails announced Plancus's arrival before he appeared in the doorway.

"Good morning, Tribune."

Glabrio tipped his head to acknowledge the greeting. Then his gaze fixed on the satchel hanging from the optio's shoulder.

Plancus set it on the floor by his desk. "Tribune Titianus sent these tablets from the Forum district. He said to be ready to join him when he came back this afternoon."

"Where is he now?"

"I don't know, Tribune."

"Well, where did he give you that?"

"He didn't. One of the Praetorians passed it on to me with his message." He pointed at the stacks of tablets Glabrio had started on the floor behind his desk. "Shall I file those for you this morning?"

"Yes."

Plancus squatted to pick up one stack. He held it in place with his chin as he stood. Without a word, he left the room.

Glabrio nudged the satchel of new reports with his foot, but he wanted to give it a good hard kick. He'd spent the night on an unyielding bed with a lumpy straw mattress in a drafty, unheated room and dined on what the garrison cook had the nerve to call breakfast. He still missed Titianus.

How had that man known he'd be there early? Had someone reported it to him, or had he merely thought out what he'd do himself and executed a countermove?

Still, he'd sent a message with the tablets that he'd be back to take Glabrio with him that afternoon, so at least there'd be something to tell Saturninus tomorrow.

But would it be something the prefect wanted to hear or only something to irritate him more?

Chapter 19

Near the Forums, morning of Day 5

With Melis beside him, Titianus left his warehouse on the Tiber and headed for the Forums to look for men who were close enough to Marcellus to be possible accomplices. They might be close friends. They might be political allies. They might even be political adversaries who hated Hadrian more than they hated each other. But they should have one thing in common.

They wouldn't be comfortable when they realized he was watching them, but what they were really thinking might be revealed best when they thought he'd stopped.

Melis was the perfect person to help him sort that out.

Slung from his shoulder, the youth had a satchel holding several blank wax tablets for making notes. He also wore the dagger Titianus had given him. He wouldn't need it, but he'd asked if he could wear it. His face had lit up when Titianus said yes.

They had passed through the Porta Trigemina and were nearing the northern end of the Circus Maximus. There were no races today, so the area around the racetrack was empty of anyone who should not overhear. It was a good place for final instructions.

"We'll reach the Forums soon. This time, we're looking for signs that two men have a secret together."

Melis shifted the strap on his shoulder. "What will that look like?"

"It could be any of several things, and they're all subtle. Standing closer than what you usually see. Glancing around to see if someone might be lis-

111

tening before they say something. Changing how they're acting if someone else joins them. Anything you think looks different from how two friends talking about routine things might look."

Melis's fast nods accompanied a grin. Sometimes his assistant thought the spying was some kind of game, even though he never let that show while he was doing it. That came from being sixteen, but this could be far more dangerous than anything Melis had done before.

"The men we'll be watching—they're very powerful, and for safety's sake, it's important they don't know what you're doing."

The grin vanished, and serious eyes accompanied Melis's slow nod.

"Try to look like you're not paying special attention to anything. Look bored, like you're waiting for a master to return. Blend into the background, like you do when you're waiting for me."

"I know what to do to stay safe." His hand settled on the dagger.

"Don't think a dagger is enough to protect you. I was in full armor with a dagger when I was almost killed, and I'd trained for years with Brutus's gladiators. If it looks like a bodyguard is watching you, pretend you see someone you know some distance away and leave."

"I will. I know how to disappear into a crowd. It's easy when you're short and ordinary like me."

"Short, yes. Ordinary, no." He tousled the youth's hair. "Probus would have my hide if I got you hurt doing this. Just remember some of these men might be very dangerous, and be careful."

Melis lowered his gaze to the pavement. They'd gone ten more paces when he looked up again. "I'm going to miss doing this when you retire." He shrugged, but that was only to hide the regret in his eyes. "I like helping you."

Titianus rested his hand on Melis's shoulder. "I like you helping. Probus did well by all of us when he added you to my familia. Some things I couldn't have done without you." After a firm squeeze, his hand dropped back to his side.

Melis walked a little taller as they passed the Great Altar of the Unconquered Hercules, rebuilt in stone after it burned in the Great Fire that Nero blamed on Christians.

Being exposed as a Christian was a death sentence then. Sometimes it still was. Glabrio's grandfather, even though he'd been a consul, had been killed by Domitian for his faith in Jesus.

Titianus's glance at Melis was quick, but it still caught the youth's eye and drew his gaze and his smile.

It was too dangerous for everyone in his house church to let the ordinary workers at the warehouse know of his own faith, but he should tell Probus and Melis, like Pompeia told him. The man who loved him like a son and the youth he'd grown fond of should join his family for eternity.

But that would have to wait until he finished this final task for Turbo.

"I'm going to walk ahead of you now so it won't be obvious we're together. You'll know when I'm pointing out someone I want to speak with. I'll let you watch him and anyone he's talking with for a while before I approach him. Watch for any changes that would say he or his companions don't want me there. Then watch what they do after I move away."

"Are you looking for someone's guilt to peek out?"

"Guilt or fear or resentment, and I know you'll spot any of that if it does. If you don't know their names, give them a number and a comment or two about what they look like. We'll sort that out later."

Titianus rubbed the underside of his chin. The cheek pieces of his helmet got in the way, and he would have preferred not to wear it. But he was well known for walking through his districts for no particular reason and for being in full armor when he did it, even if he never fastened the chinstrap. He'd draw more questioning eyes from the elites who knew of him if he wore his toga.

"Most of the ones we'll be watching will be in togas with the wide purple stripes. Make note of any equestrians or senators they talk with. Take special notice if someone who doesn't look Roman talks with them. Any questions?"

The silent shake of Melis's head drew his smile. With a deep breath, Titianus strode ahead. First stop would be the Basilica Julia as he began today's search for any beside Marcellus who might want Hadrian dead.

The Praetorian Fortress, afternoon of Day 5

When Titianus rode through the fortress gate for the second time that day, he was still mulling over what he and Melis had seen that morning.

Marcellus the Younger had been at the Basilica, and he'd been talking with Rufinus again. It was Rufinus who spotted him first, which was unfortunate. With a tip of his head, Rufinus had drawn his presence to Marcellus's attention. Whatever words were exchanged, that led Marcellus to rest his hand on Rufinus's upper arm and nod. Then they walked away together before he could reach them and start a conversation.

He'd signaled Melis to follow as they passed through the door that led toward the Forum of Caesar. But they'd disappeared by the time his accomplice reached the exit.

With Melis trailing some distance behind him, Titianus had wandered among the many public buildings, moving as if he had a fixed destination, even though he didn't. When he finally caught a glimpse of them in the Forum of Trajan, he was kept from following by Glabrio's cousin, who greeted the two as they went through an archway.

Whatever they said, Aviola headed toward him with a friendly smile and a friendlier greeting. By the time Glabrio's cousin had inquired about whether Glabrio was with him and been informed the young man was back at headquarters, they'd vanished completely. Neither he nor Melis spotted them again.

But at least his helper knew what Marcellus and Rufinus looked like, and their next scouting trip should be more productive.

At the stable, he slipped from his horse. Glabrio's stallion stood saddled and waiting for the ride to Manius's house. He'd ask Plancus later how his replacement reacted to his failed attempt to make Titianus take him along that morning, but angry or not, Glabrio was still eager to join him that afternoon.

The route from stable to headquarters passed his old quarters. A puff of dust came through the doorway, followed by a housemaid with a broom. A cart stood in the road, filled with trunks and boxes of kitchen supplies that were topped by a foot-thick down mattress.

Glabrio was moving in, and he wasn't going to be settling for the rough military life Titianus had found adequate. But even he wouldn't want to live that austere life again after knowing the pleasures of life with Pompeia.

As he climbed the Principia stairs, Victorinus came out, and the sun's rays flashed as they reflected off the lazy tribune's well-polished armor.

"Are you still here?" Victorinus's nose twitched. "I thought Saturninus was going to be rid of you by now."

Titianus's all-too-familiar disdain surged toward this tribune who served in Rome because two frontier legates his father had asked both refused to take him. Before he retired, he'd like to tell this dead weight whose centurions did everything that he should at least try to do his job, but it would be neither wise nor pleasing to God.

"He asked me to stay on for a while. I'm training my replacement for him."

Victorinus's head drew back. "Why would he do that? He hates how you do things."

It took effort not to laugh or at least smile at Victorinus's declaration of what was both true and obvious, but it wasn't time to drop the mask he'd worn for ten years.

"You'll have to ask him. If he tells you, you can tell me...or tell Glabrio so he'll be certain to make the prefect happy."

"Hmph." Victorinus stomped down the stairs, and Titianus strode past the saluting guards to the courtyard within.

Plancus saluted as he entered his old office. Glabrio sat at the desk, leaning on one elbow with his hand supporting his chin. A tablet lay open before him.

"This latest set..." Glabrio leaned back and tapped the wooden frame with his index finger. "There are some interesting charges in them."

"There's more variety from the market districts. Are you ready to go to the Baths?"

Glabrio returned the tablet to the still-to-be-read stack and put on his helmet. He didn't fasten the strap.

"Let's go. Perhaps we'll both meet someone worth knowing today."

As they passed Victorinus's empty office, Titianus tipped his head toward it. "Don't be surprised if your neighbor tells you why Saturninus wants me to train you."

Glabrio's eyebrows lowered. "Why would he do that? Isn't he the one you warned me about?"

"Because I told him he should ask Saturninus when he asked me first. I suggested he share what he learned with you so you could make our prefect happy."

Glabrio almost choked trying to stop the laugh.

It was hard not to smile himself. It was getting harder each day to hide all emotions behind a mask. He was retiring just in time.

Chapter 20

MAKING CONNECTIONS

The Baths of Trajan, afternoon of Day 5

It was handy to leave their horses and armor at the Sabinus town house, but convenience wasn't why Glabrio liked it. If Fortuna smiled, he'd get another chance to dine with Manius Sabinus.

Politically advantageous…dining with Sabinus was definitely that, but the conversation with Septimus and Sabinus had been enjoyable, too. Even Titianus had seemed less remote.

As they entered the tepidarium with two of Sabinus's slaves trailing behind them, Aviola spotted them and raised his hand. Father was seated on the marble bench beside him.

Glabrio schooled his face to keep from smiling. Father would consider meeting the tribune who irritated Saturninus good entertainment. Asking for Father's impressions later could prove enlightening as well.

"Over there." Glabrio pointed toward the two men. "That's my father with Aviola." He started toward them, and after a pause, Titianus followed.

"Father, this is Flavius Titianus, my predecessor over the XI Cohort."

"It's an honor to meet you." Titianus dipped his head and fell silent.

"It's my pleasure. My son has spoken of you."

A wry smile tugged at Titianus's mouth. "I'm sure he has. We've been touring the parts of Rome he'll be responsible for, and I haven't been easy on him." The smile vanished. "But he's taking on the most difficult districts, and I want to prepare him for the challenge before I retire."

"I've learned a lot already. That's actually why we're here." Glabrio swept the area with his hand. "Titianus is introducing me to some important people he thinks should know me as I take over."

"I, for one, am glad we met yesterday." Aviola clasped his hands around one knee and leaned back. "I sent my steward to get that amphora of Sabinus's favorite wine this morning. I'm planning a banquet this week, and Quintus Sabinus will be there. Perhaps he'll recognize it."

"He and his son are both men who can identify many of the best wines. Sabinus dines often with Emperor Hadrian, so he'll know what you're serving." Titianus wore the smile he'd shown Aviola yesterday.

Glabrio glanced at his father and caught the slight rise in his eyebrow. It would seem odd that an equestrian tribune would claim to know what the emperor and his long-time friend drank. Did Titianus have a first-name friendship with the father as well as the son?

"I appreciate you telling your manager so quickly that my steward could have the discount for friends. I've tried the wine already, and I want to get on the list of those who buy some each time you get a shipment."

Titianus turned the smile on Glabrio as if they were friends. "Remind me to do that tomorrow."

Father cleared his throat. "So, what businesses are you in besides keeping the citizens of Rome safe from harm?"

"I import wine and other foods in bulk and divide them up for sale. The wines from my own estate are among them."

"Are your wines as exceptional as Hadrian's?"

The chuckle drew Glabrio's gaze to Titianus's face. Genial eyes matched the smiling lips, but he would have sworn the usual straight lips and steely eyes were genuine, too. Which was the real Titianus?

"They're worth what I sell them for, but they have neither the excellence nor the emperor's name on the flask to bring top prices."

"Is that all you plan to do?"

"It's enough for now." Titianus accompanied his smile with a shrug.

Again, no mention of the school. If Titianus truly wanted to attract students, why not? Or was there some other reason, something related to Turbo's assignment, that made Titianus want the introductions?

"Perhaps you can change that when you retire."

"Perhaps." Titianus took a step back. "It's been a pleasure, but we need to find more of the men it's important for your son to meet before I retire." His hand swept toward a cluster of men his age and a few years older.

Father offered his gracious political smile. "It's been my pleasure as well."

As Titianus turned and walked away, Glabrio answered his father's raised eyebrow with a shrug and followed.

Serious eyes had replaced smiling ones before they reached the group. Greetings appropriate for casual acquaintances were exchanged. All expressed pleasure at meeting Glabrio, and all were ready to finish the conversation almost as soon as it started.

As they walked away, Glabrio glanced at the man beside him. The men he knew from his own years at the ludus were always glad to talk with him when they met. Had Titianus had friendships that cooled over time, or had he never formed warm friendships to start with?

Had he always been a loner? Was that by choice or forced upon him? Septimus had joked at their first dinner about him being a wolf on a blood trail who never stopped until he brought his quarry down. His father had laughingly agreed, and even Titianus smiled. But normal wolves ran with a pack.

If he had to name the animal most like Titianus, would it be a lone wolf?

A half smile tugged at the corner of his mouth. Maybe it would be a *polypus*.

Before these visits to the Baths, he would have laughed at anyone calling Titianus a polypus, but now…

He'd seen one as a child when Father took him to visit a friend at his villa by the sea. They'd gone out in a boat, and as he hung over the edge, peering into the water, he watched one change color and pattern as it worked its way along the bottom beneath them, always blending in. He'd thought the eight-legged hunter was working some strange magic until Father drew out the scroll by Plinius and showed him that changing colors like that was to be expected.

When a polypus latched onto a shellfish with its suckers, it held on so tight and pulled so steadily that the shell finally opened. Then it feasted on its victim.

Titianus often stared at someone without speaking, waiting for the building pressure to end the silence to overcome their reluctance to reveal their thoughts—that was like a polypus, too.

◆

As they walked away from the senatorial sons Titianus had trained with at the ludus, it was time to trade roles. He'd introduced Glabrio to some men who were now quaestors. The best and the well-connected would continue to rise. It was time for the consular son to introduce him to men of his father's rank. Men who might agree with Marcellus that it was time for a new emperor and choose to act on it.

He began scanning the tepidarium for likely targets for today's introductions.

The door to the steam room opened, and the younger Marcellus emerged. Right behind him…Faustus Cornelius Rufinus.

First at the Forums, now here. Coincidence or planned? They'd deliberately avoided him that morning. Would they now?

The two men exchanged words of farewell and separated. Rufinus headed toward the dressing room. But as he passed, he raked Titianus with a look of disdain. Titianus tipped his head and smiled a response, which triggered a deeper frown.

He'd wondered about Rufinus since the politically ambitious senator switched from ignoring to openly disliking him. Had Rufinus been the one who hired the assassin who almost killed him? Had he arranged for his own freedman to die before Saturninus ordered the end of the investigation of Lenaeus's murder? Or was it misdirected anger over the loss of the man who oversaw his business interests while he played at politics?

Rufinus had been rumored to be among those Hadrian would put forward for consul this year, but he wasn't. Did he blame Titianus's investigation of his freedman for that? Would that slight by Hadrian nudge him toward wanting a replacement for the emperor?

Someone bumped his arm. "Who do you want to meet now?"

Glabrio's question snapped Titianus out of his musings.

"You looked miles away. I asked you twice already."

"I was thinking." Titianus rubbed his lip. Marcellus and Rufinus…a possible combination, but only his suspicions tied them together yet. There had to be a third man as well, since the sender of the letter commented on Marcellus to the receiver.

Marcellus was sauntering across the tepidarium, pausing to exchange brief greetings with the senators he passed. Where he stopped, that was where Titianus wanted to go next.

He walked past the group that included Quintus Sabinus. He was almost to the wall when he stopped… with Saturninus.

Had he just seen all three conspirators together? In the same building, anyway.

Rufinus and Saturninus…he'd often seen them relaxing together at the Baths this past year. The ex-consul and the would-be consul…and both of them had a hearty dislike for him.

If he were honest with himself, he didn't like them, either.

God, keep me from believing the worst about any of them until I have evidence it's true.

It was time to ask questions whose answers he already knew, but Saturninus's spy couldn't know that.

"Who's that with the prefect?"

"Marcus Asinius Marcellus."

"Is his family consular?"

"His father was consul between the Dacian wars. His grandfather as well, under Nero, I think. I think he plans to be one soon. He comes to Father's banquets now."

Marcellus spoke, and Saturninus glanced at them.

"I'd like to meet him."

"We haven't talked at the dinners. He stays near the important men."

"Then let's have Saturninus introduce him to both of us." He directed a wry smile at his young companion. "If it's to be a cordial introduction, you should do the talking. Lead the way."

"You impressed my uncle. I expect you'll do the same again."

Titianus's skeptical smile was his only answer before they wove their way through the clusters of men with Glabrio leading the way.

◆

Glabrio glanced at Titianus as they approached the two men. Would he wear the serious expression he adopted each time Saturninus was present, or would he seem cordial, as he had with Father and his cousin Aviola?

"Good afternoon, Prefect." Glabrio combined the words of a subordinate with the smile of the son of a friend.

As Saturninus responded with a friendly smile, Glabrio's neck muscles relaxed. Why had they tensed so much?

Saturninus turned the smile on Marcellus. "I believe you know young Glabrio. You'll be seeing more of him around here. He's the new tribune for this district." He tipped his head toward Titianus, but his eyes stayed focused on Marcellus. "Titianus will be leaving public service in a few days."

"And I'm sure you're pleased to have such a fine young man serving under you now." Marcellus's political smile seemed almost warm, but the falseness was clear when it didn't change as his gaze shifted to Titianus and quickly back to him. "I believe my father and I will be attending your father's banquet in a couple of days. I have matters to attend to this afternoon, but I look forward to hearing how you like your new post then."

Saturninus's mouth twitched, then he directed a superior smile at Titianus.

Had he been so pointedly ignored, Glabrio would have said something to force Marcellus to acknowledge him. But Titianus didn't seem the least perturbed by the response of either of them. He merely watched them with straight lips and unreadable eyes.

"I have some senators coming for dinner, so I must leave, also." Saturninus's smile stayed friendly, but his eyes cooled. "I'll expect a report from you tomorrow."

Glabrio squared his shoulders. "Yes, Prefect."

As Saturninus walked away, Titianus's mouth twitched, as if he were trying not to laugh. But there wasn't anything funny about how he'd been treated. Or was there?

"I'm sorry."

"Why?" Titianus smiled…the last thing Glabrio expected.

"I never expected they would snub you."

"There are men whose opinions matter. There are others who don't. If you worry too much about the latter, you give them power over you they should never have." He'd been watching Saturninus until the prefect disappeared into the changing room. Then the steel gray eyes focused on Glabrio. "Show your commander the respect his position deserves while he's your commander. Show good men the respect they deserve, whether they command you or not. But what another man thinks of you…never let that determine what you think of yourself."

Titianus's smile vanished. "A wise man once told me it isn't a man's wealth or rank or family connections that determine his worth. It's his honor. Purple stripes on a tunic don't tell you whether the man wearing them is a better man than the slave walking behind him. Only how each man lives can tell you that."

Glabrio opened his mouth, then closed it. That flew in the face of everything he'd been taught. Living up to the expectations for the family Glabrio—his father had stressed that since he was old enough to remember.

Acilii Glabriones had served with distinction both Empire and Republic for over three hundred years. The grandfather who died before he was born had mostly lived that way, until he turned against Rome and became a Christian. Domitian had executed him for it, even though he'd been a consul only four years earlier. But Father had restored the family honor, as his consulship three years earlier had proven.

But he couldn't expect an equestrian like Titianus to understand, and there was no point in trying to explain it.

◆

"Titianus."

They both turned at the voice behind them, and Titianus smiled at the cousin who'd become a good friend.

"I'm free tonight, and I feel like indulging myself. So, can you join me for dinner?"

"I can."

A quick smile and a raised eyebrow were directed at Glabrio. "If you're free as well, join us again."

"I'd be delighted. Thank you." The truth of those words shone in Glabrio's eyes.

"It's only a family dinner with a few friends, but it should be livelier than last time. I'm asking your colleague's lovely new wife and brother-in-law as well. Septimus will join us, too."

Manius raised his hand, and another man in the archway leading to the outdoor swimming pool waved back. "Flaccus is waiting for me, but I'll see you later."

As he strode away, Glabrio's smile broadened to the largest grin Titianus has seen on him yet.

"It was most gracious of your cousin to include me in a family dinner."

"He sees the true value of many people, like I was telling you. He found your company entertaining last time; I expect he'll continue to invite you."

His young replacement didn't need to know how much humor Manius found in the pride and ambitious plans of young men just embarking on adult pursuits. Glabrio was no fool, and that would entertain Manius as well. But why did he have to invite Pompeia?

She would enliven the party, as she always did, and she and Kaeso were both wise enough to avoid saying anything hinting at their faith. They wouldn't put the familia at risk. But he'd tried hard to keep his private life away from the prefect's notice. That was even more important now since he wasn't certain Saturninus wasn't part of the conspiracy.

When Glabrio made his report tomorrow, what would the young man reveal about those Titianus loved to the man who might enjoy hurting him through them?

Chapter 21

BETTER COMPANY FOR DINNER

The Titianus town house, afternoon of Day 5

Sabina had just picked up Pompeia's next poem when three raps on the wall drew her attention.

"What is it, Tutelus?"

The big Syrian cleared his throat. "A messenger from your father, Mistress Sabina. He's inviting Lenaeus and Mistress Pompeia to come for dinner tonight. Titianus will be meeting you there with the young tribune. I'm to escort you all there by the usual time."

"Send him back with our acceptance and thanks." Pompeia straightened the stack of papyrus sheets they'd already looked at. "Let Kaeso know, too. I think he's in the library."

Sabina nibbled her lip. "The young tribune…what do you know about him?"

Was he the same one that Father had let her avoid the second night she was home? Why was he making her dine with him now?

"Acilius Glabrio just started his first tribune posting. He'll be taking over command of the XI Urban Cohort when Titus retires, but Saturninus asked Titus to train him before he does."

"He's the s-son of a consul. What's wrong with him that he's here in Rome, not with one of the frontier legions? Septimus said all the best want to serve out there."

"I don't know, but Titus said he's a smart one. There must be some reason. If you want, I can try to get him to tell us tonight." Pompeia rubbed her palms together. "I'm not as skilled as my husband, but I'm quite good at getting information out of people."

"No." She set the papyrus back on the table and picked up a pen. "I d-don't want him to think I'm interested."

Pompeia touched the back of her hand. "Septimus and I can keep him busy talking with us. You can talk with Kaeso or Titus or not at all, if that's what you prefer."

Sabina could have hugged Pompeia. How did her friend, who seemed so comfortable talking about anything with anyone, understand so well what a struggle it was when words came slowly and people thought your mind was slow as well?

Pompeia stepped close enough to read the papyrus Sabina held. "We have time for a few more before we leave. I wrote this one yesterday after you left. What should I change?"

Sabina scanned it, then read it silently, letting the words play in her mind.

"This is b-beautiful. I wouldn't change a thing."

Pompeia threw her arms around Sabina. When she stepped back from the quick hug, her eyes danced. "From a poet like you, that's the highest praise I can imagine."

"I've told her she could become a fine poet for years, but I'm only her brother." Kaeso's voice right behind her made Sabina jump, and she stepped sideways. She hadn't heard him come in. How long had he been there?

He wrapped his arm around Pompeia's shoulders. "Brothers can see what you don't see yourself. I'm glad you listened to Septimus and came to help."

"M-me, too."

"But just because she's written one fine poem, that doesn't mean we don't want you to keep coming every day." He pulled Pompeia closer for a squeeze, then released her. "'No matter how skilled we are, we can always improve when someone more skilled takes the time to train us.' Father used to teach that to all his students. I teach it to mine now."

"I've never been g-good at much except poetry."

"I doubt that." Kaeso picked up the poem. "Septimus says you have a beautiful voice, that you never stutter when you sing. Lyric poetry is meant to be sung." He offered a hopeful smile. "Maybe you'll bring some of yours and sing it to us?"

Her head drew back. "I've never tried that."

"Then tomorrow can be a first for both of us. First time for you to sing and for me to listen."

"But I only s-sang for my little brother."

"Think of me as your second little brother, like Pompeia does Septimus. Will you do it?" He raised his eyebrows. "For your second brother?"

Sabina dropped her gaze to the floor and traced a small circle in the mosaic floor with the toe of her sandal. Think of Kaeso as a little brother? A brother, maybe, but he was a mature man, more like Titus than Septimus, even though he and her brother were the same age. They teased and joked a lot, but beneath Kaeso's playful words, there was wisdom and strength.

Could she sing with no stutter for Kaeso, as she had for Septimus when they were young? She raised her eyes, and his smile was unchanged as he waited for her words, as he had so many times already.

"I'll try."

"Excellent!" Pompeia placed her best poem aside. "As soon as I change sandals, we can get Filomena and Tutelus and go." She wrapped her arm around Sabina's. "Dinner with Manius is always a lovely way to end a day. With you and Septimus, too, we couldn't have better company for dinner."

Sabina glanced at Kaeso, then looked away, but not quickly enough to miss the warmth in his eyes as he smiled.

The Sabinus town house, evening of Day 5

Glabrio rode up to the stableyard gate with one of his father's bodyguards behind him. While he'd gone home to get out of uniform and let his father know he'd be gone for dinner, Titianus had gone to the Subura station to do something he wouldn't explain. Glabrio had already slogged through more reports from that one station than he'd thought the whole of Rome would produce. Had Titianus gone to gather more tablets and deliver them to the fortress to tie up his morning hours again?

But whatever it was, it would take long enough that Glabrio wouldn't be the last to arrive. He'd traded his armor for the riding cloak he'd worn on his first visit. Even though the big German who'd stood in his way earlier swung the gate open, he didn't tip his head when Glabrio rode past. But nothing was going to ruin this dinner for him, not even the arrogance of a slave.

A boy of ten emerged from the portico as he reined in. "Follow me please."

Glabrio slipped off his horse, left it for bodyguard or stableman to take care of, and followed the boy into the peristyle.

As they approached the triclinium, he heard a woman's laugh. Perhaps he wasn't as early as he'd thought.

Two game tables stood just inside the doorway. To his left, two young women leaned over a tabula board. One wore a stola that marked her as a married woman, but the other didn't, even though she was old enough that she should be married, too. Just past them, Septimus and a man about his age who wore a plain tunic sat at the second table. Titianus and Manius Sabinus stood together where they could watch both games. Titianus's armor was piled by the wall.

"Glabrio, welcome." Sabinus walked toward him. "Now that you're here, we'll eat."

"My apologies for keeping you waiting. Since Titianus was still working when I went home to change…" He stopped. Excuses were never as good as being on time, but how was he to know when dinner would actually start?

"It's not a problem." Sabinus's chuckle started to raise Glabrio's eyebrow until he stopped it. "Anyone who invites Titianus has learned not to expect a precise time of arrival when he's coming from work. Sometimes he doesn't make it at all. Your father will soon know not to wait dinner on you."

"I've moved into tribune quarters at the fortress, so Father doesn't expect me every night now."

"Titus did that until he needed something more civilized for his new bride." With a sweep of his hand, Manius indicated the pretty woman rising from the game table. "This is Lenaea Pompeia, the woman who gave Titus a sufficient reason to throw out his renters and better enjoy the comforts of married life in his own town house."

Pompeia moved to Titianus's side. "I would have joined him wherever he lived, but we did need a bigger home for the school. One with a stableyard for litters and horses."

Septimus swept his game pieces into the box and stood. "One where you can go straight from entertaining him at breakfast to your classroom when he leaves to hunt law-breakers."

He rested his hand on the other man's shoulder. "This is Kaeso Pompeius Lenaeus, head of the Lenaeus School of Rhetoric, which Titus and I both attended as boys."

Head of the school—so Titianus really did have a brother-in-law who needed students. But that still left the question of why he never mentioned it during introductions. And why was his wife still working as a teacher?

The even prettier woman remained seated. Manius placed his hand on her shoulder. "This is my daughter Sabina." The smile he directed down at her bespoke fatherly affection, not just blood relationship.

Glabrio placed a hand on his chest and offered a slight tip of his head with a courtly smile. "Gaius Acilius Glabrio."

He received a gracious nod and smile in return, but she didn't speak.

A Sabinus daughter in her twenties wearing only a tunic and no stola? That suggested possibilities he'd ask Father about later.

"Perhaps he moved partly for the food." Glabrio's words drew a chuckle from Septimus. "I'm in his old quarters now. I don't know how he lived there so long. Garrison food is barely edible. I brought a chef from home."

"I'll have to remember that's a possibility if I'm not on the frontier for my first posting." Septimus nudged Lenaeus. "Kaeso's cook can tell you I like good food and lots of it, and that's what she serves every time. What Titus settled for from the garrison cook is too Spartan for me."

So, his wife's brother and familia moved in with Titianus, as well as the school, where she kept on teaching. A strange arrangement, but perhaps equestrians had stranger habits than he knew. He glanced at Titianus to find steel gray eyes watching him. More likely, this man had strange habits, even among equestrians.

Sabina stood, and her father escorted her to the host's couch, where they were joined by Septimus. Titianus and Pompeia took the couch of honor at the center.

Glabrio hesitated until Sabinus pointed at the third couch, where Kaeso had already reclined. But he should have known after the last dinner that he'd be relegated to the lower position when Titianus was there. No insult was meant by it.

The salad course was delivered. As the party dined on carrots in a white wine sauce, the conversation still flowed, at least among some of the diners. Sabinus and Pompeia chatted like old friends with Septimus adding frequent humorous remarks. Kaeso joined in occasionally, as he did himself. He wasn't surprised when Titianus spoke very little, and Sabinus listened attentively each time he did. Sabina listened to everyone, nodding and smiling at appropriate times, but she didn't speak at all.

He'd never heard gossip about any Sabinus who was simple-minded like a child. That wasn't something that could be kept out of senatorial gossip circles, even if Quintus Sabinus wanted to. Besides, there was intelligence behind those eyes that turned away quickly when he caught her watching him. She looked often at Pompeia or Lenaeus, and from either she'd get a reassuring smile.

After the salad course was cleared, the main course of a savory stew was dished into decorated silver bowls. On one side of the bowl placed before him, a mounted man with a spear followed a pair of hunting dogs as they chased a wild boar. On the other side, the boar stood over a dead dog as it stared down the hunter, now on foot with only a dagger.

He scanned the bowls of the others; none shared that ominous theme.

When Lenaeus traded bowls with him without speaking, he opened his mouth to demand an explanation. He closed it when his couch mate turned the bowl and covered part of the scene with his hand so Sabina would only see the mounted man with his dogs, not the one about to fight a boar to the death.

There must be a good reason for her presence in her father's house again. Did Lenaeus know why? Was he trying to protect her from a painful memory?

Almost certainly, Father would know as well.

By the time he'd eaten the stew and some rosemary-laced bread that came with it, Glabrio had eaten more than enough to satisfy.

"Titus, I heard good news at the ludus today." Septimus tapped his bowl, and another serving was ladled into it. "Brutus and Africanus are at Liternum. They might visit Rome for a few days."

"Are you ready to challenge him?" Titus set his bowl on the table and draped his arm across Pompeia. She leaned back into him and looked over her shoulder. When she reached up and stroked his cheek, the warmth in his eyes and crooked smile would have astounded Saturninus. It was love, not lust, that her caress excited. The tribune with no heart merely hid his well when he was working.

"Felix said he thought so. Only Africanus makes that decision. But it will be good to see them both, even if he decides I'm not up to his standards."

One clap from Sabinus, and what was left of the main course was taken away.

Septimus reached for his goblet. "Before they moved to Germania, I had no higher goal than to become good enough to fight him. Brutus told me it was a better goal to be a man of honor like you, cousin."

"I'll be telling my students that as well." Kaeso wiped his mouth with a napkin. "They'll believe it after they know you a while."

"How many students do you have?" Glabrio rubbed behind his ear. Perhaps Titianus never mentioned the school during introductions because it was too insignificant to impress anyone.

"Eight boys at the moment, but we'll be doubling after Titus retires. Pompeia has six girls and a few women."

Kaeso reached for the fruit tray, which had been left on the table after the main course had been cleared. "Titus will be teaching history and geometry. Quintilianus said geometry was invaluable for mental training with its logical progression of axioms and proofs. Titus is unequaled at forming a logical train of thought."

He tossed a grape at Titianus, who caught it before it hit him and popped it into his mouth. "There's not another mind in Rome that can beat Titus at applying logic to complex problems to solve them." He tossed a second grape, with the same result. "Couple that with understanding how men think, and the law-breakers of Rome haven't had a chance."

Titianus shrugged. "There were more who got away than you know, but that wasn't because I didn't try. Their victims deserve whatever truth we can find and what justice we can give them."

Glabrio picked up a dried fig. That seemed an obvious goal for a tribune charged with enforcing the law in Rome. So, why did Saturninus dislike Titianus so much?

"Father mentioned meeting you." Sabinus lifted his goblet to his lips and watched Glabrio across the rim as he took a sip.

His own father called Quintus Sabinus a lion of Rome, but when Glabrio asked what that meant, Father had laughed before answering. Intelligent, powerful, shrewd, a natural leader. A man you want on your side, but if you cross him, you could get mauled.

What had the elder Sabinus told his son? Glabrio swallowed, then wished he hadn't. He wasn't afraid of what the old man would have said. Titianus said the meeting went well, but the younger Sabinus's eyes were laughing as he set the goblet down.

"Father was pleased that Titianus has introduced me to both of you." Glabrio cleared his throat. "He wants me to meet all the great men of Rome."

Palm up, Sabinus swung his hand toward Titianus. "There's one of them. Learn from him what you can, and you might become one yourself." A smile played on his lips. "What is it you're so fond of saying, Titus?" He rested one hand on his chest before raising it like he was giving a speech to the Senate. "It's not the rank or wealth or family connections that determine a man's worth. It's his honor that matters most."

He reached for his goblet again and silently toasted Titianus before turning his gaze back on Glabrio. "Our fathers might not agree with that, Glabrio, but that doesn't mean it's not true. But true or not, it can be very hard to live up to. Perhaps you'll do better than I have."

He clapped his hands. "I just acquired some new musicians to share with Father. Before they go out to his estate, I thought we'd enjoy them."

The dessert course was carried in as a man and woman entered with flute and lyre.

Glabrio was not sorry for the musical break in the conversation. Father had said Quintus Sabinus was as ruthless as they came, but he truly loved Rome. Manius was expected to take his place when the elder Sabinus died.

So, why was he quoting the tribune who was notorious for his black-and-white views on right and wrong? There was no mockery in his voice as he praised his cousin.

Glabrio picked up a fruit-topped pastry and slipped it between his teeth. Father had said he could learn many things from spending private time with Manius Sabinus. It was a friendship he'd like to cultivate himself.

But when the public and private man seemed so different, what was he supposed to learn?

Sabina leaned on one elbow and stared at herself in the silver mirror on her dressing table. The evening had been pleasant enough, but the dinner at Pompeia's had been much better.

Father's chef was unrivaled, and his wine was always excellent. But with Acilius Glabrio there, she hadn't dared to relax and join in the wide-ranging conversation. In Titianus's house, no one cared how long it took her to say something. They only cared about what she said.

Filomena placed the last hair pick on the table and began unbraiding her hair. "Who was that handsome young Roman?"

"Glabrio? Someone Titus introduced to Father. He'll be replacing Titus when he retires. He's the son of Acilius Glabrio, the ex-consul." She picked up a hair pick and fingered the glass wings of the gold butterfly on the end. "I wish he hadn't been there."

The last braid had been loosened, and Filomena picked up the brush. "Why?"

"He looked at me too often, even when I wasn't speaking. And I didn't say much. He makes me nervous, and I didn't want to embarrass Father with my stutter."

"No one minded you speaking slowly before that beast of a husband and his mother. No one will now."

"That's not true. They were just acting in front of Grandfather and Father. Everyone wants to curry their favor. Even the weasel and her son acted nice before we married. We all learn how to play that game from our youth."

She shuddered "I don't want to play it again. But if someone asks Grandfather for my hand, he'll say yes if they're important enough. I shouldn't hope for more."

But no matter what she expected, she still longed for more. Someone who wanted her for herself alone…was that too much to ask?

Glabrio was handsome, and he was pleasant enough. But his smiles were political, not warm and genuine like Pompeia's and Kaeso's. His gaze felt like he saw a Sabinus, not a person in her own right, like Kaeso did.

Why couldn't she just stay with Father forever and have Septimus's best friends become her own?

Chapter 22

Doing Their Best

The Forums district, early morning of Day 6

With Melis a discreet distance behind him, Titianus entered the Basilica Julia to begin his observation of Marcellus and whomever he might be meeting.

The crowd was thinner than usual. It was a race day, and many had skipped their usual morning visit here. It was easier to watch someone, but it was too easy to be seen as well.

Marcellus wasn't among those scattered around the central chamber, but Saturninus was. He stood talking with a small group of senators by the entrance to one of the side rooms where lectures were delivered.

A walk through each main building to look for Marcellus might turn up something before Titianus rode out to the fortress to collect Glabrio. A cohort of the Praetorians kept order around the Circus Maximus on race days, but thieves enjoyed the races as much as honest people. His men patrolled the surrounding streets, and one-on-one drunken disputes over who won and who should have often flared. The senatorial son who'd never seen what could happen in the poorer part of the city should experience a race day before he was in charge.

He was within ten feet of Saturninus when the prefect's gaze locked onto him. Titianus's fist hit his chest. "Prefect."

After a single nod, his commander ignored him completely.

As Titianus moved away, he fingered his hanging chinstrap, the signal to Melis that he'd just spoken to a man the youth should start watching.

133

The tinkle of a bell quieted the conversations, and Saturninus followed his companions through the archway to take a seat.

As soon as the prefect was inside, Titianus reversed course. He slowed while he read the small painted sign announcing the title of the lecture.

The topic was arresting even though he kept moving. Seleucus Nicator—he was one of the conspirators who assassinated Alexander the Great's regent and went on to become king of the eastern part of Alexander's Empire. He, in turn, was assassinated in Thracia while on his way back to claim power in Macedonia.

Was Saturninus hoping to learn something from the past that would be useful for the future?

As he passed Melis, a snap of his fingers brought the youth up beside him. "Did you see the one I want you to watch?"

"The officer?"

"Yes. That's Prefect Saturninus. I want you to keep an eye on where he goes and whether he talks to either Rufinus or Marcellus."

"I can watch while he stays here and then follow him where he goes next."

"All right, but don't forget these men are dangerous. Stay alert. Don't put yourself at risk by trailing them into an isolated spot where they might see you and try to seize or kill you."

He tousled Melis's hair. "I can't afford to lose my future warehouse manager."

"Probus warns me each time we do this. I won't forget to be careful."

"Good. Go spy for me."

"I'll do my best." Melis flashed a grin and sauntered back to act like someone used to waiting for however long it took for a master to finish his business.

Titianus headed for the Ludus Bruti, where his horse was as welcome as he was, even a decade after Brutus had convinced him it was honor that mattered most.

If he got to see Brutus during his visit to Rome, he'd ask God if it was time to tell his mentor that honor mattered but truth mattered most. Would his friend be ready to hear the truth about Jesus?

When he entered the ludus's stableyard, his stallion stood by a feeding trough, contentedly munching some hay. A wave at the stableman drew a wave in return as he mounted and headed out the gate.

As he started up the Vicus Patricius toward the fortress, he blew out a long, slow breath. It should be a relaxing evening with his familia and maybe with Septimus and his sister. She'd been a different person with Glabrio there last night. Dinner with anyone but her family present tightened her up like an over-stretched lyre string. Anyone except his own family. With Pompeia and Kaeso, she was as relaxed as she was with her brother.

But who wouldn't feel at home with Pompeia? He'd been unable to resist her himself, even when she kept trying to discourage him.

A crooked smile leaked out. When God had other plans, nothing could keep two people apart.

Tomorrow night would not be relaxing. The banquet that Glabrio's father was giving should prove instructive, but he didn't expect pleasure from it, no matter how good the food might be.

Perhaps he should take Glabrio by his house to exchange his armor for a toga. It might go smoother if he entered the villa in civilian clothes with the consular son at his side. It would ensure his admittance without questions and lead to introductions, even if the snubs he'd receive from some might bother Glabrio, as they did at the Baths.

But it would be good for the new tribune to see who among his father's friends set the value of a person by the width of the stripes on their tunic and who looked instead at the whole man.

The Titianus town house, late morning of Day 6

With Tutelus behind and Filomena beside her, Sabina had almost reached the Titianus front door. Pompeia had said to come earlier because she wasn't teaching her Egyptians that day. They'd eat lunch together, and then she could sing them some of her poems.

For at least the tenth time, Sabina forced herself to stop chewing her lip. Why had she agreed to perform her poems for Kaeso?

With only Filomena listening, she'd tried singing the one she wrote yesterday. As it had when she was a child, singing somehow kept the words from getting stuck as she shared her thoughts.

But she never stuttered much when only Filomena was listening, so maybe it wasn't a fair test. Perhaps if she kept reminding herself it always worked before, it would work with Kaeso, too.

With Kaeso and Pompeia. It was just as much for her dear friend as it was for her friend's brother.

At least that was what she tried to tell herself. But it was Kaeso's gaze, not Pompeia's, that she felt even when she wasn't looking at him. It was his chuckles that she listened for when Septimus said something funny. It was his smiles that warmed her like a heated blanket on a cold night.

Pompeia had said she didn't need to bring her lyre. She could use theirs. It had been in their family a long time. Her mother had taught her to play it, as her grandmother had taught her mother.

Father had asked Pompeia to play for them when Glabrio joined them for dinner. She'd been almost as good as the lyrist Father had bought for Grandfather. He said Pompeia taught her Egyptians how to play, and she'd charmed Titianus with her playing the second time he dined with her at Father's house.

Would her own efforts seem feeble compared to his talented sister?

She forced her lips to straighten so Filomena wouldn't ask what brought on the big smile. Kaeso would tell her he enjoyed her playing even if it was only adequate, and he'd be telling the truth. He seemed determined to see the best in everything she did.

To see the best in her.

That morning, she'd sorted through her poems to find some that a man might like. The ones she wrote just before she married sparkled with her imaginings about the love of a good man as they started their life together. Pompeia might enjoy them. She'd been married less than a year to a man whose deep love for her showed with each glance and smile and touch. But an unmarried man like Kaeso…would he roll his eyes at the fanciful view of love that a sixteen-year-old girl once had?

After the wedding night, when her heart was shredded and any hope for love and respect from her husband had been crushed, sadness permeated everything she wrote.

Some poems from the time when her husband was away in Britannia weren't so dark. The pain had faded when his cruelty was no longer inflicted every day. Hope was hard to crush entirely when what ground you down wasn't there all the time.

But his mother remained, so any brightness was fleeting. Those poems were like flickering candles compared to the full light of day. None were suitable for sharing with the man who seemed to find something of value in everything and everyone, even the scorned, stuttering sister of his friend.

Maybe the ones written on the journey home would do, when the future no longer seemed so bleak, even if it wasn't yet clear. So, she'd brought the hopeful poems of youth for Pompeia to read and the most recent ones she felt almost brave enough to sing to Kaeso.

Almost brave enough as she walked up the street, but there was something about his eyes that would give her courage to strike the first chord on the lyre and open her mouth to sing the first word.

Tutelus knocked, and a youth opened the door. He wasn't as excited about her bodyguard's arrival as Theo had been, but he smiled as he invited them to enter.

She'd no sooner entered the atrium than Kaeso came out of his classroom. "Did you bring your poetry?"

"Yes." Sometimes it was hard to meet his gaze without blushing. This was one of those times. Her ears heated.

"A Sabinus always keeps his word. I'm glad you followed the family tradition."

"You haven't heard me yet. You might change your mind."

"Are you planning to do your best?"

"Yes."

"Then I won't be disappointed. Septimus never lies to me, and I have his word that your best is excellent."

Her ears heated again, and the grin he flashed at her only made it worse. "I'll look forward to it after class."

As he slipped back into the room where his students were bent over their tablets writing something, one thing was certain.

She would look forward to it, too.

Chapter 23

An Opportunity Worth Pursuing

The Circus Maximus, late morning of Day 6

Glabrio followed Titianus through the stableyard gate at the Ludus Bruti, and the stableman led their horses to hay-filled mangers without Titianus even asking.

They'd both trained with Brutus's gladiators. If Titianus could use this as his personal stable when he visited this part of the city, Lanista Felix would probably extend the same courtesy to him. Should he ask or just assume since it was all right when he came with Titianus?

It was a short walk to the Flavian Amphitheater, and just past it stood the uncompleted Temple of Venus and Roma.

"That's been under construction for what, six years? It's not even half finished. The whole Amphitheater was built in only ten."

Titianus drew a breath, then paused before he spoke. "The more prominent the man you criticize, the more dangerous your words. Never put it in writing, and never assume the one you speak it to won't tell another you said it."

Titianus pointed at the unfinished temple. "You aren't the first to criticize it. Apollodorus designed Trajan's Forum and Market and the Baths. Maybe he was the best architect in the world, but it was stupid arrogance for him to tell the emperor that Hadrian's own designs for the statues of the goddesses were too tall to stand up where they were seated. It didn't matter that Hadrian asked his opinion. Apollodorus was exiled and then executed."

Glabrio glanced at his companion as they continued walking down the street below the Temple and Library of Apollo Palatinus. "So, shall I interpret your silences as unspoken criticisms?"

Titianus's face settled into the emotionless mask he wore with Saturninus. "What do you think?"

"I think you're not going to tell me, and I can't safely assume anything."

Titianus's fleeting smile relaxed back into the mask. "You're right."

They continued in silence past the rest of the Palatine Hill. A sound like thunder that built and built before exploding into silence came from the Circus ahead of them. One race had finished; another would start soon.

Titianus led them northwest along the wall to a door that led to the starting gates. He knocked, and a small panel opened to reveal an ice-blue eye. When the door swung open, that eye was part of a man even taller than Father's biggest bodyguard.

"Caballus, this is Tribune Acilius Glabrio. He'll be my replacement soon."

"You'll be missed." Expected words, but the door slave looked like he meant them.

"Who's the sponsor today?" Titianus's voice had a warmer edge on it.

"Asinius Marcellus."

"Who's with him in the sponsor's box?"

"Rufinus and his son are there."

"They picked a good day to join him. Who's the sponsor for the next set of races?"

"Annius Libo."

"Rumor has it he'll be consul soon, so that's not surprising. So, who do you think will win today?"

"Hard to say since it's tied right now, but I think I know. The Blues." Caballus dropped his voice to a near-whisper. "One of the Green's stallions who'll be running in the last race was off its feed the past two days."

"We'll know by dinner if you're right. You usually are."

Caballus's crooked smile came with a wink. "You could be a richer man if you wanted."

Titianus released a slight, fleeting smile. "Or a poorer one. A race is only decided when the leaders cross the finish line."

As Caballus chuckled, Titianus tapped his upper arm. "See you next race day."

When Caballus let them out, Titianus turned toward the Forums district, and Glabrio scanned his companion's impassive face. With inside information like that, there was still time to place a bet.

"So, where do you place a bet when you aren't watching the races with friends?"

"Nowhere. I never bet. But Caballus knows racehorses, and he likes to share what he knows. It's worth my time to listen. When someone knows you care about his opinion, he's inclined to tell you the truth as he believes it to be. You never know when you might need that."

Titianus lengthened his stride. "Do you spend much time in the Forums?"

"Not really."

"They're good to patrol in the morning for watching the noble orders after they finish their salutations; by afternoon, the elite have moved on to the Baths, and the character of the crowd changes. Today I'll introduce you to some people who know what's going on near Trajan's Market and might be willing to tell you…if they think you care about their opinion."

"From what you say, I'd be a fool not to care."

"Yes, you would." One corner of Titianus's mouth lifted as laughter lurked in his eyes. "I don't gamble, but if I were a betting man, you being a fool is not a bet I'd want to take."

The Glabrio town house, evening of Day 6

When Glabrio entered the small triclinium used for family meals, Father had already been served the salad course.

"I thought you weren't coming." He picked up a purple carrot slice. "But I had enough made for two, just in case. Did Saturninus's favorite tribune keep you busy today?"

"With more than reports. He came midmorning for me. That's a first."

"What did you do?"

"It's race day, so he introduced me to the doorkeeper for the gate area."

Father's head pulled back. "Whatever for?"

"Slaves who open doors see everyone who comes through them. He maintains that showing respect to such people creates trust, and they will help you with information when you need it." One corner of his mouth lifted. "If I'd wanted to bet on the races today, I would have won. He told Titianus which horse was off its feed."

"What odds did he get?"

"Titianus? He said he never bets."

Father snorted.

"That's what I would have thought a week ago, but I've seen enough of him to take his word. What Saturninus told me about him…I've seen a different man."

"Why would Marcus mislead you?"

"I can't say that he did. I've seen what Saturninus described, but there's more to him. Last night we ate again with Manius Sabinus, and Titianus's family was there. He's a quiet man, but he's more like what you saw than what he lets his commander see."

He sat on the couch opposite his father and picked up a roll. "There was another person more interesting than Titianus's family at the dinner."

Father raised an eyebrow, asking the question.

"Sabinus's daughter was there."

"Hasn't she been married to Lucius Gallus's son for several years?" He shook out a napkin and wiped his lips. "But perhaps that's changed. Gallus's oldest son was at the races today, and I overheard someone offering him condolences. Something about a hunting accident, but he didn't seem saddened by it."

"She's living with her father now, and she wasn't wearing a stola. No one said anything about why she was there."

His father's nose scrunched. "Gallus put his wife out on his Sabatinus estate where he doesn't have to put up with her every day. I would have done the same…except I'd send her farther away than twenty miles to keep her from visiting. But perhaps the revulsion is mutual so that's not a problem."

Father selected a roll and took a bite. "I think the younger son took his wife there. If there were no children, only an insane woman would stay after that marriage ended."

"Her being widowed now—that presents an opportunity for us." His father's eyebrow rose, just as Glabrio expected. "In a few months, her grandfather will be arranging another marriage for her. From what I've seen of Sabina already, I'd find her acceptable as my wife."

Glabrio reached for a second roll. "It's not too soon to mention my interest to Quintus Sabinus. There will be competition when others become aware that she's reentering the marriage market."

"That connection would be good for your career. After Gallus became her father-in-law, Sabinus actively promoted his advancement. No one is better connected than Quintus Sabinus, and his son Manius will follow in his footsteps."

Glabrio dipped the roll in some herb-seasoned olive oil. "She didn't speak much, but she might just be shy around strangers. I think it would be a good match."

"It should be. As I recall, she used to stutter a little but not enough to make her undesirable. Lucius Gallus didn't consider it a problem at all. These past six years, he's held several important posts. Some of that was undoubtedly due to Sabinus's influence." One corner of his mouth curved. "A mostly silent woman isn't necessarily a disadvantage. Many of my colleagues would be better off with wives who don't talk as much as they do."

He took a sip of wine and returned the goblet to the table. "Sabinus is coming to the banquet tomorrow. I might mention our interest to him then."

Father picked up another slice of carrot. "I expected you to make some valuable connections staying in Rome for a year or two, but I never imagined an equestrian like Titianus would be the source. At the Baths, I found him friendlier than I expected. Saturninus has called him barely human, more like a walking statue than a flesh-and-blood man."

"He isn't as cold as he was at the start."

"Maybe he's just a man who takes a while to warm up to new people."

"I think Saturninus misjudges him. He has a quick sense of humor among his friends, even though Saturninus said he never engaged in it." Glabrio dipped the roll again.

"Maybe he's just reserved with his superiors, inclined to show them respect, and joking is the opposite of that."

Glabrio chuckled. "From what I've seen, he displays proper respect for the position, whether he respects the man or not. A man gets as much respect from Titianus as he's earned, no more, no less. He respects Manius Sabinus. Prefect Saturninus…he respects the prefect part. The man inside the body armor…not so much. He warned me the first day that I need to earn the respect and trust of my centurions if I want to do well. He even introduced me to his optios."

"Interesting. That wouldn't surprise me in a fighting legion, but for policing the city?"

"I think there's some wisdom in it. When I ask questions, his optio at headquarters words his answers carefully to protect him. I'd want him to do that for me."

He dipped in the oil again, but left the roll on the side of the dish. "I've been thinking about something else he said. The other tribunes look on me as competition, and not all compete honorably. There's one…his father got him the post because his legate friends wouldn't take him at the frontier. His office is right next to mine, but he's yet to step over and speak to me."

"Who is it?"

"Julius Victorinus."

"I know his father. Watch that one. It's not the runner who's winning a race who tries to trip the runners coming from behind."

Glabrio picked up the roll and took another bite. "When you were a tribune, did the legates all have personal bodyguards who weren't Romans?"

"They did. Why?"

"Titianus said the greatest danger sometimes came from men wearing Roman armor."

"Your tribune is wiser than I would expect for one who never served outside Rome. Why do you think the emperor always has his German guards so close?" Father's brow furrowed. "Is your tribune the man in Roman armor that Saturninus thinks most dangerous?"

A laugh exploded from Glabrio. "If he does, he has no idea what motivates his tribune. Manius Sabinus calls Titianus a great Roman and was quoting him last night. 'It's not the rank or wealth or family connections that determine a man's worth. It's his honor that matters most.' That doesn't sound dangerous to me."

Father picked up his goblet. "It might…if you weren't a man of honor yourself."

As his father drained the goblet and held it up for the wine slave to refill, Glabrio rubbed his chin. Father was a man of honor, but how many of the men who dined at his table were not?

Chapter 24

WANTING WHAT CANNOT BE

The Titianus town house, evening of Day 6

When Septimus sent word that he'd be coming for dinner, it was only right that Sabina should stay as well. Pompeia had suggested it, and Kaeso had insisted.

A partner for a few games of tabula was why he wanted her to stay… or so he said. But whatever the reason, Sabina didn't need to be asked more than once.

Now they sat at the plain wooden board that had been his father's. He picked up one of the blue-dyed antler slices.

"Pompeia likes silence while she plays, but I like some conversation."

"I noticed."

"Do you mind?"

"N-not if you do most of the talking."

"Pompeia says the only man she knows who talks more than me is Septimus."

"I l-like to listen."

"Perhaps we have two ears and one mouth because we should listen twice as much as we talk." He flipped his ear with his fingertip. "Maybe if these were bigger, I'd listen more."

"You don't need to change." A man who could sit so patiently waiting for her words to come…he didn't need to listen better.

"We all need to change something about us. We don't become everything we can be if we don't."

"Marriage changed me." She nibbled her lip. "Not for the better."

He touched the back of her hand. If only he'd leave his fingers there.

"Septimus said Gallus and his mother were cruel. I'm sorry you had to bear that."

"When I t-tried to speak, they mocked me." Maybe Septimus had already told him that, but there was something freeing about telling Kaeso herself.

"I can't understand how any man could do that to the woman he married. A man should love his wife as he loves himself. What Titianus and Pompeia have with each other is what I would like to have someday."

"Do you expect that soon?" She should want what's best for him, what would make him happy, but if he already cared about another woman…it was selfish, but that thought hurt.

Her head drew back when he chuckled. "There's something about me most Roman women wouldn't want."

"I can't imagine what." Why did she say that? The heat spread from her cheeks to her ears.

His teasing eyes turned serious; then he bounced his eyebrows at her, and the smile he wore most of the time reappeared. "Maybe someday I'll tell you, but not today."

"Whenever you're ready."

There was nothing about him that a smart woman wouldn't love to have in a husband. Her own heart already wanted him, even knowing she shouldn't let it because she wasn't going to get to choose the man she'd marry next.

The years of constant criticism had taught her how to hold back her tears until her tormentors wouldn't see, but tears triggered by kindness… those she couldn't control.

His smile faded. "Are you all right?"

"Yes. It's nothing." But it was everything…he was everything she longed for and what she'd never have.

Her brother's voice drifted through the doorway before he appeared himself. He strolled to her side and wrapped his arm around her shoulders. "Did you have a good day?"

"Yes." Any day with Kaeso and Pompeia was good, no matter what she did.

With Pompeia's arm wrapped around his, Titus entered right behind Septimus.

"Oh, Titus, you are in for such a treat tonight." Kaeso winked at Sabina and chuckled when that made her blush. "Sabina sang us some of her lyric poems today. Septimus was right; they are exceptional, both the words and the singing."

He turned his gaze from Titianus to her, and she tried hard not to look away. She tried, but she had to lower her eyes to cool the emotions he couldn't help stirring.

"I was just about to get Septimus to join me in urging her to sing them again for us this evening."

"Oh, please do." Pompeia's eager eyes made the request almost irresistible.

"Well…"

"Come on, Skylark. If not for me, do it for Titus. He's probably never heard anything as pretty as you singing your poems." Her brother could always coax her into doing something, and he knew it.

"All right." With three of them pressing her, it was impossible to say no.

"I want the one about the shorebirds first, and then Kaeso can pick." Pompeia led Titianus to their couch, and swung her legs up.

When Sabina joined her brother on the center couch for honored guests, she couldn't keep her eyes from seeking out Kaeso, reclining alone on his.

As much as she loved her brother, he wasn't the one she wanted as her closest companion at dinner. But just having Kaeso in the same room, joking with Septimus and watching her with eyes that proclaimed she mattered, was enough to made the evening even better than the day.

The Sabinus town house, late evening of Day 6

As Filomena was taking out the many small braids that created the elegant hairstyle, Mistress Sabina hummed a cheery melody. She'd used the same one while singing the words of her lakeside poems as she played the lyre for Pompeia that afternoon.

Filomena's jaw twitched. For Pompeia and that brother of hers who couldn't resist talking with the mistress.

She'd sung it again while they were eating dinner.

Applause was followed by Kaeso's voice toasting the charm of the words and the beauty of the skylark's voice. Septimus's laughter was followed by words of praise for his friend's taste in poetry and music and for appreciating how special his sister was.

It was true that Mistress's words were charming and her singing beautiful. She truly was special, but it was only natural, not praiseworthy, for a teacher like that Kaeso to see what an extraordinary woman her mistress was.

But as they were leaving, Mistress Sabina had beamed and blushed when he reminded her that he'd want to hear more of her poetry sung tomorrow.

It wouldn't do for the praise of a common man like him to become important to a noblewoman of the highest rank. But after years of belittling by her husband and his mother, Mistress Sabina was vulnerable to anyone who wanted to take advantage of her insecurity with flattering words.

If it were in her power, she'd discourage these trips to help the sister with her poetry and with teaching some Egyptian woman who had yet to appear.

But how could she protect her dear Sabina from the attentions of the brother when Septimus and Master Manius both approved of her spending time with the sister? When Septimus considered him his best friend and the master liked him as well.

She picked up the brush and drew it through the tresses she'd cared for since Sabina left girlhood behind.

"Ouch!" Mistress's hand shot up to grasp the hair close to her head. "You're pulling too hard."

"I beg pardon, mistress. I'll be more careful."

For several hours each day, they were at Titianus's town house. No one was without faults, and the teacher must have many. There should be one she could report to Master Manius to end these visits before Mistress Sabina became too fond of the teacher and the damage couldn't be undone.

The Praetorian Fortress, morning of Day 7

As Glabrio climbed the headquarters steps, he had to admit Titianus showed some wisdom by sleeping in tribune quarters. The garrison cook served slop, and the mattress Titianus left behind wasn't good enough for Father's house slaves. A night spent trying to find that one spot where the lumps were almost comfortable could leave you more tired than you were when you went to bed. But with the decent chef he'd borrowed from Father and the good mattress Father's steward had taken from a guest chamber, the place was comfortable enough now.

What he liked was how easy it was to get to his office compared to riding halfway across Rome shortly after sunrise with wagons and night workers trying to leave and day workers just arriving.

Inside the headquarters courtyard, he strode past three empty tribune offices before turning in at his own.

Plancus stood and struck his chest. "Tribune."

"Good morning, Plancus." The optio's eyes widened at his name. "What did Titianus send up for me to review today?"

"Reports from the Forums, the Circus, and the warehouse districts."

He barely stopped the sigh. Plancus would tell Titianus, and he didn't want his tormentor to know the endless mountains of reports were starting to wear him down. Glabrio's gaze turned toward his desk. The stacks on the desk were shorter than any other day.

"Where are the rest of them?"

"That's all of them, Tribune. Only the important or unusual are there now."

A crooked smile escaped before Glabrio thought to stop it. When Saturninus demanded the update on his progress in gaining Titianus's confidence, the prefect would never appreciate how significant those short stacks were. But he could view it as a small victory.

He removed his helmet and placed it on the side table. As he settled into the desk chair, Plancus stuck his head into the room.

"Can I get you anything, Tribune?"

"Not now, but maybe later."

Plancus withdrew without saluting, but there was more respect in what just happened than in a dozen fists to his optio's chest.

He'd scanned a half dozen tablets when he felt someone watching. When he glanced out the door, Titianus, arms crossed and the slightest smile playing on his lips, stood contemplating him.

"Are you ready to accompany me where I go on a typical day?"

"Of course." Glabrio snapped the tablet shut and stood.

"We'll start out at the Forums. I told the stableman to prepare your horse. He should be ready now."

What was the right amount of enthusiasm to let show? At last, he might get to see some of what Titianus was doing for Turbo. But would he recognize the difference between that and a normal day?

The Forums district, morning of Day 7

After leaving their horses at Brutus's ludus, Glabrio followed a silent Titianus as he wove through the crowds near the Forums until they reached the Basilica Julia.

In the great hall of the basilica, Titianus worked his way to one of the columns along the edge. "Yesterday I introduced you to some people who can help you do your job well. Today, you can return the favor. I know the names of many of the senators here, but I don't know which have sons or grandsons of a suitable age to be students at the school."

Titianus had a satchel slung on his shoulder. He pulled it from his side to his stomach and opened the flap. Inside were a few wax tablets. "I recommend you make it a habit to carry some of these. It's too easy to forget an important detail if you wait too long to write it down after questioning someone. Sometimes simply writing it down will make a connection or incongruity leap out at you."

"I'll do that." Yet another of Titianus's suggestions made total sense and would make his job easier.

Titianus pointed at a group of senators with his stylus. "Let's start with those."

As Glabrio identified the men with sons or grandsons the right age, Titianus wrote down their names along with the names of the ones with whom they were talking.

"Men often choose a school based on where their friends' sons have done well. Even if they don't have someone the right age now, they'll have friends who might ask for a recommendation."

Glabrio rubbed his cheek as his gaze shifted from the moving stylus to Titianus's emotionless face. Inside that helmet was a mind that understood how to run his own business. Glabrio had always thought that was what stewards were for, and a man who wanted to serve Rome at the highest levels had to have one who could run everything without his master's involvement when the province he was governing was hundreds of miles from Rome.

The only other tribune living in the fortress was Martialis, and he stayed in the Praetorian quarters only because his family villa was too far away to ride back and forth each day.

Any man who would sleep on the thin, lumpy mattress Glabrio had replaced and eat garrison slop for years while renting out his town house was either desperate for money or, as Saturninus said, nothing more than a money-hungry merchant at heart.

And yet, Titianus didn't seem to be either.

Saturninus expected a report soon, but what could he tell the prefect that would satisfy him? That Titianus wanted to map out the social networks of every senator they saw? Perhaps, but why was he doing that? If it really wasn't for finding future students, Glabrio had no idea.

Titianus town house, morning of Day 7

It was earlier than normal as Sabina approached the Titianus front door. Tutelus knocked, and the door swung open to reveal the usual youth with his friendly smile.

Pompeia had mentioned that her Romans weren't coming for class today and invited her for lunch. It was an hour until lunchtime, but they could look at more of Pompeia's poems as they waited.

At least that was what she told Filomena.

She tried not to smile too broadly, lest Filomena ask why. Lunch with Pompeia would be even better if Kaeso joined them while his boys ate in the classroom.

She waved Filomena on into the peristyle garden, but she saw Pompeia seated at the desk in her classroom, pen in hand, two papyrus sheets side-by-side on the desktop. She turned aside to join her.

"Good morning."

Pompeia jumped as she turned to face Sabina. "I didn't expect you for an hour or so." She placed the right sheet atop the left one and added a blank one above that. She set the stack aside and stood. "But I'm glad you're here now."

"I thought we c-could start early."

Pompeia's usual smile appeared. "And we can. What we need is upstairs." She waved her hand toward a student table. "Take a chair. I'll be right back."

Sabina started toward the table as Pompeia exited the room. Then she paused. Pompeia's first draft of her latest creation was waiting under that blank sheet. What would that look like compared to the polished poems she usually saw?

Her own were often quite rough, but sometimes the words came so swift and pure that the first and final versions were the same.

She went to the desk and picked up the blank sheet.

It wasn't a poem.

In Pompeia's elegant letters, words flowed across the sheet.

> When he was gone, Jesus said, "Now the Son of Man is glorified and God is glorified in him. If God is glorified in him, God will glorify the Son in himself, and will glorify him at once.
>
> "My children, I will be with you only a little longer. You will look for me, and just as I told the Jews, so I tell you now: Where I am going, you cannot come.
>
> "A new command I give you: Love one another. As I have loved you, so you must love one another. By this everyone will know that you are my disciples, if you love one another."

She lifted the edge and peeked at the sheet beneath. The same words appeared there. Pompeia was making a copy of the codex-sized papyrus that lay underneath.

"That should be fine. We'll be ready when Kaeso is." Pompeia's nearby words to the cook shocked Sabina into action.

She concealed the writings under the blank sheet again and hurried to take a seat. She had just placed her elbows on the table and steepled her fingers when Pompeia entered with a stack of papyrus held between two leather sheets bound with ribbons.

"Father used to give Kaeso and me a topic and have us both write a poem about it. I thought you'd find the difference between them amusing." With her smile broadening, she shook her head. "Father would read them aloud with full dramatic flair, and Kaeso's would have me laughing so hard I couldn't breathe. We bound the best of them."

She opened the codex, balanced it on one hand, and raised the other into oratorical position.

As she began the recitation, Sabina couldn't help laughing, but she also couldn't help thinking about the implications of what she wasn't meant to see.

Chapter 25

DISTURBING DISCOVERIES

Late afternoon of Day 7

As Glabrio followed Titianus down the steps from the Baths at the top of the Oppian Hill to the Amphitheater below, he could scarcely wait to pick up his horse at the ludus and ride home.

After a day of watching people first at the Forums and then at the Baths, Glabrio was more than ready to take off the armor and relax at his father's banquet. The Glabrio town house on the Palatine was spacious for the center of Rome, but the list of invitees was long, and the villa five miles east of Rome was a better venue for entertaining to impress.

It also offered an opportunity to watch Titianus again when he was off duty. If he could persuade Titianus to ride out to the villa with him, maybe he could get his predecessor talking about more than what could make Glabrio better at policing Rome.

If Titianus drank enough to let his defenses down, perhaps he'd say something that Saturninus could interpret, even if Glabrio couldn't.

"It will be easier for you to find Father's villa if we ride out together. We can swing by your home and pick up your toga. My manservant will help us both dress when we get there."

Titianus eyed him.

It was a simple request, and a quick yes would be the normal response. "We can."

Why the long pause, and when the answer came, why were those words tinged with reluctance? Was there something about where he lived that Titianus wanted to conceal from him? Did he even have a town house? Maybe the tribune quarters were an improvement over his own home.

After they reclaimed their horses at the ludus, they started back along the road to the fortress, but they turned off that road and rode back up to the Baths and past them. When Titianus turned in through a wide gate, the stableyard was as large as Glabrio's own on the Palatine, and a man came immediately to take their horses.

"We'll only be here a short while, so don't stable him."

The man scanned Glabrio. "Yes, master."

When Titianus dismounted, Glabrio did as well. He hadn't been invited into the house, but curiosity and the need for something to tell Saturninus drove him to stay by Titianus's side. Any normal man would have extended the invitation, anyway.

He followed Titianus through the archway into the peristyle garden.

Feminine laughter and a man's chuckle drew his attention. In a cluster of wicker chairs by a fountain with three spouting dolphins, Titianus's wife and brother-in-law lounged while Sabina stood before them, taking a deep bow.

"Oh, Skylark, if only your brother could have heard that one." Kaeso raised an imaginary goblet. "I salute your talent at capturing such delightful humor in an elegant poem. You should start a new poetic fashion."

"If he joins us tonight, you must surprise him with it. But not when he's just taken a sip or he could make a mess." Pompeia glanced at Glabrio; then her gaze settled on her husband, and she rose.

"Titus. You're home early."

"But I won't stay long. Glabrio's banquet is out at his villa." He kissed her forehead. "I came for my toga. I'll be home late."

"Or not at all. You're welcome to spend the night." Glabrio's words drew Pompeia's grateful smile. "Or bring your bodyguard along if you don't want to stay."

Titianus's broad smile was directed at his wife. "If a tribune in full armor can't ride safely through Rome at night…"

He got a slap on the arm and a roll of her eyes in return. He pointed at a bench. "Wait here. I'll be right back."

Before Glabrio could take a step, Titianus disappeared into the atrium.

"Or join us for a moment." Pompeia's hand swept toward the chairs where Sabina had seated herself next to Kaeso.

"Thank you." As Glabrio walked beside Pompeia, Kaeso raised a hand in silent greeting, but Sabina's eyes remained fixed on the teacher. The warmth of her gaze, the contented smile—both declared what he didn't want to see.

She was infatuated with Kaeso Lenaeus.

He was a commoner who lived off his brother-in-law's generosity. Not what Quintus Sabinus would choose for his granddaughter's husband, but a woman's heart could make an unsuitable choice and latch on so strongly she'd make a proper husband miserable.

Before that happened, Father needed to speak with her grandfather to arrange the marriage and cool this friendship before the teacher decided to take advantage of it.

"Thank you for offering your overnight hospitality." Pompeia's words pulled his gaze away from Sabina. "I don't know what Titus has told you, but you will be making enemies if you do your job well. A tribune in full armor might be safer than an ordinary man, but someone almost killed him last year after he left Manius's town house late."

Glabrio's head snapped toward her. Saturninus had said nothing about that. Father never mentioned any danger, either, when he suggested they request this posting. Maybe Father didn't know, but the prefect would have. Who attacked and why...those were questions any sane man would ask if he knew the tribune who served before him had been attacked and almost killed.

"How did that happen?"

"Three men jumped him. You can ask Titus if you want to know more."

"Ask me what?"

Glabrio jumped at the voice right behind him. He should have heard Titianus's hobnails on the tiles. Was he not listening or was Titianus sneaking up on him?

"About the three men and riding alone at night."

He slipped his arm around her and pulled her close for a light kiss. "I've told him about most of the hazards in Rome. I suppose I should mention that."

The smile Titianus had directed at his wife faded as his focus turned to Glabrio. "You'll be sending men to the arena. Some will blame you for their deaths. Those who care about them might want you dead as well. Or if you're getting close to an arrest, the guilty might think they'll get away with whatever they did if you die first."

Pompeia shifted away from him, and he drew her back. Then her arm wrapped around his back, and she rested her head against his shoulder.

"I'd just eaten with a fascinating woman at Manius's house, and I was thinking about her instead of watching."

So, did Titianus meet his wife through Manius Sabinus? Or maybe through Septimus and her brother.

Glabrio turned his gaze on Sabina and offered an appreciative smile. "It's a good thing I bring a bodyguard to Sabinus's dinners. There's still a pretty woman there to distract a man's thinking."

Sabina's eyes widened, but she blanched instead of blushed. Then she looked away.

Kaeso's brow furrowed; then his eyes turned on Sabina. He said nothing, and she avoided looking at either of them.

Glabrio would definitely ask Father to approach the elder Sabinus this week.

Titianus adjusted the satchel holding his toga to put it at his back instead of his side. "I don't want to be too early, but I don't want to be late. Let's go."

"I look forward to seeing you all again." Glabrio offered the two women and Kaeso his friendliest smile, but there was only one with whom he wanted a better acquaintance. She kept her gaze fixed firmly on the floor.

When Glabrio turned away, Titianus was halfway to the stableyard entrance, and Glabrio lengthened his stride to catch up.

Kaeso Lenaeus was only a teacher, and he should be no match for an Acilius Glabrio when seeking a noblewoman's hand. At least, not in the normal way of things.

But the more he saw of these people, the less he expected what was normal.

The Sabinus town house, evening of Day 7

Sabina had spoken little during her walk home from Kaeso's house. Filomena had made too many comments about how handsome Glabrio was in his uniform, but that wasn't what disturbed her thoughts.

As soon as she reached her room, she'd picked up her pen to fill the time until Septimus came home. Surely, he could answer the niggling question that kept distracting her.

Sabina blew on the wet ink of her latest composition. Pompeia would like it. Kaeso…he'd say he loved it when she sang it to him.

She sighed. Why did she have to pick up the sheet that hid what Pompeia was writing? Friends had a right to keep secrets if they wanted. Why had she been in such a hurry to see a new poem before it was finished?

She placed the papyrus atop the stack of her latest poems before staring out the window above her writing desk.

Where was Septimus? She'd left the message with the stableman to send him to her immediately upon his arrival. Would he think "immediately" meant after he spoke to Father?

It was better if Father didn't know something was worrying her. He'd expect her to tell him what it was so he could fix it. But some things only got more broken if you tried to fix them. What if this was one of them?

The knock on the doorframe startled her, and she twisted in her chair.

"I got your message. What is it?"

"Come in and lock the door."

When he turned to slide the bolt, he glanced over his shoulder at her. "It must be a big secret if you're locking Filomena out."

"I don't tell her everything."

Whenever Sabina said Kaeso's name, the twitch of Filomena's nose declared her maid's disapproval of him. It couldn't be of him as a man, for there was no finer man in either of their acquaintances. She didn't approve of the affection Sabina had for a man so far beneath her rank.

"I have a qu-question about your friends." She drew a deep breath and blew it out slowly. Sometimes that kept the words from sticking. "I s-saw something at their house."

"What did you see?" He leaned his shoulder against the window frame and crossed his arms.

"Something Pompeia was copying."

"Did she show it to you on purpose?" He'd straightened and dropped his arms to his sides.

"No." She lowered her gaze. "She covered it when I entered. I thought it was a poem she wasn't ready to show me, so I peeked when she left the room for a moment."

"Did you read it?" Was that tension or accusation in his voice?

"Some."

When she looked at him again, his lips were straight, his eyes veiled.

"What did it say?"

"I saw the name Jesus and something about how his disciples must love one another."

Septimus sucked air through his teeth. "Do not tell anyone else what you just told me, not even Father."

"I haven't, and I won't if you think I shouldn't."

"I know you shouldn't." The force behind his words made her shiver. "But what does it mean?"

He raised one finger, then pointed it at her.

"You have to swear you'll keep secret what I'm about to tell you."

Her heart sped up. What could be so bad that he'd demand that? "I swear by all the gods of Rome."

"They aren't real, so that means nothing. I want your word as my sister. Swear to me by the love we have for each other that you'll tell no one what I'm going to say."

Her breath came faster. "You have my word."

"Pompeia, Kaeso, the whole household… they're all Christians. They have been since before I met them. Father doesn't know they are. He doesn't know Titus decided to become one as well while he was recovering in this house. If you tell anyone, it might lead to them all being killed."

She bit her lip. If it put the others in grave danger, was Septimus caught up in it as well? "Are you one?"

"No, I'm not ready to do what that might require. But I must admit, I can almost understand why they are."

"Almost?"

"Kaeso has tried to explain it to me for years, but I stop him before he gets too far. It's so important to him…" He massaged his palm with his thumb. "I don't want to risk losing our friendship if I hear it all and then reject it."

With thoughts churning too much to put into words, even if she didn't stutter, she stared at him.

He moved behind her and massaged the muscles by her neck. "You're tight as a bow string. Relax. As long as you keep their secret, there's no harm done. Father was going into the library when I came in here. He saw me enter, and I don't want him asking what we were discussing, so let's go down now."

He offered her his arm. After she stood and placed her hand upon it, they headed downstairs.

Perhaps Septimus didn't want to discuss his friend's beliefs, but if Kaeso had tried for years to tell her brother everything, might he be willing to tell her? The two people she admired most had chosen a forbidden religion. The man Father admired so much had as well.

Not even Father was smarter than Titus and Kaeso, and Pompeia knew so much about so many things.

What if what they all believed was true?

Chapter 26

THE BANQUET

The Glabrio villa, evening of Day 7

As Titianus followed Glabrio toward the stables, several slaves were busy unsaddling horses and putting them into a corral. A row of elegant carriages and a few chariots, some with horses still in harness and others with their teams removed, declared this to be a gathering of the elite of Rome. Titianus had a couple of wax tablets in the satchel with his toga. Before he slept, he'd make some notes about his three suspects and the men who seemed close to them.

Glabrio rode directly to a stall and dismounted. He opened the gate himself and sent his stallion in with a slap to its rump.

"Put yours in there." He pointed to the next stall. "Someone will take care of them when they finish with the rest."

Curious eyes followed them as they walked toward the back of the villa. Perhaps it still seemed strange to the ones who knew Glabrio as a boy to see him in the armor that declared him a grown man and an officer of Rome.

They passed through a garden where the scent of roses mingled with other flowers Titianus couldn't identify. Where the garden fronted the portico, Glabrio turned away from the archway flanked by Corinthian columns and led him to a closed door to the left.

A short walk down a hall with floors made of black-and-white geometric designs ended at a staircase. They climbed it to a balcony with a railing supported by spiral columns. Halfway down the balcony, Glabrio stopped by a chamber that overlooked another garden.

"You can spend the night here. I'll send someone down to help with your toga. My room is two doors down. I'll be back shortly. Then we'll join the others."

Glabrio didn't wait for a thank you before striding to his room and disappearing inside. He'd no sooner disappeared from sight than a manservant emerged and walked toward Titianus.

"I'm Asellio. Allow me to help you prepare."

With a curl of his fingers, Titianus invited the man to follow him into the room. He pulled the toga from the satchel and handed it to Glabrio's manservant to spread out in preparation for the wrapping. As he undid the clasps on his cuirass, a wry smile formed.

His uncle Quintus liked dining in a toga. Manius did not.

Many would think it a burden to wear armor to work every day. But as long as he didn't fasten the chinstrap, it wasn't so bad. When he took off the armor one last time, would he find wearing a toga as he taught to be better or worse?

When Kaeso put on his toga each morning, it only took a few moments for Corax to toss it around him and arrange how it draped. As Asellio adjusted each pleat at the shoulder to get exactly the right spacing and curvature to each fold, it was all Titianus could do to keep from rolling his eyes. When Glabrio finally appeared in the doorway, as elegantly draped as a marble statue, Titianus stepped away from the busy hands.

"That's good enough."

The man's eyes widened, and he looked at Glabrio. The nod he got from his young master set him at ease.

Glabrio took them farther down the balcony to another set of stairs. "I asked the banquet steward to put us together." One corner of his mouth lifted. "The look on his face...it was most amusing. You present a protocol problem. Does he elevate you to where I was set to recline or lower me to where he would have put you before I asked?"

Titianus let himself grin. "It will raise eyebrows whichever way he chooses. But he should only have the problem once."

Glabrio shrugged. "I don't know about that. You might enjoy yourself so much you'll want to accept Father's next invitation."

"Next invitation?" Titianus's head drew back. The elder Glabrio would have neither reason nor desire to invite him again.

"Of course. Quintus Sabinus often invites my father, and Father invites him in return. He could easily include Manius and you."

There was no point in telling Glabrio his uncle never included him when he entertained. There could be topics of conversation that he wouldn't want a tribune of the Urban Cohort to overhear.

The hum of conversation reached them through the archway that opened into the garden visible from his bedchamber. Several reflecting pools held statues of Roman gods and goddesses and several athletic young men. Arbors covered with flowering vines shaded benches, and wicker chairs were clustered in groups of three and four around small tables holding bowls of fruit.

"Titus?" Amusement and surprise mingled in the tone of Quintus Sabinus's voice. "This is unexpected."

The eyes of the four men standing with Quintus turned on Titianus, and their expressions ranged from curiosity to indifference to mild disdain.

"It's good to see you, uncle."

"Who's the unfortunate who's drawn your attention here?"

Titianus kept his irritation at Quintus's too perceptive question from showing. He'd hoped to blend in as young Glabrio's guest while observing his quarry.

"He's come as my guest." Glabrio's look and words were the model of nonchalance, and Titianus smiled his appreciation.

"Young Glabrio. I recall meeting you at the Baths." Quintus's political smile looked almost genuine. "I trust you're taking to heart all that Titus is telling you."

"I've already learned much more from him than I expected, and I suspect he has still more to teach."

"My nephew doesn't like praise where he can hear it, but perhaps that's wise. Modesty, whether real or false, is better received by men of significance than a young man's pride."

Sabinus leaned forward and tapped Titianus's upper arm. "Saturninus showed more wisdom than I expected by having Titus train you before Rome loses his service. Rome is losing more than either of them would ever admit."

Sabinus turned back to his friends, and Titianus moved away before Glabrio said anything to raise Sabinus's suspicions about why he was there.

However...his uncle had warned him not to trust Saturninus when he was recovering at Manius's house. Would it be wise or foolish to ask the elder Sabinus who among the senators he thought was most unhappy with Hadrian? Would he just laugh and say the list was too long? That it was too hard to pick the top ones because there were so many vying for the position?

Would he suspect Titianus was investigating something and mention it to the wrong people? Suspect…yes. Mention it…probably not. His uncle had his own network of spies, and he kept a lot of information to himself until there was a compelling reason to reveal it.

But this was neither the time nor place for such questions. By evening's end, he'd know whether a visit to his uncle was a good idea or not.

Glabrio's father stood near the main entrance, greeting people as they arrived. Several ex-consuls and many of the important senators were already there. Titianus would have faded into the background to watch who arrived with whom, but his personal host had other ideas.

"There are only a few here who attend father's private dinners, and those are the only men I know very well. But they'll introduce us to others when we join them."

"We can start with those. Perhaps your cousin…"

With Titianus beside him, a smiling Glabrio started toward one of the few men in the garden above suspicion, a man who might consider Titianus's presence welcome instead of a matter of curiosity or total indifference. Or, for any co-conspirators, a threat. He'd come to watch, not to be seen, and the fewer men who drew him into conversation, the more chances he'd have to watch his quarry talking with possible allies.

Aviola raised a hand and summoned them with the curl of his fingers. Then an ex-consul and two senior senators joined him, and his focus shifted to the three important men.

A table for three under the portico was vacant, and Titianus pointed at it. "Your cousin looks busy now. We should wait to join him."

Marcellus was there already, off to the side conferring with Saturninus. Rufinus left the group of four with whom he'd been talking and wove his way through the crowd to join them.

With the low hum of many conversations, the table wasn't quite close enough to let him hear the conspirator's words. But people's faces sometimes revealed more when they thought you couldn't hear them. "We can sit."

"We will in a little while. There are a dozen or so I want you to meet. They have younger sons."

Glabrios's enthusiasm as a host was entertaining and even useful. The three whom Titianus was stalking would be there all evening. That gave plenty of time to watch without being noticed, especially if they thought he was only there to meet other men.

◆

As Glabrio introduced Titianus to some of his father's friends, he'd never been so aware of the petty jealousies and subtle acts that asserted superiority. He was careful to choose the more important men in each cluster of guests to introduce first. Many of those were gracious in their manner toward the equestrian. Some knew what Titianus did as a tribune, but most did not. The less important the man, the more likely he was to look down his nose at the equestrian who, by virtue of his social rank, could be treated as inferior.

But whether they complimented or insulted or simply ignored, Titianus responded the same. Reserved respect for their senatorial rank—that was what all received. Whether he respected any of the men themselves who wore the tunics that had stripes three times the width of his—that wasn't as clear.

But as they walked away, when the snobbish men could no longer see his face, the twitch of Titianus's lips or silent laughter in the steel-gray eyes let Glabrio figure out their place in Titianus's personal rankings.

Titianus had married far beneath his rank, but the woman he'd chosen was exactly what he wanted. That was a bad example for Sabina to see, but Kaeso hadn't looked like he was trying to repeat it.

At least not today. But tomorrow?

Father had almost finished greeting the guests. It was time to ask him to talk with Quintus Sabinus, but not with Titianus listening.

"Did you want to watch the people you already met for a while? I need to talk with Father for a moment."

Titianus pointed at the table he originally suggested. "I'll be there."

Then he sauntered over and sat, leaned back in the chair, crossed his arms, and watched.

An aged ex-consul was the last arrival, and Father had moved over to stand with cousin Aviola. Glabrio made his move.

"Father." Raised eyebrows were his father's answer. "The general who hesitates at the wrong time loses the battle and sometimes the war."

Father's nod told him to continue.

"If we're to be first to request a marriage with Quintus Sabinus's granddaughter, we need to do it now."

"If you're certain she's what you want, I can do it this week."

"This evening would be better."

Aviola chuckled. "The young are so impatient. She must be a woman of great charm to have you this eager."

Glabrio answered with a smile. His real reason was none of Aviola's business, even if he was a cousin.

"Speed might matter, Father." Glabrio squeezed his neck. "Quintus Sabinus is here, so it will be easy to tell him we're interested. She's only been back for a week, and she's not going to public places yet. But as soon as she does, many will be asking. We can't be certain he'll pick us then."

"Perhaps. But there are too many here for an official conversation. If spreading rumors was a sport, several of Rome's long-time champions are here, and many lesser competitors are as well."

"Can we at least imply that conversation is coming?"

Father squeezed his lips together to keep from laughing. "Quintus is moving, looking for his next conversation. I can suggest we talk about this soon."

Glabrio stayed by his older cousin, watching his father weave through the guests. When Father reached Sabinus, he fell in beside him. Three strides later, they stopped and stood close enough for private conversation.

Sabinus scanned the garden until his gaze locked on Glabrio. A cynical grin curved his lips. He spoke to Father, but his eyes remained focused on Glabrio. There was no reason for it, but Glabrio felt his face flush. Sabinus's noncommittal shrug drew a tip of the head and a political smile from his father.

Two other men stopped beside them, and Father excused himself to rejoin them.

"What did he say?" Glabrio fingered his toga where it draped on his left arm.

"He wasn't surprised at your interest. He said something I didn't understand about you being a friend of his nephew so he'd almost expected it."

"What does that mean?" Glabrio glanced at Titianus, sitting alone at the table where he'd left him.

"Who can say? He said to stop by sometime this week. We'll talk more then."

"Thank you, Father."

"Your friend looks lonely. Perhaps you should rejoin him."

"I will, but he's not lonely. Alone and lonely...they aren't the same thing for men like him."

A chuckle was his father's only answer.

"He's been well entertained watching everyone here." Aviola echoed his father's amusement. "And I've been entertained watching others watch him."

"Who?" Would the answer be what Glabrio needed for the report to his commander?

"Saturninus and Marcellus. The urban prefect should take a lesson from his tribune and learn how to keep his thoughts off his face. That one's like a Greek statue."

Titianus appeared to feel their gaze and turned his head to return it. He uncrossed his arms to place clasped hands on the table, but his face was as passive as a statue.

"I think I'll join him now. Maybe he'll tell me what he finds so interesting." Glabrio raised his hand in farewell and headed back to Titianus.

Perhaps he should take a lesson from the statue-man and learn to control what his face revealed as well.

Chapter 27

WHAT IF IT'S TRUE

The road back to Rome, morning of Day 8

Titianus rose when the slate-gray sky had brightened to a blue-tinged gray. With armor on and toga packed once more in the satchel, he walked to the stableyard as quietly as hobnails allowed and ordered his horse.

He'd stop by his home before going to headquarters. He could watch for Glabrio's arrival from Martialis's quarters. If Saturninus came looking for him, he'd rather not be easy to find.

Pompeia always enjoyed his surprise appearances, but not as much as he did. The bed here was as warm and comfortable as the best he'd ever used, but it held no charms when compared to the one at home with Pompeia warming him as she lay in his arms.

Besides, Glabrio should eat with his father, and he didn't want to intrude on their time together. If Marcellus or Saturninus had conversed in private with the elder Glabrio, he would have placed duty over manners and joined them, but the only one who spent too much time talking to the pair was Rufinus.

As he waited for someone to saddle his stallion, he scanned the carriages and chariots that remained. Saturninus's was no longer among them, but more than he expected had spent the night.

If he had Melis with him, he'd quickly learn who those men were. It would seem odd if he were to ask the stable overseer. The man probably wouldn't tell him anyway, and his interest could be reported to Glabrio's

166

father. That could trigger a question to his protégé about why he was there that he didn't want asked.

He mounted and nudged his horse into a walk.

The banquet had proven as valuable as he'd hoped. Marcellus hadn't liked him being there, if the frequent glances were any indication. They were accompanied by a slight scowl that vanished when someone spoke to Marcellus, only to return after the would-be consul's eyes were watching him again. Rufinus had acted the same.

He'd almost reached the conclusion that the two men who were unnamed in the letter were Rufinus and Saturninus. Both of them had watched him too much, and hostility leaked out when they weren't trying to hide it.

With Saturninus, the hostility was no surprise, but usually his commander ignored him after the first glare. He would have bet against it when he started, but he was almost ready to place his bet that the prefect was involved. Perhaps that was why Turbo chose silence when he asked.

Of course, that silence could simply mean Turbo knew so little that he wasn't ready to rule out anyone.

But knowing who the three in the letter were wasn't enough. To prevent an unknown collaborator from carrying out the plan if those three were removed, he needed to figure out where and how.

He was no closer to knowing that than when he walked out of Turbo's office six days ago.

He was far enough from the stableyard to trot. A quick tensing of his calves, and the stallion settled into the distance-swallowing pace he liked.

The murdered Greeks mentioned in the letter had died at a public ceremony.

Tomorrow would be a week, and Turbo expected a report then. He didn't have enough evidence to give any names. He might be condemning innocent men if he did.

Turbo would act as soon as he knew whom to target, and killing the wrong men would put Hadrian in even more danger. Too many relaxed when the first threat was removed, but threats often came in twos and threes.

If he were going after an emperor, he'd have one or two back-up attacks planned.

Real assassins would, too.

So, first he needed to know Hadrian's calendar to figure out where and when. The how…maybe that would become clear as the rest fell into place.

The road was almost empty. He fastened his helmet strap and urged the stallion past a trot into a canter.

God, please guide me to all who are involved. Please help me find out what they're planning, then help me stop it.

The rhythm of the hooves striking the ground and the rocking of the horse relaxed him and drew a smile.

Then the smile vanished.

What if it was God's will for the assassins to strike so Hadrian would die?

The Titianus town house, morning of Day 8

She was at least three hours early when Sabina led her bodyguard and maid up to the entrance, but Pompeia had mentioned the day before that she wasn't teaching that morning. Sabina was expected after lunch, but she couldn't wait that long to get her questions answered about what she shouldn't have seen.

Tutelus knocked, and the youth opened the door with his usual cheery greeting.

As she entered the atrium, Kaeso stepped out of his classroom, where the boys were writing on wax tablets. "This is a surprise."

"I wanted to talk with Pompeia." She did, yet she didn't. She'd have to confess to looking at something she shouldn't. That was a betrayal of trust. How would her friend react?

"She's gone to give something to a former student for her new-born daughter. She wasn't expecting you until lunchtime."

"Oh." She fought the urge to bite her lip. Last night, she'd watched the shadows cast by the moon work their way across the floor and wall for hours. It was almost dawn when exhaustion finally let her turn off her thoughts and sleep.

"Are you all right?" He stepped closer. "Since she isn't here, can I help?"

"Yes, b-but it has to be only the two of us who can hear what I say." Her heart beat faster. What would he think of what she'd done? Maybe she should have waited and told Pompeia…but it was too late to stop now. "I need to t-talk with you right away."

"The boys might need the library, so…we can go upstairs. The doors seal well. No one down here will hear us." Concern filled his eyes.

Filomena stood behind Kaeso where he couldn't see her. As Kaeso said "upstairs," her eyebrows rose and her lips tightened. The slight shake of her head was louder than a shouted "don't do that."

Sabina ignored Filomena's signals and nodded. Septimus thought no man was more trustworthy than his best friend. He was Pompeia's friend as well, and he'd never do anything to hurt her. No one deserved her trust more.

He led her up the narrow stairway to the first chamber. A chair sat by the table in front of the window with the bed to its right. Would he sit beside her on the bed? She wouldn't mind. She'd often sat beside Septimus like that while they talked. But even though Septimus called Kaeso her second little brother, it wasn't sisterly feelings she felt stirring when he was close.

He waved her into the room as he walked past to the next one, but she paused to watch him. When he came out with a chair, she glanced down to find Filomena glaring up at him, arms crossed, mouth turned down.

Sabina entered the room, and he followed. As he shut the door, she could feel Filomena's disapproval, even though she no longer saw it.

But Filomena didn't like anything Kaeso did, so what she thought didn't matter right now. Kaeso had her full trust. Nothing she didn't want would happen, and he wouldn't even do what she wouldn't mind at all.

He set the chairs opposite each other near the window. She moved her chair closer, so their knees were barely a foot apart.

His brow furrowed when she sat so close, then he relaxed. "What was it you needed to talk about?"

She looked at her sandals peeking out where her tunic brushed the floor. "Yesterday…" She turned her eyes up quickly to see his face. As always, his full attention was on her. But she couldn't meet his gaze when she confessed. She bowed her head as she drew the toe of her sandal across the floor. "I looked at what Pompeia was copying."

He drew a breath between his teeth and held it. Was that disapproval or only surprise?

"Last night, I asked Septimus what it meant. He swore me to secrecy, and I would never t-tell anyone even without that." She wiped her palms on her tunic before raising her eyes to meet his. "But I want to know why you all b-believe what you do."

His breath released, and the lips that had been so straight curved into the smile he often gave her.

"P-please tell me everything you'd tell Septimus if he asked you why."

"What had Pompeia written?" His eyes…why did they suddenly look so happy?

"Something about Jesus telling his followers they should love one another." She lowered her eyes again. "I should never have moved the sheet she put on top, but I thought she was only working on a new poem. I'm sorry."

"I'm not."

Those words startled her, and she raised her head to stare at him.

"What you saw were writings from a physician named Luke. He traveled with Paul of Tarsus as they told people about what Jesus had done for everyone."

His smile had broadened, and he leaned forward, inviting her words as he did when they played tabula.

"Wh-what did Jesus do for everyone?"

"That's the most important question." He leaned back in the chair. "He paid for the sins of all the people who ever lived and made it possible for us to approach the only true and holy God."

Her brow furrowed. "There are hundreds of gods. Which one do you mean?"

"Before I can answer that properly, I have some questions for you. Have you thought about where everything came from and how the world works? About why people behave the way they do?"

"No." She nibbled her lip. Kaeso was so well informed about everything, and she knew so little, except about poetry. But there was no disdain in his eyes as he asked, only a desire to hear her answer. Just like always.

"Septimus was studying the great philosophers before I got married and moved to my father-in-law's estate, but we never really talked about that. Father had all their writings in his library, but I mostly read the poetry he had there, not philosophy or history." She looked down. He was used to a woman who knew as much as he did, like Pompeia. "I'm sorry."

"There's nothing to be sorry about. Not knowing something is easy to fix. You and I can talk about them. It's only fair that I teach you something, with all that you've taught Pompeia and me."

He stroked his beard. "We have most of their writings in the library, but much of what's there isn't that important to learn. Some of it is even wrong."

Kaeso pinched his lip. "Before I try to explain first why I believe in God and then why I believe in Jesus, I want you to read a letter. It will start to explain why, and after you read it, you'll have questions that we can talk about. It was written by the grandfather of Titus's best friend just before he was killed in the arena for becoming a Christian."

Sabina's hand shot up to cover her mouth. "Titus's best friend was killed?"

"It was his best friend's grandfather, Publius Claudius Drusus, but Titus had met him. Publius's letter is a good starting point for us to talk about what Jesus did and why.

"Publius was well respected among the scholars who gather for lectures in the Forum. When he was in the amphitheater cell, he wrote a letter to his son who was serving in the Eastern Empire. It explained how he came to believe what he did and why he was willing to die rather than deny Jesus."

"I think Grandfather wanted to marry his daughter once. He was willing to overlook the family disgrace from that execution, but she left Rome before they could marry."

It was still a sore point with Grandfather that she'd run rather than marry him. Father had warned her to never discuss it with anyone, but Kaeso wasn't just anyone. He felt safe to tell anything.

He leaned forward, and without planning to, she did as well. "Publius liked philosophy and history, and he did a good job of explaining the essence of what Aristotle and Plato taught. Pompeia makes copies of the letter, and I can give you one." He reached out his hand, and she took it. "But you must promise me you'll guard it so carefully that no one will see it, and when you're through reading it, you should destroy it or bring it back. You can read one of our copies whenever you want, but it's safer for all of us if you do that here."

"I can hide it in my box of poetry. That has a lock, and I can wear the key on a chain." Since coming home, she'd traded the key and chain for a necklace with a circle of lapis lazuli set in gold that Mother had given her for her fifteenth birthday. She'd used that chest with its carved vines and flowers to keep her poems safe from her mother-in-law's eyes. It would protect her dear friends' secrets now. "Are you going to tell her what I did?"

"I can, if you want me to, or you can tell her. She'll be glad that you peeked because that's why I've started telling you the reason we're all Christians."

He started to release her hand, but she tightened her grip. That brought a smile to his lips.

"Maybe you'll decide what I'm telling you is the truth and become one of us. We'd all like that." He stroked the back of her hand with his thumb. She would have held on forever if he'd keep doing that, but he stopped too soon.

"Anyone in this house can tell you how there's nothing better than loving God and being loved by Him."

"Even Titus?" Her serious cousin seemed to see through everyone and everything.

"Especially Titus because he lived most of his life not knowing the one God who's real."

He stood, and as his hand dropped, she had to release it. "I have to get back to my boys, but we'll have lots of time to talk about this later. Pompeia will want to join us. She's the one who told Titus everything he needed to recognize the truth and decide to believe it."

"I'd like that."

But as much as she liked Pompeia and however good her friend would be at explaining their faith, she wanted Kaeso to tell her what he thought was the truth.

And if she decided he was right, what would that mean for the future?

◆

As the door closed behind the teacher, Filomena clenched her fists. Mistress Sabina had been weary-eyed when she came up to dress her. Since she'd barely slept at all, it was no wonder. But what had her fretting so? At the Gallus estate, she'd slept well enough, even on the nights she cried herself to sleep.

The closer they got to the Titianus town house, the tenser the mistress seemed. When she asked for Pompeia and the woman wasn't there, that brother had offered to help.

Why was Sabina so eager to talk with him instead?

And why had she gone upstairs to a bedchamber with him unescorted? To talk behind a closed door, no less.

Filomena wanted to go up there and open the door, but she forced herself to sit on the bench on the wall across from it. It seemed like forever before the two of them came out.

What had happened there? Mistress Sabina was worried when they arrived, but after a few minutes alone in that room with Lenaeus, she came out looking happy and excited.

His toga was draped like he always had it, and nothing looked out of place on Sabina, so they hadn't actually done anything. But what had they talked about that had been so urgent she couldn't wait for the sister? And why was she so happy after she talked with him?

That teacher looked too satisfied with their conversation as well.

Now the mistress sat in their library, humming to herself as she worked on a poem. But she often glanced at the open door of his classroom, and when the laughter of his students drew her eyes from the papyrus, her smile was too content.

Every day they spent in this house was dangerous for Mistress Sabina's heart. She should know better than to want a man of the lower classes, but even if she did, her grandfather would never allow it to come to anything.

But as long as Master Manius had no objection, these visits would continue. With as often as the master showed up here to eat or invited his cousin and the other two to his house, Mistress Sabina might fall for the teacher and then have her heart broken when she was married to another nobleman to seal an alliance.

There must be something about the teacher that could make Master Manius end this friendship. But what could that possibly be?

Chapter 28

A Dinner to Endure

The Sabinus town house, late afternoon of Day 8

When Sabina entered her father's house, dread of what would happen that evening coursed through her. It had started when the message came from Father that her grandfather wanted a family dinner with her at home that night. It would be the first time she saw Grandfather since she returned. What had Father told him?

As she walked past the library, she looked in. If Father was home already so she could ask, he would have been there. But no scrolls lay open on the desk, and the chairs were still precisely placed like the cleaners left them.

Tonight of all nights, she'd hoped her time would be her own. She'd expected a lovely dinner at Titus's house with conversations worth hearing and laughter when Septimus joked with Kaeso.

And every time she spoke and even when she was silent, Kaeso's gaze would rest upon her and his smile would brighten the room.

When she returned home after that dinner, she would have locked herself in her room with Kaeso's letter. She'd promised to read it right away.

Filomena always carried the satchel holding her poems, but right now it held more than poetry. The letter was concealed in the middle of the stack of poems she'd brought with her that day. If Sabina insisted on carrying it, Filomena would suspect it held something from the man her dear maid couldn't stand.

She climbed the stairs to her bedchamber with Filomena beside her.

But as soon as they stepped into the room, she held out her hand, and Filomena handed her the satchel strap.

"Grandfather will expect something more formal. Perhaps the blue linen tonight."

Filomena opened the trunk carved with a scene of a garden with a fountain. As her devoted servant leaned over the stack of rainbow-hued tunics, Sabina removed the stack of papyrus from the satchel and placed it in the poetry chest.

While her maid spread the fresh tunic on the bed and pinned most of one end of the fabric tube with silver clips to hold it on her shoulders, Sabina took off her lapis necklace and strolled to the dressing table.

She put the necklace in the jewelry box and picked up the key. With the key and its chain concealed in her closed hand, she returned to the desk and leaned over to lock the chest beside it.

When she straightened, Filomena was watching with her brow furrowed. The lock had been used to keep her snooping mother-in-law from reading her poems. The chest hadn't been locked since she returned home.

She leaned on the desk as if looking out the window, and left the key and chain behind the stack of codices when she stood. She'd put it on after Filomena helped her change.

"I want to get ready as quickly as possible so I can talk with Father before Grandfather comes."

She walked to the bed where the clean tunic lay. One by one, Filomena removed the tunic clips until the tube of fabric dropped to the floor.

As soon as she donned the new blue tunic, she returned to the desk to drop the chain over her head and tuck the key inside her tunic.

When she turned, she caught Filomena watching her in the dressing table mirror as she lay out the hair picks for the more elegant hairstyle Sabina would wear to dine with Grandfather. Her maid's eyebrows were lowered, but she said nothing.

That night, after Filomena retired to her room downstairs, Sabina would bolt her door, light the lamps by the desk, and read what Kaeso had given her.

Tomorrow she would have some questions for him, as he'd told her she should.

But first, there was a dinner to endure.

Evening of Day 8

When Sabina entered the triclinium, Father already reclined on the host couch. Grandfather was on the honored guest couch, so she chose the couch for the least important people. If only Septimus were there. He'd try to find some way to protect her from Grandfather's plans, but he was dining with friends who trained with him at the ludus. If she'd known which one was hosting, she could have sent a message, and he would have come.

The table slaves entered with the salad course of hard-boiled eggs, a selection of dipping sauces, and rolls still hot from the oven.

Grandfather selected an egg and dipped it in the mustard sauce. "I went to Acilius Glabrio's banquet last night. Titus was there with Glabrio's son Gaius." He bit into the egg, and his nod and smile declared it delicious. "Glabrio approached me to ask about you, Sabina. We agreed to speak next week about a possible union of our families."

She swallowed hard, but said nothing. Exactly what she'd feared was happening. She closed her eyes. The last time Grandfather announced whom she would marry, she'd dreamed of the love of a handsome man, the laughter of her own children, and a town house or villa to direct as its *domina*. But she'd seen that dream turn into a waking nightmare. What if the next union dragged her down into another dark, dank pit with no rope to climb out?

What she longed for was what Pompeia had, and she knew exactly who'd give it to her.

Why couldn't Kaeso have been the son of a senator so he'd be what Grandfather considered a "good match." Or even an equestrian like Titus. Why couldn't she escape the fate of an elite daughter of Rome?

But she could never ask Grandfather those questions and get the answer she longed for.

"His father said young Glabrio is very interested in you. Manius tells me he's dined here. So, what do you think of him?"

She fought off the urge to simply shrug. Grandfather would find that disrespectful, and it would be. "He seems pp-pleasant enough for one so young."

Grandfather's chuckle mocked her. "He's only two years younger than you."

"Bb-but it isn't the years, Grandfather. It's the experience." She drew a deep breath and held it. Sometimes that helped the words come. "He'd be b-better off with a wife of sixteen."

"It's a sign of unusual wisdom for one so young that he prefers a woman of your advanced years." His chuckle declared her opinion unimportant.

But it took no wisdom to see what an ambitious man would gain by marrying the granddaughter of Quintus Sabinus. Even a fool could see that.

If only she could tell her grandfather that. But she swallowed the words that would stick anyway. It was better to say nothing when nothing you said could change anything.

Father offered the plate of hot rolls to Grandfather. "He'll be older in a year and much wiser if Titus has anything to do with it."

He glanced at Sabina. "A woman as mature as Sabina needs the right man for a husband. I see no need to rush into another marriage. Marcus Gallus had us both fooled before he married her. We don't want that to happen again."

"What do you mean?"

Grandfather's goblet was almost to his lips, but he set it down without drinking.

"We thought he'd appreciate the treasure we were entrusting to him. But he and his mother abused our trust. It wasn't Sabina's choice to be dragged away from Rome and kept out of sight because she stuttered a little." Manius dipped his roll in the herb-laced olive oil. "Sabina tells me they mocked her whenever she tried to speak."

Grandfather froze with some bread halfway to his mouth, then placed it back on his plate. "They did what?"

"They mocked her and shut her away where no one would hear her. That's why we never saw her when wives were at banquets. I thought it was because her husband was in Britannia and she chose not to come. She never enjoyed dining with a crowd. Gallus always came alone, so I assumed his wife didn't like it either."

"He came alone because he and his wife despise each other. I helped Gallus as often as I could, and he advanced much more than he would have without me." Grandfather's jaw muscles clenched. "How dare he let his wife and son show such disrespect to my granddaughter."

"I'm not sure Gallus knew if he avoids his wife as much as he can. She might have held her tongue the few times he saw them together." Father gave Sabina an encouraging smile. "Sabina never let me know what they were doing. She bore it all with the strength and courage of a Sabinus." He moved an egg to his plate and spooned some honey-and-pine-nut sauce beside it. "We don't want that to happen the next time."

"Any man should be honored to marry a granddaughter of mine, and next time, he and his whole family better treat her like they know what she's worth."

"Exactly. Before you agree to a marriage, it might be wise to watch young Glabrio for a while." Father dipped the egg before taking a bite.

Grandfather nodded, and as Grandfather was looking down at his own plate, Father winked at Sabina.

She gave him the smile she knew he wanted, but deep inside where he couldn't see, her heart was dying. It wasn't her being hurt that Grandfather cared about.

What Marcus and his mother had done was no different from Grandfather lending a precious silver vase to them. Then they'd put a dent in it because they carelessly dropped it. He'd be more careful the next time he lent someone his so-called treasure, but she was still nothing more than a game piece being played in a political game both Father and Grandfather loved. They might watch for a while, but in the end, nothing would change.

She lowered her head, then lifted her napkin as if to wipe her lips. Septimus wasn't with them, so no one would notice that she wiped off a tear as well.

The Saturninus villa, evening of Day 8

Saturninus unrolled the first scroll of Thucydides's *The Peloponnesian War* to the section about Hipparchus. It was so long ago when that murder took place, and there was no way to know whether Hipparchus's assassins might have wanted to kill his brother Hippias but settled for Hipparchus because they feared their accomplices had forewarned the brother.

But it didn't really matter which of the brothers was the ruling tyrant of Athens. All that mattered was that Hipparchus had died by an assassin's hand.

A tap on the doorframe drew his gaze from the writings.

"Come in and sit." He rolled the scroll and set it aside. "You look unhappy."

Rufinus entered the library and lowered himself into the guest chair. "I do because I am."

Saturninus got a glass decanter and two gold-lined silver goblets from the side table. He filled one and set it in front of his friend before settling into his own chair again.

His guest leaned forward to pick up the goblet. Then he stretched out his legs, resting his head on the high back and closing his eyes. "Is Marcellus coming?"

"I asked him, but he sent his regrets. He was invited to a dinner where Hadrian would be present. As one who wants to be consul, it wouldn't be wise to miss it."

Rufinus's eyes opened. "I learned today that I won't be nominated as consul by Hadrian this year." He swirled his goblet. "I thought it a near certainty after the last time I dined with the emperor. I wonder what changed."

"Hmm." Saturninus set the flask down without pouring himself some. "I expected it, too. I suggested you, and he seemed receptive."

His friend's smile was fleeting. "I thank you for that. Quintus Sabinus implied he would support me when we were discussing my business agent's death." He traced the goblet's rim with his finger. "I still haven't found a good replacement for Arcanus. His skill and diligence were exemplary."

Saturninus picked up his still-empty goblet. "I don't know what's worse: losing a good man or trying to get rid of a problematic one. I was almost rid of my overzealous tribune, but Hadrian personally requested that Titianus stay on to investigate something for him."

Rufinus straightened in his chair. "What?"

"I don't know. He's reporting directly to Turbo, and neither of them have told me anything. Glabrio's son is the new tribune who's supposed to replace him. I told him to figure that out and tell me, but he can't seem to find out what Titianus is up to."

"I've seen them together at the Baths several days running." Rufinus swirled the goblet and inhaled the wine's fruity aroma. "Titianus is introducing him to people who live around there, and Glabrio has introduced him to some of his father's friends."

"I know. I was talking with Aviola when young Glabrio introduced them. Glabrio's father even invited Titianus to his last banquet at his son's request."

"What did you see him do there?" Rufinus took his first sip, and raised the goblet to his host to declare his appreciation of the quality.

"He exchanged a few words with Quintus Sabinus, Aviola, Glabrio, and a handful of others. Then he mostly talked with Glabrio's son and watched the other guests in that calculating way he has. Everyone there was senatorial except him, so they largely ignored him."

Saturninus poured himself a goblet of wine. "Ten years of sending men to the arena…it's amazing someone hasn't sought revenge for getting a person they cared about killed."

"It is." Rufinus's half-smile turned down into a frown.

"Someone tried last year. He never did figure out who hired the assassin."

"Too bad he failed…the assassin, I mean."

"Turbo wouldn't be happy if someone tried again and did a more professional job of it." Saturninus took a sip of wine.

He held it in his mouth to savor the full-bodied flavor. After the way Aviola praised it, he'd sent his steward for some of Hadrian's vintage from Titianus's warehouse. When his steward asked for the friend's price, the clerk acted like he didn't know what he was talking about. When his steward had the manager summoned, he'd asked whom the wine was for. Then he said no discount was available.

It was worth full price, but it galled that Titianus's slave had rejected the request of his owner's commander.

"Do you care if Turbo's happy?" Rufinus's mouth curved into a wry smile. "You could always volunteer Victorinus to replace him if the next attempt succeeds."

As the laughter bubbled up, Saturninus barely kept from spitting the wine on his companion. Maybe he should offer to transfer his "best man" to Turbo to join his permanent staff.

After forcing him to keep the troublesome tribune on his own staff for who knew how long, Turbo deserved it.

Chapter 29

WHAT HER CHOICE COULD MEAN

The Titianus town house, night of Day 8

Kaeso stood by the bedchamber window, watching the stars. An occasional cloud floated across the moon. For the moment, a large one was a curtain blocking both moonlight and starlight, creating darkness but no shadows.

Today had been a day much brighter than usual. How good it was that Sabina had peeked at what Pompeia had copied. Even better that she'd found the passage from Luke's writings that included both Jesus and love among the words. It must have been God's hand that gave her the urge to look and then the courage to ask him what it meant.

The more he saw of Septimus's sister, the more his heart was attracted to her. But he'd watched Father's heart break when Mother died without choosing to follow their Lord. He'd sworn to himself and God that he'd only take a Christian for his wife, and that had helped him hold back.

But if she read Publius's letter and returned with questions, would the first woman who stirred his heart become what his head had declared essential?

She was both vulnerable and strong. Her poems showed an appreciation for the beauty to be found in ordinary, even ugly things. She'd come out of the crucible of her miserable marriage wounded and yet not bitter.

And when she sang...the angels in heaven couldn't surpass the beauty of Skylark's voice.

She was a woman any man would be proud to call wife, even if that fool of a tribune she had married failed to see that.

What would she become if she let herself believe in God and chose to follow Jesus?

His smile grew in the darkness. She'd become the perfect wife for him except…

He drew a deep breath, and a sigh drained his lungs. *Except she's the daughter of a leading senator and I'm just an ordinary man.*

Septimus had told him too many stories about what was expected of the men and women of the Sabinus family for Kaeso to have much hope.

Sabina wouldn't choose her next husband. Manius's father would, and he'd use his granddaughter as a political pawn, just as he had before.

But just because Roman expectations made something look hopeless, that didn't mean it was.

Titus was living proof. He had violated the conventions of the nobility when he married Pompeia. But he'd been paterfamilias for almost ten years. He was free to make his own decisions, and he did what he thought right, even if others called it wrong.

But a Roman woman didn't have that freedom, and a noblewoman had even less freedom than most. An ordinary woman could sometimes follow her heart, but one from a family that helped rule Rome…following the desire of her heart instead of the dictates of her paterfamilias was an unattainable dream.

The moon reappeared from behind the cloud, and moon-shadows filled the room again.

Unattainable unless God wanted it otherwise. Theirs seemed a hopeless case…but he served the God of hope who could turn anything into good for those who loved him. Maybe it wasn't so hopeless after all.

But first Sabina had to believe.

The Sabinus town house, night of Day 8

When Sabina came up from the dinner, Filomena was sitting on her bed, waiting. She rose when Sabina entered.

The dinner hadn't been the ordeal she expected, but it had drained the last drop of her energy. She sat on the bed and flopped on her back. Not at all ladylike, as she'd been taught, but at that moment, she didn't care.

Filomena knelt beside the bed. "Are you all right?"

"It's as I feared. Grandfather plans to talk with Glabrio's father."

Filomena took her hand. "At least he seems like a pleasant enough young man."

"So did Marcus." Sabina sat up. "But you're right. Septimus and Titus seem to like him, at least some. Pompeia says no one is a better judge of a man than her husband. He's training Glabrio to replace him in the Urban Cohort, so Titus has seen a lot of him."

But even if he was nice enough, he was nothing compared to Kaeso. Those were not words she'd speak to Filomena, but they were still true. Both Septimus and Titus loved him like a brother.

"Grandfather and Glabrio's father were going to arrange it next week, but Father suggested delaying until they can be certain Glabrio won't be like Marcus." She sat up. "I never would have expected it, but Grandfather agreed."

She rose and moved to the dressing table.

Filomena followed. "For how long?"

"Until they're certain. That could be a week, a month, but not over a year. He wants to join a frontier legion after a year or two in Rome."

She traced the outline of her reflection on the silver mirror. "It was his father's idea to give him time to get to know important people."

The reflection of Filomena's satisfied smile behind her…it declared her maid's pleasure that a "suitable" new husband was soon to be hers. Except he wasn't the man who would suit her best since she'd met Kaeso.

"He's so pleased that he met Grandfather through Titus."

She buried her face in her hands. "Maybe it won't be as bad this time." She lowered her hands and offered Filomena what she tried to make look like a hopeful smile. "Father and Mother barely knew each other when they married, and they grew to love each other."

Her gaze settled on the poetry box. "I want to be alone now."

Filomena's head drew back. "Did you want to retire?"

"Yes, and you don't need to come back until morning."

Two quick blinks were her maid's first response. Her mouth opened, then closed. Sabina never dismissed her like that, but that letter called to her from the chest, and she'd waited too long already.

"Good night, mistress." Filomena's voice had turned formal.

"Good night." Sabina offered what she hoped was her friendliest smile and received one in return. "I think I'll write for a while, so close the door as you leave. Sleep well."

Filomena slipped out the door, pulling it shut behind her. Sabina counted to twenty before bolting it. That would be long enough for her maid to get to the stairs so she wouldn't hear the bolt slide home.

Her heart beat faster as she walked to the desk. Inside the chest that held the essence of herself in hundreds of poems lay a single letter that might change everything. Septimus had kept Kaeso from telling him too much about their god. He feared it might ruin their friendship if he decided he couldn't believe as they did.

Would she lose the two best friends she'd ever had if she couldn't believe it either?

She pulled the key out and unlocked the chest. She'd promised Kaeso she'd read it, and the promise of a Sabinus had to be kept. But that wasn't why she pulled the letter from the stack of poems and lay it on the desk before her.

A woman must keep the promise she'd made to the man with whom she was falling in love.

Chapter 30

The Letter

When Sabina took the letter from the stack of poems, her hand trembled.

How silly. There was nothing to be afraid of. She settled into the desk chair and took a papyrus sheet from the drawer. After uncapping the inkwell, she picked up her pen. Kaeso had said to come with questions, and she'd forget some if she didn't write them down.

One deep breath blown out slowly, and she began to read.

> "By the time you read this letter, I will have been executed for refusing to deny my faith in Jesus of Nazareth and offer a sacrifice to Caesar. Everything I own will have been confiscated. This letter is my only legacy, but what it contains is worth more than all my estates, more than all the wealth in the empire. I pray you will come to treasure it for the truth it contains.
>
> "I begin with how I decided the God of Israel is the one true God."

Where was Israel? If the gods of Rome weren't real, why did Kaeso think the god of a place she'd never heard of was?

On the papyrus, she wrote *Israel.*

> "The teaching of the great philosophers seemed true to me for a long time, but that was before I began to com-

185

pare them to what my own eyes have seen of the world. After much thought, I came to the conclusion that a philosophy could only be of value if it described the way the world truly is. I discovered that the philosophers I had admired most contradicted what I had seen myself. I began my search for a new philosophy without those contradictions."

What she'd seen herself. Protected as a child by Mother and Father, she'd expected only good things. What she'd seen as a woman was mostly bad…people using others for selfish reasons, cruelty because no one was there to stop what they found fun. Publius Drusus had been rich and respected, like Father and Grandfather, able to do whatever he wanted. What could have been worth more than that?

"I always considered Aristotle the wisest of philosophers, and I embraced his teaching wholeheartedly from my youth. At the core of his teaching was the existence of an effective cause for everything. I considered all I had seen of life, and if I looked deeply enough or back far enough in time, I could see the causes of almost everything. He also taught that nothing lasts forever, that everything changes over time. That was what I saw, too."

Everything had a cause? That might seem true, but what had caused Marcus and his mother to be so mean? She'd never done anything to hurt them before their cruelty started. She never even did anything deliberately to hurt them back.

But maybe there was something inside of *them* that caused it, not something she did.

"But I saw a terrible inconsistency in his teaching, and that disturbed me greatly. He taught that the universe was eternal, that it had no effective cause. But how could that be, that the universe as a whole was the opposite of all the parts within it?"

Logic. It had never been something she was good at. At least not the formal logic like Septimus was taught by Kaeso's father. What Kaeso was teaching his students. But anyone could see how this led to that and that led to the next thing when looking at how things worked. Why would the whole thing be different from the parts?

> "Clearly, there was something wrong with this idea. The universe must also have an effective cause, so I began my search for a philosophy that taught the universe had a beginning and an effective cause that started it. I found it in the Jewish Scriptures. They tell how God created everything from nothing, how He is the effective cause of the whole universe."

She'd heard stories about how the gods of Greece and Rome started the world, but there were several versions. Did any say they made everything from nothing? Septimus said not to swear by them because they weren't real. Were they just stories themselves?

What were the Jewish Scriptures? Were any in Father's library?

Maybe Septimus would know. It might be dangerous to ask Father if they were there.

"Jewish Scriptures" joined "Israel" on the sheet.

> "I also considered Plato a great philosopher, but the more I saw of men and how they lived, the harder it became for me to agree with his teaching. He taught that cities and empires could be ruled by philosopher-kings: intelligent, self-controlled men who ruled based on wisdom and reason and placed the good of those they ruled above their own desires for power and wealth.
>
> "But as I examined history, I found men like this have never ruled. Even Trajan, who provided food and education for orphans in Italia, led his legions out to conquer, killing and enslaving, making new orphans who would starve."

Sabina snorted. She didn't have to read the histories that Father and Septimus loved to know men were driven by their desire for power and wealth. Maybe not wealth, but certainly power. Grandfather and his friends were perfect examples. She sighed. And so was Father.

> "From the histories of empires and kingdoms, we know that great rulers have always done so. Trajan con-

demns the men he has conquered to die like animals in
the arena for the entertainment of the crowds. Where is
the wisdom and goodness in that? Plato was wrong about
the nature of man, so how could his philosophy be true?

"Man is not good and wise; he naturally chooses evil.
There are a few who choose kindness and mercy, but it is
cruelty and lust for power that rule. Rome is rotten at her
core, and she rules vast lands with an iron hand. Man's
love of violence led to the games."

All the men she knew went to the games. Father and Grandfather often went together. Marcus had loved them. Did Kaeso go? Somehow, she
couldn't see him doing that, and he was always at the school in the afternoon when the gladiators fought.

"I expect to die in the arena tomorrow, killed by a
lion or a gladiator's sword. Thousands of Romans, including many men whom I have known for years, will be
watching and will consider it good entertainment. Again,
I found this understanding in the Jewish Scriptures, that
man is naturally evil, selfish, rebellious against God. Man
is a sinful being."

Septimus came to Kaeso's house from his training with gladiators. Had
he watched men he knew die in the arena and enjoyed it?

"In the Jewish Scriptures, I found the philosophy
that explained everything I knew to be true about the
world, but it is much more than a philosophy. In those
same Scriptures, I met the God who made the universe.
I discovered that He cared about men enough to reveal
Himself to them so they could know Him. I learned of
Abraham, Isaac, and Jacob, and how each of them had
met God."

Her eyebrows dipped. A god who wanted mere men to know him?
What did it mean to meet a god?

She dipped pen in ink and wrote "meet god" after "Jewish Scriptures."

"I learned of Moses, who was told by God Himself to

lead the people of Israel out of slavery in Egypt because
God had promised the land of Judaea to Jacob's children."

So that was what Israel was. She'd never found Rome's history that interesting, but she'd heard of the province of Judaea. She crossed *Israel* out and replaced it with *Moses*.

> "God cared so much for His people that He gave Moses the very laws by which they should live."

Laws from a god? The Senate and the emperor made the laws of Rome, and the lawyers and praetors applied them to people. What kind of laws would a god give? Were they something Pompeia and Kaeso obeyed? She added "laws" to the sheet.

> "I learned of the many men who were prophets to whom God Himself spoke so His people, who no longer knew and worshiped Him, would return to Him.
> "From the beginning, He always wanted men to know Him and love Him. So I became a God-fearer, worshiping the God of Abraham, Isaac, and Jacob, and I studied the Jewish Scriptures daily because I could learn about Him there."

Love a god? In the stories she knew, gods wanted people to respect and fear them, but the only kind of love in those stories was a god taking a woman for his pleasure. That couldn't be what this meant.

Love joined the list for Kaeso to explain.

> "He is a holy God, and He cannot tolerate sin in His presence. But sin is not just doing the things that He has forbidden or neglecting the things He has commanded; it is also choosing to treat God as if He didn't exist."

Sin—not something she'd heard of before, at least not by that word. But she'd seen it. Doing forbidden things and not doing things you were commanded to do were obviously wrong. Treating a god as if he didn't exist—there was nothing that showed less respect than ignoring someone. That was exactly what all the state rituals that Father attended were meant to avoid. He pretended the gods were real in public, but at home he never talked like he believed in them. Neither did Septimus.

But maybe there was more to it. "Sin" joined "love" on the sheet.

> "In the Law He gave to Moses, He told His people the way to approach Him by covering their sins through blood sacrifice in their temple in Jerusalem. For over a thousand years, His people made sacrifices so they could approach Him. That ended when the temple was destroyed by Titus when he was putting down the rebellion in Judaea.
>
> "That created a terrible problem, or so I thought. God said the payment for sin always required blood sacrifice, but He let His temple be destroyed by Rome, so how was sin to be paid for? I was at a loss to explain how the true God, the one so powerful that He could make the entire universe, could allow Rome to destroy His temple and take away what allowed His people to approach Him."

Blood sacrifice to cover sin so they could approach their god? That was not what the sacrifices at the Roman temples were supposed to do. They were only meant to please the gods by showing respect. Not just to cover sin, whatever that meant, but to be the only way to pay for it. What was the difference between covering and paying?

She dipped the pen and wrote, "Why blood and what does it do?"

> "Then I met a man who could explain it all. He told me of Jesus of Nazareth and how He came from heaven to make the final sacrifice for sins. He was the Son of God. He was sinless, and He made Himself the perfect sacrifice for all sin when He was crucified. After three days, He rose from the dead, proving His claim to be God."

Her hand shot to her mouth. Jesus made himself the sacrifice through crucifixion? Why would he do that? There was no more horrible way to die. Rose from the dead? People didn't do that. Dead was dead.

> "The grandfather of my friend actually knew men who had been with Jesus after He rose. There could be no

doubt of the truth that Jesus was the Son of God and the final perfect sacrifice."

Did people really see Jesus alive again after he'd been executed and buried? That seemed impossible to believe. But if someone she trusted completely told her they'd seen a dead man alive and walking around, that they'd talked with him, would she believe it?

If Septimus or Kaeso told her? She'd have to at least wonder if it was true.

"At last I understood it all. The temple could be destroyed because God had made the perfect blood sacrifice Himself—Jesus on a cross more than eighty years ago. The temple and its sacrifices were no longer needed, so He had Rome destroy it so people would no longer cling to the old ways.

"The coming of the Messiah, of Jesus, was foretold in the Jewish Scriptures hundreds of years before He came, and God kept the promise He made to His people. There was no need to continually sacrifice animals to cover my sin with their blood. To be saved from my sin, I only had to believe in Jesus as the sacrifice for all sins, including mine. It all made perfect sense, and I finally knew the truth."

Did it make sense? How could this be the truth? Kaeso believed it. So did Pompeia. Could they be right?

"When I went the first time to worship with my friend, I actually met God myself. I felt His love surround me, and now He lives in me. I am never alone."

Publius met this god? How could a god live inside a man? One more thing for the list.

"That day when I decided to believe, to repent of my sins and commit myself to Jesus as my Lord, all the worry and sadness in my life was replaced by peace and joy. For the first time, I knew what it was to be fully alive.

"I want you to experience this yourself. For you to

know this perfect love deep in your soul—that will be my dying prayer."

Peace, joy, fully alive? Perfect love deep in one's soul? What did all that mean? Those words joined the others Kaeso would have to explain.

"Following Jesus is like a perfect marriage; denying Him would be like committing adultery against the most loving, beautiful, faithful wife a man could have. I could never betray my Lord that way. I have chosen death instead.

"I will die soon, but I have no regrets. I am content to die because it isn't death that matters. It is whether you have accepted Jesus as Savior. Death is terrible apart from Jesus. Without Jesus, I would be lost, in hell, forever separated from God. With Jesus as my Savior, death has no power over me, and I don't fear it. It will just usher me into life with Him in heaven.

"Jesus told us that He is the way, the truth, and the life. He promised if a man would believe in Him and follow, he would know the truth, and the truth would set him free. If you let Him, Jesus will show you what is true. Open your mind to Him. Open your heart. Know the truth and be free like I am, even in this prison as I wait to die. I will be praying for all my children to choose to follow Jesus until I take my final breath and even after that, for life with Jesus is eternal."

Know the truth and be free, even in a prison waiting to die. Her hand shook as the pen tip touched the surface of the ink. She hadn't known what to expect, but it wasn't a god who wanted to give people peace and joy and life even after you die.

Sabina made the final entry on the papyrus. "Know the truth and be free."

She capped the inkwell and wiped off the pen tip with a small piece of cloth. While the ink dried enough to be placed in the chest without marking the page pressed against it, she stood by the window, watching the night sky.

A large cloud slipped across the moon, throwing all into darkness. All except her room with its lampstand by the desk.

By the time the moon reappeared, the ink was dry. She stacked her questions atop the letter and returned them to the chest, placing several poetry sheets above them. The key turned in the lock, and she hung the chain around her neck again.

She blew out each lamp and slipped into her bed, drawing the sheet up to her chin.

In the darkness, she watched the moon shadows as they moved across the wall. She could close her eyes, but it was too hard to keep them shut. Too many questions swirled in her mind, and she'd find no peace until she had answers.

Was there a truth here that could set her free, no matter what the future held?

Tomorrow she would find out.

Chapter 31

Difficult Questions

The Praetorian Fortress, morning of Day 9

When Titianus entered the fortress, he rode to the back side of Martialis's house and tied his horse there. If Saturninus happened to be at headquarters, he'd rather slip in and out without his commander seeing him.

It was a short distance to the praetorian prefect's quarters, and he kept a brisk pace to reduce the risk of someone from the Urban Cohort seeing him and telling Saturninus he was there.

When the guards at the entrance to Turbo's office opened the door, the prefect looked up from the reports.

Turbo smiled, and Titianus's stomach clenched. If the curve of Turbo's lips meant he expected a report he could act upon, he was going to be disappointed.

Titianus stopped in front of the desk and saluted.

"What do you have for me?"

"A report on my progress to date. I started with ex-consul Marcellus and his son, as we discussed before. As yet, I don't have evidence that either Marcellus is plotting against Hadrian. I've been watching those with whom they meet, and there are two others whom I've seen with the younger one often. But I have nothing definitive yet."

"Who are they?" A satisfied smile warmed Turbo's eyes, but that wasn't going to last.

"I can't tell you yet."

Both smile and warmth disappeared as he said "yet."

"Are you protecting someone?"

"I might be protecting an innocent man from being accused of something he hasn't done. It's been my practice with Saturninus not to reveal whom I suspect until I have enough evidence to be certain. He wasn't happy with me at times, but protecting the innocent is as important as catching the guilty."

Turbo's eyebrows lowered. "I want the names."

Titianus stopped the swallow before Turbo could see. "If the ones I'm considering turn out to be innocent, can you guarantee that nothing will happen to them before I can find the ones who are truly guilty? It won't protect the emperor to have the wrong men punished while his enemies keep plotting."

More than once, Titianus had been beneath the arena where the lions were caged. The big cats stared at him, tails twitching, and always one licked its lips. Turbo's eyes were dark brown, but other than the color, they were too much like those ruthless amber eyes in the deafening stillness of this office that felt like a cage.

Turbo's unspoken answer was no, so his response must be as well.

"The friends of an innocent man wrongly punished become enemies if they weren't before. Even the friends of a guilty man can seek revenge. I don't want what I do to make more enemies for my emperor than he already has."

Turbo's humorless laugh echoed in the room. "I can see why Saturninus was eager for you to retire."

"I appreciate the great honor of receiving this assignment, but if how I work isn't what you need, I'll step aside for another."

"No. You're exactly what Martialis said you were. I should have expected this." One corner of Turbo's mouth lifted in a wry smile, but his eyes remained cold. "Is there something I can do to speed up your investigation?"

"If the Greek assassinations set the pattern, I need to know what public ceremonies Hadrian will be participating in for the next two or three months. That should help narrow down the likely place of the attack, and that will help me identify those involved."

Turbo's head tipped back, and he looked down his nose at Titianus. "I can have that list for you by this afternoon."

Titianus had spent most of the last three years with a commander who disliked him. He was finishing his service to Rome angering two prefects at once. But he wouldn't have innocent blood spilled if he could prevent it.

"It is possible the Greek references only meant assassination and told us nothing about where. In case we read that part wrong…if there are any private gatherings where either Marcellus is likely to be near Hadrian, I should know about those, too."

"Are there specific hosts you need to know about?"

Titianus's mouth twitched before he stopped it. That question was a trap. Anyone he named would become Turbo's target. "Only those you think I should."

Turbo's jaw clenched until he flexed it. The humorless smile returned. "If I knew which posed a threat, I wouldn't need you."

Titianus chose silence as the best response.

The prefect leaned back in his chair and crossed his arms. "I'll expect progress and a report in four days. You're dismissed."

"Yes, Prefect." Titianus's fist hit his chest before his parade-turn. He strode to the door, pulled it open, and marched past Turbo's guards.

He'd almost reached Martialis's quarters when his stomach unclenched. He'd be back for the list after lunch, but until then, what should he do?

God, please guide me to the proof I need by that deadline. Turbo has no qualms about punishing the innocent on the way to finding the guilty. Please don't let me and mine be among them.

The Titianus town house, afternoon of Day 9

On other days, Sabina had been eager to reach Pompeia's house by lunchtime. Dining with her friend was followed by sharing some poems and relaxed conversation about many different things. Pompeia had even set up another loom by her own in the weaving room off the peristyle.

But today it was Kaeso's company she wanted. She had questions to ask, and he had the answers. But Pompeia could answer them, too. If she'd come at the regular time, he might wonder why she spent so much time with Pompeia without asking them.

Today, she timed her arrival to when Kaeso dismissed his students to go train with gladiators like Septimus did or to whatever else younger boys liked to do.

When the door slave let them in, the wisdom of Sabina's plan was confirmed.

"Sabina." Kaeso stepped out of the library, still in the toga he usually shed as soon as his students left. "I was afraid you weren't coming. Pompeia should be back shortly to answer any questions."

"But I want you to teach me. You're a wonderful teacher, and I know I'll learn better." She pointed at the room where they'd spoken yesterday. "Up there would be nicely private."

"It would…" Caution tinged his words. "I'm honored that you think I teach well, but are you certain you want me and not Pompeia?"

"I'm sure." Being with him, no matter what they were doing…she wanted that more than anything she'd ever wanted before.

"Stay here." Sabina took the satchel from Filomena and started up the stairs. When she looked over her shoulder to see if Kaeso was following, Filomena had moved behind him.

Her maid's gaze was fixed on him, and hatred shone in her eyes.

But he didn't see it. His back was toward Filomena, and his eyes were fixed on Sabina. He stood, unmoving. Then she smiled at him, and he followed her up the stairs.

When he entered the room where they'd talked before, Sabina swung the door shut. But just before it closed, Filomena cleared her throat. Determination straightened her mouth and lowered her eyebrows. Determination…but determination to do what? Sabina would ask her later, but if Filomena was determined to speak against Kaeso, that was not something she would allow. Not in her hearing and not to other people, either. Filomena could keep any critical thoughts to herself.

The door clicked shut, and she slid the bolt over. Not Filomena, not anyone would interrupt what Sabina had been eager for since she read Publius's first words to his son.

She sat near the middle of the bed. That left plenty of room for him on either side of her, but he'd still be close enough for them both to read something. He should have joined her, but he stood three feet away, and he didn't move when she patted the bed to invite him to sit. Why didn't he?

Kaeso cleared his throat. "I can explain any questions you have about what we believe and why, but I was only six when I decided I would follow Jesus. I can't really remember what it was like not to. That's why I think Pompeia might be better at answering some of your questions."

He had lowered his voice and glanced at the closed door, then took a step closer.

"She was twelve when we became Christians." His voice was even quieter. "So, she started out closer to where you are than I did. Mother never stopped worshiping the gods like she'd learned from her mother, and she trained Pompeia in the Roman way."

"What about your father?"

"He stopped believing in the gods long before he became a Christian. He used to quote Seneca often."

One hand rested over his chest as he raised the other in his best oratorical style. "'Religion is regarded by the common people as true, by the wise as false, and by rulers as useful.'" Kaeso returned to his usual relaxed stance. "Father still taught Stoic philosophy to our students after he learned there was one religion that was true. It's expected, and the Stoics did write many worthwhile things. But he stopped teaching it as the greatest wisdom known to man. He asked his students to think about the statements that were only partly true or even wrong. He would guide them to see where the logic broke down."

A corner of his mouth lifted. "Titus excelled at that. Maybe that's why he's such a superb investigator."

He took another step, leaned over, and tapped her list. "You started doing that right here. I teach my boys like Father taught me. Knowing what the philosophers said and being able to see both what's right and what's wrong is important for a noble Roman who will someday help rule the empire. Truth will always stand up against the questions you ask."

His eyes turned once more toward the closed door before refocusing on her. "But it can be easier to get your question answered when someone had that question themselves. Some things I never had to wrestle with like Pompeia did."

"But I want you to explain it to me first. If I still have questions when you're done, we can talk with Pompeia together." She patted the bed beside her. "Please sit. We need to be able to read some of the passages together so you can explain all that I need to know."

He hesitated, then sat and held out his hand. She handed the list to him, but the copy of the letter stayed in her own lap.

His eyes were solemn as he scanned what she'd written; then his smile grew. "Your questions are excellent. They go right to the heart of what we believe."

He glanced over at the letter. "I often start by telling my students the history behind something. That's a good place for us to start. It's where Publius did."

He touched the second phrase on her list. "Jewish Scriptures. They tell about the Jewish God. He's my God, too. We'll start here because it's part of why the Jews worship God so differently from what Romans do. Jewish religion is not based on tales about what many gods are supposed to have done sometime or other. It's based on history, not myth, with stories about real people and real events and how God dealt with them. The record of what God has done is in the Jewish Scriptures, which have been written down and then copied exactly for hundreds of years."

"Not s-stories, but history?"

"Yes, written down and carefully copied to prevent changes, and the oldest parts were written more than a thousand years ago. The Jews divide it into three parts: the Law, the Prophets, and the Writings. The first part was written by Moses. Some of it is the history of the ancestors of the Jewish people from when Abraham was first called by God to leave behind the false gods of his fathers and go to the land God had promised to his descendants. I won't tell you the whole history, but Abraham fathered Isaac, who fathered Jacob. God Himself renamed Jacob Israel, and that's why the Jews call themselves the sons of Israel." He touched the crossed-out word. "I see you had a question about that at some point."

Sabina nodded. "I f-figured out it meant the Jews."

The approval in his eyes...it felt good to know he thought she was smart.

"When there was a bad famine, Israel and his whole family moved down to Egypt. Later they were made slaves of Egypt's ruler, but God used Moses to free them and lead them back to the land He'd promised to Abraham. The rest of the books of the Law tell about that journey and describe Jewish law. God Himself gave Moses the laws that His people must obey, and Moses wrote them down. Twice actually. Once when they were first given at the start of their journey to the promised land, and then just before Moses died and the people of Israel conquered what's now Judaea and some areas surrounding it. The laws tell how people should live to please God."

"Do you follow those laws?"

"Some, but not all of them. They were God's old covenant with the descendants of Abraham. When Jesus came, He made a new covenant with all people, not just the Jews, and there are some things in the new covenant that replaced what was in the old. But even though we Romans were never under the whole Jewish law, we are under the new covenant that Jesus set in place. We still want to make the right choices and live the way that pleases God, so there are many things in the Jewish law that we do follow."

Sabina drew her finger down the first four entries. They'd talked about three, but not the strangest one. "We skipped past one question. He wrote that the four men you mentioned met their god. What happens when someone meets a god?"

He looked at the list. "I'm going to answer that one later. There are some things you need to know before you'll understand."

"Publius said later that he met his god, too." Should she ask the next question? It was so personal, and maybe he wouldn't want to say. "Have you m-met your god?"

"Yes, and I'll tell you about it, but first I need to explain some more things."

Meeting your god—that sounded so important; it was hard to wait for the answer. But patience was a virtue. Her lips twitched. At least a dozen times, Kaeso and Pompeia had looked at each other, said "Patience is a virtue" at the same time, and then laughed. It was a family motto that held happy memories. And now it was playing in her mind, too.

If only that could be something she and Kaeso passed on to their own children.

Kaeso's lips were straight as his finger started at the fifth word. But as he scanned down to the last phrase, they curved into his best smile, and her heart beat faster when his gaze turned back on her.

"We'll jump ahead to sin and blood and come back to love. God's great love for us can only be understood after we know how serious sin is and what it costs to pay for it."

He leaned closer. He probably only did it to see the letter better, but it didn't matter why as long as he did.

"Show me where you were reading when you wrote down sin."

"Here, where it says your god can't stand sin. But then it says sin could be covered by a blood sacrifice. Why did a blood sacrifice work?"

"I can't answer that. I'm only a man, and although I try to understand what I can about God, there are things that are beyond me. The life of an animal is in the blood. Maybe that's part of it, but I don't know if it is. But if God told Moses to tell the people of Israel that a blood sacrifice is the only thing that can cover sin, I can be certain it does. He also told Moses that the blood of an animal covered sin for a while, but it didn't take it away for good.

"Publius didn't write it in his letter, but the animal they sacrificed couldn't have anything wrong with it. It had to be the best they had, not a cast-off with defects. The closer to perfect the animal was, the better."

"But no animal is perfect."

"And no man is either. At least not any man like you or I know. That's why God came to earth Himself as Jesus and became the perfect blood sacrifice to not just cover sin but take it away permanently."

He shifted on the bed and twisted to face her.

"It's because God loves us and wants us with Him. But by His very nature, He can't abide sin in His presence. It's in our nature to do what we want, whether it's good and pleasing to God or not. That's what sin really is—all the things we do that separate us from God. It builds a barrier we can't take down or get over ourselves."

"So, do you sin?"

No man was perfect, but Kaeso was as close as she'd ever seen.

"I don't want to. I try not to, but yes. Even the best people we know can't completely keep from sinning, so our own actions keep us from being with God. The effect of our sin doesn't go away if we ignore it or try to forget we did it. It's got to be paid for to be removed."

He picked up her hand and held it between both of his.

"That's why God came to earth as Jesus to make that perfect payment for all of us. He took the punishment for our sins so we wouldn't have to. Because of His love for me, He cleared away the barrier I'd built. All I have to do is believe Jesus did what He said He would, and that barrier is gone."

His thumb stroked her wrist as she stared into his eyes. They'd never seemed brighter. She trembled, but it was his words even more than his thumb that caused that.

"Jesus promised His followers that believing in Him would make them children of God, that we would have a life that didn't end at death, but stretched on without ending." His thumb stopped as his grip tightened. "Because I believe in Him, I'll spend eternity with Him."

"Publius wrote that was why he wasn't afraid to die." She nibbled her lip. "Are you?"

"I'm not afraid of death, but I wouldn't be telling you the truth if I said I wasn't afraid of some of the ways a person can die. Rome doesn't like Christians because we won't take part in the rituals for the state gods. Many people just pretend they believe in the gods and do what's expected. Your father is one of those. But for me to do that"—he shook his head—"I'd be denying Jesus is my Lord. God commanded us to worship no other god but

Him. Some die in the arena for refusing to pretend. Sometimes a governor decides to kill us. That happened in Bithynia and Pontis. I pray I'd be able to remain true to my Lord if I ever face the choice Publius did."

"I don't want anything to happen to you." The mere thought…she blinked fast to hold back the tears.

He grinned at her. "Neither do I."

Then he released her hand, and his eyes returned to her list. His face was so peaceful, as if he saw nothing to worry about. But just being a Christian…that was so dangerous if anyone found out.

It was a good thing she'd sent Filomena out and locked herself in the room while she read. Filomena would never deliberately betray her friends, but a single slip of the tongue in the presence of the wrong person…Sabina shuddered at the thought of where that might lead.

"Are you cold?"

"No." How could she feel cold when he sat beside her, eager to share what he believed mattered most?

Chapter 32

TIME TO STOP

With her finger, Sabina traced Publius's words at the end of the letter. Everything he described—she wanted it. But didn't you have to know someone before you could follow him?

"I think I left what might be the most important question off my list. Peace, joy, feeling fully alive…everything Publius describes depends on me believing in Jesus. But how can I believe in someone when I don't know anything about him?"

"I can help with that." He handed the list back to her. "Would you like to read what Jesus did from beginning to end? To think about what my father and Pompeia studied when they were trying to understand what Publius believed and why he thought it worth dying for?"

"I would."

Her answer brought his grin back.

"I have my father's codex of the gospel written by Luke. Remember I told you he was a physician who sometimes traveled with Paul of Tarsus when he was going around the Eastern Empire telling people about Jesus."

Sabina nodded.

"Luke was with the first believers in Jerusalem for a couple of years while Paul was in prison in Caesarea. He wrote two codices: one telling what Jesus said and did and one telling how the news about Jesus and His sacrifice to rescue us started spreading through the empire."

"So, it's a history?"

"A history and much more. He told us at the beginning of his writings that he talked with many of the eyewitnesses who saw Jesus when He was teaching in Galilee and Judaea and when He went to Jerusalem to be killed. Luke came to Rome with Paul for his trial and was here when Paul was killed for his faith.

"Father met Jesus the first time he read Luke's gospel. That's why it was his favorite. I'll lend you the first codex. Then you can think about some of what Jesus taught His disciples and what happened when He went to Jerusalem to sacrifice Himself for my sins." He took her hand. "For your sins, too."

His dead father's favorite codex. Could there be any treasure more precious to him? Perhaps he was trusting her with it because she was Septimus's sister, but her heart whispered it was because he was starting to care about her like she cared about him.

"I'll guard it well. When I'm not reading it, I'll keep it where I keep what's most dear to me."

She pulled the key on its chain out of her tunic. It had been next to her heart, and it felt warm in her hand. "I have a chest for all my poems. I kept it locked so my mother-in-law would never see them. It will protect your codex from prying eyes, too."

◆

The eagerness in her eyes—nothing could have made Kaeso happier at that moment. This must have been how Pompeia felt as she first shared about Jesus with Titus.

"I'll make sure you have it just before you leave today. We don't leave any of the Christian writings out where someone might see them."

"I can put it into my satchel right away and keep it with me. May I keep the letter to read again?"

"You may. If you don't mind, I'll tell Pompeia what we talked about. Then she and I will both be praying that you hear God calling you."

"Calling me?" Her fingers covered her mouth as her eyes widened. "Would your god talk with me like he did with Moses?"

This had to be better than talking with Titus. Her cousin never showed emotion back then, and seeing her excitement and that slight uncertainty was a memory he'd treasure if she became a child of God. No, after she became his sister in Christ. That seemed almost certain now.

"Usually not. Mostly it's something inside you that hears and responds."

Her brow furrowed, and that triggered his grin again.

"Don't worry if you don't understand that right now. You soon will."

Trust replaced confusion, and she clutched the letter and questions to her chest. "I can hardly wait."

He was about to respond when a knock on the door stopped him. He held one finger to his lips before rising to let whomever it was in.

◆

Filomena sat on the bench where she could see the closed door and fumed.

Why was Sabina putting her heart and her reputation at risk with the teacher? Telling her to stay in the atrium. Leading him upstairs and going alone into a bedchamber. Closing the door. That click was a bolt locking it. No decent noblewoman would closet herself away with a common man like that. She wouldn't even do it with a young nobleman who wasn't her husband or brother. Eyebrows would rise even at an uncle or cousin.

Gallus had been a horrible mistake, but Master Sabinus would be careful to avoid another brute like that. A fine young man from a consular family was already eager to have her as his wife.

But what if she did something with the teacher that she shouldn't? All the visits here needed to stop. Her infatuation with that Kaeso needed to end before something happened that couldn't be undone.

Pompeia came in from the peristyle and stuck her head into the library where Sabina should have been. "Filomena, where is Sabina?"

Filomena pointed at the closed door, and the sister climbed the stairs. But when she tried the door, it wouldn't open.

They had bolted the door. If he wasn't trying to get Sabina to do something she shouldn't, why was it bolted?

When the sister knocked, it was only a moment before the door opened.

The teacher was still wearing his toga, and relief flooded Filomena.

His sister walked into the room before he closed the door again. The click of a bolt sliding into place again was unmistakable.

Nothing appeared to have happened to Mistress today, but was that only because his sister interrupted them?

She chewed her lip. There must be something that could get Master Manius to forbid these visits. But how could she find out what it was? And once she did, how could she convince the master to keep her beloved Sabina from ever seeing the brother and sister again?

The Sabinus town house, late afternoon of Day 9

When word came that Mistress Sabina needed to come home for dinner, Filomena struggled to keep her delight from showing. Every time they ate at Titianus's house, the conversation walking home was all Pompeia said this and Kaeso said that.

Tonight, Master Manius had invited Glabrio for dinner with both their fathers. Mistress Sabina was to be there to meet the ex-consul who might soon be her father-in-law.

That marriage needed to happen before her Sabina gave her heart completely to the teacher. It was too obvious that she already cared for him. Her smile grew when he entered the room. Her eyes lit up when he praised her as a poet and singer. But even when they simply sat and talked, she glowed with happiness.

It might not be love yet, but it was close. If her heart wasn't to break again when she married the man her grandfather chose, spending time with Kaeso must stop.

And the way to get Master Manius to end it might be opening.

When Sabina and the other two came out of the bedchamber, Pompeia had stood on the balcony beside her while Kaeso went to his room two doors down. He came out with a codex, and when he returned to the pair, Sabina opened her satchel for him to slip it inside.

Then, for the rest of the day, she kept that satchel at her side instead of giving it to Filomena. That wouldn't have been odd if they'd been in Pompeia's classroom writing and correcting poems, but they'd gone to the weaving room.

There was no need for a satchel there. And when it was time to head home for a bath and an elegant hairstyle for the dinner, as Master Manius had requested, the cord for latching the satchel had been slipped through the loop and then knotted to make it harder to open undetected.

Then Mistress Sabina had even carried the satchel herself, which drew a raised eyebrow from Tutelus, even though he never reacted to anything the mistress did.

But the final proof there was something in that codex she didn't want anyone to see was locking it in the poetry chest and wearing the key as soon as they got home.

Filomena gathered up the linen tunic with a garland of embroidered leaves and roses around the bottom and some clean undergarments before following Sabina to the town house's private bath.

She helped Sabina undress, and her heart beat faster when the mistress lifted the key chain over her head and placed it by the clean clothes. It might not be long now until she'd have what she needed to protect Sabina from herself.

After applying scented cleansing oils and scraping them off with a strigil, she held Sabina's hand as she stepped into the tub of hot water for a soak.

"I left the binding cords that match the garland in your room, mistress. Did you need anything before I fetch them?"

Sabina settled onto the underwater bench that let the water cover her shoulders. "I n-need for this dinner to be over, but that's not something you can get me." Her smile was sad before she shrugged, rested her head against the rolled-up towel that padded the edge, and closed her eyes.

With the key hidden in her clenched hand, Filomena slipped from the bath chamber and scurried to Mistress Sabina's room. When she entered the bedchamber, she bolted the door and unlocked the chest.

She lifted out the codex the teacher had sent home with Sabina. No title was visible on the leather cover, but two curved lines touched at one end and crossed near the other, looking like a fish. With tightened lips, she opened to the first page.

> "Inasmuch as many have undertaken to compile a narrative of the things that have been accomplished among us, just as those who from the beginning were eyewitnesses and ministers of the word have delivered them to us, it seemed good to me also, having followed all things closely for some time past, to write an orderly account for you, most excellent Theophilus, that you may have certainty concerning the things you have been taught.
>
> In the days of Herod, king of Judea, there was a priest named Zechariah, of the division of Abijah. And he had a wife from the daughters of Aaron, and her name was Elizabeth."

A history about events in Judaea? Why would Lenaeus be giving her that to read? Why did Sabina treat it like something secret?

She flipped ahead, scanning past a story about some older woman who was supposed to be barren having a son who would serve their god. Then an angel appeared with a message for a virgin.

> "And behold, you will conceive in your womb and bear a son, and you shall call his name Jesus.
>
> He will be great and will be called the Son of the Most High. And the Lord God will give to him the throne of his father David, and he will reign over the house of Jacob forever, and of his kingdom there will be no end."

A son born to a virgin was also the son of the most high…what? A king who would rule forever over a kingdom that would never end? That didn't sound like something that could happen, so maybe it wasn't a history.

She jumped ahead several pages.

> "In the fifteenth year of the reign of Tiberius Caesar, Pontius Pilate being governor of Judea, and Herod being tetrarch of Galilee, and his brother Philip tetrarch of the region of Ituraea and Trachonitis, and Lysanias tetrarch of Abilene, during the high priesthood of Annas and Caiaphas, the word of God came to John the son of Zechariah in the wilderness."

Maybe it was a history. Why else would it list an emperor and the Roman governor with some kings? But what did it mean when it said the word of God came to the man who was the baby from the first story?

She turned the page.

> "Now when all the people were baptized, and when Jesus also had been baptized and was praying, the heavens were opened, and the Holy Spirit descended on him in bodily form, like a dove; and a voice came from heaven, "You are my beloved Son; with you I am well pleased."
>
> Jesus, when he began his ministry, was about thirty years of age, being the son (as was supposed) of Joseph, the son of Heli,…"

The long list of names ended with "son of Adam, the son of God."

Filomena closed the codex and stared at the cover. This was about someone named Jesus, and she only knew of one of those that anyone might write about.

Kaeso was a Christian, and he was trying to convince Sabina to become one, too.

She returned the codex to the chest and locked it. With the chain and key gathered into her hand to hide them from the mistress's eyes as she returned them, she carried the cord down to the bath chamber.

When she entered, Sabina was still relaxing in the hot-water tub, water up to her neck, a slight frown curving her lips. Her eyelids opened long enough to see who entered, then closed again.

As Filomena returned the key to its place by Sabina's clean tunic, she couldn't stop her own smile. The teacher himself had given her the weapon she needed to stop them meeting.

Sabina would tell her to leave as soon as they went upstairs so she could read what Kaeso Lenaeus gave her. As soon as the mistress closed the door, Filomena would be free to talk with Master Manius about the danger Lenaeus posed.

It was just as Filomena predicted. As soon as she finished arranging the many small braids in an intricate pattern and securing them with jewel-topped hairpins, Mistress Sabina had told her she wanted to be alone until it was time to go down to dinner with her grandfather and the two Glabrios.

Filomena paused on the balcony after pulling the door closed behind her. When she heard the bolt slide across, she started downstairs. Sabina wouldn't be coming out soon when she had that codex to read.

Master Manius sat at his library desk, a scroll open before him. She rested her hand on her chest, where her heart beat as if she'd just run to the Baths and back. When she revealed Mistress's secret, would he get angry? Would that anger be directed at her? Would he ask how she came to know what she did and punish her for looking at what Mistress Sabina had meant to keep from her?

No matter. This was the only way to protect Sabina from Lenaeus, and nothing would stop her from seeking what was best for the person she cared about most.

In the doorway, she cleared her throat. "I beg pardon, Master Manius, but there's something you should know."

He looked up and gave her a slight smile. "What is it?"

"It's for your ears only." She closed the door behind her and bolted it.

The master's smile had flipped to a frown and his eyebrows lowered when she faced him again. "Is something wrong?"

"Mistress Sabina…she spends a lot of time at your cousin Titianus's house." She took a deep breath.

"I know that. She enjoys sharing her poetry with Titianus's wife."

"She does, master, but her brother is there, also, and he spends time with her as well."

The master crossed his arms. "I would expect so. She and Septimus eat with them often."

"Yes, master, but…well…he's trying to convince her to become a Christian, and I'm afraid of the danger that poses for Mistress Sabina."

"I see." He covered his mouth with his hand and rubbed his jaw. "I'm glad you warned me. You are to tell no one else because you're right that it could be dangerous. The wrong person knowing could get her killed."

He massaged the back of his neck as his eyes bored into her. "I know how loyal you are to Sabina, and I trust that you'll do everything you can to protect her from anyone who would want to hurt her."

"I will, master."

"Your silence is the best way to do that."

"Yes, master. I would never tell anyone anything that could hurt her."

"Good. I'll take care of this problem in an appropriate way." He flicked his fingers. "Go."

Chapter 33

Not for Her to Choose?

Relief washed over Sabina's maid's face before she bowed and left the room, but as soon as she disappeared through the doorway, Manius rolled his eyes and released a deep sigh. If what she'd just told him was true, it might be a huge problem for Sabina and his whole family. But there was one person who would know the truth of the situation.

Through the open door, he saw a housemaid dusting a statue.

"Urtica."

The girl scurried over. "Yes, master?"

"Go tell the stablemen that Septimus is to come to me the moment he gets home."

She left as quickly as she came. It was almost dinner time. He shouldn't have a long wait.

Manius sat at his desk with the scroll of Tacitus open before him, but he wasn't seeing the words written upon it. His mind kept drifting to the problem that hung over his household.

Where was that son of his?

When Septimus finally entered the library, Manius rolled up the scroll and pointed it at the guest chair. "Bolt the door and then sit."

The bolt slid into its slot with a click. As Septimus lowered himself into the chair, Manius set the scroll aside and pressed steepled fingers against his lips.

"Is Kaeso a Christian?"

"What makes you ask that?" Septimus's jaw twitched. His son still had much to learn about masking his nervousness when avoiding an answer with a question.

"Because he has a codex of Christian writings…and he lent it to your sister."

The breath Septimus drew was deep, and he held it longer than Manius expected. Would his silence be followed by a lie?

"Yes."

"How long have you known?"

"Kaeso has been my closest friend since we were fifteen. I can't say exactly when he told me, but it's more than three years."

After that confession, his son relaxed in the chair as if nothing were wrong.

"Has he tried to persuade you to join him?"

"He's told me what he believes. He thinks that it's true and that the truth of it will finally persuade me."

"Finally?"

"I haven't made my mind up. I know what it might cost if I became one. I'm not ready to pay that price."

"Is his sister one?"

Septimus's silence was louder than any shout.

"You just answered without words. Does Titus know?"

Septimus opened his mouth as if to speak, but no sound came out. Then he released a deep breath. "Titus is alive because they prayed for him. He was bleeding from his ear, barely breathing when I got him here. I thought he'd die at any moment, but Pompeia had him taken upstairs. That's where they prayed."

He rubbed the sides of his nose. "A man doesn't survive a broken skull. That's what the physician said he had. Knowing that, it would be hard for a man not to believe the prayers to their god did something."

With his elbow on the desk, Manius leaned his forehead on one palm, and sighed.

"Has Kaeso convinced your sister yet?"

"I don't know. She does admire him. She's going to take anything he says seriously."

"Only admires him?"

"Well…that's all it is at the moment, but I don't think it will stop there. I can see he suits her better than any other man I've known. I don't think it will be long before she sees it, too. She doesn't love him yet, but if I were to place a bet on it, I'd bet she soon will."

Manius closed his eyes and scrunched them. "Hmph." He'd thought

Pompeia would help Sabina get back the confidence Gallus and his mother had stolen from her. She had, but if he'd known that friendship with the sister might lead to love for the brother…

"It's not as bad as you think, Father. You should see her when she's with them. She's like she was when we were children. She's happy. He treats her like she's a treasure. We both know she is, and he sees that, too. I'm sure he only wants what's best for her." He cleared his throat. "You're not going to find a better husband for her, no matter how important that man's family might be."

"Your grandfather is planning to arrange her marriage with Glabrio."

"Can you stop him? She'll do it if that's what Grandfather orders her to do, but it could break her heart…again. She doesn't deserve that. She sacrificed once for the family. Why can't she have the man who can make her happy for the rest of their lives?"

Manius leaned on the desk, eyes closed, nose and mouth covered with steepled fingers. She didn't deserve that, and Kaeso was one of the finest young men he'd met.

"Don't say anything to her because I might not succeed." He leaned back and rested his hands on the arms of his chair. "I'll see what I can do to get her the desire of her heart, if you think that's what your friend is."

"I do think he will be, if he isn't already."

He pushed up out of the chair. "Not a word to her about our conversation. And not a word to your friend."

Septimus's nod was slow, but his smile was one of his broadest.

Manius draped his arm across Septimus's shoulder as he passed. "Your grandfather should arrive shortly. There's time for some tabula before he comes."

As they strolled into the peristyle on their way to the gameboard in the triclinium, Manius rubbed his jaw. Young Glabrio was eager to unite with the Sabinus family. Ex-consul Glabrio considered it a good political move. Father would be weighing the advantages of accepting the proposed union versus waiting for a better one. Sabina dreaded becoming only a game piece in political maneuverings one more time. Septimus expected him to change what seemed inevitable. Dinner should be…interesting.

Manius was not winning the tabula game when his father arrived early for dinner. He'd expected the early arrival, even counted on it for the chance to defer any decision on Sabina's next husband to a future meeting with Glabrio and his son.

"Good evening, Father." He leaned back in his chair as Septimus made another move that guaranteed his son's victory. "I'm glad you're early. You've just spared me from a humiliating defeat at the hands of your grandson."

Father's chuckle drew Septimus's grin.

"But I've been playing distracted. I've been thinking more about what we planned for tonight, and I'm not certain it's the right time."

"Why not?" His father moved Manius's game piece, placing it where he would have himself. How much they thought alike amazed him sometimes.

"Gaius Glabrio seems on the surface to be a nice enough young man with impeccable family connections and a bright future, but I'm in no hurry to marry Sabina off until she's fully recovered from her time with Gallus's wife. I found her stutter was barely noticeable when she left, but she came home with too many words giving her a problem every time she speaks. You may have noticed the other night that she hardly talked at all."

Septimus made his next move, and Manius responded. He was definitely going to lose this game, but he was playing something more important than tabula now.

"I think a few months with Septimus and Titus's wife should fix that. She's already a little better since she started visiting Pompeia."

Septimus made his next move, and his grandfather picked up a game piece that Septimus had just removed from the board. "You and your sister were close before she married. What do you think?"

"I agree with Father. A delay will do no harm, and it might do a great deal of good."

Quintus replaced the polished stone. "Very well. We won't finalize anything tonight. We'll agree with enough to keep the union of our families on the table, but with no time set for a final decision." He grinned at Septimus. "Watch and learn how we do that. You'll need to know yourself before long."

Manius moved his next piece. He was halfway to victory in the game Septimus wanted him to play tonight. "I'll send for her when we're about to start eating so she won't have to converse with either Glabrio too much."

Father's eyebrows lowered. "But she will have to talk with them at dinner, and she'll need to make a good impression."

Septimus made the winning move and leaned back in his chair. "She will, and if they listen, they'll see she's worth hearing, even with the stutter. She and I can share the third couch, so she'll be more relaxed. That will help." He chuckled. "Young Glabrio's been working with Titus for a while now. He should be used to someone he respects not talking much."

Father scooped Manius's remaining pieces off the board and into a pile, ready for the next game. "Sometimes, the less a person says, the easier it is to respect them."

Manius joined Septimus in a hearty chuckle. He couldn't agree with his father more.

Manius was playing tabula with his father when Gaius Glabrio was escorted into the room. Like Titus, he came in armor and carried a satchel.

"I see Titus has taught you the value of taking notes."

Glabrio's hand rested on the satchel. "He carries two or three tablets, but I haven't seen him use more than one."

"Have you looked inside one?" Septimus raised one eyebrow. "He uses a secret shorthand he invented himself. You might want to carry double what you've seen him use."

Father placed his game piece before his gaze swept Glabrio from helmet to sandal and back. "So, you've been working with Titus for a week. I told you to listen closely to what he tells you. What have you learned that you didn't know before?"

Glabrio's eyebrows rose, then dipped, and Manius fought to keep his mouth straight. The young tribune hadn't expected an interrogation.

Father's eyes lit like a cat playing with a mouse. "Start with something practical if that's easier."

Glabrio squared his shoulders, like a boy reciting for his tutor. "Silence is a powerful way to get people to tell you something."

"Watch how Titus uses silence. He's a master. Go on."

The young tribune smiled as if Father had commended him, but his father's cool eyes said otherwise.

"Give slaves and noncitizens a chance to tell you the truth because they want to. Using the torturer is worse than useless because anyone will lie to end the pain. Partial information is best kept to yourself until you know enough to act wisely."

Manius placed his game piece and crossed his arms. "Even if the one wanting that information is your commander?"

"Maybe. Saturninus hates that, but Titianus often does it."

Father made his next move. "What's he taught you of a more…philosophical nature?"

One corner of Glabrio's mouth lifted. "That's a much longer list, but it might prove more useful over time. The general way of looking at things can lead you astray. Rank, wealth, and family position don't define your worth as a man. Honor is what matters most. You might find it where you least expect, and it might be lacking in men you thought had it."

"That sounds like my nephew. Go on, if there's more."

Glabrio still wore his helmet, so he rubbed under his chin. "Only some men's opinions matter, and never let theirs affect your opinion of yourself. The genuine respect of those who serve you is valuable, and their loyalty can give you success where there might have been failure. The slaves of a household often know things their master won't tell you. If he hasn't earned their loyalty, it's easy to learn what he doesn't want known."

"Hmph." Father eyed Glabrio. "So, is your opinion one he thinks matters?"

"I hope so. If not now, I hope to change his mind. His respect is worth earning."

Father tightened his lips. "I suppose it is." His social smile returned. "Is that all?"

"Not quite. Those who have accomplished the most don't feel a need to make others feel small to make themselves feel important. What passes for friendship often isn't. The friend of your father isn't necessarily your friend."

"I never realized my nephew was such a philosopher." Father reached across his chest and massaged his neck. "That's quite a lot for one week. Anything else?"

"A warning. Truth and justice matter, but pursuing them can make you enemies in both low and high places. The commander of a legion, even one at war, might find his greatest enemy wears Roman armor."

Father's chuckle sounded genuine, but Manius couldn't always tell.

"Titus should know about making enemies." Father set down the polished stones he'd been holding. "He's sent enough people into the arena for what they've done, and he's made powerful people lose wealth they had no right to have anyway. He got his wife because of it, but he was almost killed by an assassin."

Glabrio's head drew back.

"He didn't tell you that's why he married his old teacher's daughter?" Father's face faked surprise, but Manius saw the laughter in his father's eyes.

"No. He mentioned the attack, but not what happened later."

"He was riding back to the fortress after dining here. Some thugs jumped him." Manius leaned on the game table. "He was in full armor, but that doesn't help much when there are three of them. Septimus got there just in time to stop them killing him. We kept him here while he recovered."

"Did he catch the one who hired them?"

"He didn't have to." Father placed his next game piece. "I took care of the problem while he was recovering. He is, after all, my nephew. Even if he doesn't think that matters, I do."

"It might be a while before your father arrives." Manius pointed at the second game table. "I want to finish this game with Father. Shed your armor, and you two can play a while."

Septimus pulled out a chair for Glabrio before settling into his own. Glabrio, after hesitating as if he wanted more conversation with two powerful men, left his armor in the corner and joined Septimus.

Manius's mouth twitched as he subdued a grin. Young Glabrio didn't realize he'd just done him a big favor. Titus's protégé didn't yet know how risky a conversation with his father could be if you tried too hard to impress him and failed.

The tabula games were only half over when the elder Glabrio was shown into the triclinium. Manius rose as Glabrio stepped into the room. Showing proper respect to an ex-consul was always a good first move toward getting what he wanted.

"Welcome to my home. This is the first time I've had the pleasure of you joining us, but I hope to have it often repeated." He stepped away from the table. With a sweep of his hand, Father invited Glabrio to sit.

Glabrio settled into the vacated chair. "It's a pleasure to join you so soon after the banquet to discuss the joining of our families."

"It's always a pleasure to be in company together, no matter what the reason." Father rolled a game piece between his fingers. "I'm glad you mentioned your interest in Sabina. It's never too early to begin thinking about the future." He returned the black stone to the pile. "But it's somewhat premature to be deciding it."

Glabrio's eyebrows lowered.

Father offered his friendliest smile. "It would be a fine thing for two families such as ours to consider at the right time. Gaius here"—his hand swept toward the tribune—"is an admirable young man whom I would be pleased to assist in his career."

He rubbed his chin as his eyebrows also lowered. "But it hasn't even been two weeks since Sabina became a widow. It would spawn unwelcome gossip about her regard for the memory of her husband if we act too quickly. It would also suggest an insensitivity to the great loss his father has suffered if we were to commit to a second marriage less than two weeks after young Gallus died. A month or two at least and perhaps as much as six would be more appropriate before anything is arranged."

Gaius Glabrio straightened in his chair at the other game table. "Isn't it already more than a month since her husband died? I heard the message was delayed because it was sent in the ordinary military dispatch to his father, and Gallus didn't bother to forward it to his wife for several days."

The elder Glabrio's mouth twitched, but his son wasn't looking at him to read that signal to be silent while the older men talked.

Father's laugh sounded amused, but his eyes suggested he wasn't. "While that might be true, some truths should be left unsaid. We all might think that odd, but grief makes people do strange things. Most of us know better than to put such thoughts into words where others can hear."

The young man flushed three shades of red. "I beg your pardon. I should have made allowance for the effects of grief over the loss of a son and husband. I meant no disrespect to the Gallus family or your granddaughter."

"Quintus knows that wasn't your intent, Gaius." Glabrio punctuated a cautioning glance toward his son with a slight shrug toward Father. "We men of experience make allowances for the impetuousness of the young, especially when matters of the heart might be involved. Gaius has seen enough of your granddaughter to be impressed already. It's only natural for a young man to be eager in these matters." His mouth curved into a political smile. "We remember what it was like to be young, don't we, Quintus?"

Manius moved to the edge of the table where the two lions of Rome sat. "I believe Titus has been impressed by the potential of your son." He picked up the goblet he'd been using while they played and raised it toward

Gaius. As the young man's focus bounced between him and Father, Manius chuckled. "It takes some skill to know what my cousin really thinks, but the signs are there for those who can read them. He's fond of saying that rank, wealth, and family position don't define a man's worth. Honor is what matters most. I think he sees it in you."

Glabrio senior leaned back in the chair. "Honor does define a man, but we all know that family connections are important."

Quintus picked up two game pieces and tumbled them against each other in his hand. "They are, and in a few months, when a suitable period of mourning has passed for Sabina, perhaps we'll do something about that." Raised eyebrows accompanied Father's nod before his fake friendly smile reappeared. "You and I both know we don't have to be related to someone at the moment to begin furthering his career."

Glabrio senior rose and walked to his son's table. "As you say, the conventions of mourning should be observed, and then we'll discuss the future." Glabrio rested his hand on his son's shoulder. "We'll be looking forward to that."

Manius turned to the wine steward. "Send someone to tell Sabina and the kitchen we're ready to dine." He gestured toward the couches. "Shall we?"

An ex-consul needed no guidance on which couch to take. He settled onto the center couch in the place of highest honor, and Gaius reclined beside him.

Manius caught Septimus's eye before joining Father to take the second-place position on the host couch, and the smile his son returned radiated appreciation of this first step toward freeing Sabina to make her own choice of the man she would wed.

Chapter 34

Taking Care of Danger?

Filomena paced the floor in Sabina's bedchamber. What had been decided between the two *patres familias* of the Sabinus and Glabrio families? Had the two patriarchs set a date for Sabina to marry young Glabrio? Would that marriage agreement mean the end of visits with Lenaeus before he led Sabina into danger?

"That was interesting and very strange."

She startled at Mistress Sabina's voice behind her.

Sabina sat on the bed, flopped onto her back, and spread her arms. "I was certain Grandfather would introduce me to my future father-in-law, but not a single word was uttered about me marrying Glabrio."

"No talk of a marriage at all?"

"Not unless they were speaking in a secret code known only to a paterfamilias who gets to control everyone's lives."

"Does that seem likely?"

"No. I'm only joking. Grandfather and Glabrio's father talked to each other and Father about things that have nothing to do with me."

She sat up and kicked a beaded sandal off. "It was mostly about who was serving where right now and what was going on in the Eastern Empire and across the frontier. I never knew Grandfather kept track of so many people, and Father knew almost as many. But I never dined with Grandfather's senator friends before, so maybe they all know everyone."

The second sandal followed the first. "Actually, Grandfather didn't say anything about what each person was like. Only where they were serving.

But from what Septimus has said, he likes to learn secrets about people, and secrets aren't much use if you don't limit who else knows them. Glabrio's father wasn't as cautious, but nothing he said was mean-spirited."

She slid the filigree gold bracelet off her arm and laid it on the pillow. "Remember how Asinia used to complain about missing out on all the gossip because her husband hadn't let her stay at the town house in Rome? I bet she was a vicious cat who loved to spread the cruelest gossip, true or not. One thing I love about Pompeia is she never says anything mean about anyone."

Filomena managed a subdued smile, but what the mistress loved about Pompeia shouldn't matter soon. "What about Tribune Glabrio?"

"He and Septimus talked about training at the ludus…which trainers they'd had, which ones they thought best. I found it terribly boring compared to what Septimus and Kaeso talk about. Glabrio likes the games. He bragged on his father getting the best seats down close."

She shuddered. "It reminded me too much of that husband of mine and his bloodthirsty friends. Glabrio was surprised that Septimus goes so seldom, but I'm glad he doesn't." She wrinkled her nose. "I don't know why anyone would want to watch men killing each other for no good reason. Kaeso never goes."

"But your father and grandfather like the games, too. Don't they always sit down by the sand?"

"They do, but I'll never understand why."

Sabina went to the dressing table, and Filomena followed.

One by one, she pulled the jeweled hair picks out, and Sabina's braids cascaded down. "The tribune must have talked about something else. Did you get to know him better?"

Sabina rolled a hair pick between her fingers. "He said he'd moved into the tribune quarters where Titus used to live. He took a chef with him because the food was so bad, and he took part of their library. He said he likes poetry."

"He does?" Filomena began unwinding the many braids. "Did Master Septimus tell him how wonderfully you write and sing?"

"No, he didn't, and I could have hugged him for that. I'm sure Grandfather would have made me perform for them all if he had. There's not much else about me he can praise to his senator friends."

"Master Septimus would scold you if he heard you say that."

"He would." Sabina picked up the hand mirror. "So would Kaeso.

They both call me Skylark, and they listen to me…really listen." She set the mirror down. "But, I must admit, it surprised me that Glabrio did as well. I avoided talking as much as I could, but when I had to, he really looked at me and listened like he wanted to hear my thoughts. I don't think he was pretending."

"Then he's nothing like your dead husband. Glabrio sounds like a good man, like your brother."

"Yes, I suppose he is. But since nothing was said, I don't have to worry about that tonight."

"Was that all they talked about?" The last braid was unwound, and Filomena ran a comb through the free-flowing tresses.

"No. Glabrio suggested he and Septimus should go to the Circus together this week. Septimus said he'd already arranged to go with Kaeso but only to the afternoon races after he finished teaching for the day. But if Titus was willing to let Glabrio off duty, he could join them."

Sabina set the hair pick down. "He didn't seem eager to do that until he asked if I was going, too. As soon as I said I might, he switched to saying he'd love to go with us. He'll talk with Titus and see."

Filomena suppressed a smile. Many thought the races a romantic way to spend time together. "What did Master Manius say about that?"

"Nothing." Sabina stood. "You can go now. I want to write for a while, and it will go better if I'm alone tonight. I'll see you in the morning."

"Good night, mistress."

When Filomena stepped onto the balcony, Sabina closed the door behind her. The bolt slid over, and Filomena's eyebrows plunged.

Master Manius said he'd take care of the problem, but Mistress Sabina was behind that locked door reading the Christian codex the teacher had given her. The master hadn't said anything, or else Mistress Sabina was defying him.

Laughter came from the circle of wicker chairs where the five men had gathered by the peristyle fountain for a final drink and conversation. The master still had guests, so maybe it was only because there were others in the house tonight. Maybe he'd take care of the danger Lenaeus posed tomorrow.

The Ludus Bruti, morning of Day 10

Titianus sat at the desk in Brutus's office with Turbo's list in front of him and an open blank tablet beside it. Two lists actually: one with public appearances for the next three weeks and another with private gatherings for the next two. The ones where the prefect expected Marcellus to attend were marked with an M.

All the public and some of the private affairs were marked with a T. Turbo planned to be at those. The prefect would have his own most trusted guards with him. Any assassin who wanted to live beyond thrusting his blade into his target would be a fool to try anything when Turbo was there.

But some of the private gatherings were marked with an S for Saturninus. At the top of the private list, Turbo had written that Titianus knew about those already. But why would Turbo think that? Or did he write it knowing full well it wasn't true?

First was a dinner at the palace with Turbo present. Hadrian's German guards and Turbo's Praetorians would be there, so he could rule that one out.

Second on the list was a dinner at the Sabinus villa closest to Rome. Neither S nor T appeared beside it, but Hadrian was probably safer there than in his own palace. Quintus was the emperor's personal friend, and his uncle knew enough about anyone else he would invite to know if they might want to kill Hadrian.

Quintus Sabinus's network of spies was as good as the emperor's own. If they caught wind of something, they would tell Quintus's spymaster Festinus. If he put the most trusted ones watching the suspects, would his uncle learn something to pass on to him?

He drummed on the frame of the blank tablet with the brass stylus Brutus had left behind. If only Brutus were still in Rome. The equestrian whose gladiators had trained him and more than half the senatorial sons could have steered him toward the most likely suspects or ruled some out. Brutus would have kept their conversation secret as well.

Would it endanger the innocent to ask Quintus whom he thought wished Hadrian harm? Wishing and acting were worlds apart, but sometimes the thought was punished the same as the deed.

He rubbed both sides of his nose.

In three days, he had to report something to Turbo. But what that could be when he still knew nothing…

God, please guide me to the truth before innocents get hurt.

He heaved a sigh and read on.

Hadrian was hosting other dinners at his palace on the Palatine Hill. Both Turbo and Saturninus would be present at those. In between, Saturninus was entertaining Hadrian, but Turbo was invited as well. No M by that entry, and Turbo and his Praetorians would be watching anyway.

His head drew back at the next entry: a banquet in six days at the younger Marcellus's villa. An S but no T labeled that one. Was Turbo really not attending, or did the prefect not want him to know ahead of time whether he was?

With his elbow resting on the desktop, he covered his mouth with his palm and rubbed his face. Saturninus might play that trick on him, but suspecting Turbo was probably paranoid.

"Guest lists not known" followed the Marcellus banquet. Only a list of hosts, and he had no personal knowledge of most of them.

But Quintus and Manius would. Manius he would trust with most things, except his family being Christian. Quintus...could he trust his uncle to keep secret what he asked when the safety of the emperor Quintus called friend was in the balance?

A pattern of knocks on the bolted door announced the arrival of his own spy. Since Turbo drafted Titianus to hunt assassins, Melis had been riding his mule up from the warehouse and waiting to see whether he was needed that day.

Titianus slid back the bolt, and the youth entered.

"Stabularius said you were here already. I beg pardon if I made you wait, master. I ran an errand for Probus, and it took longer than he expected."

"He's probably not happy that I've been needing you every day for the last week, and there's no end in sight."

"I rise early to get a few things done before I leave, and there's time when I get home to help with some of the rest that's hard for him to do."

Titianus tousled Melis's hair. "I'm glad you lighten his burden for me. Since before I was born, he's taken good care of business for both my father and me. I expect you'll do the same for me and my sons."

Melis's eyebrows popped up, and a grin split his face. Titianus laughed. "We're not expecting a child yet. You'll be among the first I tell when we are."

Titianus pointed at the guest chair, and Melis sat, still grinning.

"Stabularius is brushing your stallion. He takes good care of us."

"Glabrio has taken over my fortress office, so Saturninus had Victorinus asking my optios if I was working out of their stations. He'll never discover that Felix is letting me use this office to keep what I learn secret, and Glabrio thinks I only leave my horse here." Titianus pointed at the strongbox. "Felix put an extra lock on that, and I have the only key. There couldn't be a more secure place than a ludus with gladiators challenging anyone who tries to enter."

He closed Turbo's tablet and put it in the strongbox with the notes he'd made of his and Melis's observations. The lid closed with a satisfying thud, and he dropped the hasp over the iron loop before securing it with his lock. A good tug to ensure it was latched, and he straightened. He draped the key chain around his neck and slipped the key inside the cuirass.

"Salutations should mostly be over. Let's go see if you can overhear what no one wants me to know."

"Mostly the same three men?"

"Yes, and anyone they talk with too quietly." He tapped Melis's chest with his finger. "And for Probus's sake, don't forget these are dangerous men."

As Titianus headed for the Forums to look for Marcellus, Rufinus, and his commander, he looked down at the still-scrawny youth at his side. Probus wasn't the only one who would grieve if something happened to his talented spy.

Chapter 35

What He Believes

The Praetorian Fortress, early morning of Day 10

Yet again, Glabrio had dropped off his daily written report of Titianus's activities with Saturninus's optio. Plancus had found out the earliest the prefect ever arrived, and living in tribune quarters made it easy to fulfill his duty without speaking to the man who got more irritated each time he failed to find out what Turbo had Titianus doing.

Saturninus had complained that his oral reports had all been the same. With good reason—whatever Titianus was up to, he kept it well concealed.

But with a little creative effort, he made each written one different. One day they walked through the Forums and found some history lecture that had many senators watching it. Titianus counted them and wrote down their names. The next day he commended one of his patrols for catching a thief in the act. Another day he rode through the warehouse district and talked with the *vigiles* centurion about a night fire that was arson.

They often visited the Baths for more introductions to men from consular families and senators who wielded a lot of power. If Saturninus was there and saw them, he'd mention the men they were talking with at that time. Maybe there was something hidden in this. Titianus said when they started that the introductions were for getting more students in his brother-in-law's school, but he never mentioned the school to any of them. However, that inconsistency was something Glabrio kept to himself.

If there was something unusual but obviously irrelevant to whatever Turbo wanted, he'd end the report with that.

The optio never said Saturninus wanted more than he was doing. As long as he dropped off a new tablet, he was reporting as ordered without betraying the man who was sharing both practical advice for doing his job and surprisingly accurate observations of how Roman society worked and what was wrong with it.

He would be sorry when Titianus retired. Who would have thought he'd enjoy the company of the tribune Saturninus had called not quite human?

Yesterday, Titianus had mentioned the many evenings he'd enjoyed playing boardgames with the Praetorian tribune who also lived in quarters. Glabrio had begun spending entire evenings at the fortress if Father was dining out. Tabula with Martialis would provide some diversion.

When he reached Martialis's office, no one was there. As he walked away, a voice came from behind him.

"Glabrio." Martialis and his optio strode toward him. "Did you need something?"

"I was just looking for you."

"We were at camp worship. Now that you're living in the fortress, it's good to make an appearance there."

"Does Titianus go?"

"He did before his time at Sabinus's house. When he came back here for a few weeks while the workmen were knocking out some walls to make classrooms at his town house, he didn't."

"He said you and he used to play tabula most evenings. When I'm not eating somewhere else, would you care to join me for dinner and games? I brought a chef from home, so I can promise a respectable meal."

"I'd like that, but we played latrunculi more. It kept our strategic thinking sharpened."

No surprise there, but if anyone didn't need his sharpened, it was Titianus.

"I like that better, too. When Titianus finally retires, my evenings will be entirely my own. I dine some with my father, but I'll mostly be here."

"I'll look forward to it." Martialis followed his optio into his office, and the door closed.

As Glabrio headed back to his own office, he fingered his lip. Had something happened at the Sabinus house that made Titianus stop going to the mandatory worship of the state gods? Mandatory for the soldiers. Saturninus told him it wasn't mandatory for his officers, but Titianus often did unnecessary things to show respect for his men. Joining their worship would fit that pattern. But why the sudden change?

Now that he thought about it, he'd never heard Titianus mention any of the gods whose names popped up in everyday speech. Fortuna never smiled when Titianus spoke, and he never uttered "by Jupiter and Mars."

When they'd stopped for Titianus's toga, he'd waited in the peristyle with Titianus's wife and her brother. He hadn't noticed an altar for the household gods, but it was probably in the atrium, like at his father's house. But what was on it?

What was it about a stay at Sabinus's house that stopped him going to fortress worship? If he got his wife because he recovered from the attack there, was she responsible for the change?

And if she had been, was her brother part of the reason as well?

The Titianus town house, afternoon of Day 10

Kaeso was in his classroom, putting away the scrolls he'd used that day when he heard Theo greeting Tutelus.

At last! He'd been praying for Sabina since she left with the codex yesterday. Prayers for God to enlighten her mind and open her heart to hear Him calling her.

"Go on to the peristyle. I want to speak with him alone." Sabina spoke so softly. Was he not supposed to hear?

"Would your father think it's proper? Or Glabrio?" Filomena's voice was just as quiet.

"Father trusts us both completely, and rightly so. What Glabrio thinks doesn't matter."

"But your grandfather—"

"He hasn't committed me to that marriage yet. I'll do what I think best until then."

Yet. Kaeso cringed at that word. As Septimus had feared, Sabina would seal another political alliance. What good was wealth and privilege when she lost the right to follow her heart? Would their still-healing skylark lose the joy she'd recovered when she was forced back into a cage?

His lips tightened, then relaxed. Maybe it wouldn't be so bad this time. At least Glabrio seemed like a decent man. But what would he think if she decided to follow Jesus? Domitian had executed his grandfather for making that choice. Would the grandson be an understanding husband if his wife did the same?

"Kaeso?" He turned to find serious eyes and no smile. The satchel hung from her shoulder. She'd guarded Father's codex carefully, just as she'd promised.

"I'm returning your codex."

His shoulders sagged. She'd seemed so eager to see what was in it after reading Publius's letter. "Did you finish it?"

"Yes, b-but there are so many things in it I don't understand, and others that…frighten me if they're true. But there's also something about it that makes me want more, much more."

She pointed toward the balcony and the chamber where they talked before. "Can we go up there again and talk about it? I have so many questions."

It was hard not to grin. God was calling, and she was starting to hear. But woman-to-woman might be better than asking a man. Especially a man who found her attractive.

"Pompeia is in the weaving room. I'm sure she'd love to answer them. I'll get her."

He started toward the door, but she moved into his path.

"Please don't. I w-want you first, and if I'm still confused, then Pompeia can join us." She licked her lips. "I feel in here"—she tapped her chest—"that this might be the most important thing I ever do."

"It is."

Her eyes widened, and he almost reached for her hand to reassure her.

"But you'll soon see there's nothing to fear."

"You don't know my questions."

"I've probably asked them myself and found an answer to many."

She started up the stairs ahead of him. When they reached the balcony, she drew a deep breath and stepped into the room. He got the chair from the next room and closed and bolted the door. She'd already turned the chair by the desk to face him, and he placed his chair in front of her.

"Ask your questions. Anything you want. I'll try to answer them all."

She twisted her gold bracelet as she stared at the floor. Then she raised her eyes to his.

"I d-didn't expect it would begin like the histories Father loves. He has so many of them by people I've never heard of. He told Septimus at breakfast about a new one he likes because the writer gives the names of the local governors to show when things happened. He said that made what the man wrote more believable. Augustus ordering a census, then Jesus starting to travel and teach in the fifteenth year of Tiberius with Pontius Pilatus as governor. Three tetrarchs, even some high priests named—Luke did everything Father expects from a good historian."

"I agree. I like that attention to detail as well. It says the writer does his best to be accurate. Father always looked for that before adding something new to our school library."

"But then there are things that don't seem like history. Things that don't happen to real people."

The bracelet twisting stopped when she looked at his eyes. Then she refocused on the bracelet, and the twisting resumed.

"For example?"

"Jesus b-bringing dead people back to life. Him being born to a virgin. That doesn't happen. Even in the stories about how demigods came to be, the Greek gods lie with a woman, so even if she was a virgin, she's not when the baby is born." She offered a sheepish smile. "But Father and Septimus say those are only stories. I know they're right, so I guess the comparison is rather silly."

"But it's still a good question. Every baby we've ever seen came from a man lying with a woman. Even with an angel appearing out of nowhere and telling her she'd bear God's Son, Mary questioned whether it could happen. It was strange. Impossible, actually. But since God made everything that we see around us, He can easily make a baby some special way. I don't understand exactly what God did, but that's because my mind has its limits."

"I hadn't thought of it like that." She rubbed her palm with her thumb. "I guess that's true for all the healings. Even the boy he raised from the dead and the local ruler's daughter." She smiled at him. "You just answered a lot of my questions."

The smile faded. "But the things that frighten me…it's some of the things Jesus said we have to do." She took the codex out of the satchel and placed it on her lap. With her fingertip, she traced the fish.

"Let's go to that part, and we can work our way through it."

She thumbed through several sheets and finally pointed at the letters halfway down the sheet. "There's a long part here where Jesus is teaching a large group of people who came from all over that area. He's telling them how they must live. Some of that…I don't think I can do it."

"What do you think you can't do?"

"Love my enemies. Forgive the people who've deliberately hurt me." With eyes lowered, she gripped the codex. "Septimus said someone murdered your father. That's how Titus met you and Pompeia...when he was looking for the murderer."

When she raised her head, her eyes glistened. "Finding my father dead like Pompeia did...I can't imagine anything more horrible. Surely your god doesn't demand that you forgive the one who did that."

"Did you get to the part where Jesus was crucified?"

"Yes." She wiped the corner of her eye. "I've never seen a crucifixion. I don't even want to think about how horrible those are. I skipped over most of it."

"Remember how Publius wrote that God said blood sacrifice is the only thing that covers sin so we can approach Him?"

She nodded.

"That crucifixion was the sacrifice that paid for the sins of all people for all time. For my sins because I know what Jesus did there." He tapped his chest before pointing at her. "And for yours if you decide you'll let it. God gives each of us that choice, and I hope you'll choose what I did."

He took the codex from her lap and flipped to a page near the back. "You'll want to go back and read that part carefully, no matter how hard it is. Jesus said something at the beginning of it that helps me understand love and forgiveness."

With his finger pointing at the vital words, he handed it back to her. "Read to me what Jesus said while the soldiers were nailing Him to the cross."

"'Jesus said, "F-father, forgive them, for they do not know what they are doing."'" One hand flew to her mouth. "How could he say that when they were the ones killing him?"

"Because God loves us. Agape love, not affection like we usually have for one another. Those words show the depth of Jesus's love for us, even for those soldiers for whom that was just one more day with three more executions."

He leaned forward to trace the words. "The centurion and the troop on the hill that day...they were Roman soldiers who thought they were executing two criminals and an enemy of Rome. They had no idea what they were really doing, that God had planned it from the beginning, but they still needed forgiveness for that and for everything else they'd done that separated them from God. They didn't know they were fulfilling God's promise to provide the perfect sacrifice to break down the barriers we built ourselves."

"I've always thought love was the deepest and noblest kind of affection."

"Some kinds of love are, but did you notice the Greek word Jesus uses for love is 'agape?' What He means by love isn't simply affection for someone, like how I love Pompeia and Septimus as my sister and friend and how she loves Titus."

He wouldn't say it aloud, but what he felt for Sabina was already closer to the second kind of love than the first, even though he never intended that to happen and nothing would ever come of it.

She fingered her lip. "Agape is not the word I use for love when I write in Greek."

"Because it's not like the other kinds of love. It doesn't mean the way we feel about someone. It's more about how we treat them. It's where we want what's best for them, even when they want to hurt us. Even when they've actually done it."

"How do you ever love that way?"

"On my own, I couldn't, but once I become a child of God by believing in Jesus and what He did, He makes it possible." He almost touched her hand where it lay on the codex, but he pointed at the words instead.

"Forgiving...that's a big part of loving like Jesus tells us."

She turned back to the first page she'd shown him. "This part here right after 'Love your enemies.' I suppose it's a list of things I should do."

Kaeso took the codex and read where she was pointing. "'Love your enemies, do good to those who hate you, bless those who curse you, pray for those who mistreat you. To one who strikes you on the cheek, offer the other also, and from one who takes away your cloak, do not withhold your tunic either.'" He handed it back. "Those are part of it."

"They never hit me, but all the other things he says you have to forgive—those are what Asinia and my husband did to me...for six years. I never said or did anything to hurt either of them, but I hated them for it." She nibbled her lip "Maybe I still do, at least some. But I feel sorry for her, too. She did love her son. She thought I wasn't good enough for him, and maybe that's part of why she was so mean."

Her eyes narrowed. "But don't you hate the man who killed your father?"

"I can't say I haven't struggled with that, because when it first happened, I did. But I asked God to help me forgive, not because I wanted to, but because I knew He wanted me to. And He has. The man who murdered Father was murdered himself, so I'll never know if it was his own idea or whether he did it for someone else. I've worked on forgiving that person, too, just in case."

"Worked on forgiving?"

"For something that painful, it's not something I can do once and be done with it. Sometimes something happens that stirs up the old feelings of anger, and I find I haven't completely forgiven the one who made me angry. But each time that happens, God helps me forgive again. It's His Spirit living inside me, like Publius described, that helps me do it."

She leaned forward, lips straight, eyes focused on him, and his heart rate ramped up. He'd never had someone to share his faith with like this, and God was reaching her with his words.

Holy Spirit, keep showing me what she needs to hear to want more.

"How did your god's spirit get inside you?"

"I was only six when I decided I believed in Jesus, so for you it will be more like what Father and Pompeia did. You confess your sins, which are all the things you've thought and done that built a barrier between you and God, and you ask God to forgive you. When you believe Jesus's death on that cross was the sacrifice that paid for those sins, you become a child of God, and God's Spirit lives in you."

Her brow furrowed. "I don't understand what you mean."

"I'm not sure how to put into words what that feels like, and I haven't yet told you all you'll need to understand." He tapped the codex. "But you've already started doing what Jesus said we should do."

"I have?"

He took the codex from her lap once more and turned to a place near the middle. "'And I tell you, ask, and it will be given to you; seek, and you will find; knock, and it will be opened to you. For everyone who asks receives, and the one who seeks finds, and to the one who knocks it will be opened.'"

He handed it back to her, and as she took it from him, he took her other hand. "Nothing matters more than truth, and Jesus said He is the way, the truth, and the life. If you decide to follow Him..." He closed his eyes and in the warmth of God's presence, he felt God's pleasure with what they'd just done.

His eyes opened. "I'm no poet, but even if I were, I'd never find the right words to describe the joy and peace that will bring."

Her eyes glistened with the start of tears, but the quiver of her lips steadied into her brightest smile.

"May I keep your father's codex á while longer?" Her finger traced the fish. "I want to read it again a little at a time and then ask you questions. A few each day instead of all at once."

"There is nothing that would give me more pleasure. Luke wrote a lot about what Jesus did and some about what He taught. But John was the disciple who was closest to Jesus, and he wrote down what Jesus taught His most committed followers in private. It's almost like sitting with Jesus and hearing His words yourself. We can look at that, too."

"I'd like that."

"Then we'll do it. Pompeia can join us or not, as you wish. But I know she'll be as happy as I am that you want to learn about our Lord. Tomorrow we'll start."

"You know so much, and I want to learn all you know." She steepled her fingers and pressed them against her lips. "And when you've explained it all...maybe it will be time for me to follow Jesus like you do."

He lacked the skill of the impassive Tribune Titianus for concealing emotion, but even Titus would have failed at hiding the delight her words inspired. There would be many more conversations, and God knew where they would end.

But Kaeso didn't have to see Filomena to know she was fretting downstairs. They'd been behind a closed door long enough today, so he stood.

"I know some, but I'm still learning, too. What I do know is God loves me enough to pay for my sins Himself so I can be with Him, like Publius explained in his letter. When you decide to believe and follow Jesus, you'll feel that love surround you, just as it does me."

Sabina clutched the codex to her chest and beamed as she stood. While she tucked it back into her satchel, he moved his chair against the wall. There was no point in hauling it back and forth between the rooms when they'd be using it in here every day.

As he unbolted and opened the door, he tried to keep his smile from becoming a sappy grin. Filomena would misinterpret that for certain.

Pompeia would be delighted if her dearest friend became their Christian sister, and there was one thing that could make it even better. After she did, would Septimus finally let him explain why he should join the children of God as well?

Chapter 36

The Only Good Choice

The Sabinus town house, evening of Day 10

Manius sat at his library desk, drumming on it with a stylus. The messenger he sent that morning to tell Titus his family was dining here had returned after finding him alone in the Forums. Titus knew he wanted to speak privately before they ate, but it was past time for his cousin to appear.

Or not. He should be used to Titus's frequent delays when he was working. But he'd never had anything this important to ask him before.

The click of hobnails on marble announced Titus's arrival before he appeared in the doorway.

"You said we needed to talk." He lifted the helmet from his head and tucked it under his arm. "Is anything wrong?"

"Maybe. Close the door and bolt it."

Titus's eyebrows rose, but he didn't ask why. Manius pointed at the guest chair.

His cousin set his helmet on the floor beside it and sat. "How can I help?"

Manius rubbed his mouth. This man was so different from the other men he spent time with. With most, he'd have to phrase a hard question just right before asking it, and he still might not get a truthful answer. With Titus, blunt and to the point was best, and the answer would be either truth or silence.

"Last night, I learned Kaeso has given Sabina a codex of Christian writ-

235

ings. I asked Septimus if that meant his friend was a Christian. He said yes. When I pressed him, he said you and Pompeia were as well."

Titus's emotionless tribune mask appeared. "That's true."

"When I asked about whether Sabina was, he didn't know, but he said she admired Kaeso and would take anything he told her seriously."

Titus nodded and remained silent.

"Sabina might be easy to influence, but you're no ill-treated young woman falling in love with a man who's kind and smart and treats you like you're truly special. Kaeso could easily persuade Sabina to believe some superstition, but you'd be as hard to convince that something false was true as any man I know."

Titus leaned back in the chair, and the trace of a smile curved his lips.

"So, before I talk with her about it, I need some answers from you."

"Ask your questions. I'll try to provide them."

"When did you become one?"

"When I was here waiting for my balance and vision to return to normal."

"Why would you even consider doing that?"

"Septimus brought me here with a broken skull. I was near death when Pompeia and Kaeso asked their God to heal me. I never believed in any gods, but I would have been a stubborn fool not to consider whether a god who could keep me from dying might be the one God with real power."

He leaned forward, crossed his arms, and rested them on the desk. "I had a lot of questions. Pompeia answered some of them and gave me a codex like Sabina has when I wanted to know more. Then what I felt here"—he tapped his chest—"I understood here." He touched his head. "God is nothing like the characters in the stories of the Roman gods. He's real."

Titianus's steel gray eyes bored into Manius. Without a doubt, his cousin believed what he was saying.

"Do you think Sabina will become one?"

"Maybe. If she really thinks about, I expect she will. Once you see the truth, it's hard to resist."

"Truth?" Manius rolled his eyes. "I know you think honor and truth should decide everything, but clinging to them can get you killed. She'd be in mortal danger." His palm covered his mouth, then fell away. "How is she going to do all that's required of the wife of a leader of Rome? So much of it involves publicly worshipping the state gods."

"I don't think she can, but there is a way to protect her."

"What could that be?" Palms up, Manius held out both hands and shrugged.

"Let her marry Kaeso. She can live in my household in safety and find happiness with a man who will love her as much as I love Pompeia."

Manius snorted. "Even if I wanted to, that's not mine to decide."

One corner of Titus's mouth lifted. "No one understands what motivates Quintus Sabinus better than you. If I were a betting man, I'd bet you can get him to approve their marriage."

Manius shook his head. "You and Septimus give me more credit than I deserve. No one controls what Father does except my father."

"I think Quintus's love for his son could make him choose the best for his granddaughter."

When Titus chuckled, Manius's head drew back.

"And he's never had to make a decision when so many children of God are praying for him to choose what's best." Titus's half-smile turned into a full one. "If God can stop me dying, He can open your father's eyes to see the right thing to do."

Manius stared at his cousin. There was a strange logic to that argument. The worst thing that could happen was Father would refuse to listen to reason. But was Titus's suggestion the best thing?

"I can offer no guarantees, but I'll try."

"That's all God asks of any of us." His cousin's smile faded. "But it could put us all in danger if you reveal our faith."

"He won't commit her to any marriage without discussing it with me first. I'll watch for the right time to propose that he let her choose her husband. I'll think of some reason that will sway him."

"I'll be praying for you…and her." Straight lips and serious eyes confirmed that promise.

"I guess that can't hurt."

"Nothing could help more."

An ironic smile was Manius's only response. His cousin truly believed that. The gods Manius knew about didn't listen to a man's prayer. But Titus wasn't easily fooled. If he thought he was still alive because of a prayer to his god, maybe he was.

"Dinner awaits us." Manius rose. "You were a little late, and I've made us even later. But if Father agrees, you and I will be talking more about your god."

Titus scooped up his helmet and grinned. "I'll look forward to it."

The Titianus town house, morning of Day 11

Pompeia was dozing when Titianus tucked the light blanket around her and slipped from their room. Kaeso would still be in his chamber, reading from one of the Gospels and praying.

He'd awakened before the first hint of gray lightened the night sky and prayed himself. Now that he had the answer to those prayers and the scattered clouds were awash with pink, Kaeso needed to know what he'd decided to do. Kaeso should know, but it would only worry Pompeia more when there was nothing she could do to help.

He tapped on Kaeso's door and opened it without waiting for an answer. His brother-in-law turned from his desk as Titianus closed the door.

"I wanted to talk to you before Pompeia gets up." Titianus ran his hand through his hair. "After much prayer, I've reached a decision." He sat on the bed, and Kaeso shifted the chair to face him.

"What is it?"

"Every day is one day closer to an attempt to kill Hadrian. Turbo is already angry at me because I won't tell him the names of the men I suspect at the moment. If I tell him and I'm wrong, he'll have already acted against them, maybe even killed them before I can find who's really involved. If they strike before I'm sure, Turbo will blame me because I didn't tell him. I'll be a dead man, and they could seize all my property. My will leaving everything to Pompeia and you won't be worth the papyrus it's written on, and you'll all be on the street."

Kaeso blew out a long breath between pursed lips. "So, what have you decided?"

"I'm going to lure them into the open before they move against Hadrian. I'll be the bait, and when they try to silence me, Glabrio and my men will be watching to stop them before they can kill me." He rubbed his palms on his thighs. "I'd like you to be praying more while I'm doing this. For wisdom in deciding what to do and for protection when I do it."

Kaeso set the codex on the desk and crossed his arms. "I can see why you don't want to tell Pompeia."

"She always prays for me when I go out each morning. That's already enough. I don't want to worry her more."

"So, you don't care if I'm more worried?" Kaeso's mouth smiled, but his eyes were serious.

Titus leaned forward and punched his arm. "That's what brothers-in-law and brothers-in-Christ are for. As long as you're praying, I don't have to worry as much."

He stood. "Join me for breakfast. I want to get to the ludus before Melis comes today. I need to make a list of names for him to memorize before we go to the Forums. He'll need to listen for anyone mentioning them as he pretends to wait for me."

Kaeso returned the codex to its drawer in his cabinet and locked it. He dropped the key chain over his head and pulled the door shut behind them.

As they started down the stairs, Titianus glanced at Kaeso and gave thanks once more for the blessing of both bride and brother that God had given him.

The Ludus Bruti, midday of Day 11

The sun was directly overhead when Titianus entered the ludus stableyard for the second time that day. Melis was half a block behind him. Normally, the youth would have walked the final blocks beside him, but he'd told his spy not to approach him until they were out of sight from anyone they had seen in the Forums and to walk on past if it looked like someone was following him.

The wrong person realizing they were together could put Melis at risk the next time Titianus left him spying.

When the youth walked past the gate, Titianus's heart rate ramped up. Who was trailing him?

His stallion was tied by a manger with a clear view of the gate, so he strode to the horse and acted like he was going to mount.

No one walked past.

"Master."

Titianus startled and spun to find the youth right behind him.

"I came around through the front, so if I missed seeing someone, they wouldn't see me follow you in here."

Titianus rested his hand on Melis's shoulder. "Good idea. Let's do that in the future." He tipped his head toward the entrance, and they headed to Brutus's office.

Once inside, Melis bolted the door and took his seat by the desk while Titianus got a wax tablet from the strongbox.

With stylus in hand, Titianus leaned on the desk. "So, we saw Saturninus and Rufinus in the Basilica before I moved on to make them think I was ignoring them. Did Marcellus join them?"

"No. But for a while, they joined five other senators who were arguing about the division of Italia into the new provinces. Three were angry that Hadrian, not the Senate, was going to appoint the prefects for them and give them power like the consuls of Rome. Then one got them gossiping about who the first set would be and how to get considered for future appointments. Rufinus and Saturninus looked at each other a lot and didn't say what they thought."

"Were any of them on the list I showed you this morning?"

"No."

"Did you recognize any of them."

"Yes."

Titianus pushed the tablet toward him. "Write them down. It might be important later."

Melis took the stylus he offered. "When the prefect and Rufinus left that group, they said something that might be important."

Titianus's raised eyebrows asked the question.

"They were talking about some special entertainment at Marcellus's villa that should delight many in the Senate, especially with all the turmoil over the new Italian provinces. They didn't say what. I would have heard more, but they went into one of the lecture rooms and took seats at the far side."

"Which talk?"

"Something about the wall being built in Britannia. I stayed outside to follow them again, but they came out separately and went different ways when the talk was over."

"Marcellus is giving a banquet in five days, and Hadrian will be there."

He squeezed the back of his neck and scrunched his eyes. If he was right about who, he'd just discovered where and when.

God, please let this be it. Please guide and protect me as I try to stop it.

Saturninus had been trying too hard to discover what he knew. First thing tomorrow morning, he'd catch Saturninus in his headquarters office and satisfy some of his prefect's curiosity.

By tomorrow afternoon, if they moved against him, he'd know if his suspicions were right.

Chapter 37

What Sabina Needs

The Circus Maximus, afternoon of Day 11

Like an approaching thunderstorm, the pulsing rumble from cheering fans beat against Glabrio as he led his party into the Circus. It was early afternoon because they'd had to wait for Kaeso to release his students, and a race was just ending. The sun beat down on the crowd, and the aroma of two-hundred-thousand sweating fans assaulted his nose and overpowered the scent of roses that lingered in Sabina's hair.

It was too late to get the best seats where he usually watched with Father in the rows right by the track. Those were reserved for senators and their families, but they still filled fast.

But he was in uniform, and the usher led them down to the back of the equestrian seating where there was still some room. The man had raised an eyebrow at Kaeso with his blue tunic stripes instead of the noble purple that he and Septimus wore, but at least he didn't challenge a commoner sitting with a tribune and a second senatorial son.

Sabina walked between him and Septimus with Kaeso bringing up the rear. With her sitting beside him, he'd be able to talk with her between races, despite the murmur of conversations around them. She was shy about speaking in the dining rooms, and he'd always been on a different couch, which made private conversation impossible. That shouldn't be a problem here with them forced to sit close by the lines inscribed into the marble benches. Since she was going to be his wife, they should start getting to know each other.

He led them along the row and squeezed past the knees of those already seated until they reached four seats together. But when he turned, it was Septimus who was behind him.

Had he deliberately slipped past his sister to put her next to his friend or had Sabina made that choice? Glabrio stopped his eyebrows from dipping and forced the growing frown to turn into a slight smile. He'd been practicing what he'd seen Titianus do so often, but he hadn't expected to use his new skill today.

The six teams of acrobats with their trained horses entered the track and spread out along the *spina* that ran down the middle, three teams on each side of the wall. Being late had put Glabrio's party midway between the best team in front of the imperial box and the team farthest from the finish line. A trumpet fanfare started pairs of horses connected head to tail cantering in circles with a man standing on the first horse's back. Another blast of the horns and the men leaped into the air, turned a somersault, and landed on the back of the trailing horse.

Sabina's arm shot out with her finger pointed, and her gasp was followed by her grabbing Kaeso's arm and burying her face in his shoulder. "I c-can't watch this. They're going to get killed."

He chuckled as he patted her hand. "Keep watching. It's safer than it looks. They do this every race day."

She lifted her chin to look at his face. "Well, if you think they're safe enough…" She released his arm and turned back to watch the performance. He made no move to sit closer, but she stayed too close for Glabrio's comfort.

He struggled to keep the frown off, and he won. It wouldn't do for the teacher to think he was jealous. It couldn't be jealousy when there hadn't been time to grow an emotional attachment, but he did feel protective of what her grandfather and Father had decided for both of them. If she was to become his wife, it should be his arm she was grabbing, even if they'd barely met and hadn't had a single private conversation.

Septimus glanced at the pair, and his mouth twitched. But the grin he'd kept from his lips showed in his eyes. Her brother was encouraging them, and from the look in her eyes when she glanced at Kaeso, she didn't need much encouragement.

The teacher was harder to read. His eyes stayed friendly and unperturbed whether he looked at sister or brother. But he lived with Titianus. Maybe he hid what he really thought as well.

As the crowd shouted its approval, the acrobats made their final bows and trotted toward the exit on the end opposite the starting gates. The next race would begin shortly, but the fire of anticipation he usually felt was absent.

He needed to spend more time with both of them. Kaeso didn't seem the kind of man who would try to steal another man's woman, especially if he was becoming a friend. Or was he? He was making no obvious attempt to win her affection, but it was happening anyway.

Did Kaeso know of the intended marriage? Would he discourage her if he did? Or would he only realize he needed to move quickly to get her to commit to him? She'd bring a dowry that would free him from dependence on the generosity of a brother-in-law.

But surely her father wouldn't approve of her marrying the son of his own son's teacher, no matter how much he liked the young man himself. And even if he would, Quintus Sabinus would never let his granddaughter lower herself that much.

That thought restored his smile, but it didn't last.

Manius had quoted Titianus at their second dinner. "It's not the rank or wealth or family connections that determine a man's worth. It's his honor that matters most." When Glabrio repeated it to Quintus Sabinus as something Titianus had taught him, her grandfather only replied that it sounded like his nephew. He didn't say whether he agreed or not.

He scrunched his nose to shake off the uncertainty. Father claimed there was no one more politically savvy than Quintus Sabinus. Throwing away an alliance by letting his granddaughter marry a common teacher was something that lion of Rome would never do.

Near the Sabinus town house, late afternoon of Day 11

By the time they returned to the town house, Septimus had made his decision. Each time he saw his sister and his best friend together, it was more obvious they were meant for each other.

Obvious to him. Probably obvious to her. But maybe not obvious to Kaeso.

If Father could persuade Grandfather to let Sabina choose, her choice should know what was coming. Nothing could be harder on her than revealing her desire to marry him only to have him act shocked by the suggestion.

Her first husband's rejection had destroyed her confidence. If Kaeso didn't want her, it was better if she thought it was Grandfather who said no.

As they climbed the steps that led from the valley by the Amphitheater to their town house in the Fagutal atop the Oppian Hill, Glabrio made certain he walked beside her and offered his arm should she need support. She hadn't, or maybe she had but she didn't want to encourage him. But the smile on his lips remained the same, and his eyes revealed no disappointment when she proved capable of climbing without his help.

Glabrio seemed like a good man, and he'd probably be a decent husband. But Sabina deserved more than decent treatment. She deserved love.

Septimus led the group around to the stableyard entrance. The front door was closer, but Glabrio was more likely to mount up and leave if they said their farewells outside the house.

"It was a l-lovely outing, but I'm quite fatigued. I b-believe I'll go rest before dinner." Sabina offered her social smile to Glabrio and a warm one to Kaeso. "Have a good evening."

Both men's eyes followed her as she entered the peristyle.

"I see Father's stallion is gone. I wonder where he's dining tonight." Septimus adjusted his toga at the neck. "I'll enjoy an evening of solitude for a change."

"Father is expecting me, so I'll bid you both a good evening as soon as I get my helmet." Glabrio disappeared into the peristyle to fetch it, and by the time he returned, the stableman had finished saddling his horse. He mounted and, with a casual wave toward Septimus, rode out the gate.

"Time for me to go home, too."

Kaeso hadn't taken three steps before Septimus fell in beside him. "I have something to ask you." He dropped his voice to a whisper. "But not where ears can hear."

They strolled out the gate and headed toward Titianus's town house, which lay on the other side of the Baths.

They'd walked half a block when Kaeso stopped. "No one can hear now. What it is?"

"What do you think of Sabina?"

"She's part of the reason you turned out so well." He tapped Septimus's arm with his knuckles.

"Probably, but that's not what I'm asking. What do you think of her… as a woman?"

One corner of Kaeso's mouth lifted. "Other than maybe my sister, she's the smartest woman I know. I'm glad she comes so often to spend time with Pompeia. They're kindred spirits in many ways."

Septimus tightened his lips. Kaeso could make it as hard as Titianus to get an answer. "That's not what I'm asking, and you know it. Do you like her…as a woman, not as your sister's friend?"

The playful glint in Kaeso's eye dimmed. "Of course I like her. Did you know I've never heard her say a single hateful thing about her husband or his mother? The only people I know who would do that are my Christian friends."

He rubbed his jaw. "I can only marry a Christian woman, but aside from that, she's everything I'd like in a wife. She isn't one yet, but if she were, I'd be so…pleased and proud if she wanted me." His mouth drooped. "But I know your grandfather will select her next husband. A teacher with a small school, even one that trains the sons of senators like you…I'm not important enough myself to ever be considered suitable."

One corner lifted into a wry smile. "I don't have even a hundredth of what it takes to be equestrian. And the school…I own the scrolls in my library, but my brother-in-law owns where I live and work."

He shrugged. "Glabrio seems like a good man, and he comes from a consular family. Your grandfather will agree to their marriage. Titus has seen a lot of him, and he thinks Glabrio's a better man than most with his background. There's a good chance he can make her happy. I think he'll at least try."

Septimus rested his hand on Kaeso's shoulder. "Nothing is certain until it's accomplished. Grandfather doesn't always do what everyone expects. Sometimes he delights in doing the opposite."

Resignation colored Kaeso's single laugh. "That might be, but not in this case."

"Haven't you told me a thousand times your god can make all things work for good for those of you who love him?"

"I have, but what I want most isn't always what's best for everyone."

Septimus nodded, but he didn't agree. There was a good chance Father would succeed in convincing Grandfather to let him pick her husband, and Father would pick Kaeso without regard for wealth, rank, or connections. But in case he was wrong, it was better if Kaeso didn't hope too much for what seemed impossible. Then if it happened, he would enjoy it even more.

Chapter 38

The Attack

The Praetorian Fortress, early morning of Day 12

Titianus left his stallion in the fortress stables and told the stableman to leave him saddled. What he needed to do shouldn't take long.

As he approached Saturninus's office in the Principia, he fingered the hanging chinstrap. If he were meeting with Turbo, he'd fasten it. With Saturninus, he never did. But if he did today, would the prefect notice and wonder why?

Anything that bothered his commander was a good thing this morning. He fastened the strap.

If all went as planned, by this afternoon at the earliest, someone would try to kill him. Then he'd only need to find the ones who hired him.

Or her. If he wanted to kill a man, he'd hire a woman to do it. Even most men who protected themselves with bodyguards would never see that coming.

Titianus didn't know Marcellus and Rufinus well enough to predict, but Saturninus wouldn't expect a woman to be as skilled with a weapon and ruthless about using it as a man. He might expect poison from a woman's hand, but never a dagger thrust.

Would Hadrian?

As he passed his old office, he glanced in. It wasn't Plancus at the optio desk. He made a sharp turn and entered.

"Where's Plancus?"

The man who normally served Saturninus stood and fisted his chest. "Good morning, Tribune. He's at the fortress hospital. He started vomiting at breakfast. Prefect Saturninus assigned me to help Tribune Glabrio until he recovers."

Titianus barely stopped his eyebrows before they dipped. Saturninus never lent out his personal staff to help anyone. Had he had something added to Plancus's food so the prefect's man could spy on them?

He tightened his lips to stop the smile and barely kept from rolling his eyes. That his prefect would poison his optio seemed unbelievable on the surface. But so did an urban prefect plotting to kill an emperor with two men wanting the consulship.

If Plancus was still sick tomorrow, what would that mean?

God, please guide me to the truth without others like Plancus paying for it.

"Tell Glabrio I'll be back to speak with him before he leaves here."

"Yes, Tribune." As Titianus turned to leave, the sound of a fist striking a chest followed him. After the quiet efficiency and subdued respect displayed by Plancus, would Glabrio find the eager attention to his every word that Saturninus demanded from his aides as unhelpful as he had?

Saturninus's door was closed when Titianus reached it. One of the guards slipped inside to announce him, closing the door behind him.

It should have opened to admit him immediately, but it didn't. As the delay dragged on, Titianus spread his legs and rested one hand on his sword with the other behind his back, like a legionary at parade rest.

At last, the door opened, and the guard saluted as he strode in to set a trap…or be caught in one.

When he reached the desk behind which Saturninus sat, he struck his chest and stood at attention. "Prefect. I've come to report, consistent with what Turbo is allowing."

"What Turbo allows? Do you forget you still report to me, Tribune?" Saturninus closed the tablet that lay before him and clasped his hands atop it. If looks could burn, Titianus would be on fire now.

"No, Prefect. That's why I've come to tell you I have two suspects in the private matter I'm investigating, and I expect to have the names of the other participants shortly. It's my hope that I'll be requesting permission to resign within a week. I should have sufficiently trained Glabrio to take over policing my part of Rome by then as well. I thought you should know this now."

"What is the private matter?"

"I'm not allowed to tell you."

Saturninus's teeth clenched. "And you won't name the suspects either?"

"No, Prefect, I'm not allowed to tell you any details. I haven't told Turbo yet, either. But I should have all the evidence I need to be certain who they are shortly, and then I'll tell him. Perhaps he'll tell you."

Anger flared in Saturninus's eyes, but he faked a smile. "I'm sure he will. You're dismissed."

"Prefect." Titianus struck his chest again, executed a parade turn, and marched from the room.

As he walked across the courtyard, he released a deep, slow sigh.

If all went as he hoped and it was God's will, he would be resigning again within the week. There were four more days until Marcellus's special event that should make the senators happy. If he didn't catch the would-be-assassins before then, he'd get them during Marcellus's surprise.

But four days should be plenty of time to lure Hadrian's enemies out of the darkness so Turbo could arrest them. That would ensure Hadrian's continuing rule until he died a natural death.

Or someone else tried to kill him. Most emperors hadn't died during peaceful slumber. But that wouldn't be Titianus's problem once he formally retired. He'd given Rome and her emperors ten years of his life. That was enough from any man. Only God deserved more.

He swung by Glabrio's office again, and his replacement sat with tablets surrounding him, reading the morning reports. As he passed Plancus's desk, the prefect's optio stood to stop him.

Glabrio looked up. "It's fine, Hortus. Titianus can always come in."

Closing the door would be pointless. Saturninus's man would probably listen at it, and the wood was too thin to block all the sound.

"Can you meet me at the Subura station an hour before noon?"

"I can. Should I bring anything?"

"Only the usual." Glabrio was staring at his neck, and Titianus released the chinstrap. Now he had two men wondering why he'd fastened it. Perhaps he'd tell one later. "I'll see you then."

As he headed back to the stables, a satisfied smile grew. If Saturninus was involved with the plot, he'd be warning his fellow conspirators as soon as he could. They'd believe their capture was inevitable if they didn't stop him before he told Turbo.

Gellius would make certain no one listened at the door in Subura, and Glabrio wouldn't expect to be told everything when he heard of the expected attack. With a squad of men nearby, his diligent replacement would make sure the assassin didn't succeed, and they'd capture the attacker alive so he could find out who hired him.

If he were a betting man, he'd bet he'd be a target by midafternoon, and he'd soon have the evidence he needed to be allowed to resign once more.

The smile drooped into the straight lips he'd hidden behind for so many years. What if he was wrong about Saturninus? What if it wasn't Marcellus's special gathering where the attack would come? What if…there were too many what ifs to be certain he'd made the wisest choice, even though he'd prayed.

God, please guide me to the truth before anyone innocent is hurt. If I've been wrong about what I thought You told me, get me back on the right path before it's too late.

Near the Ludus Bruti, morning of Day 12

It would be a few hours before Glabrio met him at the station, so Titianus rode to the ludus. He'd been prowling around the Forums every morning since he started this case. It might seem suspicious if he stopped now. Saturninus thought he was still hunting more accomplices.

But it was the last time he'd take Melis with him. Probus would be getting his assistant back for good. If an assassin was hunting him, he didn't want his irreplaceable manager-in-training getting killed by accident.

When Titianus rode through the gate, Melis was saddling one of the ludus mules while four bodyguards lounged under the portico. He checked the two cinches one last time before trotting over.

"Does Felix know you work for him, too?" Titianus slipped from his horse.

"No. Well, maybe. I'd rather be doing something than nothing while I wait, and I like mules."

"Where are the guards going?"

"There's a ship in Portus with some officials from Antioch. They wanted protection before coming into the city."

"Do you know their names?"

"Yes. Should I tell you?"

"No. Just checking." Titianus's smile was wry. Melis always had an answer when he asked for some detail, even when he didn't need it. It had become a game with them.

The youth trotted to a bench by the ludus entrance and returned with his satchel. "Two blank tablets and two styluses in case you need the spare."

Titianus slung it onto his shoulder. "Forums today. Same as we've been doing. See if anyone is talking about Marcellus's gathering in four days. I have a partial guest list, but I'd like to know what people think the surprise will be."

Melis's mouth twitched as he replaced his cheerful smile with the sulky look of an overworked slave. Then he disappeared into the ludus.

Titianus went out the gate. Melis would follow half a block back after coming out the front door so no one would think they were together. That had been Melis's idea; it was a good one.

If the youth had been born Roman and in an equestrian family, Titianus would be encouraging him to try for a tribuneship with the Urban Cohort. But since he wasn't Roman, that wasn't an option. Even after Probus got too old for the work, running the warehouse would keep no more than half of Melis's mind busy. Maybe the young man himself would have ideas about what he could do with the other half.

He was halfway to the forum when it happened, and Titianus didn't see it coming.

A hand grabbed the edge of his helmet at the cheek-guard hinge. He didn't need to see it to know a knife was coming to slice his throat open.

But the assassin had counted on his grip on the helmet letting him bend Titianus's head back far enough. Without that, the cheek guards would block the knife.

If the chinstrap had been fastened, like most soldiers did, he'd be a dead man now.

Instead, he let his knees buckle, and the thug was left holding only brass.

But as he tried to rise, the man slammed the helmet into his head, knocking him to his hands and knees. A hand grabbed Titianus's hair and pulled his head back, exposing his throat.

Before the sharpened steel could slice him open to bleed to death, Melis plowed into the assassin from the side, bowling both Titianus and the thug over. The knife was knocked loose and flew several feet away, clattering when it hit the pavement. The hand gave up its grip in his hair, and the assassin lurched toward his dagger.

But Melis, still on the ground, scrambled after him, dagger drawn. He slashed at the man's leg, and blood oozed along the length of the cut.

The man spun and kicked the dagger from Melis's hand, and it sailed through the air until it hit the wall. Then he kicked Melis in the head before punching him. The youth collapsed onto his stomach. As the would-be murderer scooped up his own knife, Melis scrambled to his feet and leaped onto the killer's back, wrapping his legs around the waist and one arm around the neck.

He'd punched the man's jaw several times when the assassin drove his knife into Melis's thigh and tossed him off.

But by then, Titianus had regained his feet. With sword drawn, he charged.

Before he could reach him, the man spun and ran.

If Titianus gave chase, he could catch him and find out who hired him. But Melis was bleeding heavily. If he didn't get that stopped now, his brave young spy would die.

He knelt beside the youth.

"I'm sorry he got away, master. I tried to stop him."

Titianus untied the sandal strap that wound up Melis's calf and pulled the sandal off. As he worked the strap free from the sandal, he paused to tap Melis's shoulder.

"That's all right. I let him get away." The strap was almost free. "It's more important to stop that bleeding than to stop him."

Melis reached toward to his dagger, lying about six feet from them, and flexed his fingers. "My dagger...I cut his leg."

Titianus had seen, but Melis would want to tell him. "Where and how long?"

"Left calf on the back, length of my hand."

"Then my men can find someone who saw where he went. You did well."

He picked up the dagger and handed it to Melis after kneeling once more by the bleeding leg. The youth wiped it on his tunic and slipped it back into its sheath.

Titianus wrapped the strap tightly around the thigh above the wound. "Probus isn't going to be happy about this. He told me to keep you safe and out of trouble. He said you'd be impossible to replace." He tied the knot that would keep it tight enough to slow the blood loss until he could get Felix's help stopping it. "I agree."

After putting his helmet on, he scooped up Melis. "It doesn't look too bad. Nothing a lanista can't take care of, and the ludus is close."

Melis rested his head against Titianus's shoulder and closed his eyes. "You were right. A dagger isn't enough."

"But your courage was. You just saved my life." He offered the youth a grateful smile, but with his eyes closed, Melis didn't see it. "Pompeia will be thanking you for that."

"I'd do anything for you and the mistress."

The youth went limp, and Titianus lengthened his stride.

"Oh, God, don't let him die. Holy Spirit, please heal him. In Jesus's name, I ask you to heal him." Some prayers were too important not to speak them aloud, even if only in a whisper.

The four blocks to the ludus seemed like four miles. As he entered the stableyard, the stableman sprinted into the hallway that led to the ludus office.

Titianus had barely reached the doorway when a trotting Felix met him.

"What happened?"

"Someone tried to slit my throat, and Melis tackled him before he could. Stab wound in his thigh. He was bleeding heavily when I tied it off."

As they spoke, Felix led them into the barracks, and he waved Titianus ahead of him into an empty chamber.

"Thrax!"

A passing gladiator stuck his head into the room.

"Send Lepidus for Galenos, then get armed. You're going to bodyguard Titianus."

"Thank you, Felix. I saw the man, and Melis cut him. I'll get my men from the Subura station to fan out and search for him. I want him alive to tell me who hired him."

If he were a betting man, he'd bet on Rufinus. Or maybe Marcellus, but he couldn't rule out his commander.

Titianus rested his hand on Melis's shoulder. "He doesn't look like much, but he has the courage of a lion and a mind as sharp as anyone I've ever met. After Galenos treats him, can you get him to my town house? Pompeia will want to look after him."

"I can."

Thrax appeared in the doorway, armed with a sword, a dagger, and a scowl that should scare anyone.

Felix tipped his head toward the gladiator. "He's Brutus's best body-guard. Keep him as long as you need him. Go hunt."

As Titianus left the room, he paused in the hallway to look once more at his little spy and his gladiator friend. Men who only considered the stripes on a tunic when deciding a man's worth were utter fools.

Chapter 39

Like a Real Person

The Subura station, morning of Day 12

When Titianus entered the station with Thrax beside him, Gellius rose to salute him. But his fist froze halfway to his chest when he saw the red on the leather skirt where Melis had bled. "Are you hurt?"

"It's not my blood, but you'll be hunting the one responsible for it. Summon the men and gather the ones who can find out whether a wounded man has been seen."

"Some are on patrol, but they'll be back soon for lunch. Of the men here now, that's Asellus, Barbus, and Juncus."

"Titianus?" Glabrio came from his office, wax tablet in hand. "I thought I heard your voice. I came early. Figured I'd get ahead on the repo—" His gaze locked on the bloody leather. "What happened to you?"

"An assassin."

Gellius came back from the common area with sixteen men behind him. When Titianus turned to face them, all stood at attention.

"You will be looking for a man about my height with black curly hair and a gash on the back of his left calf about the length of a hand. He was last seen half way between the Ludus Bruti and the Forums. He tried to kill me, and I want him brought back here alive and able to talk. Any questions?"

No one spoke. "Then go hunt."

As they filed out the door, Titianus turned back to Glabrio.

His protégé rubbed his lip. "This is the second attempt to kill you in a year."

"That I know of." Titianus pointed toward the office, and Glabrio led him back to the desk. Titianus settled into the guest chair.

"Saturninus didn't even mention the first one." Glabrio set the tablet back on the stack and sat. "So…is this something that happens to every tribune, or is it only you who makes deadly enemies?"

"If you do your job well, you'll make some of your own. This one wasn't supposed to strike before this afternoon."

Glabrio's eyebrows shot up. "You scheduled an attack on yourself?"

"No, but I told someone something that I thought might trigger one. I overestimated how long it would take him to get an assassin hired. That's why I wanted you down here before lunch. You were going to lead a small troop to watch over me and stop whoever tried before they killed me."

"You used yourself as bait?" Titianus almost laughed at Glabrio's wide eyes and gaping mouth, but his protégé wouldn't understand what was funny.

"I might still be. If you really want someone dead, you hire more than one killer to make certain."

"Who was this someone you told?"

"I can't tell you that yet." He rubbed his jaw. "But perhaps I can soon. When my men bring in the one Melis cut, I'll find out who hired him."

"Is this part of what Turbo has you investigating?"

Titianus donned his emotionless mask. "I'm not free to tell you that, either."

"If you can't tell me that, at least you can tell me what happened."

"I was going down to the Forums from the ludus when he jumped me. My assistant warehouse manager was close enough behind me that he stopped the killer from slitting my throat." He flipped the dangling chinstrap. "If this had been fastened, I would have been a dead man before Melis could respond. When the one who attacked me grabbed it to jerk my head back, I slipped out of it. Melis tackled him and cut his leg before he ran."

Glabrio pointed at Thrax, who stood outside the doorway. "What does your manager do that he needs an assistant built like that?"

"Thrax works for Brutus. Melis is sixteen, short, and scrawny, but never let the age or size of a man limit what you think he can do. He took a knife in the thigh as he kept me from being killed. I took him to the ludus for

Felix to tend, and Felix wouldn't let me leave without a bodyguard. He gave me Thrax until I don't need him."

"But if your man cut the killer's leg, why did he get away?" One corner of Glabrio's mouth lifted. "You're not so old and slow that you couldn't have caught a limping man."

"Melis was bleeding too much to leave him. Your men will be able to find where he went and bring him to me."

When Titianus said "your men," he triggered Glabrio's smile.

"You were right about respecting the junior officers and letting them know it." Glabrio placed his hand on the stack of reports. "They separate the commonplace from the unusual and bring what's important to my attention." A satisfied smile curved his lips. "When I ate at Manius's house with his father and mine, Quintus Sabinus himself wanted to know what I'd learned from you. That was one thing I mentioned." He chuckled. "He said you were more of a philosopher than he expected."

"A word of caution."

Glabrio's brow furrowed. "What?"

"Watch my uncle's eyes closely as you listen to his words. What seems a simple question might hide a trap, and what seems like a trap might just be him playing with you. He's not as straightforward as Manius, and saying too little to him is safer than saying too much."

Glabrio blew his breath out slowly. "I'll remember that. We should be related soon by marriage. Father and he agreed on a few months delay while Sabina is in mourning."

Titianus blanked his face. "Time and Quintus Sabinus…you can never predict what they'll do."

Glabrio seemed like a decent young man, but Titianus would do what he could to prevent that marriage. Sabina and Kaeso belonged together, just as he and Pompeia did. God had arranged his own marriage, and he was already asking God to do the same for his cousin and his friend.

The Ludus Bruti, late morning of Day 12

The straw mattress on the rope bed at the ludus wasn't quite as soft as Melis's bed in Probus's apartment, but it was close. He'd awakened to find Felix, arms crossed, standing beside him. When he tried to sit up to see what the physician was doing to his leg, Felix's meaty hand landed on his shoulder and pushed him down.

"Let Galenos finish."

Melis wasn't going to argue. Even the attempt to sit up had made his head spin.

"That should do it." Galenos wiped his hands on a towel and pitched it toward a bloody pile by the cell door. "If it starts bleeding again, send for me."

"He's going to Titianus's town house now. When the tribune stops in to get his horse and the boy's mule for Thrax, I'll tell him."

"Thrax is one of the best, but for a runt, this one did a good enough job as bodyguard." Galenos rested his hand on Melis's other shoulder. "Don't do anything to make it bleed for a few days."

"I'll try not to." Melis had never seen a smile on Galenos before.

The physician slapped his shoulder and picked up his satchel from the other cot.

As Felix walked him from the room, the lanista looked back over his shoulder. "You." He pointed at Melis. "Don't try to go anywhere. The men will be here with a stretcher to take you to Titianus's shortly. They better find you lying there resting."

"Yes, Felix." He offered a crooked smile to the lanista and got an upward twitch at the corners of the lanista's mouth in return. But that almost-smile was as meaningful as a grin on most people.

He blew out a slow breath and closed his eyes. Good enough job as a bodyguard. Those words were the highest praise he'd ever received.

The Titianus town house, early afternoon of Day 12

Four gladiators carrying a stretcher and a bodyguard armed with two daggers and a spine-chilling glare had drawn gazes and comments between the ludus and the town house. The stretcher-bearers probably tried to be careful, but the occasional jostling shot bolts of pain through Melis's leg. Pugnus had carried him upstairs like a small child, and the master's wife and brother-in-law had overseen him being put in a bedchamber.

Now he lay on a pillow-soft bed off the peristyle balcony of his master's house. He'd dozed off almost as soon as his head hit the pillow, and when he awoke, he was alone.

The gurgle of fountains in the garden pool below was a far cry from the rumble of wagon wheels and the curses of oxen and mule drivers when traffic was moving too slowly.

The bruises on his forehead and jaw where the would-be killer had kicked and punched him were tender, and his thigh ached where the knife had gone in. But Master Titus was still alive, and that was worth every bit of the pain and more.

Had Probus been told he'd be late getting home? He tried to sit up and thought better of it. The room didn't spin like it had at the ludus, but it wasn't quite steady, either.

A soft tap on the open door drew his gaze.

A pretty young woman near his own age stood in the doorway with a tray. "We thought you might be ready for something light to eat. Mother baked rosemary rolls this morning, and there's cheese and raisins and dried dates."

As she spoke, she placed the tray on the chair from the writing desk and moved it over beside his bed. "How are you feeling?"

"Well enough."

"Can I get you anything else?"

That was something he asked Probus, not something a pretty woman asked him.

"No. I thank you for bringing this."

She stepped back. "Don't hesitate to ask for anything. We're all so thankful to you for saving Master Titus. Everyone is going to be glad when he retires and stays here teaching instead of going out looking for dangerous people who do horrible things to others."

The people at the town house might be glad, but he would miss the days spent by his master's side, exposing the secrets that brought justice to the victims and made the guilty pay for their crimes.

"Would you like another blanket?" She opened a cabinet to reveal spare pillows and blankets. "Or maybe a couple of pillows so you can sit up a little?"

"Thank you, but no. I'm fine now."

Feeding him was one thing, but treating him like a guest in the house?

"Everyone will be glad to hear you're awake and feeling better."

His brow furrowed. "They won't care."

Why would they? He'd never been to the town house before.

"Of course they will. We all want you to get better, almost as much as

Master Titus does, and he cares a lot about you. Probably as much as you care about him."

His head drew back. How should he respond to that? Master Titus appreciated what he did, but as for caring for him as a person...

He shook his head. Probus did, but it was hard to believe anyone else would. No one cared when he was a child. Until Probus bought him, no one gave him the chance to show he was worth caring for.

"If you need anything, just call. One of us will be up to help you."

"Thank you...what's your name?"

"Lilia." She flashed a smile and stepped out the door.

His gaze settled on the tray. A cloth with a stitched green vine and red flowers sat under the plate, and someone had laid out the food in a pattern, like he'd seen done for masters and mistresses, but never for their slaves.

He closed his eyes. Perhaps someone did care about him, at least a little.

The Titianus town house, late afternoon of Day 12

When Melis awoke again, the patch of light on the wall across from the window had moved enough to declare the day mostly gone.

A hand shaking the foot of his uninjured leg had awakened him. He cracked his eyelids open to see whose it was. Would it be Lilia?"

He'd only eaten a slice of cheese and a few bites of a roll before the need for sleep won over the desire for food. Would she ask him if that meant he wasn't as well as he'd said?

A stern-faced Master Titus, still wearing his helmet, stood in front of him. He must have come up the moment he got home if that brass still sat on his head.

"How's my bodyguard feeling?" Straight lips relaxed into a slight smile.

"Good, master."

The master took off the helmet and set it on the floor. "I sent word to Probus about what you did. He'll probably scold me for almost getting you killed the next time he sees me."

He moved the tray to the writing table and sat. "Felix tells me you lost enough blood you should take it easy for at least a couple of weeks." His eyes narrowed, but Melis saw the smile mixed in with the glare. "I'm debating whether you can do that if I let you go back to the warehouse."

"I can." Melis's mouth twitched. He could still do some of what he usually did when he sat at a desk. If he tried to do the rest of it, Probus would stop him...if he saw before Melis did it.

"We'll see if you can stand doing nothing here for a few days. Then I'll decide."

"The one who tried to kill you...I'm sorry he got away. But with Thrax watching...will you be safe?"

"My men are searching for him. You cut him enough they should find him by tomorrow. As soon as I learn who hired him, I'll be safe again." Titus tapped Melis's upper arm. "Teachers seldom make dangerous enemies, and I expect to be hunting assassins for only a few more days."

The master's smile turned wry. "Probus will be glad when both of us stop."

"I won't." Melis looked away from the face of the man who'd taught him so much about right and wrong, duty and honor. The man who'd seen what he could do and let him do it. "I've liked helping you."

"You've been a great help." Titus's lips straightened. "As I carried you to Felix, I thought you were dying because you saved me. I'm glad I was wrong."

There were only two men Melis would gladly die to protect. His gaze returned to one of them. Did he dare ask about what he thought he'd heard as the sounds of the street had grown softer and louder and softer again until they turned into silence?

"I heard you ask your god not to let me die. But which god is that?"

Titus's eyebrow rose, then settled back into place as one corner of his mouth lifted. "What did I say?"

"You asked someone called Holy Spirit to heal me...in Jesus's name."

"I didn't think you heard that." The half-smile turned into a full one. "What I'm going to tell you should not be shared with anyone without first asking me if you can."

"You know I can keep secrets."

"This secret is one that could kill me and several others."

Melis inhaled sharply. "Then I'd die before telling anyone."

Titus settled back in the chair and crossed his arms. "When you came to see me at the Sabinus town house the day after I was attacked, the only reason I was still there was through God's mercy. I was dying with a broken skull in that stableyard when Pompeia had them take me upstairs. She and Kaeso asked God for my healing in Jesus's name. Septimus had gone for Galenos."

He pointed at Melis's bandage. "He's the one who treated your leg. They both expected a dead man when he reached me. I had the blood in my ear and the bruise behind it from a broken skull. He couldn't explain how I was still alive with that, but Pompeia did when I asked her later."

"There's a god who can stop men dying?"

"There is, and He's the God I worship and follow."

Melis chewed his lip. "I'd like to know about him.

Titus leaned forward and placed his hand on Melis's upper arm. "We don't just know about Him. We know Him."

Melis's eyebrows dipped. "There's a difference?"

"A huge difference. You'll be here while you heal, and I'll introduce you to Him."

"Like meeting a person?"

"Yes. I prepared for that by reading a letter written by my best friend's grandfather, Publius Drusus. It tells why he believed in Jesus and was willing to die for that belief."

Melis's head drew back. "He died for believing what you do?"

"He was killed in the arena. He wouldn't offer the libation to the Roman gods and the genius of the emperor."

"Why wouldn't he? It's only a little wine and a few words."

"Because the God we worship is real. He's not just a story someone made up generations ago or some powerful man like the emperor. He tells us to worship only Him, and for Publius, that meant dying."

Melis rubbed his mouth. What kind of god could be worth dying for? "Could it mean the same for you?"

"It could, if someone outside our familia finds out about my faith. I'm trusting you not to tell anyone."

"I won't. Not even Probus."

"I'll probably tell Probus myself before much longer, and when I do, I'll let you know he's in on our secret."

"I won't tell anyone without asking you."

Titianus slapped his spy's arm. "I know. You wouldn't have risked dying to save me if you weren't a man I could trust."

A man he could trust. Hearing Master Titus say it aloud filled Melis with pride.

Titus scooped up the helmet and put it back on his head. "I have to join Manius and Quintus Sabinus tonight to get their help hunting assassins. I'll get you a copy of the letter before I leave. After you read it, you'll have questions. I had many, so don't hold back from asking everything. I'll probably be home too late tonight, but tomorrow we can talk."

"I'll be ready."

Titus's nod before he strode from the room filled Melis with anticipation like nothing he'd felt before. Master Titus had talked to his god like a real person he knew. Would Melis soon be doing that himself?

Chapter 40

Family Connections

The Sabinus town house, evening of Day 12

His cousin hadn't specifically invited him, but when Septimus arrived to dine with Sabina at his house, Titianus had learned that Manius and his father were sharing a family dinner alone. Manius had said drop in anytime, and tonight he wanted more than food and conversation.

He wanted help saving an emperor.

When he rode into the stableyard with Thrax beside him, Manius was showing Quintus the young stallion he'd just bought.

"You in full armor and a bodyguard with you?" Manius strolled over to join him as he dismounted.

"Brutus's lanista insisted. Someone tried to kill me again."

Manius chuckled. "You're joking, of course."

"No."

As Manius's frown appeared, Quintus joined them. "Do you think it was ordered by the same man as last time?"

"I have some suspicions, but it's premature to share them."

"Hmph." His uncle's lips tightened. "In other words, you think it might be, but you don't have enough evidence to convict at a trial."

"I'm not free to say."

"So, it probably is. Septimus saved you last time. Why are you still alive this time?"

"I had my warehouse manager's assistant along to help me watch people. He tackled the assassin as he was about to slit my throat."

Quintus rested his hand on the neck of Titianus's stallion. "A warehouse worker? Why not one of your soldiers?"

"Melis blends into the background. He looks like just one more slave waiting for a master to finish his business. But his mind is dagger-sharp, and sometimes he spots things even I miss."

"Stay for dinner, and you can tell us all about it. That should prove entertaining." Manius pointed toward the canopy where his slaves dined. "Your man can eat with mine."

"Thrax, we'll be staying a while. Get some dinner." As his guard slipped off the mule, the big man's scowl was replaced with an almost-smile.

With Titianus beside him, Manius started their stroll into the house. "Did you kill the assassin?"

"He got away. He'd stabbed Melis in the thigh while he was hanging on the killer's back. I needed to get the bleeding stopped."

Quintus moved to Titianus's other side. "A talented spy is valuable, but one who would risk dying for you…that's priceless. Are you going to free him?"

"Not yet. He's only sixteen." Titianus fingered his lip. Melis deserved the best he could give him.

"But I could free my manager. Probus bought Melis as a boy of twelve, and he looks on him as a son."

They had reached the private dining room. "I could give citizenship within two weeks to two faithful servants if I free one to buy and adopt the other."

Manius was close enough to give him a nudge. "Like I did with Corax."

Quintus's eyebrows dipped as he turned his gaze on Manius. He received a shrug and a smile in return. "As we both know, Father, some shortcomings of Roman law can be overcome by clever application of other parts of it. It was Titianus's idea to keep a boy from being tortured, not mine, but I should have thought of it."

Titianus set his helmet on the floor inside the triclinium. "Before we dine, may I ask the two of you something in confidence?"

Manius's eyebrows lowered. "Behind a locked door?"

"That would be best."

Manius snapped his fingers, and the wine slave who was getting a third goblet from the cabinet turned to face him.

"Take the Falernian to the library." As the wine slave left the room, Manius gestured for Titianus to go ahead of him. "Whom should we be careful to not tell what you ask?"

Titianus's jaw twitched. He'd prayed before coming, but this still felt dangerous. *God, please let me asking them be a good idea.*

"Everyone."

Quintus's head drew back. "What could be that secret?"

It was too late to turn back, even if he wanted to. "Something that could cause the death of an innocent person if the wrong man learns I'm asking."

Manius looked at his father. Raised eyebrows got a nod in return. "What you ask us will go no further."

Quintus's hand swept toward the library door. "Privacy awaits, and we'll do what we can to help."

Manius entered the room last and bolted the door.

"Saturninus has been fuming over something you're doing that he can't figure out." Quintus chuckled. "He turns an odd shade of red when he mentions you sometimes. Is this about that?"

"Probably, and what I'm about to say must go no further than the three of us."

"You already have our word." One corner of Quintus's mouth lifted. "As my nephew and his cousin, you can be assured we'll both keep it."

Titianus drew a deep breath and squared his shoulders. "I've been tasked by Turbo with finding some men who might be conspiring against Hadrian. Not just people who dislike him and criticize some of his actions, but those who might try to remove him from power by killing him."

Quintus snorted. "I see why Turbo chose you for this, and why he doesn't want Saturninus knowing what you've learned. Our urban prefect isn't the most careful man about what he says when he's had enough good wine."

He rubbed the underside of his jaw. "Right now, the list of those who dislike Hadrian is longer than usual. I can't name any who would act on it, but many are angry with him for dividing Italia into four regions under legates whom he will appoint and give consular rank. To treat Italia as nothing more than a group of administrative units and the prefects not being appointed by the Senate, that has many seething."

"There's more." Manius sat on the edge of his desk. "He also took the cases that were usually tried in the courts in Rome and put them under the authority of his legates out in what amounts to Italian provinces. That's being seen as an insult to the entire Senate and a total disregard for the way things have always been done."

Quintus moved to the wine cabinet and poured himself a goblet. "The senators who would be genuinely sorry to see something happen to Hadrian might be fewer than those who would applaud his retirement, by whatever means. But being unhappy with an emperor is a far cry from trying to kill him."

His uncle's eyes narrowed. "But I think you already knew everything we've told you, and you have something specific you want from me. What is it?"

Titianus suppressed a smile. He hadn't asked for anything, yet his uncle knew it was coming. His uncle's reputation for seeing past the words being spoken to the thoughts lurking behind them was well deserved.

"There's a banquet in four days at the younger Asinius Marcellus's estate where Hadrian is going to be present. Do you know anything about it?"

"Of course." Quintus took a sip. "Manius and I are both invited. We've been promised some rare entertainment...something never before seen in Rome."

"Do you have any idea what that is?"

"Such secrets usually get leaked by someone wanting to show off how much they know, but this time I haven't heard anything." Quintus set down the goblet. "But whatever it is, I can add something to the dinner that should prove amusing."

His uncle's slyest smile appeared. "I can bring a guest with me. It will be good sport to bring my notorious nephew along. Some will find it shocking if they don't already know that the incorruptible Titianus is my nephew. I'll watch the reaction of others as I introduce you, and you can watch the reactions of everyone to Hadrian."

Titianus let his smile grow but stopped short of the grin that offer deserved. "I'd like that, but I'll be in uniform and fully armed, just in case."

Manius joined Quintus in a chuckle. "That's all the better, cousin. Some might not believe you were really you if you dressed like an ordinary man. Stop by that morning, and I can tell you our plans for getting there." He straightened and moved toward the locked door. "If you have nothing else that requires secrecy, let's eat."

As Titianus followed his uncle from the room, it was clear he'd have to expand his instructions to Glabrio. Wealth, rank, and family connections really didn't determine the value of a man, but they might play into how much help he could give when you needed it.

Chapter 41

UNCOMFORTABLE CONVERSATIONS

The Praetorian Fortress, early morning of Day 13

Titianus fastened his chinstrap as he climbed the steps to reach Turbo's office. What he had to report was less than Turbo wanted, but at least he had something.

Unlike with Saturninus, who'd left him waiting yesterday to show who was in command, the guard opened the door with its eagle wings and thunderbolts the moment he arrived, and Titianus stepped inside. Turbo summoned him with a curve of his fingers, and Titianus marched forward, stopping four feet short of the desk to salute.

"Report." Turbo pushed a tablet aside and leaned back in his chair, arms crossed.

"Two things, Prefect. I told someone whom I expected to tell Marcellus and his co-conspirators that I would soon have enough evidence to identify all who were involved. Someone hired an assassin to attack me yesterday. He was injured by my assistant, and I expect my men to find and arrest him today. I will then be able to discover the name of the one who wanted me dead. That might allow me to solve this case."

"You used yourself as bait?"

"Yes, Prefect."

"Hmph." A wry smile appeared and vanished as quickly as it came. "Martialis told me you'd do all you could to solve this. Give me the name of the person you told."

"The assassination attempt came much sooner after that conversation than I thought possible. So, I can't be certain it was related. I can't accuse a man who might be innocent."

Turbo's mouth twitched before turning down. "And the second thing?"

"The banquet Marcellus is hosting is a matter of much discussion among the senators. Word is there will be surprise entertainment there, but no one seems to know what it will be. But I have an invitation to go as a guest, and I'll be watching everyone."

Turbo's frown had grown deeper as he spoke, but Titianus needed the next answer. "You didn't mark that banquet as one you'd attend. Will you be there?"

Turbo's eyes remained cold, but his frown turned into a smile. "I'll be there. Anything else?"

"No, Prefect."

"Then you're dismissed."

Turbo opened the report and ignored Titianus as he saluted and marched from the room.

As he left Turbo's headquarters, he started toward the stable where he'd left Thrax. But before he'd gone fifty paces, he turned toward the Urban Cohort offices.

With Melis injured, he needed another pair of eyes. Glabrio should be willing to provide them at the Forums and then the Baths. Whoever tried to kill him might reveal themselves when he showed up alive.

It would be enough for Glabrio to think he merely wanted to see who hated him. If his men found the assassin alive and he could get the man to talk, his replacement would be backup as he went after the men who wanted Hadrian dead.

The Rufinus town house, early morning of Day 13

The salutation would begin shortly, and Faustus Rufinus rolled the scroll of Tacitus and slipped it back into its cubicle.

"Faustus."

The voice from the doorway triggered a shiver even before he turned. Quintus Sabinus stood with arms crossed and two scary Germans standing behind him.

Rufinus plastered what he hoped was a confident smile on his lips. "Sabinus. You're visiting early. To what do I owe this pleasure?"

"I think you already know." Sabinus strolled to the desk and picked up a stylus. "Someone tried to kill my nephew yesterday...again." He rolled it between his fingers. "After the last time, I thought we'd come to an understanding about how foolish it would be to try again."

"I didn't try to kill him last time. I'm not trying now."

Rufinus leaned against the wall and crossed his arms. "I wouldn't object if someone else killed Titianus, but I'm not fool enough to order it myself. As you well know, clients often do things their patron didn't request. My man had accidentally killed a man and started a fire, but Titianus would never have believed either was an accident. Wouldn't you try to kill the man who wanted you burned alive before he could kill you?"

He straightened. "I didn't order your nephew's death last time, and I give you my word as a Roman that I have no intention of doing anything to hasten it now."

Sabinus's gaze locked on Rufinus's eyes, and they stared at each other for three times longer than Rufinus found comfortable. Then the old crocodile's frown relaxed into a political smile.

"I think I believe you...this time." Sabinus set down the stylus. "But if you hear who just tried or who plans to, you'll let me know immediately... if you want my continued support."

"Your support?" Rufinus mirrored Sabinus's fake smile. "This year's consuls were announced, and I'm not among them. Last time we met here, you said you thought I'd make a good one." He cleared his throat. It might be unwise to ask, but he had to know. "Did you advise Hadrian against me?"

Sabinus's chuckle was the last thing Rufinus expected.

"Not at all. When Hadrian asked, I told him I thought you'd serve Rome well. You're still on his list for the future...and you will be as long as you're on my list, too."

"I'm very pleased to hear that. Serving Rome well, as you have for years, is my highest goal."

Sabinus's lips twitched. The old lion didn't believe him. Even though Sabinus might not agree on what serving well required, Rufinus had spoken the truth. But changing the subject now was wise.

"Will you be attending the special affair Marcellus and I are hosting this week? Hadrian will be there, and it should provide a surprise for all involved."

"Manius and I will both be attending. What do you have planned?"

Rufinus chuckled. "Marcellus would be angry if I revealed that, even to you." He forced a friendly smile. "Maybe especially to you, since you and Hadrian are so close."

"Perhaps I'll bring something to add to the entertainment."

"If you wish, but it will already be a memorable evening."

Rufinus's secretary knocked on the open door. "All is ready for you, master."

Palm up, Rufinus swung his arm toward the door. "If you'll excuse me, Sabinus. My clients are waiting, and I'm sure yours await you as well."

Sabinus offered a warm smile with chilling eyes. "Until the banquet, then." He strode from the room, and his Germans fell in behind him.

Rufinus pursed his lips. Quintus Sabinus was definitely in for a surprise at the banquet, but he might not enjoy it.

Early afternoon of Day 13

Titianus sat with Glabrio beside him in the men's dressing room at the Baths of Trajan. The marble bench wasn't comfortable, and Glabrio's nostrils sometimes flared when a particularly filthy man walked too close on his way to disrobe. But his protégé hadn't complained.

Glabrio had wondered about the wisdom of leaving their armor at Manius's town house when someone might be hunting him, but pointing at Thrax had silenced him.

Rufinus and Marcellus had both passed through on the way to their daily conversations with other important men. Both had glanced at him with their usual condescension, but neither had seemed surprised to see him. That left only one known suspect for hiring the assassin.

Saturninus.

But it could be another co-conspirator he hadn't identified yet or simply someone who wanted revenge.

He sighed.

"Should we be doing something else now?" Glabrio leaned his head against the wall and closed his eyes. "Maybe go inside and watch people while we bathe?"

Titianus had just opened his mouth to agree when the click of hobnails on the marble floor drew his gaze. Asellus from the Subura station stopped in front of him and saluted.

"Tribune, we caught him."

"Go tell Gellius we're on our way."

Titianus stood and summoned Thrax with a curl of his fingers. "Armor first. Then I'll show you the best way to interrogate to get what might be the truth."

It took half an hour before Titianus entered the station. Gellius saluted them both. "He's in the back cell."

Titianus paused with his hand on the cellblock door handle and turned to Glabrio. "When I say 'Send for Bassus,' ask me who that is."

He pulled open the door, and the smell of human waste assaulted his nose. Carrying a lighted torch, Gellius led them down the pathway between cells and unlocked a door. Shackled to the opposite wall was a man who looked Syrian. His left calf was bandaged.

"That's him." Titianus crossed his arms. "You shouldn't have failed to kill me, and you shouldn't have killed my slave. Whoever hired you, he didn't pay you enough for what your failure will cost you. Your freedom is forfeit. You are now a slave of Rome, but how you will serve is mine to decide."

He turned to Glabrio. "Obviously not a citizen." Then he fixed his stare on the assassin. "Gellius."

"Yes, Tribune?"

"Send for Bassus."

Gellius stuck his head out the door. "Asellus. Get Bassus."

"Who is Bassus?" Glabrio had stepped up beside him.

"My station torturer." Titianus let a wry smile appear. "He enjoys the work, so he takes his time, but I don't mind waiting. It won't be too long before we know who hired this one. That's the man I want. This one...he's only the way I'll find the one really to blame."

A strangled gasp came from the chained would-be killer.

Titianus rubbed beneath his chin where the helmet wasn't blocking. "As my prisoner, you have two choices. You can tell me now who hired you and where I can find him. Or you can wait until Bassus comes and tell me after he's spent some time with you. If you tell me the truth without Bassus's help and I find the man responsible for you attacking me, Bassus won't have to deal with you before you leave here."

"I'll tell you. I swear. It's Gaius Barbatus, and I can show you where he lives. You sent his brother to the arena for killing a citizen he was robbing. Barbatus wanted to make you pay." It wasn't warm in the cell, but sweat beaded on the thug's lip. "That's the truth. I swear it by all the gods of Syria and Rome. You don't need Bassus."

Titianus donned his fiercest scowl and glared at the man as he repeated Barbatus's name and the plea for mercy several times.

"Gellius."

"Yes, Tribune."

"I won't need Bassus today. If this one fails to deliver up Barbatus or Barbatus isn't guilty, Bassus can have him tomorrow."

Titianus turned and strode from the room, and Glabrio followed. They entered the office, and Titianus put his helmet on the desk.

Then he dropped into the desk chair, leaned back, and clasped his hands atop his head while Glabrio settled in across from him.

"That's how you get a man to tell you the truth willingly. I almost never need to use Bassus as more than a threat to get a slave or foreigner to talk. A man under torture will say anything to get the pain to stop, and you can never be sure of the truth of it. But fear will wring the truth out of most men."

"I can see that. So why do the others use their torturers routinely?"

"Perhaps truth and justice matter more to me. I hope they will to you."

Glabrio's solemn eyes and slow nod were exactly what he'd hoped for.

Titianus stood. "Let's return to the baths to bathe this time."

As they started up the hill to Manius's house to leave their armor there, relief flooded Titianus. A man like Barbatus would only hire a single killer at a time. As soon as the arrest was made, it should be safe to return Thrax to Felix.

But he'd hoped the assassin was hired by one of his three suspects. Now he was back to nothing but suspicion and speculation and no hard evidence against any of them.

"Thrax."

The bodyguard moved beside him. "Yes, Tribune?"

"I think you can go back to the ludus tonight. As soon as Gellius arrests Barbatus, I won't need your protection."

His words triggered a scowl. "Felix said to stay until there was no danger. Can you tell me you're in no danger whatsoever? None at all?"

No one was ever completely safe in Rome.

"No."

Thrax's mouth straightened. "Then you have to feed me for a while longer." Straight lips turned into a grin. "Ciconia is a much better cook than ours."

The grin was catching, but Titianus managed to keep it down to a slight smile. He had an image to maintain while he still wore tribune armor, but Glabrio's snort almost made the grin break through.

Chapter 42

Discovered

The Baths of Trajan, afternoon of Day 14

When Glabrio rode into the ludus stableyard, he'd asked where Titianus was. As usual, his mentor had started his day at the Forums, watching the senior senators and whoever conversed with them. Glabrio still hadn't figured out why he was mapping out social circles among the elite, but if he were a betting man, he'd wager it had something to do with the Turbo problem. Titianus still hadn't mentioned his brother-in-law's school to anyone.

He almost laughed when he found Titianus in the Basilica Julia. He was used to having his scrawny spy blend in with the clusters of slaves waiting for a master to finish a conversation. Thrax was trying to be his second set of eyes, but he was four inches taller than most of the Romans and had biceps bigger than many men's thighs. He didn't fit in with the manservants who seldom did anything more strenuous than wrapping their master in his toga. That scowl would make anyone think twice before snapping their fingers to summon him.

So, when Glabrio tracked him down and suggested they go to the Baths to meet people, Titianus welcomed the change.

But meeting people wasn't Glabrio's goal anymore. Thrax would go, too. He was only borrowed, not a member of Titianus's familia, so he might not know what he shouldn't say when Glabrio asked a question.

One of Manius's house slaves had come with them to watch their clothing, so Thrax stayed within ten feet of them.

As they strolled toward the pool large enough for swimming laps, Glabrio spotted Saturninus at the far end. Two Greek-looking men stood listening to him, Rufinus, and Marcellus. Only the Greeks had wet hair.

"I didn't know our commander liked to swim."

Titianus's head snapped sideways to put them in his field of view. "I never tried to figure out what your commander likes, but Victorinus could probably tell you."

"Could, but probably wouldn't. If glares were daggers, I'd bleed daily."

Saturninus and the senators were looking away when Titianus slipped into the pool. "I think I'll swim some." Before Glabrio answered, he stretched out in the water and, with long, smooth strokes, swam to the far end. There he stopped, turned to face Glabrio, and settled into the water so only his head was out.

For a man wanting to swim, he was oddly stationary. But...Saturninus and the others were within earshot.

Thrax moved up beside Glabrio and crossed his arms. He scanned the men near the soaking Titianus and said nothing.

A bodyguard saw everything in a household, and one who was only hired might be willing to tell what he saw. With Thrax right beside him and Titianus too far away to hear, his chance had come.

"Fortuna certainly smiled on Titianus when his slave tackled the one who tried to kill him. Or maybe it was one of the other gods who watched over him. Or maybe one of Lenaeus's. He'd have to move his school if Titianus died."

Thrax glanced at him, then turned his gaze back on Titianus.

"Sharing the house the way they do, are Lenaeus's household gods on the atrium altar with Titianus's?"

"The only statues in the *lararium* niche are busts of Augustus, Trajan, and Hadrian."

"Are they in the peristyle instead?"

"I don't pay attention to how the rich people I guard decorate." Thrax's sneer relaxed into a wry smile. "The only thing I care about is whether their kitchen feeds me well, and his does."

Glabrio smiled to disarm him. "Is the family altar where they do the morning rituals for the ancestors in the peristyle, like ours is?"

"I've never seen them do it." The gladiator's eyes narrowed. "But why are you asking me?"

Glabrio's mouth started to open, but he shut it. What question could he ask that would distract enough to make his questions seem casual…and harmless?

"Hmph." Thrax tipped his head to look down his nose. "If you're so curious about him and his family, you need to ask Titianus."

He turned and moved several feet away before crossing his arms and watching Titianus once more.

Ask Titianus. Glabrio's lips tightened. An obvious suggestion, but what if he wouldn't answer? Worse still, what if the answer he received was the one he was afraid of?

The Titianus town house, evening of Day 14

Titianus and Thrax had ridden in silence from Manius's stableyard to his own. It had been a disappointing day.

One swim away from identifying more conspirators—with each stroke and kick, he'd felt closer to finding others who were in on the plot. But it was only two well-known actors now appearing in Euripedes's *Medea* at the Theater of Marcellus. That was in his district, and he'd seen them both perform. Both good actors, but not assassins.

They were barely through the gate when Thrax moved up beside him. "There's something you should know."

Titianus reined in. "What?"

"Felix told you I'm Brutus's best bodyguard, and I am. I don't just watch for enemies with weapons. I watch for anything not quite right with the people around you." His hand rested on his dagger. "I saw something today."

Titianus twisted in the saddle to face him straight on. "Tell me."

"Glabrio…he might not be one to trust as much as you do. He was asking me about what you do at home. Questions about something he doesn't need to know."

Titianus stiffened. "What did he ask?"

"Where your family alter is. What household gods you have on it, both you and Lenaeus. Where you do your morning rites."

His stomach clenched. "What did you tell him?"

"He needed to ask you. Then I moved away from him to end his questions."

"A good answer. Thank you for telling me."

With a fleeting smile and a tip of his head, Thrax reined away to put the mule in a stall before joining Titianus's people under the canopy for dinner.

Titus rubbed his lower face. Glabrio was much too observant and much too good at interpreting what he saw. He slipped from his horse, handed his reins to Stabularius, and went to find Kaeso.

His brother-in-law was in his classroom, placing scrolls on each table for the morning class. "Did you have a good day?"

"No, and it just ended badly." He went to the corner farthest from the door and summoned Kaeso with a curl of his fingers.

"What happened?" Kaeso's words were whispered.

"Glabrio is asking about our religious practice so we need to be careful about what he sees."

"We could let him come no further than the stableyard so he doesn't see anything. Or we could dig out the old statue and incense plate Glyptus used to fool the people who came to pay respects to Father. I think everything got packed when we moved here. Ciconia can probably find them if they didn't get thrown away or put together something else that will do."

Kaeso rubbed the back of his neck. "I expect Sabina will decide to join us very soon, so I should warn her, too."

"Does Septimus know that she's close to faith?"

"I don't know. She promised to keep what we talk about secret, so she probably hasn't told him."

Titianus blew his breath out slowly. "Well, Glabrio is a good man, and even if he finds out, he probably won't tell anyone about us. He knows his own grandfather died for his faith, and I don't think he would put friends at risk of that."

"Then it's probably a good thing Sabinus plans for her to marry Glabrio rather than someone who wouldn't protect her." Regret and resignation tinged Kaeso's voice.

"He won't do as a husband. He'll rise through the political posts and end up a consul like his father. Even if he tries to protect her, she'll be too visible in Roman society to remain undiscovered."

Kaeso's shoulders drooped. "I'd love to solve that problem by marrying her myself, but Quintus Sabinus would never choose me over Glabrio." He shrugged. "He'd never choose a man like me over anyone."

"Manius would. I've already talked with him because Filomena told him Sabina had your copy of Luke's writings. He asked me about it as soon as he could. He'll try to convince his father to let him choose." He tapped Kaeso's chest. "And his choice is you."

Kaeso closed his eyes and tipped his head back. "God, let it be so."

"As you always say, God can work all things for good." Titianus draped his arm across Kaeso's shoulders. "He certainly did for Pompeia and me. I think he might for you."

The Titianus town house, early afternoon of Day 15

When Kaeso closed the codex of Luke and offered it to her, Sabina reached out to take it.

"It must have been so wonderful to listen to Jesus, to talk with him after he rose. It must have hurt terribly to see him go back to heaven, to never see him again."

"But remember He said He'd be sending what the Father promised. They were to wait in Jerusalem until He did."

"I wish we had more of the story."

"We do. I have what Luke wrote telling how the message about Jesus spread from Jerusalem through Asia and Greece and on to Rome. We'll get to that, but before we do, I want you to read the gospel of John." He unlocked the small cabinet he'd moved into the room and took out a codex. When he handed it to her, she pressed it to her chest.

Kaeso sat down and pointed at the codex. "John was one of the three closest to Jesus, and reading what he wrote makes me feel like I'm sitting at Jesus's feet, listening."

"That sounds w-wonderful, but..." She hung her head and sighed.

He leaned forward and touched the back of her hand. "But what?"

"If I decide to believe, how can I live like a Christian if I'm forced to marry Glabrio? A husband sees everything he wants to. If he discovers my faith, I wouldn't be the only one in danger. That could put you all at risk, too."

"It can be done. We have a Christian brother who's at one of his distant estates at the moment, so you haven't met him. He was Publius's closest friend. For thirteen years, he's had to keep his faith secret from everyone but his secretary Glyptus. Glyptus got the papyrus and waited while Publius wrote his letter down in the cells under the arena. Publius made them promise to read the letter before sending it on to his son."

He pointed at the satchel. "You read a copy of the copy they made of the parts that weren't personal. They studied the letter with my father as they tried to figure out why Publius chose to die. They're both believers and worship with us when they're in Rome."

"But he's a man and a paterfamilias and can go where he wishes, do what he wants. Grandfather will choose whom I marry." With closed eyes, she shook her head. "Once I'm married again, my husband will dictate what we do for public worship. Glabrio will be an important man like his father, so he'll expect me to be seen at public ceremonies with him."

She wiped at the corner of her eye. "I wish I could choose my husband this time."

"I wish you could, too."

Was that longing in his eyes, as there must be in hers? Why did she have to be a Sabinus, bound by tradition to serve the family through marriage?

"Grandfather hasn't announced anything yet. I thought he was going to the first time Glabrio and his father came to dinner, but he said nothing. Father told me that first morning that he'd give me the few months of the typical mourning period. But if Glabrio doesn't want to wait, I can't imagine that Grandfather won't say do it sooner. Even if he doesn't, he'll arrange another noble marriage when those months have passed."

He took her hand in both of his. "One of the blessings of being a child of God is how amazing things you'd never expect sometimes happen. Don't despair." He squeezed her hand, and even though that couldn't change the future, somehow it helped. "We're all praying for God's protection for you and for His will to be done. Two of the gifts God bestows on His children are hope and joy."

Joy...Pompeia had already explained how they could have joy even in times of sadness and loss, even when their father was killed. But Sabina longed to have happiness as well as joy.

Only one man would make the finest of husbands; one man could fill all the empty places in her heart.

But it did no good to dream of being Kaeso's wife. Grandfather would never approve, and his decision was as binding as Roman law.

Outside the Titianus town house, late afternoon of Day 15

As Sabina left the Titianus town house, her satchel hung from her shoulder. From within it, the gospel written by John called to her. A quiet dinner with Septimus and maybe Father awaited her. Then she'd read and think and ask God to show her what she needed to do.

But as Graptus closed the door behind her, Glabrio approached and fell in beside her.

"I was in the area, and I thought we could talk as I walk you home."

She shifted the satchel in front of her and gripped the strap with both hands. Even though she wanted to, she couldn't say no. He hadn't done anything to deserve such rudeness.

"Of course."

He tapped the satchel. "There must be something important in there for you to hold it so tightly."

"My p-poems. I only have one copy."

"I hear they're exceptional. Perhaps you'll share them with me sometime."

"Septimus thinks everything I do is good, even when it isn't."

They were nearing the Porticus of Livia, and Tutelus usually took Sabina along the side street so she wouldn't run into people who wanted to talk. But with Glabrio beside her, it wasn't Tutelus choosing the route.

Ahead were several women about her age, and two were the last people she wanted to know she was back in Rome.

But the entrance to the porticus offered an escape into the maze of art galleries, and she took it.

He followed her in, and they entered the inner garden with the Altar of Concordia at its center.

"Concordia...the goddess of agreement in marriage. She's a worthwhile goddess to have in the household shrine of any who are newly married. Perhaps, she'll have a place in our future."

"Or perhaps not." She looked away from the white marble altar dedicated to a Roman goddess who wasn't real. "Harmony happens when both are kind to each other."

He rubbed under his chin where the cheek guards weren't in the way. "Titus and his wife seem so well suited to each other. Do they have Concordia among the gods in their house?"

"No."

"Which gods do they have?"

The hair on the back of her neck rose. Why was he asking?

"I haven't noticed."

His brows dipped. "Haven't noticed, or there aren't any there?"

She didn't mean to act surprised, but her head drew back before she could stop it.

Glabrio lowered his voice to scarcely above a whisper. "Pompeia and Kaeso are Christians. I think Titianus might be as well. Do you know how dangerous that makes them if they're trying to get you to be like them?"

"They aren't dangerous. I've never felt safer than when I'm with them."

"I don't want to see you hurt, Sabina. Being friends with Christians isn't safe."

"I know they're Christians, and I'm willing to risk it. I've almost decided to become one, too."

He froze midstride. "But why would you do something so stupid?"

Was this her way to escape? If he thought Christians were dangerous and being one was stupid, maybe she could get him to tell his father she wasn't a suitable wife.

But if not Glabrio, Grandfather would be picking the son of another leader of Rome. At least Glabrio was a nice enough man. Titus and Septimus both liked him. But would he allow her to practice her faith and worship with her friends?

"B-before I answer that, tell me why your grandfather gave up everything and died for his faith in Jesus."

He shrugged. "That was before I was born. Father has never talked about it."

"Aren't you curious? He had everything a noble Roman should want. Bringing honor to your family by serving as consul, more wealth than most senators, a worthy son to carry on after him. Why would he throw all that away and die, too, for a man who was executed on a Roman cross sixty years earlier?"

He stroked under his chin where the helmet didn't block. "I don't know. I never found it important to think about. Father has no interest in it, and I mostly study what's in our library. It's better than most here in Rome."

"Does it have what your grandfather had in his library about Jesus?"

"I never saw anything."

"Then it's missing what matters most."

His silence...did it mean he wondered if what she said was true?

"If you want, I'll ask if you can come learn with me."

"Well...I don't think so." His answer was no, but uncertainty lurked in his eyes.

"They won't tell anyone you're interested. People will just think you've become a friend of Titus. My father comes often for Titus's company."

He shook his head and frowned. "I'm not at all interested in their faith." The frown faded away. "But I might come to dine with Titus after he retires...if he invites me. My father and Aviola like him. I value his friendship."

"He p-probably values yours." She glanced toward another exit that would put her close to the side street Tutelus used. "I need to get home for dinner."

"I would go with you to see if I could join you, but Father's expecting me tonight."

Sabina touched his wrist. "Thank you for caring about the risk, even though it's one I'm not afraid to take."

"I won't tell anyone what I already figured out. I won't reveal what you told me. I hope I'm wrong about the danger, but be very careful anyway."

"I will."

Tutelus led them out of the portico and toward the narrow street that led home. But when she glanced back, Glabrio stood watching her. He'd put on a mask like Titus wore when on duty. Then he turned and slowly walked away.

Chapter 43

Decision

The Titianus town house, afternoon of Day 16

Kaeso's students had just left, and he was filing scrolls when Sabina bounced into the room with the biggest smile.

She took his hand. "I need to talk with you upstairs right now."

He set the remaining scrolls on the desk. "Lead the way."

Filomena didn't glare at him as they passed. Her shoulders sagged, and defeat filled her eyes. He drew a breath between his teeth. What had Sabina so happy and Filomena so sad?

By the time he reached the head of the stairs and entered their study chamber, she had his copy of John's gospel that he'd given her yesterday in her hands. He hadn't even closed the door when she started talking.

"I r-read the first part, and I've decided. Above all else, I want to be a child of God." She opened the codex.

"'The t-true light that gives light to everyone, was coming into the world. He was in the world, and the world was created through him, and yet the world did not recognize him. He came to his own, and his own people did not receive him. But to all who did receive him, he gave them the right to be children of God, to those who believe in his name, who were born, not of natural descent, or of the will of the flesh, or of the will of man, but of God. The Word became flesh and dwelt among us. We observed his glory, the glory as the one and only Son from the Father, full of grace and truth.'"

She bounced on her toes as she beamed at him. "I can't explain it, but the moment I read it, I knew I wanted that more than anything I've ever wanted."

Her radiant smile triggered his biggest grin. "Being a child of God—it's even better than the best you can imagine."

"B-but that wasn't the best part." She turned her gaze back on the words Pompeia had copied for him so many years ago. "'John testified concerning him and exclaimed, "This was the one of whom I said, 'The one coming after me ranks ahead of me, because he existed before me.'"' Luke wrote about that. 'Indeed, we have all received grace upon grace from his fullness, for the law was given through Moses; grace and truth came through Jesus Christ.' That's what Publius was telling us."

She clutched the open codex to her chest. Her eyelids closed, and she tipped her head back. When her eyes opened, their sparkle triggered silent alleluias as he watched his prayers being answered.

"When I read this next part..." She bit her lip, but that was from joy, not nervousness. "'No one has ever seen God. The one and only Son, who is himself God and is at the Father's side—he has made him known.'"

She closed the codex and traced the fish on the cover before turning glowing eyes on him again. "Then I said, 'God, Father of Jesus, please make Him known to me. Please let me become one of Your children, like Kaeso.' And I felt something in the room with me, urging me on to take the risk and become a Christian like all of you." She placed a hand over her heart. "No, not something, Someone. Like when you watch me so expectantly when I'm going to sing a new poem. Like what I was about to do truly mattered."

"That's the Holy Spirit. He is how God is present with us here and now."

"Then Filomena knocked on the door and told me Father wanted to see me right away, so I locked your codex in the chest and went to him."

The glow in her eyes faded.

"What did he want?"

"I don't know. When I got to his library, Titus had just arrived. He was in uniform and looked deadly serious. Father said he'd speak with me later."

"With Titus, that doesn't mean anything. He just had his tribune face on."

"I was glad he interrupted. I wanted to tell you right away, so I got the codex and we came before Father could send for me again."

He took her hand. "I'm so glad you did. Pompeia will be as pleased as I am. So will Titus."

But that wasn't quite true. They would be pleased, but nothing they felt could match the joy coursing through him at that moment. She would be his sister-in-Christ forever, even if she never became his wife.

"So, now I've decided, what do I do next?"

"Remember how Publius wrote about repenting of your sins and asking God to forgive them because Jesus paid for them?"

She nodded. "I can do that."

"That's next. Then you'll tell God you believe in Jesus and want to follow Him as your Lord."

She covered her mouth. "I'm not s-sure what to do to follow Him."

"That's why we read and study the writings God has given us. He teaches us what that means and reminds us how He wants us to live."

"C-can I keep coming here for you to help me with that?"

"Pompeia and I would both be sorry if you didn't."

"Father was going to a banquet tonight with Grandfather. But he needs to know as soon as I can tell him." She chewed her lip. "He's not going to be happy about it."

"We'll be praying for you."

Did she suspect what his most heartfelt prayer was? Probably not, and he wouldn't tell her. If what he longed for wasn't God's will, it was better if he suffered that disappointment alone.

"I think it will go smoother than you expect. It's safe to tell your father, but we have to be careful who we tell while Rome still bans our faith."

"Can I tell anyone else?"

"Maybe. You'll find the Holy Spirit will let you know when to speak and what to say if you ask Him. When you saw what Pompeia was copying...that was God starting you on the path to bring you to this point. Everyone in this familia follows Jesus as Lord. Tutelus knows we're Christians, but he's not a brother yet." He gave her a crooked smile. "Theo is convinced he will be. If he does join us, Titus will have to buy him from your father so he won't have to fight in the arena again."

"Filomena knows, too. She asked what I was reading, and I told her. She's upset because she's frightened about what might happen to me, but when she sees how happy it makes me, she'll understand why I had to join you. I think she'll join us after I explain it all to her. If Grandfather marries me to Glabrio, she can help me keep it secret. But maybe something will happen, and he won't."

"Only God knows our future." *Oh, God, if only she could join us in this familia as my wife.*

"I w-want to tell Pompeia. Then we can study." She handed him the codex and headed downstairs toward the weaving room.

He waited until she was out of earshot to release a deep sigh. He'd never met Quintus Sabinus himself, but from everything Septimus had told him, it would take God's own intervention for a man like that to let his favorite son's daughter marry a man like him.

But bigger miracles had happened.

Chapter 44

Marcellus's Surprise

The Marcellus estate, evening of Day 16

As the time approached when wagons and carriages could finally enter the city, the lines could stretch more than a mile at each city gate. When Titianus's men let the first ones in two hours before nightfall, the drivers traded the frustration of going nowhere for the irritation of moving at a snail's pace. But he hadn't expected a line at Marcellus's stabling area.

His stallion was used to crowds and noise in the heart of the city, but the spirited team yoked to Quintus's chariot resented the wait. After several minutes of dealing with them, Quintus handed the reins to Manius, who soon handed them to the charioteer who stood behind them.

Manius moved to the side where Titianus's normally stoic mount had turned fidgety at the nickers of the mare behind them.

"With our four Germans, your man doesn't need to stay. We planned on you spending the night with us, so he can wait for you at Father's villa."

From the placid mule on the other side of Titianus, Thrax cleared his throat. "He offered. I heard Marcellus shows off his wealth by feeding us bodyguards well."

The chariot lurched as they moved forward. One more carriage and it would be their turn to unload.

It wasn't the food that made Thrax insist, and they both knew it. "I'll tell Felix of your extreme dedication to duty in giving up what the Sabinus kitchen serves." One bounce of his eyebrows drew Thrax's almost-grin, which turned into his bodyguard frown as quickly as it had appeared.

They rolled forward again and stopped. As Quintus and Manius descended from the chariot, Titianus dismounted.

"Don't leave without me. Too many know drunken senators can forget and ride home without their guards. That makes an easy target." Thrax held out his hand, and Titianus handed him the reins.

"I won't. You're the one who'll know how to get my horse back."

As Thrax trotted after the Sabinus guards, Quintus tipped his chin at him. "It wasn't good food he came for. Marcellus's generosity doesn't extend to slaves."

He drew a finger along his jaw. "I'll ask for him next time I need an extra guard." One eyebrow rose. "Or is it only for you he does more than is required?"

Titianus answered with a shrug.

They entered the garden, where a large number of couches were arranged around low tables. A quick count found twelve sets of three couches. With three reclining on each, that made a hundred guests. Nothing odd in that, but off to the side, there were five platforms, each one a foot taller than the one below it. What that was for...he had no idea.

They were not among the first to arrive. Sixty, maybe seventy men stood in groups of two to five, and all had two wide purple stripes on their tunics, pronouncing them senators. In togas as white as a launderer could make them, over half looked ready to launch into oratorical performances with the slightest provocation. At least twenty had the wide purple stripe on the edge of their toga that declared them currently magistrates of at least *praetor* rank. Two that he saw were this year's consuls.

Saturninus stood with his back toward Titianus's party, dressed in a purple-banded toga and tunic, talking with the consuls.

Titianus lifted off his helmet and tucked it under his arm. The red horsehair crest made him too tall. In armor, he stood out like a wolf among sheep. But he would have looked scarcely less out of place had he worn his off-white toga and his tunic with merely equestrian stripes.

Some of the men he recognized from Glabrio's banquet. Most of those glanced at him and then looked away as if he were invisible, but a few noses twitched or nostrils flared at the sight of him, which spawned a smile on Quintus that looked quite genuine.

But the solid purple tunic and toga of an emperor was absent. The guest of honor was not yet here.

"Time to circulate." Quintus returned a wave to Glabrio's father on the far side of the gathering. "I let Marcellus know I'd have a guest I'd like reclining near me. His secretary replied that would be no problem." Eyes sparkling like a mischievous schoolboy, he chuckled softly. "I didn't tell him who it was."

Titianus scanned the crowd as his uncle sauntered toward a cluster of men his own age. Then a man striding out of the house toward them caught Titianus's eye. When he was twenty feet away, Titianus caught his.

Rufinus's head drew back, and his eyebrows plunged. A scowl started before he could stop it, but it only lasted a moment. He directed a political smile and slight tip of the head toward Titianus, then pivoted toward Saturninus. Standing close behind, he spoke into the prefect's ear. Saturninus twisted until his gaze fell upon Titianus. His mouth twitched before he turned back to respond to something the consul said to him.

Rufinus joined a group that included Lucius Gallus and turned his back toward Titianus.

"He claims he didn't hire the assassin." Quintus's near-whisper in Titianus's ear made him jump.

"He didn't. It was the brother of a man I sent to the sand." Titianus's gaze stayed fixed on Rufinus. "For a man with my job, not every enemy wears purple stripes." He looked at Quintus over his shoulder. "But some of them do."

A commotion by the door through which Rufinus had come drew everyone's attention.

Marcellus entered the garden with Hadrian at his side. Four steps behind them came Turbo, and Titianus was no longer the only armored equestrian in the group. Behind Turbo came Martialis with a squad of Praetorians. Half went one way, half the other until they encircled the dining party, spacing themselves out evenly and standing at parade rest.

Hadrian, with Turbo at his side, strolled over to join Saturninus and the consuls, and the rest of the diners returned to their conversations.

Martialis joined Titianus. "Turbo told me how you used yourself as bait." His voice was a near-whisper. "But he decided the risk was too high to use Hadrian himself to lure your quarry into the open, and he couldn't persuade the emperor to miss the surprise he'd been promised by a man he trusts as a friend."

"My prefect?"

Martialis nodded.

"Who's your young friend, Titus?" Quiet words right behind him startled Titianus again. When he turned to face his uncle, laughing eyes revealed that was deliberate.

"Quintus Rammius Martialis, tribune of the Praetorian Guard. He and I lived in quarters at the fortress."

Titianus held his hand palm up toward Quintus. "This is Quintus Flavius Sabinus, my uncle."

"I'm honored to meet you." Martialis donned the political smile and polite eyes he'd no doubt learned from his father.

"Martialis. Your father was Prefect of Egypt when Turbo was military prefect there. Lasting friendships can come from serving together. Genuine friendships." He rested a hand on Titianus's shoulder. "You'd be wise to keep your friendship with this one when he retires."

Martialis squared his shoulders as if that were an order. "I intend to."

"When they begin seating for dinner, come find me." With an enigmatic smile, Quintus moved away to join Manius and a group of praetors.

"So, that's the infamous Quintus Sabinus. I've heard stories…"

"And they might be true. Or not. A man who likes playing with other men's minds will always have stories about him."

"Hadrian thinks he can trust him."

"And he can. You might find honor where you least expect it…part of the time, anyway."

"That sounds like something you'd tell Glabrio. He's been quoting you to me when we play latrunculi."

"I did."

"I'm glad he's decided to live in quarters. His chef serves better food than our garrison cooks, and even though he's not quite as good as you at the game table, he presents a challenge."

The musical reverberation of a brass gong echoed through the gathering.

"Time to join my uncle. The food should be exquisite, but I'd rather be eating at the garrison with you."

Martialis returned to his centurion by the entrance, and Titianus worked his way past the couches toward Quintus, who stood next to Hadrian. As the emperor invited Quintus to recline at the table of highest honor with his upturned hand, Quintus smiled and pointed toward him. The solemn-faced emperor fixed his gaze on Titianus. Then whatever his uncle said drew a laugh and a slap on the shoulder from Hadrian.

Quintus moved to the next table where Manius already stood and spoke in his son's ear. They shared a chuckle, and by the time Titianus reached them, they had taken the couch of honor and saved a place for him.

The salad course was served, and Titianus settled in for a delectable meal and an earful of political conversation he took no part in. His contributions were the moments of silence when watching the speaker made them pause and ponder what was safe to say while he listened.

As the final course was being cleared, the gong sounded again. Saturninus, Marcellus, and Rufinus rose and stood together in front of Hadrian.

Turbo swung his feet off his couch, and draped the strap that held his sword across his chest. Titianus did the same.

Saturninus cleared his throat. "As you all know, it can be hard to keep a secret in Rome, even among friends sworn to secrecy." Chuckling spread from table to table. "But my friends and I"—he held his hands out to Marcellus and Rufinus—"have succeeded." He clapped his hands once. "Set up the chairs."

A flurry of motion followed, where a dozen of Marcellus's slaves carried chairs to the platforms and began setting them out.

He turned to the emperor. "Caesar Traianus Hadrianus, we know of your love for the performances of the classics of Greek theater, but every classic play was performed a first time. And while the lyrical performance of a Greek tragedy or comedy never ceases to delight, Latin is the language of power and glory."

He held his hand toward Marcellus, who stepped forward to speak. "We also know of your love of history, both studying great events of the past and performing mighty deeds of your own for historians of the future to celebrate. We considered presenting a story of Philip of Macedon, who did great deeds until his life was cut short and his son went on to achieve even greater glory. But that story has been told enough times."

Rufinus stepped forward. "So, in this time of prosperity and peace under your leadership that exceeds Alexander's greatest accomplishments, we present a play in your honor. But the spirit of our times is better served by comedy, not tragedy. So, in the spirit of the greatest comedies of Aristophanes and Plautus, we present *The Wolves*, a satire in Latin on Roman family life, performed by the actors who delighted you in *Medea* at the Theater of Marcellus...and written by the three of us."

Marcellus pointed toward the chairs. "If you'll all find a seat, we can begin."

Titianus covered his mouth and closed his eyes. It wouldn't do to laugh aloud, even though he was struggling not to shake from it bubbling up inside him. Saturninus would never understand. For two weeks he'd been hunting assassins, and they turned out to be playwrights.

He looked over at Turbo. The prefect's lips twitched, and an ironic smile crept out. His gaze turned on Titianus, and he shook his head. Then he rose and followed Hadrian to the honored seating at the front of the platform.

Manius nudged Titianus. "Let's go enjoy Rome's latest literary master-piece." Manius's grin was contagious, but Titianus fought against letting his own out.

He pursed his lips and relaxed them to achieve his usual emotionless face. His commander was one of the playwrights, and if he put on his tri-bune mask now, it would be easier to show no emotion if the play turned out to be bad.

Chapter 45

FINAL REPORT

The Praetorian Fortress, morning of Day 17

For what might be the last time, Titianus left his stallion at the fortress stables. One visit to each prefect, and then he could retire to civilian life. After the last two weeks, a toga sounded much better than armor for his work uniform.

First, a stop at Saturninus's fortress office to once more request permission to resign. Then, his final report to Turbo.

His hand rested on the satchel he'd carried for ten years. It held only one tablet today—his letter of resignation. He expected to leave it for Saturninus's optio to give to him when he finally showed up.

After last evening's performance, the prefect would be recovering from the volume of wine he'd drunk in response to the many toasts offered by genuine friends and by those only seeking his favor. It wasn't a literary masterpiece, but it had been good enough. It was mostly the play and not the playwrights that drew the audience's laughter, his included.

After that, he had some farewells to say.

Inside the Principia, he passed what was once his own office. Plancus raised a hand in greeting, and he turned in. "Is Glabrio here?"

"Not yet, Tribune, but I expect him any time. He gets in almost as early as you did."

Titianus let his mouth twitch, then relax into a slight smile. "Take good care of him. He deserves your best, as you've always given me."

Plancus's broad smile was met by one of Titianus's own.

"I've noticed, and I will."

A few more steps took him to the prefect's office. As he expected, Saturninus wasn't there. He handed Hortus the tablet. "For Prefect Saturninus as soon as he arrives."

The optio took it. "As soon as he arrives."

As Titianus walked away, it took a struggle to get the smile off his lips.

It was a short walk to the Praetorium, and when he approached the guards at Turbo's door, one knocked and stuck his head inside even before he reached them. Then he held the door open.

Titianus fastened his chinstrap and entered.

Turbo looked up from the reports spread around his desk. "Titianus."

"Prefect." Titianus struck his chest. "I wish to make my final report."

Turbo closed the tablet in front of him. "Proceed."

"Before the performance last night, I believed the letter you showed me was sent between Saturninus and Rufinus, but I had no solid evidence to prove it or to tie them to an assassination plot. Since last night, I'm convinced they were only discussing possible plots for their play, and there was never any intention to harm Emperor Hadrian."

Turbo's mouth twitched. "You read the letter and saw a threat to the emperor, as I did." One corner of his mouth lifted. "We were both wrong. Their only threat to Hadrian is from telling other men with no more talent than they have that the best way to earn his favor is to write him an equally bad play. But it could have been worse."

"The play or the plot?"

"Either and both." He leaned back and crossed his arms. "I didn't like you withholding their names, but in this case, that proved wise. But now that you've completed this assignment, I have another if you want it."

Titianus froze. With the way Turbo "asked" before, he couldn't turn down the last one. What would this one be?

Turbo chuckled. "No, it won't be as difficult or as dangerous as this could have been. One of my senior tribunes is moving on to his first political post. When he becomes *questor*, I'll need a new tribune. I'd like it to be you."

Relief surged through Titianus. It was an offer he'd have no trouble refusing.

"I'm honored by your offer, but there are others who would accept it eagerly and benefit more. As Prefect Saturninus would tell you, I'm really an equestrian businessman, and after ten years, it's time for me to look after business."

"I understand." Turbo leaned forward and clasped his hands. "But if you change your mind, let me know. You're dismissed."

Titianus struck his chest, executed a parade turn, and left the office of the man in whom power and honor were mostly compatible.

As he headed to the Principia to check for Glabrio one last time, he undid the chinstrap. When he got home, he'd take off the helmet one last time and put it on the rack where he hung his body armor. He'd keep it all there...for a while.

He was almost to his office when Plancus came out, carrying a stack of tablets held in place with his chin.

"Tribune Glabrio is in."

Titianus tapped his arm as they passed and got a smile in return.

Glabrio sat at his desk with the stack of unreads still taller than the reads. But he closed the one before him and leaned back with a smile when Titianus entered.

"Martialis told me what happened last night...and what Turbo had you doing." He blew out a breath. "Better you than me. At the start, I believed you when you said you were figuring out who knew and liked whom so you could get students." His eyes narrowed. "But that made no sense when you never told anyone about the school."

"Sometimes what you do serves two purposes. I will be using what I learned to find new students. We can teach twice as many after I join Kaeso in a teacher's toga."

"I learned a lot about watching people at the Forums and Baths." His smile faded. "Bolt the door and sit."

With the door closed, Titianus settled into the guest chair and crossed his arms. He'd heard that said too often lately, and his stomach clenched every time.

"I talked with Sabina about what she's learning in your house. I know your family secret, and it's safe with me."

"I expected it would be, but it's good to hear you say so."

"You've taught me a lot about many things. Not just what I'm supposed to do, but about people and what's important. About judging each person by who they are and not where they came from. About who's worthy of trust and respect. I'm planning to continue as you've been doing. Getting to the truth and delivering justice matter."

"Good. One more word of advice. Be careful in the exalted company your father keeps. Being your father's son doesn't protect you from all enemies. It could put a target on you for one who wants your father's friendship only as long as it benefits him. False friends can quickly become enemies."

"You mean Saturninus?"

"Among others. To men like him, without my armor, I'm only a merchant rich enough to be equestrian, but nothing more. When I begin teaching, they'll think even less of me. It won't be long before they don't think of me at all. But even as a consul's son…" Titianus massaged his hand. "Maybe especially as a consul's son, there will always be people who want to tear you down, and the better you are at doing something, the more enjoyment some will get if you falter."

"I'll be careful. You've opened my eyes to the resentment behind smiling masks and how hard it can be to find true friends."

"Martialis will be one, if you let him. I think he'll find one in you as well." Titianus rested his hands on the arms of the chair. "When you have nowhere better to go, you're welcome to drop in for dinner with me anytime, like Septimus and Manius do. No advance notice is needed. There's always room for one more man of honor at my table."

Glabrio's smile reflected Titianus's own. "I was hoping you'd say that, and I will."

Chapter 46

The Proper Arrangement

The Sabinus town house, early morning of Day 17

As Sabina entered the triclinium, Father pushed away his breakfast plate. She'd planned her entry for when it was almost time for the salutation. If he had people waiting for him and some might be close enough to hear shouting, he wouldn't yell as long or as loud after she shared her news. The most wonderful news she'd ever had, whether he thought so or not.

She closed her eyes and tightened her lips. When she relaxed them, the sappy grin had relaxed into a happy smile.

She marched into the room and stood before him, gripping her palla in sweaty palms. "May I speak with you, Father?"

"Go ahead."

"C-can we go to the library? I don't want any to hear but you."

"We can." He drained his goblet and swung his legs off the couch.

He led her into the room and sat halfway on the edge of his desk. "Bolt the door and tell me."

As she slid the bolt home, her breaths came faster. *God, please give me the words to say without freezing.*

Counting each step, she walked over to stand before Father, back straight, chin high.

"Yesterday I made a decision, Father." She drew a deep breath. Sometimes that helped the words come out.

"What did you decide?"

Father hadn't waited for her to finish, like he usually did now. His smile

298

had hardened into the political one he'd learned from Grandfather, and his eyes had veiled, too. But no matter what he did, it was time to speak the truth and ask for deliverance from a future made dangerous by her choice.

"I'm a Christian."

Father's mouth twitched, then settled back into the formal smile. "What do you want me to do about that?"

Her head drew back. Was he joking? His eyes were serious, so maybe not. Did he really want her to answer?

God, give me the right words and make them come out quickly.

"I want you to get Grandfather to spare me from sealing an alliance. Don't make me marry Glabrio. Let me stay here with you and Septimus and his friends."

"His friends. Aren't they your friends, too?" Father's voice was too calm.

"Very much so."

Father fingered his lip. "Why do you want to stay with them?"

Sabina gripped her left hand with her right. If only it was Kaeso's hand. He gave her confidence whenever she lacked it.

Pompeia was a dear friend and kindred spirit, and every day together made their sisterly bond stronger. But she loved Kaeso as a man. Her heart soared and her mind filled with poetry each time she imagined them spending days and nights together for the rest of their lives. But if she told Father that, would he forbid her seeing him again?

"You don't have to answer that yet. I had a conversation with Titus a couple of days ago about whom you should marry. Would you like to know what we discussed?"

"Yes, Father." It was a good thing she hadn't eaten yet. Nothing would have stayed down.

"When I asked him, he told me everyone in his household is a Christian, that you soon might be telling me what you've just said. He pointed out the problems of you making a political marriage, and I agreed."

Sabina gripped a chair back to steady herself. What was he saying?

Father's political smile relaxed into a real one. "He proposed a way to avoid insulting my fellow senators when we decline their marriage requests. But I need a few answers before I can do as he suggested."

"What are the questions?" Her heart was beating like it did when she'd chased Septimus as a child.

"It's too soon for me to tell you, but whatever I do, it will be in your best interest."

Father stood. "But I'll suggest to your grandfather that I be allowed to choose your next husband. If he agrees, I'll look for someone it will be safe for you to marry."

He came to her and wrapped an arm around her shoulders. "I have salutation now, and you need to eat. Father and I are going to a banquet this evening. I should get a chance to ask him soon."

In her best interest...no one fit that better than Kaeso. Septimus could persuade Father to do almost anything. Could he suggest Kaeso in a way that would make Father agree?

"Thank you, Father."

He pushed a loose strand of hair behind her ear. "Don't thank me yet. I can't promise Father will grant my request, but...we'll see."

He turned her and gently pushed her toward the door. "Why don't you go up and write a poem about this? The next time I eat with Kaeso, you can sing it to us."

In the doorway, she glanced over her shoulder. Why was Father smiling like Septimus had just told his best joke?

Afternoon of Day 17

Manius sat at his library desk, dressed in his toga, rolling a stylus between his fingers. Father was riding in from his villa, and they would be going to the Baths to circulate among friends, allies, and enemies before going to a banquet at Aviola's town house.

Which presented a problem. Aviola and Glabrio were cousins, so the elder Glabrio was certain to be there. Each time Manius saw him, he made some comment implying their future relationship through marriage.

He had to convince Father today to put an end to those expectations... or at least not to confirm them.

When Father stepped into the library, Manius invited him to sit in the guest chair with a sweep of his upturned palm.

"Compared to Marcellus's play last night, this should be a quiet evening, but it might be amusing. Some of the reactions to Titus being there in armor were as entertaining as the play. There were three who seemed particularly nervous when I introduced him as my nephew. I wonder why."

"Perhaps they'll be there tonight, and you can figure that out."

"Perhaps. But I think I'll tell Festinus to check into them when he reports tomorrow. If my master of spies can't find something, their unease might mean nothing. The way Titus looks at you without speaking...it has that effect on people. But if they're doing something they wouldn't want our tribune of the Urban Cohort to know, that's information I want at my fingertips."

Father stretched out his legs and crossed them at the ankle. "At the Forums this morning, I ran into the elder Glabrio. He's even more eager about his son marrying Sabina than he was. We were interrupted, but I think I'll agree to the marriage tonight. We just won't make the public announcement until her three months of mourning are over."

Before he could stop himself, Manius sucked air between his teeth. "You can't do that. It could lead to her death and will certainly lead to embarrassment for you and the whole Sabinus family."

Quintus's head drew back. "What are you talking about?"

Manius barely stopped himself from rubbing his neck. Nervousness was not the signal he wanted to send Father. Titus had warned they might all be in danger if he revealed their faith. He'd told his cousin he'd find another reason to convince Father, and he meant it. But he could give Father no other explanation for that marriage to be fatal.

And he had an overwhelming sense that he should tell Father the truth, even though no one else should know. No one kept potentially lethal secrets better than his father, and no one protected those he considered family better.

"You're taking a long time to answer. Why?"

"Because you won't like the reason, but when you hear it, you'll know I'm right."

He didn't believe in Titus's god, but the urge to tell Father got stronger and stronger. Was that a nudge from the Christian god? Titus would laugh if he told him he'd thought that...or would he? He'd said his god could open Father's eyes so he'd do the right thing.

"Tell me." Father leaned back in the chair and crossed his arms.

"If I do, it stays strictly between the two of us."

"I taught you how to keep secrets. You don't need to question whether I can. Tell me."

"She's a Christian, so you can't let her marry into any of the families we thought appropriate."

Father's eyes bulged and his mouth opened, but no words came.

"But I can stop people from asking you about marrying her so we don't offend any of them."

Father's hands dropped to the chair arms. "How are you going to do that?"

Not a question, but a challenge. If Titus's god was real enough to reach Father, he'd better start doing it. It was too late to take back what Manius had already revealed.

"I know who would marry her and keep her secret. He'd make her a happy woman as well."

"Who?" Cold eyes and a near-sneer—that look had earned Father the nickname "crocodile."

Should he reveal Kaeso's name? But Father would never yield without a specific plan.

"Titus's brother-in-law."

Father looked at him sideways. "Why won't it bother him that she's a Christian?"

Silence wasn't the best answer, but anything he said put his friend at risk. All his friends.

Father leaned forward. "Is he one?"

He could sidestep the question now, but in the end, Father needed to know. "Yes."

An odd growl came from Father's throat. "Is his sister one? And Titus?" Quintus's eyebrows plunged. "Lenaeus…isn't he Septimus's closest friend?" His eyes narrowed to scarcely a slit. "Has Septimus become one, too?"

It might be stupid to sail a ship under towering thunderclouds with lightning striking the sea around you, but what other choice was there?

"There are more Christians connected to this family than you want to know about. It's better if I don't share all I know."

Quintus gripped the arms of the chair. His knuckles whitened, and his breaths came faster. "Are you one?"

"Not yet, but I've been considering it."

"Well, I forbid it."

Manius massaged his neck. He could say nothing and let Father assume he'd obey. Or, as Septimus often said, he could be a man of honor and tell Father the truth.

"Father, you know I couldn't honor you as my father more than I always have. And you're not just my father. You've been my closest friend since I became a man."

Father's smile was that of a victor. Manius drew a deep breath and blew it out. Obedient son or man of honor? His next words would decide.

"But if I become convinced that what the Christians believe is true, I'll have no choice but to believe it myself. I know how much you care about some who already believe. Like them, I can keep it secret from those who would strike at us because of it. At the end of our lives, it's not power or wealth or family reputation that matters most. It's truth."

Father's nostrils flared, and the icy anger in his eyes would make a brave man shiver. His mouth opened as if to speak, then closed.

Manius waited in silence. His father could strip him of everything, but the embarrassment, no, the disgrace of all of Rome knowing what his favorite son had chosen would probably kill him if anyone learned why.

Then Father's shoulders sagged. "You are my son. Nothing can change that." A sigh drained his lungs. "Do with Sabina what you think best, and I'll approve your decision. Believe what you must, but don't tell me about it. As long as I don't know you've changed, I can tell anyone you're a loyal son of Rome, and they'll believe me. That should be enough to protect you as long as you don't betray what you are yourself."

One corner of Father's mouth lifted as he shook his head. "So, your cousin Titus, the most single-minded enforcer of Roman law I've ever seen, worships the one god Rome has outlawed." The second corner rose to make an amused smile. "Huh." Another headshake. "For how long?"

"About a year."

"Hmph." Father ran his hand through his thinning hair. "Well,"—he blew out a long breath—"your cousin's secret is safe with me. Your family spends so much time with him, even a hint of it might throw suspicion your way. If I say nothing, no one will suspect the incorruptible tribune has abandoned his dedication to Rome. Turbo trusts him completely. If a man like him can fool everyone, I guess you can do the same if you try."

"You don't need to worry that I can't. With you as my teacher, I've learned from the best how to keep secret what must not be revealed." He rose, walked around the desk, and wrapped his arm around his father's shoulders. "And no matter what I decide about this, I'll still be a loyal son of Rome." After one quick squeeze, he stepped back. "And I'll always be proud to be your son."

He tipped his head toward the door. "Shall we go to the banquet?"

His father's sigh accompanied tightened lips. A roll of Father's eyes finished with another shake of his head. "Dinner should prove entertaining.

Young Glabrio has turned into another Titus, and it's driving Saturninus to distraction. Perhaps I should suggest the young man deserves a more appreciative commander like Turbo. That should get a reaction." He chuckled as if their earlier conversation had never happened.

As they walked through the atrium to where their bodyguards and valets waited, Manius glanced at the man who had guided him through life. Who would have thought he'd even consider what Father believed could be wrong?

But he loved his father too much to leave things as they were. He tightened his lips to stop the smile that would make Father ask what he was thinking.

If I decide what Titus claims is true, I'll become a Christian. And if that happens, I won't give up until I persuade you to join me.

The Sabinus town house, morning of Day 18

When Sabina rose from the dressing table, her hands trembled. She took Filomena's hands, and the trembling stopped.

"I w-wonder if Father asked Grandfather last night. I tried to stay awake, and I almost did. But he got home so late that I dozed for a while, and when I woke, he was already asleep."

She pressed her palms against both cheeks. "If Grandfather said yes, wouldn't Father have awakened me to let me know?"

"I can't say what the master would have done." Filomena pushed a loose strand of hair behind Sabina's ear.

"Maybe there was no chance to ask Grandfather, or maybe he said he'd have to think about it. Maybe Father wanted to wait until he had an answer."

"Maybe if you go down to breakfast now, you can know instead of worry." Filomena pushed a slipping hair pin back into place.

Sabina took her maid's hand. "What would I have done without you these past six years? You're right. I shouldn't just fret. I need to be brave and go find out. Pompeia and Kaeso pray about everything, and they don't worry much. I need to remember to do the same now."

She gave a squeeze before releasing her hand. "I know you didn't like them because you thought they weren't good for me, but no one could be better."

"I talked with Ciconia yesterday while you studied. She's cared for Pompeia like I have for you. Everyone in that familia is Christian. She explained some things. She said we could talk more today. I think I'll offer to help in the kitchen so we can."

Sabina slipped her arms around her faithful friend. "I'm so glad. I want you to know this happiness, too." She stepped back. "Even if Grandfather insists on choosing, at least I'll have one person to share my secret."

She squared her shoulders. "Septimus always says b-bravery isn't the absence of fear. It's doing what you should even when you're scared to death. It's time for me to be brave."

She headed downstairs.

At the door to the triclinium, she paused. Father sat on the edge of the couch. As he reached for another hardboiled egg, he glanced at her. Then he swirled it in his favorite sauce and took a bite.

"I was beginning to wonder if you'd get here before salutation." He summoned her with a curl of his fingers. "I won't torture you with suspense. Your grandfather has given me authority to choose your next husband."

Her shoulders sagged as relief coursed through her.

"But I have some very strict requirements that he'll have to meet."

"Wh-what, Father?"

His face looked too solemn.

"I've come to enjoy your company enough that it will have to be someone who spends most of his time in Rome. Since he'll probably come with you to dine here, it also needs to be a man whose company I can enjoy."

She fought the urge to nibble her lip. *God, please let him see that's Kaeso.*

"That means he has to be smart and well informed. You wouldn't want a stupid man, anyway. But some intelligent men want a wife who's not as smart as they are, and that rules out some possibilities."

"I d-do prefer smart men, like you and Septimus." One little nibble wouldn't hurt. The smartest man she knew was Kaeso. Septimus thought so, too. If she asked him, he could point that out to Father. *God, let Kaeso be the one Father chooses.*

"Since you don't enjoy public gatherings, it would be better if your future husband didn't have high political ambitions." Father dipped the egg again and ate what remained. "Especially since you've made that dangerous decision that would be impossible for him to hide."

He reached for another egg and dipped it in the second sauce. He took a bite and smiled his approval.

"It's better if a husband and wife can agree on the most important things to have harmony in their marriage, like your mother and I have. So, since you tell me you're determined to believe like your friends, you need a man who can at least hide your faith, and it would be better if he shared it."

Another dip, another bite, and the egg was gone.

"So, all things considered, I'm planning on you marrying Kaeso."

It was her first squeal of delight since she became a woman. She threw her arms around him and knocked him back onto the couch. He pushed her up so he could sit again, and patted the couch for her to sit beside him.

"I'll take that as your approval. That's a good thing. I already sent an invitation to come for dinner tonight to celebrate."

He wrapped his arm around her. "Your grandfather is joining us. When he gets to know your Kaeso, I'm sure he'll approve of my choice."

She snuggled into his shoulder and sighed the most contented sigh of her entire life.

"Thank you, Father."

Thank you, God, for everything!

Chapter 47

WHAT MATTERS MOST

The Titianus town house, one month later

If anyone had told Manius Sabinus two months ago that he would have traded a son-in-law from a senatorial family with a town house in Rome and several estates for a man whose fortune was almost entirely based on the scrolls in his library, he would have laughed at the absurdity of it.

Now he stood at the base of the balcony stairs as Sabina threw a kiss down to him before disappearing into a bridal chamber in his cousin's town house. He was a betting man, but like his father, he only bet on sure things. That Sabina and Kaeso would be happy together was a bet he'd gladly make.

It had been a good celebration despite the small number in attendance. Or perhaps because of it.

Grandfather had declined to come. Although he conceded that his granddaughter's new husband was highly recommended by the senators whose sons studied with him and was entertaining to converse with while dining, he'd chosen a dinner with Hadrian over the wedding.

Surprisingly, young Glabrio had come, but he left before dinner to join his father. He didn't want the elder Glabrio asking why he went to the wedding of the woman he was supposed to marry himself.

Melis, Titianus's new freedman who'd fought an assassin to save his master and still limped because of it, had gone to the servant's quarters hand-in-hand with the pretty cook's helper and the rest of Titus's familia. Tutelus, Sabina's bodyguard who'd escorted their party from the Sabinus town house, went with them.

It was time for Septimus and him to go home themselves. He'd arranged for his Germans to come after dinner and bring horses, so he strolled with his cousin and son into the stableyard to wait.

Titus had installed benches under the portico for the people who escorted their students. Manius settled onto one and stretched his arms out along the back.

"Well, Titus, having you as a cousin has proven highly diverting this past year. First you and Pompeia, now Sabina and Kaeso. Throw in an assassination attempt and some political intrigue, even though it wasn't real, and you've kept me well entertained."

"Glad to be of service." Titus leaned against the portico column. "It wasn't my intention when I started."

"Knowing you has been thought-provoking as well. I'm sure Glabrio would agree. I never expected the unyielding tribune who requires rock-solid evidence before making an accusation to be so philosophical. You haven't won me to your way of thinking on everything, but I've learned more from you and Septimus than I ever expected."

Septimus sat on the bench beside him. "What, Father?"

Manius stood. Head high, arm raised in his best oratorical stance, he cleared his throat. "It's not rank or wealth or family connections that determine the worth of a man. It's his honor."

Septimus chuckled, and Titus smiled.

"You two and Kaeso—you've shown me how true that is. You all live it, and I'm proud to call you friends." He placed his hand on Titus's shoulder. "But there's something missing from Titus's favorite saying."

As his wisest cousin's steel-gray eyes warmed, Manius's own smile grew into a grin. "And even though honor is important, it's truth that matters most."

Brummbar and Barin came through the gate, leading the two extra horses. After Manius mounted, they all rode toward the street. But before they passed through the gateway, he looked back at Titus. His cousin raised a hand in farewell.

Truth did matter most...but what was the truth? What Titus had told him about the Jesus he followed seemed unbelievable. How could something so unbelievable be true? But if it was true, how could a man not decide to believe?

Finis

I'd Love to Hear from You!

If you enjoyed this book, it would be a real gift to me if you would post a review at the retailer you purchased it from. A good review is like a jewel set in gold for an author. Other great places to share reviews are Goodreads and BookBub. If you've read others in the series, it would be great if you post a review of those, too.

I'd also love to hear from you at carol-ashby.com or directly at carolashbyauthor@gmail.com.

Want to hear about upcoming releases in the Light in the Empire series and free gifts only for newsletter subscribers?

For free gifts and other special offers, advance notices of upcoming releases, and info about my latest writing adventures, please sign up for my newsletter at https://carol-ashby.com/newsletter/.

Light *in the* Empire Series

What Matters Most is the eleventh volume in the Light in the Empire series, which follows the interconnected lives of seven Roman families during the reigns of Trajan and Hadrian. Each can be read stand-alone. The twelve novels of the series will take you around the Empire, from Germania and Britannia to Thracia, Dacia, and Judaea and, of course, to Rome itself.

Coming in in 2022: Please Help Me Choose!

Who would you like to see in a future story?

I grew to love several of the characters in *What Matters Most* while I was writing. That usually happens, and sometimes a future story takes shape in my head even before I finish. But more often the next hero or heroine is chosen because readers tell me who needs to come back as a story lead.

Readers who loved Galen as a teen in *Blind Ambition* wanted to see him as a grown man, so he became the hero in *Faithful*. People who asked for Brutus and Africanus to have their own story found out what happened to them in *Honor Bound*.

Since people kept asking what happened to Leander's beloved but long-lost sister in *True Freedom*, it was clear Ariana would need her own story in *Hope Unchained*. People who met Ursus in *Hope Unchained* asked what happened to him, so he returned with his childhood name of Matti in his quest to know God better in *Hope's Reward*.

In *What Matters Most*, Septimus, who was rather like a Great Dane puppy in *Honor Bound,* comes back four years older, and Tribune Titianus from *More Than Honor* and *True Freedom* faces the most dangerous assignment of his life. I'm SO glad people asked for still more of them after the earlier books.

But there are many more characters in the books of the series that I would like to spend more time with, and I hope there are some for you, too. Who would you most like to see in a future story? What was it about them that made you want more of them? I'd love to hear what you think. It will guide what I write next.

Some possibilities:
Aulus of *True Freedom?*
Glabrio of *What Matters Most?*
Septimus or Manius of *Honor Bound, More Than Honor,* and *What Matters Most?*
Someone else I haven't mentioned? (I can't wait to see who shows up here!)

Please tell me who you'd love to see again as a comment at carol-ashby.com or directly at carolashbyauthor@gmail.com!

I'm thinking about writing a short story or novella about someone from Sextus's or Calvia's households in *Honor Bound* or Gracchus of *Hope Unchained* and *Hope's Reward* to give to newsletter subscribers. Which would you rather have?

Please go to my website, carol-ashby.com, and share your thoughts in the comment box. Sign up for the newsletter, and you'll get the story when I finish it. Looking forward to hearing from you!

Historical Note

Senators and Equestrians in the Early Roman Empire

Under the Roman Republic, the Senate consisted of men from the upper class who were not specifically elected to the Senate but who had been elected to their first magistrate position of questor by the public assemblies of male citizens called *comitia*. A man was normally a senator for life, but he could be expelled from the Senate for "misconduct" as defined by the senators at the time. While there were originally 100 members, the number of senators increased to 300, then 600 in 80BC, then 900 under Julius Caesar.

Officially, the Senate advised magistrates, but its power increased after the end of the Second Punic War with Carthage (201 BC). It prepared legislation for a formal vote by the assemblies, handled government finances, oversaw the state religion, and dealt with foreign powers. From the 2nd century BC until the beginning of the Empire under Augustus, the Senate was the government of Rome.

Serving in the Senate was an unpaid position, so a private source of a large income was needed. Senators were banned from making money in commerce by the *lex Claudia* in 218 BC. Senatorial wealth was based largely on land ownership, with profits from agricultural activities and ownership of rental properties being legal ways to make money. For some senatorial families, pursuit of political power was the main goal of life. This was largely achieved through personal relationships among the senators. Marriages, divorces, and friendships were often used to acquire political advantage. This remained true during the Empire.

Consuls were elected every year, so political campaigning and developing political alliances were never-ending activities. Bribery and corruption were often part of the campaigns, which were all paid for with personal money and money from political allies.

There were a few dozen families that provided most of the consuls, and building one's own political alliance while undermining others was common. Coming from a consular family had great importance, and even under the empire, the descendants of men who were consuls during the Republic were called *nobiles* (nobles).

After Augustus established himself as the first emperor, the power of the Senate was greatly decreased, but Augustus chose to call himself "first citizen" (*princeps*) to make it appear the Senate still controlled Rome and her empire. This pretense was continued by later emperors until Diocletian revamped imperial administration in AD 285.

Augustus decreased the number of senators from over 1000 to fewer than 600 and set a property requirement of 250,000 *denarii*, the equivalent of a quarter million daily wages. The imperial Senate still controlled the state treasury, administered some peaceful provinces whose governors they appointed, and became a legislative body issuing *senatus consulta* that had the force of law. Provinces on the frontier where legions were based and the province of Egypt, which was the source of much of the wheat eaten by the one million people living in Rome itself, were Imperial provinces. The emperor appointed legates, the legion commanders who also governed a province that contained a single legion, and governors over the legates when more than one legion was based in a province.

With many emperors, being a senator who angered the emperor was potentially deadly. Many old senatorial families chose to retire from politics, although some individuals were executed or "chose" to commit suicide to avoid confiscation of their property from their heirs. Some upper-class male citizens from the provinces who met the property requirement joined what had once been an Italian-only Senate. Trajan, who was born in Spain, became the first non-Italian emperor. Hadrian, the son of Trajan's cousin and his own adopted son, was also born in Spain.

Some emperors were notorious for executing senators they thought might be plotting against them. Tiberius, Caligula, Claudius, Nero, and Domitian are well known for executing inconvenient senators, so when a new emperor announced he would not kill senators, the pronouncement was welcomed. But it wasn't completely believed, and it wasn't always true.

An emperor unpopular with the Senate sometimes had his rule ended by conspirators who killed him. Caligula and Domitian were assassinated, and Nero committed suicide because he expected it.

Trajan had been a popular emperor who died a natural death, and Trajan's Praetorian Prefect Attianus stayed on with Hadrian. While Hadrian was away from Rome, Attianus charged four ex-consuls with attempting to assassinate Hadrian during his first year as emperor (AD 118), and the prefect presented evidence that forced the Senate to vote for execution. Although Hadrian denied involvement, the Senate blamed him, and many would have welcomed his speedy death.

The second noble order of Romanes were the equestrians (*equites*). They originally formed the cavalry of Republican Rome, but by imperial times, they were the wealthy business class (*ordo equester*). After the *lex Claudia* forbade senators from being involved in commerce, equestrians took over most financial opportunities in Rome and the provinces. These included banking, operating mines, importing and exporting goods, money lending, and tax farming. They also received government contracts for road building and supplying the military.

To be enrolled as an equestrian, the minimum financial worth was 100,000 denarii. Although many were wealthy enough to qualify as senators, most chose to remain in the private sector growing their wealth instead of governing. Some pursued military careers or salaried positions administering the empire.

Only senators could serve in some of the most important government positions. The Prefect of the City (*praefectus urbi*) had many administrative duties, including the distribution of free grain to citizens, and was, in essence, the mayor of Rome, outranked only by the emperor. He was selected by the emperor from among the senators and served until the emperor chose to replace him. It was a very powerful and highly respected position.

The urban prefect commanded the Urban Cohort , which was essentially the daytime police force of Rome. In AD 120, Rome had about a million residents and was divided up between four tribunes with six centurions under each. It was organized much like a legion.

The Praetorian Prefect was also appointed by the emperor, and he was always an equestrian. The Praetorians were organized and trained like a regular legion. Part of the Guard traveled with the emperor when he left Rome, and part remained in Rome to discourage attempts by political rivals to replace the emperor in his absence.

Large crowds can quickly lead to riots. With 250,000 attending the races and 50,000 attending the gladiatorial games, a large military presence was desirable. A Praetorian cohort of between 800 and 1500 men was assigned to keep order at the Circus Maximus on race days, at the amphitheater while the games were in progress, and at the theater during performances.

The city prison was run by the Praetorians, and executions decreed by the emperor or the Senate were their responsibility. A centurion with a detachment of Praetorians might be sent far from Rome to carry out an execution, bringing the head back for public display in Rome. Although not part of their official job description, they often played a crucial role in deciding who would be the next emperor.

In *What Matters Most*, the hostility between Hadrian and the Senate is the backdrop for the investigation of an assassination plot that becomes the equestrian Tribune Titianus's final case. Although Titianus is a tribune of the Urban Cohort reporting to Urban Prefect Saturninus, he is loaned to the Praetorian Prefect Turbo for this delicate assignment because of his reputation for incorruptibility and his lack of entanglement in the political alliances of the senatorial class.

The importance of political alliances combined with the authority of the *paterfamilias* to determine whom the sons and daughters of senatorial families married. The paterfamilias was the oldest male member of the family, and he owned all the family property and could dictate what his adult children did until he died.

For Sabina, that was her grandfather, Quintus Flavius Sabinus. Her father Manius still didn't own property and still had to obey his father, even though he was Quintus's grown son with grown children of his own. Quintus arranged Sabina's first marriage to the son of a man who sought Quintus's political favor. It was customary for young noblewomen to marry between fourteen and sixteen years of age. Young noblemen married later, but it was still common to marry in their early to mid-twenties to a young woman selected by their fathers or by their grandfathers, if still living.

Sabina knew her duty and responsibilities as the seal on an alliance her grandfather wanted, so she suffered without complaining. At the beginning of the story, she is freed from a miserable marriage by the death of her husband. As a still-young woman of twenty-two, she expects to seal another alliance by marrying another man selected by her grandfather.

For more about life in the Roman Empire at its peak, please go to carolashby.com. Articles on law enforcement in the city of Rome and the power of the paterfamilias are there.

Many of the characters in *What Matters Most* are based on historical people. To the extent possible, I've stayed true to what is known of them in the historical records.

Special effort was made to get the historical details right for Hadrian and Turbo and for the men from consular families.

Several of the characters in *What Matters Most* have either served as consul or want to be consuls. Under the Republic, consul was the second-highest level of the *cursus honorum,* which was a sequence of political offices of increasing importance. Consuls had both military and political responsibilities, and all had military experience because they served as military tribunes before starting their political climb. The two consuls were elected by an assembly of the people to govern Rome and its provinces together for one year. One was in charge, and they alternated being in charge each month. After that, they served as the governor (proconsul) of a province.

After Augustus established the empire, most of the former responsibilities and power of the consuls were transferred to the emperor. Consuls were nominated by the emperor and then formally elected by an assembly of the people. Several consuls were selected each year, with the first pair of consuls serving that year (ordinary consuls) giving their names to that year in the Roman dating system. The consuls who served later in the year were suffect consuls. The ordinary consulship was more prestigious than the suffect because the year was named after them.

After finishing their few months as consul, the ex-consuls became governors of the provinces that were administered by the Senate. Egypt and the provinces on the frontier where legions were stationed were imperial provinces, and their governors were chosen by the emperor. The governor of an imperial province with one legion was usually the legion commander (legate). If there was more than one legion, their legates were subordinate to the provincial governor.

The four consuls that Titianus discussed with Turbo were executed by Praetorian Prefect Attianus for allegedly plotting and unsuccessfully attempting the assassination of Hadrian in AD 118. The prefect presented sufficiently convincing evidence to get the Senate to condemn them, but many in the Senate were angry that they were forced to do that. Hadrian claimed it was done without his authorization, but many senators suspected that he ordered it.

Upon his father's death, Hadrian had been entrusted to the care of Trajan, who was his father's cousin, and Attianus. Attianus was suspected of helping Trajan's wife Plotina write Trajan's will herself after Trajan had died of a fever he caught while campaigning in the East. In that will, Hadrian was officially adopted and made Trajan's successor as emperor. Attianus had a personal attachment to Hadrian, so it's easy to believe he might have acted on his own to protect his almost-son, but he also might have been following the orders of his emperor.

All four of the executed men had been highly regarded by Trajan and would have been potential contenders to become emperor if the succession had been murky because Hadrian wasn't officially Trajan's adopted son.

Hadrian's relationship with the Senate remained strained for his entire reign. It's likely that he appointed his trusted friend Turbo as Praetorian Prefect from AD 125 to 134 so someone loyal would be keeping an eye on the politically ambitious members of the Senate for him.

THE EXECUTED CONSULS:
> A. Cornelius Palma Frontonianus, consul ordinarius in AD 109.
>
> C. Avidius Nigrinus, consul suffectus in AD 110, replaced as governor of Dacia by Turbo shortly before his arrest.
>
> L. Publilius Celsus, consul ordinarius in AD 113.
>
> Lusius Quietus, consul suffectus around AD 117, Roman Berber prince and general over the Moorish auxiliary cavalry. He was the governor of Judea in AD 117 who suppressed the Jewish Kitos rebellion before Hadrian replaced him shortly after Trajan's death. Quietus died on his way home to Mauritania, and many suspect-

ed Hadrian had him murdered because of his popularity with the armies and his closeness to Trajan, making him a dangerous rival for the throne. After his death, a revolt broke out in Mauretania, Quietus's home province, and was suppressed by Turbo.

MORE HISTORICAL POLITICAL CHARACTERS

Hadrian: Caesar Traianus Hadrianus, Emperor of Rome, AD 117 to AD 138.

Turbo: Q. Marcius Turbo, trusted friend and general for Trajan and Hadrian, Praetorian Prefect AD 125 to 134. Directed the main Roman fleet during Trajan's Parthian war, put down revolts in Egypt, Cyrene, and Mauritania, commanded the legions on the Danube, and governed first the two Mauritanias and then Dacia. For the last two years (story is set in AD 127), Hadrian's most trusted general had commanded the Praetorians, who served as imperial bodyguards and kept watch on any political unrest in Rome.

Saturninus: M. Lollius Paulinus D. Valerius Asiaticus Saturninus, consul AD 125, Urban Prefect AD 124-134.

M'. Acilius Glabrio or Aviola: suffect consul under Nero in AD 54; alive when son/grandson executed in 95.

M'. Acilius Glabrio: consul in AD 91. Exiled by Domitian and executed in AD 95 for treason for becoming a Christian.

M'. Acilius Glabrio, consul in AD 124, and proconsul of Africa in 139/140.

M'. Acilius Aviola, consul in AD 122, cousin to Acilius Glabrio.

M. Asinius Marcellus (deceased): consul in 54. According to Tacitus, he was an accomplice in illegally changing a will, a capital crime. His death sentence, pronounced in a Senate trial, was commuted by Nero because he was the great-grandson of Asinius Pollio, whom Nero admired.

M. Asinius Marcellus: consul in 104.

Q. Rammius Martialis: Prefect of Egypt AD 117-119 while Turbo served there as military prefect.

L. Aurelius Gallus: suffect consul sometime between AD 129 and 132.

D. = Decimus L. = Lucius, M = Marcus, M'. = Manius, Q. = Quintus

(There were only 20 common first names in use at this time, so abbreviations were often used.)

HISTORICAL LITERARY FIGURES

Marcus Fabius Quintilianus (AD 35–95): celebrated orator, rhetorician, Latin teacher, and writer.

Marcus Annaeus Lucanus (Lucan, AD 39-65) poet; writer of epic poem about the Julius Caesar-Pompey Civil War, friend then conspirator against Nero; forced to commit suicide.

Quintus Horatius Flaccus (Horace, 65-8 BC): leading Roman lyric poet during the time of Augustus.

Publius Papinius Statius (AD 46-96): composer of epic and shorter poems, including odes.

Titus Maccius Plautus (Plautus, c. 254 – 184 BC) playwright whose comedies are the earliest complete Latin literary works.

Aristophanes (c. 446 – c. 386 BC): playwright of ancient Athens called the Father of Comedy.

For more about life in the Roman Empire at its peak, please go to carolashby.com.

The Epistle of Publius

HOW ONE MAN CAME TO FAITH

In *The Legacy*, Publius Drusus was a scholarly man who loved philosophy and history and taught his sons that the Roman gods were only characters in stories. But his desire to understand the world and why it was the way it was led him first to belief in the creator God of the Jews and then to believing that Jesus was his savior. As he sat in a cell under the Flavian Amphitheater awaiting his execution for his faith, he wrote a final letter to his son Titus, who was serving as a tribune in Thracia. He hoped to explain how he got to that point and to convince Titus to embrace the Christian faith as well. With the personal portions meant only for Titus removed, here's the version of the Epistle of Publius that Pompeia copied for Glyptus to deliver to other believers around Rome.

THE EPISTLE OF PUBLIUS CLAUDIUS DRUSUS

By the time you read this letter, I will have been executed for refusing to deny my faith in Jesus of Nazareth and offer a sacrifice to Caesar. Everything I own will have been confiscated. This letter is my only legacy, but what it contains is worth more than all my estates, more than all the wealth in the Empire. I pray you will come to treasure it for the truth it contains.

I begin with how I decided the God of Israel is the one true God.

The teaching of the great philosophers seemed true to me for a long time, but that was before I began to compare them to what my own eyes have seen of the world. After much thought, I came to the conclusion that a philosophy could only be of value if it described the way the world truly is. I discovered that the philosophers I had admired most contradicted what I had seen myself. I began my search for a new philosophy without those contradictions.

I always considered Aristotle the wisest of philosophers, and I embraced his teaching wholeheartedly from my youth. At the core of his teaching was the existence of an effective cause for everything. I considered all I had seen of life, and if I looked deeply enough or back far enough in time, I could see the causes of almost everything. He also taught that nothing lasts forever, that everything changes over time. That was what I saw, too.

But I saw a terrible inconsistency in his teaching, and that disturbed me greatly. He taught that the universe was eternal, that it had no effective cause. But how could that be, that the universe as a whole was the opposite of all the parts within it?

Clearly, there was something wrong with this idea. The universe must also have an effective cause, so I began my search for a philosophy that taught the universe had a beginning and an effective cause that started it. I found it in the Jewish Scriptures. They tell how God created everything from nothing, how He is the effective cause of the whole universe.

I also considered Plato a great philosopher, but the more I saw of men and how they lived, the harder it became for me to agree with his teaching. He taught that cities and empires could be ruled by philosopher-kings: intelligent, self-controlled men who ruled based on wisdom and reason and placed the good of those they ruled above their own desires for power and wealth.

But as I examined history, I found men like this have never ruled. Even Trajan, who provided food and education for orphans in Italia, led his legions out to conquer, killing and enslaving, making new orphans who would starve.

From the histories of empires and kingdoms, we know that great rulers have always done so. Trajan condemns the men he has conquered to die like animals in the arena for the entertainment of the crowds. Where is the wisdom and goodness in that? Plato was wrong about the nature of man, so how could his philosophy be true?

Man is not good and wise; he naturally chooses evil. There are a few who choose kindness and mercy, but it is cruelty and lust for power that rule. Rome is rotten at her core, and she rules vast lands with an iron hand. Man's love of violence led to the games.

I expect to die in the arena tomorrow, killed by a lion or a gladiator's sword. Thousands of Romans, including many men whom I have known for years, will be watching and will consider it good entertainment. Again, I found this understanding in the Jewish Scriptures, that man is naturally evil, selfish, rebellious against God. Man is a sinful being.

In the Jewish Scriptures, I found the philosophy that explained everything I knew to be true about the world, but it is much more than a philosophy. In those same Scriptures, I met the God who made the universe. I discovered that He cared about men enough to reveal Himself to them so they could know Him. I learned of Abraham, Isaac, and Jacob, and how each of them had met God.

I learned of Moses, who was told by God Himself to lead the people of Israel out of slavery in Egypt because God had promised the land of Judaea to Jacob's children. God cared so much for His people that He gave Moses the very laws by which they should live.

I learned of the many men who were prophets to whom God Himself spoke so His people, who no longer knew and worshiped Him, would return to Him.

From the beginning, He always wanted men to know Him and love Him. So, I became a God-fearer, worshiping the God of Abraham, Isaac, and Jacob, and I studied the Jewish Scriptures daily because I could learn about Him there.

He is a holy God, and He cannot tolerate sin in His presence. But sin is not just doing the things that He has forbidden or neglecting the things He has commanded; it is also choosing to treat God as if He didn't exist.

In the Law He gave to Moses, He told His people the way to approach Him by covering their sins through blood sacrifice in their temple in Jerusalem. For over a thousand years, His people made sacrifices so they could approach Him. That ended when the temple was destroyed by Titus when he was putting down the rebellion in Judaea.

That created a terrible problem, or so I thought. God said the payment for sin always required blood sacrifice, but He let His temple be destroyed by Rome, so how was sin to be paid for? I was at a loss to explain how the true God, the one so powerful that He could make the entire universe, could allow Rome to destroy His temple and take away what allowed His people to approach Him.

Then I met a man who could explain it all. He told me of Jesus of Nazareth and how He came from heaven to make the final sacrifice for sins.

He was the Son of God. He was sinless, and He made Himself the perfect sacrifice for all sin when He was crucified. After three days, He rose from the dead, proving His claim to be God.

The grandfather of my friend actually knew men who had been with Jesus after He rose. There could be no doubt of the truth that Jesus was the Son of God and the final perfect sacrifice.

At last, I understood it all. The temple could be destroyed because God had made the perfect blood sacrifice Himself—Jesus on a cross more than 80 years ago. The temple and its sacrifices were no longer needed, so He had Rome destroy it so people would no longer cling to the old ways.

The coming of the Messiah, of Jesus, was foretold in the Jewish Scriptures hundreds of years before He came, and God kept the promise He made to His people. There was no need to continually sacrifice animals to cover my sin with their blood. To be saved from my sin, I only had to believe in Jesus as the sacrifice for all sins, including mine. It all made perfect sense, and I finally knew the truth.

When I went the first time to worship with my friend, I actually met God myself. I felt His love surround me, and now He lives in me. I am never alone. That day when I decided to believe, to repent of my sins and commit myself to Jesus as my Lord, all the worry and sadness in my life was replaced by peace and joy. For the first time, I knew what it was to be fully alive.

I want you to experience this yourself. For you to know this perfect love deep in your soul—that will be my dying prayer.

Following Jesus is like a perfect marriage; denying Him would be like committing adultery against the most loving, beautiful, faithful wife a man could have. I could never betray my Lord that way. I have chosen death instead.

I will die soon, but I have no regrets. I am content to die because it isn't death that matters. It is whether you have accepted Jesus as Savior. Death is terrible apart from Jesus. Without Jesus, I would be lost, in hell, forever separated from God. With Jesus as my Savior, death has no power over me, and I don't fear it. It will just usher me into life with Him in heaven.

Jesus told us that He is the way, the truth, and the life. He promised if a man would believe in Him and follow, he would know the truth, and the truth would set him free. If you let Him, Jesus will show you what is true.

Open your mind to Him. Open your heart. Know the truth and be free like I am, even in this prison as I wait to die. I will be praying for all my children to choose to follow Jesus until I take my final breath and even after that, for life with Jesus is eternal.

Discussion Guide

1) In the beginning, Titianus is four days from finishing his service as a tribune of the Urban Cohort. His reputation for incorruptibility forces one last case on him that could prove fatal. How did he respond? Have you ever thought you were finally through with something only to find you have to continue? How did you respond?

2) Sabina was a typical daughter in an elite Roman family, where it was normal for political alliances to be sealed by a marriage. She expected the first marriage her grandfather arranged to turn out well, as her own parents' arranged marriage had. What happened? How did she respond?

3) When Sabina, the sister of Kaeso's best friend Septimus, comes home as a widow with a terrible stutter and a fear of returning to Roman society, what do Kaeso and his sister Pompeia (Titianus's wife) do to help? What did that mean for Sabina? Have you had the chance to help someone recover their confidence after something went horribly wrong? What did you do?

4) Glabrio was eager to get to know Titianus's powerful relatives, Manius and Quintus Sabinus. Why was that important to him? When he learned Sabina was free to marry again, what did he do? Have you or someone you know ever been in a situation where getting someone to be your friend could bring big advantages? What happened?

5) Glabrio was supposed to take over Titianus's command after a very quick explanation of what every tribune did, but the delay in Titianus's resignation forced him to train Glabrio more thoroughly in his own procedures while hiding what he was investigating from their commander. How did that affect Glabrio?

6) Pompeia and Kaeso welcome Sabina and encourage her to focus on her gifts instead of her defect. What was the result of that encouragement? Kaeso thinks it was God who led Sabina to see the writings that betrayed they were Christians, and when she asked about it, he was thrilled to explain and teach her. Have you ever had the chance to

share your faith because a friend asked you a question about it? What happened?

7) Glabrio's grandfather had been a consul of Rome. Then Emperor Domitian exiled him. Four years later, Domitian had him executed for the treason of becoming a Christian. That was thirty years before this story, so Glabrio never knew his grandfather or wondered about his faith. What happened after he learned some of the people he liked and admired were also Christians?

8) Manius had not suspected his friends (Titianus, Pompeia, Kaeso) were following the outlawed Christian religion until Sabina's maid told him Kaeso had given her some Christian writings. How did he respond to that disclosure when he first heard? Has anyone ever been surprised to learn you're a Christian? How did they respond?

9) Quintus Sabinus had considered revealing someone was a Christian to be a good way to get rid of them. What did he do when he learned people he cared about followed Jesus? Have you seen friendship change the attitude of someone who was hostile to Christ and to Christians?

10) *What Matters Most* is a story of duty and honor, of empathy and encouragement, of friendship and love that open the door to faith and a future blessed by God. What touched you most? What made you think about what your own choices would be?

WHO WOULD YOU LIKE TO SEE IN A FUTURE SHORT STORY OR NOVELLA?

I grew to love several of the characters in *What Matters Most* while I was writing. That usually happens, and often the next story for a character takes shape in my head even before I finish. Sometimes it's requests from readers that reveal who should be the focus of a future story. There are many people in *What Matters Most* and all my other novels that I would like to spend more time with, and I hope there are some for you, too. Who would you most like to see in a future story? What was it about them that made you want more of them? I'd love to hear what you think.

Please go to my website, carol-ashby.com, and share your thoughts in the comment box. Sign up for the newsletter, and you'll get the story when I finish it. Looking forward to hearing from you!

Glossary

Amphora: a tall clay jar with two handles and a narrow neck used for transport of liquids

As: in Imperial times, a copper coin worth 1/16 denarius, 1/4 sestertius, 1/2 dupondius

Aureus: a gold Roman coin worth 25 denarii

Atrium: the open central court of a Roman house with enclosed rooms on all sides

Castrum: military fortress, fort, or camp

Centurion: 1st level officer over 80 men; rises through the ranks based on merit

Client: one with obligations to a patron; could be of same or lower status as patron. When slaves were freed, the former owner became their patron.

Cognomen: the third name of the 3-part Roman name, the surname or family name

Consul: highest elected political office, nominated by emperor; presided over Senate and judged special cases, could become governors of some provinces after serving

Damnatio ad bestias: condemned to the arena to be killed by beasts

Denarius: silver Roman coin worth 1.13 drachmas; worth about one day's living wage

Domi tribunorum: tribune's quarters in a Roman fortress

Domina: female head of a Roman household

Domus: town house of the upper classes and wealthy freedmen with indoor courtyards (atrium and peristyle), many rooms, and a garden

Dupondius: Roman brass coin worth 1/2 sestertius or 1/8 denarius

Equestrian order: 2nd highest class of Roman citizens; required personal wealth greater than 100,000 denarii

Falernian wine: most renowned Roman wine from Mt. Falernus in Campania

Familia: the Roman family unit consisting of the paterfamilias, his married and unmarried children regardless of age, his son's children, and his slaves

First table: the main (second) course of a three-course Roman dinner

Second table: the dessert (third) course of a three-course Roman dinner

Freedman: a freed slave who owes support and service as a client to his former owner

Gladius: short thrusting sword used by the Roman military and some gladiators

Kalasiris: a close-fitting Egyptian tube dress with straps

Lanista: the head trainer of a gladiatorial school

Lararium: household shrine, often a niche in an atrium wall

Latrunculi: military strategy board game involving trapping and removing captured stones

Legate: commander of a legion

Legion: unit of the Roman army consisting of about 6000 Roman citizens

Ludus: (plural l*udi*) gladiator training school; also rents bodyguards

Ludus Bruti: gladiator school belonging to Marcus Brutus

Ode: a lyric poem in the form of an address to a particular subject, often elevated in style or manner and written in varied or irregular meter; a poem meant to be sung

Optio: (plural *optiones*) Roman junior officer ranked below centurion

Palla: rectangular cloth wrap worm by Roman women

Paterfamilias: (plural *patres familias*) Oldest living male of an extended Roman family, the patriarch who owns everything

Patronus: patron; expected to provide some material benefits for their clients, both freeborn and freed

Peregrine: a person who is not a Roman citizen

Polypus: octopus

Praetor: a Roman magistrate ranking below consul, serves as a judge

Praetorian Guard: military unit serving as bodyguards and intelligence agents for the emperor

Praetorian Prefect: an equestrian serving as commander of the Praetorian Guard

Praetorium: residence (building or tent) of the commanding general (prefect or legate)

Principia: headquarters building of military fortress, fort, or camp

Questor: the first magistrate position on the political career path for senators

Quintilian rhetoric: taught the good orator must also be morally sound, i.e., be good man

Raeda: a four-wheeled closed-in carriage

Rhetor: a teacher of rhetoric or oratory, which was used in court, public speeches, and writing

Rhetoric: the art or persuasion, including the concept, style, memory, and delivery

River Styx: a river in Hades across which Charon carried dead souls fpr a fee (Greek mythology)

Salutation: daily ritual during which prominent citizens received clients and others seeking favors

Salve: hello, standard Roman greeting

Second table: the dessert (third) course of a three-course Roman dinner

Senatorial order: highest class of Roman citizens; required personal wealth greater than 250,000 denarii

Sestertius: (plural sesterces) bronze Roman coin worth 1/4 denarius

Salve: hello, the standard Latin greeting

Solis: Sunday

Spina: a wall running down the center of racetrack to separate teams going in opposite directions

Strigil: an instrument with a curved blade used to scrape sweat and dirt from the skin

Sui iuris: independent of their paterfamilias, most often through his death

Taberna: tavern or shop selling prepared food

Tablinum: the main office and reception room for the Roman master of the house

Tabula: popular Greco-Roman board game, often played with betting, similar to backgammon

Tepidarium: the warm room at a Roman bath complex with radiant heat from floor and walls

Thermae: a Roman bath complex, the "baths

Tribune: high-ranking officer from equestrian or senatorial order

Triclinium: dining room with couches arranged along three sides of a low table

Turma: a cavalry unit of 30 men commanded by a decurion

Urban Cohort: one of four military police units under the urban prefect; 1 tribune over 6 centurions and about 500 men

Urban prefect: senator serving as quasi-mayor of Rome with administrative and judicial powers to maintain order in the city; commander of the Urban Cohort

Vale: goodbye, the standard Latin farewell

Vestibulum: passage between the outer door and the interior of a town house (domus)

Vigiles Urbani: "watchmen of the City," firefighters and night watchmen of Rome

Scripture References

Chapter 24: When Sabina sees what Pompeia is copying.
   John 13:31-35 from ESV

Chapter 32: When Filomena looks at the codex Sabina brought home
   Luke 1:1-5, 2:31-33, 3:1-2, 21-23 from ESV

Chapter 35: Discussion between Sabina and Kaeso of the gospel written
      by Luke
   Some events Sabina refers to: Luke 1:5, 2:1-3, 3:1-2
   Jesus forgiving on the cross: Luke 23:34 from CSB
   Loving your enemies: Luke 6:27-29 from CSB
   Ask, seek, knock: Luke 11:9-10 from ESV
   Jesus the way, the truth, the life: John 14:6 paraphrased

Chapter 43: When Sabina is reading from the gospel written by John
   John 1: 10-18 from CSB
   1:18 is a paraphrase based on CSB and ESV
   John 1:18 (paraphrase): No one has ever seen God. The one and only
      Son, who is himself God and is at the Father's side—he has made
      him known.

Acknowledgements

Most of all, I thank God for this opportunity to tell this story of how true friendship can create openings for sharing our faith with people who don't yet know our Lord. I had great fun doing that for several of the characters with each very different from the others.

No one can write the best book possible without the help of many others. Here's a few who helped me more than I can express.

I'm especially thankful for Lisa Garcia, my top alpha beta and dear friend who's helped me with every book in the series. I can count on her to see the places that need additional work to get the story right. I wouldn't be able to write the spiritual scenes well without her prayers and her feeling for exactly how they should be to seem real. She's so good at spotting typos that I'll never need a copy editor. Her prayers always bless me in writing and in life.

I want to thank Sherril Stinnett, who's also been my invaluable alpha beta for *Honor Bound*, *Hope's Reward*, and *More Than Honor*. She's wonderful at spotting when something isn't quite right so I can fix it. I can tell she's praying when I'm writing the hard sections, especially where faith decisions were being made.

Christine Dillon, the inspiring author of the Grace series, was also a beta reader for this book. With an author's eye and the spiritual insight of a missionary, her help with a manuscript is always a blessing. It's such a pleasure to have her as my fellow author buddy.

Terry Shoebotham is my local writing buddy and prayer partner for writing and so much else in life. She's a joy to talk books with, and I'll be so blessed when we can meet again in person to discuss our writing projects.

I want to thank Andrew Budek-Schmeisser for being my critique partner, prayer partner, and good friend as I've written so many of these books. Whenever I needed prayers for something that was giving me problems, I could count on him. Despite serious health problems, he's always been willing to share his knowledge of good writing, his spiritual insight, his artistic insights on the covers, and his expertise with horses, combat, low-tech field medicine. He's also helped me with *The Legacy, Faithful, Second Chances, True Freedom, Hope Unchained, Honor Bound, Hope's Reward,* and *More Than Honor* and with many brainstorming sessions about characters for future volumes. None of the books would have been the same without him.

I also want to thank Katie Powner, my long-time critique partner, for her prayers and wise comments. She is an award-winning author herself whose debut novel, *The Sowing* Season, was joined this October by *A Flicker of Light.* For wonderful contemporary reads, you can't beat Katie's novels.

Thanks also to Mesu Andrews for praying with me for inspiration and for meeting deadlines when they got way too close. As a leading writer of Biblical fiction, she shared her author insights on important spiritual scenes, too. Ancient history nerds belong together, and I can count on her to share my excitement about archeological discoveries from Old Testament and Roman times.

My line editor, Wendy Chorot, has once more brought her deep spiritual insight and her editorial skill to bear to make the spiritual scenes feel like real life. Working with her is always a delight.

Roseanna White has designed another gorgeous cover that captures the location of the story and some of the key characters. I can't figure out which of her covers I love most. Each time I think she can't top the last one, she does.

I especially thank my son Paul, who provided the body for the man in the toga, and my daughter Lydia, who provided the woman's body. Roseanna replaced their heads with heads that fit the characters. I sew the clothing that's historically correct, and they pose however Roseanna needs them. They've both been four different people on the covers now. That toga is 18 feet long and 7 feet deep at the center of the arc. It takes me many minutes to wrap it just right to get the folds to drape properly, more or less. With plenty of laughter as we tried over and over, we got close enough. I can always count on my kids!

But my special thanks go to my wonderful husband, Jim. That's his arm holding the sword this time, so the cover is a family portrait, sort of. He spent more than an hour with me watching a video from a UK professor on how two servants would drape a toga and figuring out how to do it alone as I practiced on him before trying to drape our son. His humor, kindness, and patience are the model for the best of my heroes. I'm so blessed to be his wife.

About the Author

Carol Ashby has been a professional writer for most of her life, but her articles and books were about lasers and compound semiconductors (the electronics that make cell phones, laser pointers, and LED displays work). She still writes about light, but her Light in the Empire series tells stories of difficult friendships and life-changing decisions in dangerous times, where forgiveness and love open hearts to discover their own faith in Christ. Her fascination with the Roman Empire was born during her first middle-school Latin class. A research career in New Mexico inspires her to get every historical detail right so she can spin stories that make her readers feel like they're living under the Caesars themselves.

Read her articles about many facets of life in the Roman Empire at carolashby.com, or join her at her blog, The Beauty of Truth, at carol-ashby.com.

LIGHT *in the* EMPIRE SERIES

The Light in the Empire Series follows the interconnected lives of four Roman families during the reigns of Trajan and Hadrian. Join them as they travel the Empire, from Germania and Britannia to Thracia, Dacia, and Judaea and, of course, to Rome itself.

Forgiven

Are some wounds too deep to forgive?

With a ruthless father who murdered for the family inheritance, Marcus Drusus plans to do the same. In AD 122, Marcus follows his brother Lucius to Judaea and plots to frame a zealot for his older brother's death. But the plan goes awry, and Lucius is rescued by a Messianic Jewish woman. Her oldest brother is a zealot and a Roman soldier killed her twin, but Rachel still persuades her father Joseph to put his love for Jesus above his anger with Rome and hide Lucius until he heals.

Rachel cares for the enemy, and more than broken bones heal as duty turns to love. Lucius embraces Joseph's faith in Jesus, but sharing a faith doesn't heal all wounds. Even before revealed secrets slice open old scars, Joseph wants no Roman son-in-law. With Rachel's zealot brother suspecting he's a Roman officer and his own brother planning to kill him when he returns, can Lucius survive long enough to change Joseph's mind?

Blind Ambition

Sometimes you have to almost die to discover how you want to live.

It's AD 114 in the Roman province of Germania Superior, and being a Christian carries a death sentence. Tribune Decimus Lentulus is on the fast track for a stellar political career back in Rome. When he's robbed, blinded, and left for dead, a young German woman who follows the Way finds him. Valeria knows it's his duty to have her and her family killed, but she chooses to obey Jesus's command to love her enemy and takes him home to care for him.

It's not his miraculous recovery that shakes Decimus to his core. It's the way they love him like family and their unconcealed love for Jesus. In spite of himself, he falls in love with the Christian woman Rome wants him to kill. Can Valeria hide her faith to follow him into the circles of Roman power? Or should he abandon his ambition to help rule the Empire and choose to follow a different way?

The Legacy

When Rome has taken everything, what's left for a man to give?

Betrayed by a ruthless son who'll do anything for power and wealth, Publius Drusus faces death with an unanswered prayer—that his treasured daughter, Claudia, and honorable son, Titus, will someday share his faith. But who will lead them to the truth once he's gone?

Claudia's oldest brother Lucius arranged their father's execution to inherit everything, and now he's forcing her to marry a cruel Roman power broker. If only she could get to Titus—a thousand miles away in Thracia. Then the man who secretly told her father about Jesus arranges for his son Philip to sneak her out of Rome and take her to the brother she can trust.

A childhood accident scarred Philip's face. A woman's rejection scarred his heart. Claudia's gratitude grows into love, but what can Philip do when the first woman who returns his love hates the God he loves even more?

Titus and Claudia hunger for revenge on their brother and the Christians they blame for their father's deadly conversion. When Titus buys Miriam, a secret Christian, to serve his sister, he starts them all down a path of conflicting loyalties and dangerous decisions. His father's final letter commands the forgiveness Titus refuses to give. What will it take to free him from the hatred poisoning his own heart?

Join the people you met in *Second Chances* eight years earlier in this tale of betrayal, hatred, love, and forgiveness, where even bad things can work together for good.

Faithful

Is the price of true friendship ever too high?

In AD 122, Adela, the fiery daughter of a Germanic chieftain, is kidnapped and taken across the Roman frontier to be sold as a slave. When horse-trader Otto wins her while gambling with her kidnappers, he entrusts her to his friend and trading partner, Galen. Then Otto is kidnapped by the same men, and Galen must track them half way across the Empire before his best friend loses a fight to the death in a Roman arena.

Adela joins Galen in the chase, hungry for vengeance. As the perilous journey deepens their friendship, will the kind, faithful man open her eyes to a life she never dreamed she'd want?

A trip to the heart of the Empire poses mortal danger to a man who follows Jesus, especially when he must seek the help of an enemy of the faith for Otto to survive. Tiberius hunted Christians when he governed Germania Superior and banished his own son when he became one.

When Tiberius learns sparing Galen offers a chance at reconciliation, he joins the trio on their journey home. Can his animosity toward the followers of Jesus survive a trip with the Christian man whose courage and faithfulness demand his respect?

Follow the continuing saga of the people you met in *Blind Ambition* from the frontier of Germany to the heart of the Empire.

Second Chances

Must the shadows of the past destroy the hope of the future?

In AD 122, Cornelia Scipia, proud daughter of one of Rome's noblest families, learns her adulterous husband plans to betroth their daughter to the vicious son of his best friend. Over her dead body! Cornelia divorces him, reclaims her enormous dowry, and kidnaps her own daughter. She plans to start over with Drusilla a thousand miles away. No more husbands for her. But she didn't count on meeting Hector, the widowed Greek captain of the ship carrying her to her new life.

Devastated by the loss of his wife and daughter, Hector's heart begins to heal as he befriends Drusilla. Cornelia's sacrificial love for Drusilla and her courage and humor in the face of the unknown earn his admiration…as a friend. Is he ready for more?

Marriage to the kind, honest sea captain would give Drusilla the father she deserves…and Cornelia the faithful husband she's always longed for. But while her ex-husband hunts them to drag Drusilla back to Rome, secrets in Hector's past and the chasm between their social classes and different faiths erect complicated barriers to any future together. Will God give two lonely hearts a second chance at happiness?

Join the people you met in *The Legacy* eight years later in this tale of hope and a future never imagined until God opens the door.

True Freedom

The chains we cannot see can be the hardest ones to break.

When Aulus runs up a gambling debt to his father's political enemy, he's desperate to pay it off before his father returns to Rome. His best friend Marcus suggests they fake the kidnapping of Aulus's sister Julia and use the ransom money. But when the man they hired kidnaps her for real, Aulus is catapulted into a desperate search to find her.

Torn from his childhood home by Rome's conquering armies and sold as a farm slave to labor until he dies, Dacius's faith gives him strength to bear what he must and serve without complaining. After a deadly accident makes him one of Julia's litter bearers, he overhears Marcus advising her brother to kidnap her. When Dacius almost dies thwarting the kidnapping, a Christian couple pretend Julia and Dacius are their children to keep her brother from finding them before her father returns.

But pretending to be free again makes returning to slavery more than Dacius can bear, while acting like a common woman opens Julia's eyes to dreams and destinies she never knew existed. With her brother closing in and her father almost home, can she find a way around Roman law and custom to free them both for the future they long for?

Find out what happens to Ariana's brother Diegis twelve years later in this tale of hope and a future never imagined until God opens the door.

Hope Unchained

Can the deepest loss bring the greatest gain?

Rome's conquering army took Ariana's family and freedom, but nothing can take her faith in Jesus. When she rescues a tribune's wife from certain death, her reward is freedom and a chance to free her brother and sister. But first she must catch up with the slave caravan before they vanish forever, and tracking them from Dacia to the coast seems impossible for one woman alone.

Discharged from the legion with a hand crippled by a Dacian knife, Donatus faces a future without hope. When the tribune asks him to escort Ariana on her quest, it's the only work he can find. It means four weeks with a Dacian woman and a gladiator bodyguard, but it takes money to eat. A man without options must take what he can get.

But a lot can happen in four weeks. Even battle-hardened men can be touched by love and forgiveness, and it's easier to face an enemy with a sword than to face the truth. When his moment of truth comes, what will Donatus choose, and what will that mean for both of them?

If you read *True Freedom* and wondered what happened to Leander's beloved sister Ariana, you can find out in *Hope Unchained*.

Honor Bound

Can the deepest loss bring the greatest gain?

Marcus Brutus owns estates, ships, and gladiator schools that increase his fortune daily, but his greatest treasures are his honor and his wife. When she reveals her faith in Jesus before dying after the birth of their son, he's consumed by hatred for the unnamed Christian woman who led his beloved to abandon the Roman gods, making him lose her in this life and the next.

For fifteen years, Licinia's father hid her Christian faith. But now her father is dead, and a ruthless political enemy is hunting for anything to destroy her brother. When she becomes the target, her brother sends her to their estate in Germania. But is that far enough to protect her from an evil man who will stop at nothing?

When a carriage accident leaves Brutus injured and his best friend near death after rescuing Brutus's son, Licinia welcomes and cares for them. But her strange habits and his friend's unexpected recovery make Brutus suspect she's the Christian who corrupted his wife. When her brother's enemies come for her, does honor require him to protect her or turn her over as an enemy of Rome? And when Licinia's heart is drawn toward the pagan man who makes money off death, can she reconcile her growing affection with her love for Christ?

If you read *True Freedom* and wondered what happened to Africanus and Brutus, you can find out in *Honor Bound.*

Hope's Reward

Must the secrets we hide destroy our hope for a future?

For a gladiator slave, each time you step on the sand, it's kill or die. When Ursus decides to follow Jesus, he must choose to die the next time he's ordered to fight…or run away. He runs, taking again his childhood name, Matti. But he isn't just trying to escape. He's running to Thessalonica, where he hopes to find other Christians like the woman who led him to faith.

When Felicia's new husband, Falco, almost kills her in a fit of rage, her uncle won't help her end the marriage with his business partner. He will send her to her sister in Thessalonica, but only if she tells no one she plans to divorce Falco and demand her dowry back before she gets there. When Matti interrupts a robbery too late to save Felicia's money for traveling by sea, he offers to bodyguard and escort her overland to their mutual destination.

After Matti risks everything to save her from Falco's assassins, Felicia fears taking the danger to her sister's family. When his Christian friends take them in, she discovers the deepest desires of her heart. But will the secrets of Matti's past make a future together impossible?

If you wonder what happened to Ursus in *Hope Unchained*, he's the hero in *Hope's Reward*.

More Than Honor

Duty and honor had anchored his life, but only truth could set him free.

Devotion to duty and dogged determination make Tribune Titianus the most feared investigator of the Urban Cohort. Honor drives him to hunt down anyone who breaks Roman law, but it becomes personal when Lenaeus, his old tutor, is murdered in his own classroom. Why kill a respected teacher of the noble sons of Rome, a man who has nothing worth stealing and no known enemies? Had he learned something too dangerous to let him live?

Pompeia was only a girl when Titianus studied with Father before her family became Christians. She and her brother Kaeso can't move their school from the house where their father was killed. But what if the one who killed Father comes to kill again? Kaeso's friend Septimus insists they spend nights at his father's well-guarded home. But danger lurks there as well. As Titianus hunts for the murderer, will he discover their secret faith and arrest them as enemies of the Empire?

When Titianus gets too close to finding the killer, the hunter becomes the hunted. While he recovers at his cousin Septimus's house, Pompeia becomes the first woman to touch his heart. But a tribune's loyalty is sworn to Rome, no matter how he feels. When her faith is revealed, will truth and love mean more to him than honor? Does honor require more than devotion to Rome?

If you're curious about what happened with Manius's family, Kaeso's family, and Titianus a year before *What Matters Most*, you can find that story in *More Than Honor.*

I'd Love to Hear from You!

If you enjoyed this book, it would be a real gift to me if you would post a review at the retailer you purchased it from. A good review is like a jewel set in gold for an author. Other great places to share reviews are Goodreads and BookBub. If you've read others in the series, it would be great if you post a review of those, too.

I'd also love to hear from you at carol-ashby.com or directly at carolashbyauthor@gmail.com.

Want to hear about upcoming releases in the Light in the Empire series and free gifts only for newsletter subscribers?

For free gifts and other special offers, advance notices of upcoming releases, and info about my latest writing adventures, I hope you'll sign up for my newsletter at carol-ashby.com.

Who would you like to see in a future story? Help me pick what to write next!

I grew to love several of the characters in *What Matters Most* while I was writing. That usually happens, and sometimes a future story takes shape in my head even before I finish. But more often the next hero or heroine is chosen because readers tell me who needs to come back as a story lead.

Readers who loved Galen as a teen in *Blind Ambition* wanted to see him as a grown man, so he became the hero in *Faithful*. People who asked for Brutus and Africanus to have their own story found out what happened to them in *Honor Bound*.

Since people kept asking what happened to Leander's beloved but long-lost sister in *True Freedom*, it was clear Ariana would need her own story in *Hope Unchained*. People who met Ursus in *Hope Unchained* asked what happened to him, so he returned with his childhood name of Matti in his quest to know God better in *Hope's Reward*.

In *What Matters Most*, Septimus, who was rather like a Great Dane puppy in *Honor Bound*, comes back four years older, and Tribune Titianus from *More Than Honor* and *True Freedom* faces the most dangerous assignment of his life. I'm SO glad people asked for still more of them after the earlier books.

But there are many more characters in the books of the series that I would like to spend more time with, and I hope there are some for you, too. Who would you most like to see in a future story? What was it about them that made you want more of them? I'd love to hear what you think. It will guide what I write next.

Some possibilities:
    Aulus of *True Freedom?*
    Glabrio of *What Matters Most?*
    Septimus or Manius of *Honor Bound, More Than Honor,* and *What Matters Most?*
    Someone else I haven't mentioned? (I can't wait to see who shows up here!)

    Please tell me who you'd love to see again as a comment at carol-ashby.com or directly at carolashbyauthor@gmail.com!

I'm thinking about writing a short story or novella about someone from Sextus's or Calvia's households in *Honor Bound* or Gracchus of *Hope Unchained* and *Hope's Reward* to give to newsletter subscribers. Which would you rather have?

Please go to my website, carol-ashby.com, and share your thoughts in the comment box. Sign up for the newsletter, and you'll get the story when I finish it. Looking forward to hearing from you!

www.ingramcontent.com/pod-product-compliance
Lightning Source LLC
Chambersburg PA
CBHW030358200726
48286CB00015B/1617